CURSE OF THE GARGOYLE

What the critics are saying...

ജ

"Tara Nina has crafted an facinating story mixing the paranormal world with that of a traditional Scotish male.... nyone looking for a hard to put down read will enjoy this spicy, mesmerizing story as much as I did." ~ *The Romance Studio*

"Blending the appeal of the Scottish male revered for his sense of duty and strength with a blend of the paranormal Tara Nina has created an interesting story of a modern woman and her fight to save a group of brothers cast into the curse held by the stone that has kept them safe for hundreds of years." ~ *Fallen Angels Review*

"This book is a very quick and interesting read with very steamy scenes in it. I would like to read of the rest of the brother's stories." ~ *Night Owl Romance*

An Ellora's Cave Romantica Publication

www.ellorascave.com

Curse of the Gargoyle

ISBN 9781419956508

Edited by Briana St. James
Cover art by Philip Fuller

Electronic book Publication March 2007
Trade paperback Publication June 2007

This book is printed in the U.S.A. by Jasmine-Jade Enterprises, LLC.

Content Advisory:

S - ENSUOUS
E - ROTIC
X - TREME

Ellora's Cave Publishing offers three levels of Romantica™ reading entertainment: S (S-ensuous), E (E-rotic), and X (X-treme).

The following material contains graphic sexual content meant for mature readers. This story has been rated S-ensuous.

S-*ensuous* love scenes are explicit and leave nothing to the imagination.

E-*rotic* love scenes are explicit, leave nothing to the imagination, and are high in volume per the overall word count. E-rated titles might contain material that some readers find objectionable—in other words, almost anything goes, sexually. E-rated titles are the most graphic titles we carry in terms of both sexual language and descriptiveness in these works of literature.

X-*treme* titles differ from E-rated titles only in plot premise and storyline execution. Stories designated with the letter X tend to contain difficult or controversial subject matter not for the faint of heart.

Also by Tara Nina

ꕥ

Arian's Angel

About the Author

ꕥ

Tara Nina is a romantic dreamer whose dreams are now a reality through the publication of one of her romantic fantasies. She resides in Northern New Jersey along with her husband, two children, two dogs and a cascade of supportive friends and relatives.

Tara welcomes comments from readers. You can find her website and email address on her author bio page at www.ellorascave.com.

Tell Us What You Think

We appreciate hearing reader opinions about our books. You can email us at Comments@EllorasCave.com.

CURSE OF THE GARGOYLE

Dedication

ஜ

My warmest thanks go out to my newfound friends in the sisterhood of the Sizzling Scribes. If not for their support, this book would not have been completed.

Thank you, Briana, for your efforts in this endeavor.

Thank you, C.H. Admirand, without your constant nudging, advice and friendship I would not be where I am today.

Trademarks Acknowledgement

ஜ

The author acknowledges the trademarked status and trademark owners of the following wordmarks mentioned in this work of fiction:

Band Aid: Johnson and Johnson Company

Dramamine: Pfizer Pharmaceuticals

Oscar: Academy of Motion Pictures Arts and Sciences

Chapter One

Fall 1740

Heart of Grampian Mountains, Scotland

ꟷ

'Tis taken a fortnight but the deed's done. My brathairs *are safe for the time being. My husband and his clan have hidden them well.*

By the grace of my Lord, I promise to find the way to set them free of the curse of Hume MacGillivray. May his dark soul find the path to the fires of hell where he belongs for the wrath of evil he has placed upon my kin.

Akira MacDonnell (daughter of Farlan MacKinnon)

Ericka read her favorite passage from the supposed diary of Akira MacDonnell for what must have been the millionth time. Closing the tattered cover, she clutched it against her chest as turbulence bounced the plane.

Aunt May better be right. With her eyes shut tight, one white-knuckled hand gripped the armrest and her feet pressed against the floor as if she could stop it with an imaginary brake pedal. God, she hated flying. Flying! She hated traveling, period, but Aunt May had insisted she join her in Scotland. As the plane leveled off and the turbulence passed, Ericka released the breath she hadn't realized she held.

"It's all right, dear." The elderly lady next to her patted her hand. "Not much longer and we'll be landing."

Ericka attempted a weak smile, then leaned her head against the window. To abate her fear, she concentrated on the many lights dotting the landscape below and swallowed back her nausea.

After working for several years with Aunt May, she should've gotten used to her eccentric ways. Ericka sighed heavily, fogging the window against her cheek. True, her aunt had created the perfect job for her as the head of research for the Center of the Restoration of Folklore and Mythology. The position allowed her to work mainly from home with the occasional venture into the office downtown, which kept her travel phobia under control.

Gulping at the knot in her throat, Ericka rubbed the moisture from the glass. Being on a plane headed for Scotland stirred the cauldron of nausea to life in her stomach. She took a deep breath and tried to keep down the slim remnants of airplane food she'd eaten earlier.

And why was she several thousands of feet above ground on this plane anyway? Oh, yeah, she silently reminded herself. Aunt May bought a castle. Not just any castle but *the* very castle that haunted her dreams, Castle MacKinnon. But how was that possible? The castle wasn't real. Ericka had never been able to authenticate the diary of Akira or anything else pertaining to Clan MacKinnon. Cupping her forehead, she stared at the book her aunt had given her.

Had there truly been an Akira MacDonnell? Or was the story in her hands just that…a story created by an imaginative woman long ago and not a diary as her aunt claimed it to be?

Akira's depiction of her family and their vile end at the hands of a former clansman tore at Ericka's heart. Without any proof of their existence other than the book in her lap, she refused to believe the events were real.

Curses don't exist and neither does the Castle MacKinnon.

The sooner she made Aunt May see the truth, the quicker they could get past this one particular Scottish myth and chalk it up to being just that…a myth. A story for mothers to read to their children at bedtime, nothing more. But was it? Ericka bit her lip and pressed farther back into her seat.

What if Akira's tale held a hint of truth to it? That little smidgeon of doubt teased her analytical mind and led her to do the one thing she swore she'd never do. Fly.

As the announcement to prepare for landing came across the PA system, her heart skipped a beat and she automatically tested her seat belt. She didn't know which she hated worse—takeoff, landing or flying in general.

Once the plane touched down, relief that it landed without crashing into a ball of flames washed over her. Though her legs ached from hours of sitting, she was one of the first to grab her carryon and stand in line to exit the plane. Glimpses of the sun's rays greeted her through the large windowpanes of the airport terminal in Glasgow, Scotland, as she made her way to baggage claim. Thankfully, it didn't take long to get through customs.

Wouldn't have to deal with this if I'd just stayed home, she huffed. After safely tucking away her passport and ticket in her carryon, she struggled to push the cart full of her luggage to the outer door. Relief washed over her at the sight of a balding man holding a sign with her name. Thank god Aunt May had arranged for someone to pick her up. Ericka extended her hand.

"Hi. I'm Ericka Russell." She smiled weakly over the rumble of her stomach. *How could it even think of food after such a horrendous trip*?

"Name's Ned," he replied in a thick Scottish brogue with a stiff shake of her hand. "Yer aunt sent me to pick you up."

He grabbed the luggage cart without another word and walked away as if assuming she'd just follow.

Ericka called out. "Excuse me, Ned. Would you mind if I took a moment to visit the ladies' room?" A stiff nod as he pulled the cart to a halt and leaned against it was his only reply. Racing to the nearest restroom, she went about her business, then washed her face and hands in a flurry. Moments later, she silently shadowed the balding Scotsman to the parking lot.

"How long a drive is it?" she asked as Ned loaded her luggage into the trunk.

Slamming the lid closed, he replied. "Three, maybe four hours, depending on the weather. May as well settle in, lass. There's hot tea in the thermos and oat cakes in the bag on the seat for you. It should be enough to hold you over 'til we get there."

He opened the closest passenger door and placed her bag inside.

First the turbulent flight from hell and now an eternity trapped in a car. The air around her seemed to thicken and her chest tightened as she tumbled into the backseat. The old sedan didn't have power windows, so she turned the handle twice. Just knowing the tiny gap existed for fresh air allowed the constriction in her chest to ease slightly.

A loud clap of thunder rumbled, followed by a downpour when they reached the motorway. She leaned back, popped another Dramamine pill and chugged water from the bottle she pulled from her bag. Travel was not her forte. For the past three years she'd left the traveling up to her aunt.

Why had her aunt made her do this? Her stomach quivered and threatened to revolt. *Must've drunk too much water with that pill.*

On the slim chance it would help settle her stomach, she pulled an oat cake from the bag and nibbled at the pleasant taste of oatmeal with a hint of honey. Staring through the onslaught of rain, Ericka caught glimpses of haystacks, open fields and the occasional cottage or small village, but not many people. But what did she expect? Nobody in their right mind would be out in a storm like this.

Casting a glance at her quiet chauffeur, she sighed. Nobody but her and a balding Scotsman.

*****

"Lass."

Ericka snapped upright at the sound of an unfamiliar Scottish brogue. She gasped, realizing she'd fallen asleep in the backseat. Jetlag. It had to be jetlag that caused her to sleep in a moving vehicle. Ned's smiling eyes met hers in the rearview mirror.

"We're here, lass." He stepped out of the car and opened her door.

Sliding out, she stood beside the car, ran a hand across the bun of hair at the nape of her neck and adjusted her glasses. The rain had stopped and the vision before her stilled her movements as she took in her surroundings. Mist lingered in the tinted gray skies above the castle, adding to its haunting appearance.

Scanning the castle walls, it appeared to her that most of the stone had been refurbished. Yet there was one exception that captured her gaze, the tall, spiraling center tower. It seemed century-weathered with every crack and crumbled stone visible. The tower's fragile state was oddly out of place compared to the rest of the structure, yet hinted to its once great strength.

Lifting her gaze upward, Ericka froze, her breath stilled. Her pupils dilated at the sight of a ghostly figure in the window at the top. When she blinked, it disappeared. But was it ever truly there? She squinted, but saw nothing. It had to be a figment of her tired mind.

She repositioned her glasses again, then smoothed the front of her blouse and skirt. *Mustn't appear out of sorts.* Ericka tucked a loose strand of hair behind her ear. Aunt May needed someone to guide her in the matters of this castle and she didn't intend to let her down. No matter what it took, she planned to find out the truth behind this castle's history.

Gravel crunched beneath her feet as she followed Ned across the driveway. A magnificent carving of a kilted man in a battle stance was etched in the mahogany wood grain of the double front doors. Was it the crest of the MacKinnon clan? Could the Scotsman in the image be one of the MacKinnons? She'd have to research the door's origins. Hopefully, her aunt hadn't based her purchase on the realtor's word and the door's carving. The crest could be a fake that coincidently resembled the same one on Akira's supposed diary.

Instinctively, she clutched the bag's handle, the precious story she'd studied and researched for months nestled inside. Though she discovered vague references to the clan in early Scottish history, so far every lead had come up empty and unsubstantiated. Was it possible they were one of the many clans disbanded during the repression of the Jacobites in 1746?

Ericka traced the proud male figure with her fingertips. A vague feeling of warmth filtered across her skin. She pulled back, touching her fingertips to her lips. Had she actually felt heat from the door? It had to be because the castle was heated. She snorted at her jumpiness.

Timidly, she outlined the strong features of his face. Once again, warmth coated her fingertips as they feathered across the masculine lips of the kilted god on the door. But this time, she didn't jump.

Was this man a MacKinnon? Did they ever truly exist? Part of her hoped so as she trailed slowly down his broad chest. The warmth increased, crept through her palm, up her arm, then sent chills skittering down her spine. Before she could react, the door opened, leaving her hand lingering in midair.

"Ericka!" Aunt May grasped her hand and tugged her into a hug. Jeweled fingers clasped her shoulders as bright red lips planted a kiss on each cheek.

"It's so good to see you. I'm so glad you didn't chicken out. How was your trip?"

The simple reminder of the flight sent her stomach into somersaults. She swallowed hard, then forced a smile. "Fine. Everything went as expected."

"Oh, Ericka. Ever the practical one." She spun around. The many bangles around her wrist jingled when she waved her hand in the air. "I know you hated it. But trust me, you're going to love it here."

I hope you're right. Ericka shook her head. Ned disappeared down the hall with her luggage in hand, leaving her no choice but to follow her aunt.

The stone entryway walls were covered every few feet with tapestries depicting scenes of beautiful country. Each pictured a place Ericka could only assume was located in the highlands of Scotland. People and animals appeared captured in the motions of everyday life in ancient times. One particular picture pulled her in. Seven kilted men of various ages stood behind a trio of ladies seated in a garden.

Dark eyes beckoned her to the color-faded wall hanging. A strong jawline accentuated his kissable-looking mouth. Absently, she licked her lips. Dark hair pulled back in what she assumed was a ponytail made her fingers twitch to loosen his hair from captivity and let it fall around his shoulders. A red and green plaid draped from left shoulder to right hip. A white tunic fit taut to the broad expanse of his chest.

The rugged Scottish apparel looked good on him, but she felt it would look better in a pile around his feet. *Where had that thought come from*? she chastised herself as she continued to study the portrait.

Upon closer inspection, a gold brooch pinned on the plaid at his left shoulder sparked her interest. It held a crest similar to the carving on the door. Between the book, the door and now this brooch. Coincidence? Was it a lead to the mysterious MacKinnon clan? Excitement pinged through her. Here was finally something concrete to research more fully.

A sigh escaped as she followed the slope of his shoulder to flexing thick biceps. His hands lay poised on the hilt of a downward-pointed sword. Skilled hands, she bet. A man with hands like those knew how to work a sword as well as a woman's body. She felt a flush of heat course through her body and she shivered.

My god, it's just a portrait, she chided herself mentally. Yet the thought of him warmed her belly. Forcing her gaze up, she noticed he stood stationed off-center to the left behind the middle woman. As if magnetized by his form, her gaze drifted to the hilt of his sword once more, then dipped downward. His lower torso, hidden from view, led her imagination into a frenzy of speculation as to what lay beneath his kilt.

Unconsciously, she tilted her head sideways as if doing so she could get a peek beneath. He was a huge man with long muscled legs. She bit her lip at the prospect of what else lay hidden on the man. His cock must be proportionate to his size—most likely thick enough to drive a woman insane while making love. Her breath increased with the notion.

"Enchanting, isn't he?" Aunt May whispered in her ear.

Ericka jerked upright, adjusting her glasses. A warm sensation seeped into her cheeks. *Caught ogling an image.* She'd forgotten Aunt May stood next to her as she examined the tapestry. Hesitantly, she glanced at the male figure, who now stood with a wry smile upon his lips. Was that there before? She blinked and forced her attention to her aunt.

"I was inspecting the detail, trying to place a date of its origin," Ericka pronounced. A flustered tone tinged her words, though she'd tried to sound professional as always.

"Yeah, that's what I thought you were doing. But I have to tell you, that Gavin's the most handsome of the seven." She sighed audibly, turned and strutted toward the open door at the end of the hallway.

Ericka's mouth dropped open. Did her aunt think that these men were the MacKinnons? Glancing back at the tapestry, the man's dark eyes twinkled.

Oh god! She closed her eyes tight, took a deep breath then peeked at the tapestry once again. Normal. The eyes seemed normal now. She spun away.

I must be exhausted. That's it. I'm too tired to think straight.

Two steps. That's all she took before the hair on the back of her neck rose. Glancing over her shoulder, she gasped. A wink!

Did he just wink? That's not possible.

Jetlag. Exhausted. My eyes must be playing tricks on me. I need to lie down. I need rest. Ericka gripped the bag and hustled after her aunt. She wanted to get as far away from that portrait as possible.

* * * * *

Aye, how the memory of their laughter haunts me. The tricks thou didst play upon me whilst we were young. A simple twist of a lock of my hair doest I crave from any hand of the seven. Separation brings agony. Agony brings pain. Night after night, little rest does my body yet receive. Protect thy brathairs *at all cost 'tis my solemn oath.*

Ericka jerked upright. The skin of her arms prickled with alarm. A sensation of no longer being alone rippled through her system. Slowly, she shifted on the bed. At first sight, the woman's shape appeared hazy and unclear. Rubbing the sleep from her eyes, she stood. Was the other woman real or a figment of her imagination? She couldn't tell.

She swallowed hard, but could not force any words to form. Who was she? What did the woman want? And most of all...why wasn't Ericka scared? A stranger was in her room, but instead of fear, curiosity flowed in her blood. She could see the back of a red-haired woman seated at the desk. A thick

Scottish female brogue spoke a passage. From the subtle movement of her arms, Ericka could tell she was writing. Without a sound, she eased closer until she stood within inches of the woman's back.

Careful not to touch the woman or breathe upon her hair, Ericka leaned forward and peered over her shoulder. The handwriting was immaculate. The flow of the letters was flawless as the woman placed quill and ink to parchment instead of pen to paper. She'd seen this woman's handwriting before, but where? The answer sat poised on the edge of her gray matter, hidden behind a veil of fog.

Ericka digested every word the woman wrote. She felt the heartache radiate off the redhead's body. It permeated her senses and almost brought tears to her eyes. The woman missed someone…*brathairs*…*brathairs*. The term rattled around her brain before it struck a familiar chord. Gaelic! *Brathairs* meant brothers in Gaelic. She dared to exhale, grateful she had retained something from the Gaelic to English dictionary she used to translate Akira's diary.

The woman set down the quill and closed the leather binding over the parchment. A crest of a kilted man singed into the leather cover reminded her of the door and the replica of Akira MacDonell's diary. Could this be the real diary? She swallowed at the sudden knot in her throat. But she didn't believe it existed.

She lifted her gaze to the mirror above the desk. Lost green eyes in the face of a beautiful redhead stared back at her as if she wasn't there. But which of them wasn't? Searching the mirror, Ericka's image didn't reflect. Only the redhead and the room decorated in an ancient era appeared in the reflection.

Ericka's breath caught in her throat as she gazed about the room. An overstuffed mattress covered with heavy furs lay near the window, which was covered by dark drapes. Stepping backward, she stumbled, knocking over a privacy screen and nearly falling into a chamber pot.

Scrambling to gain her balance, Ericka grasped at the first solid piece of furniture she could reach…the desk. Frightened, she held on to the rough edge as she dared to glance around. The room was not at all as it had appeared when she entered it several hours earlier. As quick as she spun around, the room disappeared and the sensation of falling swirled around her…

Gasping for breath, Ericka sprang upright with the sheets twisted around her waist. Beads of perspiration trickled from her hairline. Moisture formed above her lip. Shakily, she grabbed the lace netting encapsulating the four-poster bed and pulled it back.

The desk chair sat empty. There was no sign of the woman or the leather binder in which she had written. Sheets swaddled her body as she forced her feet to the floor and stood. After untangling the sheets, she stepped one foot forward. The plush carpet and the four-poster bed complete with modern-day pillows, sheets and comforter were back in the room. The nightstand with a crystal lamp stood beside the bed. The painting that hung on the wall above the bureau…

Three long strides and she stood in front of the bureau. The painting had been in her dream. A redheaded woman sat on a bench in front of a tree surrounded by shrubs and flowers. The woman in the portrait looked similar to the woman Ericka had seen in her dream, but older. If the woman she dreamt about was Akira, then could this be her mother…the mother of five of the seven brothers she'd read about?

Did the MacKinnons truly exist? They couldn't have. She'd found no evidence of their existence. But were this castle and its surroundings evidence enough? If it wasn't for this damn castle and the carved crest on the front door and the diary being the same, she'd chalk it all up to being a myth. She needed proof, something to validate their authenticity. This whole thing could be an elaborate hoax. After all, it was her job to prove whether the myths her aunt collected from around the world were created from fact or pure fiction.

What about the woman in her dream? On tiptoe, she reached across the bureau and ran a hand across the textured cloth of the painting. Trembling fingertips traced the gold crest pin attached to the left shoulder of the woman. In every discussion she had with her aunt about the MacKinnons, her aunt wholeheartedly believed in their existence. She even believed this was their castle, their home.

Ericka took a deep breath and stumbled back to bed. Her head felt as if someone stood inside her skull with a handball racquet and slammed her brain from side to side.

If this castle was the MacKinnon clan's home, there had to be proof. But today was not the day for her to think about it. She told her aunt she only needed a few hours' rest. But the way she felt, she didn't plan to leave the bed until the morning.

Ericka's brain churned. She'd never dreamt so vividly before. It was as if the woman had truly been in the same room with her in the exact same time. She turned over, burying her head under the feather pillow, trying to halt the onslaught of confused thoughts. *I never saw pictures wink 'til now. It must be jetlag causing this. I've never flown before, must be jetlag.*

A slight chill fleeted across her body and sent her snuggling deeper under the covers. Every muscle relaxed as the cool sensation turned to warmth and an essence of safety filled her soul.

* * * * *

"Well?"

"'Tis done. Thy seed is planted." An audible sigh echoed her words as the apparition moved to the settee and flounced onto its cushions.

"You don't seem happy. I thought this was what you wanted…to free your brothers." Bracelets jingled as May moved to sit next to her ghostly friend.

Akira sighed again. "Aye, 'tis not a simple feat to slip into the stone. In all of these two hundred years he's slept unharmed and not aware of thy world outside his shelter. What happens if this doesn't work? Will he return to sleep? Or will he lay awake for the rest of eternity aware of the stone around him? 'Tis why I never before crossed into his thought."

May leaned back against the cushions, arms crossed upon her chest. "Then we'll just have to make sure everything goes as planned. Won't we?"

Chapter Two

ཇ

Ericka walked through the castle door and into the rear garden. Manicured hedges lined the walkway. Rosebushes and flowerbeds were in full bloom. Hints of their fragrance filled the air as she continued to explore. Exiting through the rear garden gate, the beauty of the land stole her breath. A field of heather stretched for acres, ending as it blended into the woods. A slender path wove its way through the plush surroundings, tempting her to follow its secret trail.

Several yards into the field, she knelt to gather a few stems of heather. The creak of the garden gate invaded her silent reverence. A tall, dark-haired man stood, hands on hips, dressed completely in Scottish attire. His stance seemed familiar, but she couldn't place from where she thought she knew him.

The masculine vision in a knee-length kilt, tunic tucked in at the waist, sword draped at his side, commanded Ericka's attention. Scrutinizing every inch of him, her gaze scoured his handsome face. A square jaw with lips set firm hinted at his ability to kiss. She didn't have a clue why that thought popped into her head, but his sensual stance had her licking her bottom lip in anticipation of how sweet he might taste. His dark as coal eyes startled her when they met across the field. She gasped. He couldn't have seen her.

Not heeding the trail, his steps seemed deliberate, crushing all in his path. She wanted to run, but froze in place. The intense glare of those dark eyes held hers captive. Her vocal cords refused to utter even the slightest of sounds. The man was getting closer. A scowl clouded his good looks and his dark eyes seemed furious. Her heart pounded as the blood rushed through her veins.

If he caught her, what would he do? Who was he? Seconds before he reached her, she willed the strength to move and bolted like a rabbit being chased by a wolf.

Heather slapped against her bare legs and stones bruised her tender feet as she raced for the cover of the woods. Close behind, heavy footsteps thundered. She urged more speed to her tiring legs and overrode the pain shooting from her aching feet.

Should have exercised more and what happened to my shoes?

Addled thoughts ground through her brain. Panic pushed her on. Just a few more steps and hopefully she'd escape the giant brute hot on her tail. Her overworked lungs burned, but he easily closed the distance between them with his steady gait.

As she reached the tree line, a strong arm wrapped around her waist and jerked her to a halt. A sweaty hand slapped across her mouth, muffling the scream in her throat. Her bare feet swung out from underneath her as she hung in his viselike grip several inches from the ground. His hot and rapid breaths heaved across the top of her head.

The feel of his heart pounding as he held his body pressed against her back matched the overexerted rhythmic speed of her own heart. Caught, but not for long. She sank her teeth into his palm, dug her nails into the arm banded around her waist and twisted until her heel connected with his knee.

"Agh!" He stumbled slightly off balance and she slid from his hold. Though her teeth didn't break the skin, red bite marks riddled his palm and deep nail scratches scored his arm.

"You fiery-headed wench!" His other hand whipped into her hair before she could gain her footing and balled fist-tight into her auburn locks.

Ericka fell backward against a chest of steel. His height towered over her short five-foot-two frame. The arm around her waist crushed her against the length of his body. Raggedly, she gasped for air as she tried to wiggle free.

A chuckle rumbled deep in his throat. Her eyes widened with shock as she realized the more she fought, the more he seemed to enjoy her struggle. His response was evident in the growing thickness pressing against the small of her back.

The feel of his massive size thrilled her senses. Who was he? And what did he want with her?

"How many times must I ask you not to leave the castle walls? 'Tis not safe out here." His fist knotted in her hair, stretching her neck back while his lips pressed close to her ear. The heat of his breathy words sent tingles down her spine.

Who did he think she was? She had never met this man before. A man this hunky she definitely would have remembered.

His grip loosened from her hair then slipped to her chin, tilting her head at an angle that exposed her neck.

"Please stop…I'm…" She started to tell him of his mistaken identity but the words caught in her throat when his lips lavished the tender spot. The gentle sucking of her skin between his teeth sent arrows of warmth and wetness to her pussy. His cock grew more rigid against her back. Instantly, her nipples pebbled. Why was her body reacting so fiercely to his touch?

The grip around her waist relaxed as his hand splayed across her belly. When his thumb brushed the underside of her breast, her body tensed. He was a stranger and yet she couldn't bring herself to stop him. She craved his touch. Had it been the wild pursuit across the field of heather? Or was it simply the man that had her adrenaline flowing and her body reacting to his magnificent build?

"M'Gaol."

His soft endearment struck a chord of heat within her soul. His voice, deep yet tender, sent shivers down her spine. All rational thought disappeared from her brain.

"Why must you disobey me so?" he whispered against her neck as he trailed light kisses from neck to shoulder. He eased the strap of her nightgown from her shoulder until it could move no farther, leaving her breasts trapped against the lace of the gown.

Sliding a hand under the lace, he freed a tender mound. Apt fingers tweaked the aching nipple into a reddened peak and she felt the inner muscles of her pussy clench as if the two were connected. Opening her mouth, she intended to stop him but no words would form. Instead, an unstoppable moan escaped as his fingers strummed her breasts to perfection, making her body hum with need.

"Ah, at least part of you obeys me," he whispered as he adjusted her body into the crook of one of his strong arms. In this position, she felt off balance with her head pressed against his chest and her hands grasping at his tunic. A soft laugh escaped as he nuzzled her pert nipple then sucked it into the warm moisture of his mouth. Her eyes automatically fluttered shut as his tongue danced around the hard bud.

Ericka gasped between clenched teeth as her hands latched into his hair, loosening the long dark tendrils from its ponytail. At first, her intention had been to jerk him from her breasts, but she couldn't. Tender circular ministrations of his masterful tongue and gentle nibbles of his teeth persuaded her to let him linger.

This couldn't be happening. Clutching a fist tight in his hair, she knew she should stop him, but it felt *so* good.

His other hand slipped to the lower edge of her nightgown and raised it, allowing him access to her moistened panties. The moment thick skilled fingers lifted the lacy edge, Ericka grabbed his wrist. She knew she should stop, but the heat of his hand the brush of his fingertips under the edge of her waistband had her trembling with need.

Unhindered by her hand, he slid his fingers into the warmth of her tender folds. Weakened knees threatened to crumble the instant his thumb brushed her clit as another finger penetrated her pussy. Her body's traitorous response was instantaneous.

Ecstatic moans escaped her lips as his finger rocked in a gentle to-and-fro motion and his thumb massaged her clit to the edge of oblivion. His mouth sucked her nipple as if it gave him nourishment. Harder, faster, she grasped his hand, encouraging the rhythm. Her other hand tangled in his hair, urging his mouth to continue the tortuous pleasure.

What was wrong with her? Part of her knew she should stop him, a total stranger. But, oh god, how the mystery man worked her body. Rocking harder against his hand and fabulous fingers, she was so close to orgasm.

As if he knew she wanted more, he slipped in another finger while massaging her swollen clit in harder circles with his thumb, sending sparks throughout her bloodstream and flooding her system with passion-filled fire. With her eyes closed, Ericka's head thrashed against his chest as the dammed-up river exploded.

Her juices flooded his hand. He shifted her limp body upright as he whispered raggedly against her ear. "Remove your undergarment."

Ericka trembled with need, residing in a wanton haze of desire as she slid her panties down. His intent was clear. She couldn't stop. Hell, she wouldn't stop, not when she needed to feel his cock inside her so badly.

With her panties around one ankle and her nightgown bunched above her waist, he nudged her legs apart with his thigh. The glide of his cock between her dripping pussy lips from behind until it brushed against her swollen clit teased her unmercifully. His fingers eased the head into her tight, wet entrance.

The head alone was larger than either of the two men she'd experienced sex with in the past. She gasped, hoping he would fit. Not an ounce of her wanted to end this unusual sexual experience. It didn't matter that he was a stranger, dressed in ancient clothes. She had to have him buried deep, fucking her hard.

Sex with a stranger. Why not? She sighed audibly as he coaxed his cock farther into her aching slit.

His left arm encircled her waist as his chest pressed against her back, gently easing her forward. With her hands braced against a tree, she spread her legs farther apart as he gradually entered her slickness.

"*M'Gaol*. So tight and wet, I think you enjoy the chase. It excites you." His words were hoarse against her ear.

He pushed farther, stretching her tight pussy muscles, trying to ready her for the entire length of his cock, stopping when she whimpered. Tender kisses caressed her neck as his fingers massaged her throbbing bud.

"'Tis not our first time together, and yet I hurt you?"

Biting her lip, she couldn't bring herself to answer. Painful pleasure oozed through her pussy. Though his cock was the largest she'd ever had, she wanted more. She needed to feel him buried to the hilt. Never had a man so sexually talented ever wanted her. She wasn't about to lose this chance to enjoy such pleasure simply because of a little pain. Instead of a vocal reply, she surged backward, taking more of him in with her movement.

He answered her gesture with a movement of his own. Plunging into her tightness, he steadily increased his rhythm, timed faster and faster, harder and harder until neither could bear any more. Waves of warmth and wetness crashed around them as he buried his shaft to the hilt and released his seed.

Arching back, her auburn hair scattered across her shoulders as she stretched her neck, tilted her chin upward and screamed her release. His hands cupped her breasts while his cock lay sheathed by her pussy. His warm lips pressed tender kisses upon the side of her head.

She reached over her head to gather his face in her hands. She wanted to taste his lips, feel his tongue on hers. Rough! Like sandpaper.

Her eyes flew open. Belvedere, her aunt's English Springer, stood straddled over her on the bed. Doggy breath greeted her along with a lavish rough tongue covered with drool-filled kisses.

"Crazy puppy, get down," she commanded as she pushed him off. He jumped to the floor. Barking and yelping, he raced out the partially opened door.

"Needs to go to doggy school," she muttered, flopping back on the pillows and brushing doggy slobber from her cheek.

Her clit tingled. Her nipples ached. A dream. She sighed. It had all been a dream. Disappointment flushed her system. A dull ache throbbed between tender thighs. Need, desire and sex—or the lack thereof—had caused this incredible dream. It had to be the flight combined with the medication she'd taken that added to these hallucinations. A picture didn't wink. And a gorgeous man didn't appear out of thin air, chase you down and make love to you. She snorted, shaking her head.

She sat up, pulled back the netting and swung her legs over the side. Morning sunlight spilled in through the open curtains. With her chin lifted toward the light, her eyes closed as she reveled in the remnants of the dream still vivid in her mind. The thought of his hands upon her skin and his lips upon her breasts sent a renewed rush of heat to her pussy. Her inner muscles quivered and her clit ached. Her eyes snapped open at the overactive reaction her body applied to a dream.

Forcing her body to move, she stood. After a few steps, the weakness in her thighs surprised her. It felt as if she'd been riding a horse for a week. At the sight of a vase upon the desk, she gripped the dresser for support. How did that get there?

A large crystal vase sat filled with heather in the center of the desk. She took a deep breath. *Get a grip.* It had to have been Aunt May who placed them there. It was her favorite flower and Aunt May knew it.

Ericka did several deep knee bends, trying to loosen the stiffness in her legs, which in her opinion, was from all the walking during her travels. She wasn't used to traveling, so that had to be it. She pulled fresh clothes from the drawers, then ran a hand across the flowers. Tiny soft purplish-pink petals fluttered through her fingertips as she sniffed their unique fragrance. An inaudible sigh escaped as she left the room. This wasn't anything a nice hot shower wouldn't fix.

* * * * *

The feel…the taste…the scent of her lingered. A throbbing need for her was great as he commanded his body to move. His limbs did not listen. His eyes remained closed.

Though his body did not physically respond, he wanted her. The need to feel her tight wet pussy gloved around him thrashed through his system. Somehow, he had to get out of here.

But where was here?

He could not be sure. Darkness surrounded him. The need to breathe seemed suspended, though his mind was awake. Thoughts flooded his brain. Visions of people and places flashed behind closed lids.

The face of the last person he remembered seeing sat poised clear as day. Hume MacGillivray, the devil, he did this somehow. Pain rumbled around his skull. Hunger for freedom pounded the walls of his mind. Revenge. *I need to seek revenge.*

And you shall.

A whispered sweet Scottish brogue penetrated his prison.

Akira?

'Tis me, brathair.

Where are we? Show yourself, so I may see thee.

'Tis hard to explain. As far as seeing me, search your memories. Ye shall see me there.

Explain yourself, lass! What sort of prison does this be?

'Tis a prison formed of a curse.

A curse? His thoughts switched to a forcible rumble.

The sight of a single man burned behind his closed lids. If he could reach his sword, he'd rip the ghostly remnants to shreds. Hell, if he could just move his hands, he'd tear the man limb from limb. But he could not so much as lift a finger imprisoned by the words of another.

Hume MacGillivray. The name echoed in his thoughts.

Calm yourself, brathair. *He has long since passed into the gates of hell.*

By the hand of my kin, I hope. Which of our brathairs *sought out our revenge*?

Akira paused and did not answer.

Akira?

Rest, my brathair. *Soon ye shall be free.*

Akira! his mind shouted.

Rest.

Rest! How can one's mind rest when all that's available is thought?

The memory of his wife immediately captured his interest. Tavia taunted his senses. Her beauty filled his thoughts. Long auburn hair flowed in the wind as she ran. The scent of heather teased his nasal passages as if he chased the creature of his desire once again. The rapid rhythm of his heart as he closed the distance on his prey revisited his dream. The anticipation of capturing the gentle beauty had him hard and hungry for a sample of her fine womanly attributes…her breasts, her lips and her sweet pussy.

She ran faster than he remembered and seemed eager to escape. His wife was not one to make him work this hard for their enjoyment. Her body was built for pleasure…his pleasure. Always, he made sure she knew the joys of total fulfillment, though this time seemed different.

The chase teased him greatly. But the bite to his hand and the swift kick to his knee had dampened his mood if only for a moment. Was that a new twist to their lovemaking? Where had Tavia learned such a thing…this infliction of pain in order to heighten their pleasures? But the game had been worth it. If he could smile, his lips would have covered his face.

The memory of her taste danced upon his tongue. The apt response of her breasts to his touch sensitized his frozen fingertips. The warm, wet tightness of her body as it consumed him, twitched the nerves of his shaft. Yet something was different.

Though her clothing appeared strange, its soft texture enticed him. Her scent seemed similar, yet different. The way his cock fit tight inside her luscious body had him wanting to fuck her again. Her breasts seemed fuller in his hands and the memory had him craving to suckle from them. The roundness of her bottom as it cushioned his rocking motions while pounding her pussy helped bring him splendid release. And her face, he couldn't see her face. In his rush to have her, he'd taken her from behind.

She cried as though it was their first time, but he'd had her many times. The exquisite pain of entering her tight canal thickened his member to the brink of explosion. The thought of being inside her made his heart ache. Her feel, her smell, the taste of her skin were different from memory, yet enticing. He had to have her.

Damn Hume MacGillivray! Damn this curse! Akira! Ian! Padon! Someone, anyone, set me free!

Chapter Three

ஐ

"Good morning, Ericka. Slept well, I hope?" Aunt May's cheerful greeting, the bright morning sun, the fresh crisp air and the scent of flowers greeted Ericka the minute she stepped onto the patio.

"As well as could be expected. I do apologize for not making an appearance at dinner," Ericka replied. After pouring a cup of coffee, she took a seat at the table.

Restful sleep had eluded her for most of the night. First, she dreamt of a woman visitor. When she overcame that vivid imaginary intrusion, her second dream started with a wild chase through a heather field and ended with the wettest dream she'd had in a long time. Ericka crossed her legs, hoping to alleviate the sudden ache of her clit at the memory of the fantasy man.

"No apology necessary, you were exhausted." Aunt May smiled.

Before Ericka could reply, a short, round, gray-haired woman brandishing a flour-covered rolling pin bustled through the door.

"Mistress, you promised." The red-faced woman sputtered in a thick Scottish brogue. Flour sprinkled from her hair and clothing as she animatedly waved the rolling pin in air. "You promised things like this wouldn't happen if I came to work for you. You promised!"

"Good morning to you too, Margaret. Pleased to see you're in such good spirits this morning." Aunt May rose to face the woman.

"Knew better than to come to work here." Margaret's head shook, causing a white cloud to float around her.

Ericka stifled a laugh behind her napkin. Margaret's appearance reminded her of a cartoon character who'd been hit with a bag of flour.

"Margaret, I'd like you to meet my niece, Ericka Russell," Aunt May continued in a soft relaxed tone. Bracelets jingled as she swept her arm toward Ericka.

"Pleased." Margaret nodded curtly and attempted politeness through thinned lips.

"Calm yourself and tell me what's happened." Aunt May grasped the woman's shoulders.

"She's at it again! You promised you'd keep 'er out of my kitchen! Can't work under these conditions! Gonna quit, I tell you!"

Aunt May turned the woman toward the door. "Show me what she's done."

Margaret stomped through the doorway, muttering. "Should've never let Ned talk me into this."

"Ned's wife. Best darn cook and housekeeper around. Guess we better go see what's cooking in the kitchen," Aunt May whispered to Ericka.

Upon entering the kitchen, Ericka gasped. She couldn't believe her eyes. Pots that should have hung from the ceiling rack were strewn everywhere. Flour covered the counter, walls and floor. Water overflowed the sink and mixed with the flour on the floor, turning into a gooey mess. Eggs were splattered against the refrigerator door and dripped, mixing into the oozing concoction.

Gazing around the room, she followed a trail of paw prints. Belvedere stood in the center of the mess. His tongue worked overtime, sampling the uncooked goods.

Amazing work for a puppy. How had he caused such a mess? Ericka shook her head. Margaret said "she". Didn't Margaret know Belvedere was male?

"Add a little heat to this and we've got ourselves a cake," Aunt May quipped.

Ericka laughed, but Margaret saw no humor in the situation.

"Margaret, why don't you go get cleaned up? Ericka and I can take care of this." Aunt May suggested as Ericka scooted Belvedere out the back door.

As soon as Margaret was gone, they started cleaning. Ericka swept the loose flour into a pile, while Aunt May scrubbed the counter.

"Any idea how this happened? And who did you promise to keep out of the kitchen? Margaret mentioned a she?" Ericka shot a raised eyebrow look over her shoulder at her aunt.

"Akira."

Ericka's sweeping stuttered to a halt. "Akira? You don't mean the one from the diary, do you?"

"You know another Akira? We really don't have to do this. It was her tantrum. We shouldn't have to clean this mess. You hear me, Akira?" Turning her gaze upward as she spoke, Aunt May stopped cleaning and dropped her rag in the sink.

Ericka followed her gaze, but saw nothing. Aunt May had lost her mind. She tsked. Akira wasn't real. That dog of hers had to have made this disaster.

"Come on, Ericka, let's go. She won't clean this as long as she thinks you will." Bejeweled fingers grabbed Ericka's arm and led her toward the door.

"But, Aunt May, I don't think Margaret…"

The moment the door closed, pots banged and the sound of a whirlwind whistled from inside the kitchen. Peering in the window, Ericka's jaw sagged. Pots flew back into place. The flour, eggs and gooey mess disappeared. Within a split second, the kitchen was clean. Ericka lifted her glasses, then rubbed her palm against her eyes. Unbelievable. That didn't just happen.

Aunt May peeked in the window beside Ericka. "Good. She's really not a bad ghost. It's just her way of releasing frustration. Come and sit in the garden with me."

She turned and walked down the path, bracelets jingled with every step.

Replacing her glasses, Ericka gawked at the spotless kitchen. *Must still be asleep*. She pinched herself. *Ouch*! *Nope, not asleep*. As she rubbed the forming bruise on her arm, she followed, trying to think of a rational explanation for the events she had just witnessed. Somehow, she must've bumped her head. *That's it*. She decided. *Haunted castles weren't real. Must've bumped my head during the night*.

Bewildered and confused, she sat on the bench beside her aunt. Only when Aunt May grasped her hand did she attempt to focus her thoughts.

"I want you to look at this place with an open mind, Ericka. All your life you've been practical, analyzing everything for the truth and a reason for being. Maybe, some things exist without any scientific or historical reason to back them."

"Aunt May, there's an answer for everything. You just have to know where to look."

"Then explain the kitchen." Aunt May smiled, releasing her hand as she leaned back on the bench.

"I…" Ericka bit her lip. At the moment, she couldn't.

"You can't. Akira did it." Aunt May laughed. "And that's that."

"There is no Akira." Heat flushed her cheeks as Ericka stood and spun around to face her aunt. Though she had no reasonable answer for what she saw, she refused to accept her aunt's way of thinking. There had to be a logical explanation. Ericka continued to try to reason with her aunt. "There are no such things as ghosts. And no matter what you think, I don't believe in curses either. Given a certain amount of time and the right equipment, I'm sure that I can determine what happened in the kitchen. And I'll find the truth behind this castle."

As if drawn to it, Ericka turned to face the hulking, gray stone structure. What truths were hidden within its walls? Without looking, she knew her Aunt May had risen from the bench and now stood behind her.

"Believe me when I tell you this…you're looking at Castle MacKinnon."

"What do you base that on? A crest carved in the door? Anyone could have done that. Quite possibly it's a replica. And god knows what the realtor told you." Ericka huffed in frustration.

"There was no realtor."

"What?" Ericka paused as the reality of the situation settled into her brain. How had her aunt bought a castle without a realtor? Had someone seen her as a target, an elderly, rich woman easily parted from her money? Nausea churned in her stomach as a new idea sprang to life amid the onslaught of rampant thoughts. She should have recognized sooner that her aunt's behavior had turned into an obsession with this nonexistent clan.

Aunt May returned to the bench, sat down and crossed her arms over her chest.

"There was no realtor involved. I found this place all on my own." For a moment, she hesitated. "Well, I did have a little help."

"I don't understand. Who helped you? Who conned you into buying this place?"

Ericka fisted her hands. Her aunt spoke in riddles and she didn't have time for this. If she acted quickly enough and informed the authorities, maybe they would catch the thief and retrieve her aunt's money.

"No one conned me, as you so politely put it. Akira led me here and I bought it from the owners for a reasonable price."

"Now we're back to this ghost."

Totally frustrated, Ericka plopped onto the bench beside her aunt. With her forefinger and thumb, she lifted her glasses and pinched the bridge of her nose. Not only was *she* suffering from some sort of jetlag craziness, her aunt had obviously bumped *her* head and lost *her* marbles.

"Just once, believe the impossible. Don't search for a reason or a truth. Accept what you've seen without documentation to prove it." She shot a sideways smile at Ericka as she continued. "Akira has haunted and protected this castle for over two hundred years. And I think it's time you find out why."

Aunt May pulled a tattered leather journal from her pocket and handed it to Ericka.

Shakily, Ericka traced the faded crest of the MacKinnons etched in the cover. Akira's diary. The one she saw in her dream. The one Akira wrote in as she watched.

"By chance, I found this in an old bookstore in Lochaby, which was going out of business. All the books were packed in crates. You bought the crates sight unseen and took your chances. Of course, I bought several." Aunt May's eyes sparkled. Ericka knew her love of books and was surprised that she didn't buy the whole store.

"I spent the rest of that day in my hotel suite with these books scattered about. And this one…" Her aunt ran a finger over the crest as she paused. "This one caught my attention. That night was the first time Akira reached out to me."

"Sure it wasn't a dream?" Ericka asked, staring at the tattered cover…the proud Scotsman held his sword drawn ready for battle. With a ginger motion, she flipped through the yellowed pages. This volume seemed thicker than her copy.

"It wasn't a dream. Akira made a connection with me through that diary." Aunt May's head shook as she spoke.

"But the book you gave me—" Aunt May cut her off before she could finish her sentence.

"A friend of mine who owns a small press put that version together. It gave you just enough information to capture your interest, but not enough to tell you their entire life story." Aunt May's arm draped across her shoulders.

"I don't understand." Disbelief surged through her veins as she stared at her aunt.

What made her aunt do that? As far as she knew, Aunt May had never before deliberately withheld information pertaining to a research project. What made this project different? How was she expected to do her job without *all* of the available information? Ericka swallowed hard, tamping down her rising anger. Forcing a level of control to her voice that she didn't feel in her gut, she continued.

"My job is to research the myths that you find. Why did you not give me everything? I thought we were a team."

"Greed." Aunt May laughed as she stood. "I wanted to keep their story to myself. But then I came to realize that not only did Akira need me, she needed you too."

Long after Aunt May left, Ericka sat, gently turning the fragile parchment pages as if each were a newborn kitten and she afraid to drop it. More pages. So much more information. Scanning the paragraphs of feminine Gaelic script, she realized she needed the Gaelic to English dictionary she kept in her bag.

She hurried into the castle and up the stairs. After retrieving the dictionary, she returned downstairs, wandered through the castle and out into the rear garden. Weeds were scattered amongst the roses and hedges, but the place seemed familiar. The garden gate hung ajar and creaked as she pushed it open. Ericka gasped. Heather stretched for acres, touching the woods on the opposite side.

The field from her dreams. How could it be? *I must've seen it from a window yesterday.*

She deeply inhaled the heavenly scent. After walking a few feet, she sat cross-legged, surrounded by the tall flowers and placed the dictionary and diary in her lap. A déjà vu sensation filtered through her system and a chill skittered down her spine. Warmth pooled in her pussy as a flash of the dream entered her thoughts. Her inner muscles ached for the length of his cock embedded deep, his fingers gripping her hips as he rode her to oblivion. Nervously, she licked her bottom lip and dared a glance across her shoulder. No tall, dark handsome man followed. She snorted at her own stupidity. Fantasy man didn't exist. It was all a wet dream.

Icy coldness shrouded her aura even though she sat in the sun. *I must be coming down with something.* Shivering, she tried to shake it off, but the sensation lingered.

Picking up the diary, she read a passage.

Hume MacGillivray returned to the clan today.

How did she do that? Scanning the page again, she read the Gaelic as if it were second nature. She hadn't used the dictionary. Maybe, they were words she already knew from her prior study of the replica diary. But this page wasn't familiar. It wasn't one from her copy.

"Read. Don't question."

A thick female Scottish brogue echoed. Nearly jumping from her skin, Ericka huddled low in the long stems of heather. Had she heard someone? Darted glances about the field gave the impression she was alone. Was someone hiding in the flowers?

"Read!" This time the voice snapped.

She spun on her knees, searching the perimeter for the perpetrator of the voice. Seeing no one, she sat back on her heels. *Now I'm hearing things.* She laughed to herself and settled back into a comfortable reading position. Once again, she opened the diary to read. Not sure how she was accomplishing it, she read the Gaelic and understood each word.

Hume MacGillivray returned to the clan today. 'Tis many years since we've seen him. Though he appears frail and subdued, I feel a strength within him. His presence contains an energy. One I do not recognize.

Gavin accepts him with open arms. Proclaims his return as a gift from god and thanks the monks which saved him. But I…I choose to seek him out with caution. The presence I feel is shrouded in darkness and darkness leads to evil.

Ericka stretched her neck from side to side and adjusted her glasses. Akira knew something wasn't right, yet her brother failed to listen. Typical male. He refused to listen to a woman, guess he got what he deserved, she silently scoffed.

A sharp pain burned inside her skull.

Never speak ill of my brathair! The words rumbled inside her head behind the burning pain, scorching all thought.

That voice again on top of a migraine. Ericka removed her glasses and pressed her palms against her temples in a futile attempt to subside the blaring pain.

Believe what you like! But 'tis me, Akira, who speaks to you.

Akira? Ericka refused to believe it was Akira. The diary dropped from her lap and tumbled into the heather as she shot to her feet. Both hands clutched her head, fighting the blinding pain bouncing around her skull. She squeezed harder and covered her ears, as if by doing so, the voice would go away.

How else do you read Gaelic so well?

Crazy, I've slipped into a world of craziness. It must still be jetlag. Ericka closed her eyes until the dizzying pain subsided. When it passed, she opened her eyes. A ghostly vision of a green-eyed, red-haired woman stood directly in front of her. The diary floated in midair, extended from a transparent hand.

Be sure to finish this if you plan to help me.

All air rushed from Ericka's lungs as darkness surrounded her. Pure icy coldness swept across her body, causing her leg muscles to weaken and she folded to the ground.

* * * * *

"What did you do?" May demanded as soon as the door to Ericka's room closed behind Ned. He carried Ericka inside and upstairs after May found her unconscious in the heather field. She tucked the covers up around Ericka's cold body.

"I simply helped her read Gaelic the same way I helped you."

"Oh," May spoke. "Akira, dear, you must realize that not everyone likes it when you enter their minds."

Before Akira could protest, May's hand shot up in halt. "Ericka is the daughter I never had. She understands me and loves me in a way no one else ever has and I won't let you torment her. I want you to give her a chance to accept you at her own pace."

Akira vanished the moment Margaret entered the room carrying a fresh pitcher of water, a glass and a cloth on a tray.

Promise not to torment her. May paused in the thoughts she sent out to Akira. *Or I'll take her home and you'll wait, oh…perhaps another two hundred years for the one who could set your* brathair *free.*

* * * * *

Ericka woke to a cool cloth across her eyes. She started into an upright position and grabbed her glasses from the nightstand. Fully dressed with the exception of her shoes, she was in bed. But how?

The last thing she remembered…Akira!

Jumping from the bed, she spun full circle, searching under the bed, the ceiling and even the closet for the slightest inkling of the otherworldly being. If there was such a thing. She shook her head in disagreement with her thoughts as she sat on the edge of the bed.

The diary lay open on the nightstand. Obviously, someone—or something, she sighed—left it there on purpose.

The passage on the page drew her in as if it spoke to her. Lifting the book, she read.

'Tis for all and none to see.

The king within his castle center

His essence captured by thy brush

Bold 'n strong forged for the master

Go forth 'n touch his claymore strength

'Tis giveth the answer which ye seek.

It made no sense as she read it again and again.

A riddle! Why would Akira's diary contain a riddle? She skimmed back through the pages and read. The reasoning behind the riddle became clear.

Hume MacGillivray was determined to destroy the MacKinnons even after casting the supposed curse upon the brothers. Lowering the book to her lap, Ericka stared into space.

This book gave her more insight into the MacKinnon clan than the replica she owned. Akira's fears rippled through Ericka and tugged at her heart.

Seven brothers turned to stone by a curse. One crazy clansman with revenge on his mind and a determined sister to save her brothers sounded like a farfetched, sci-fi, B-movie. But did it happen? She fingered the book, skimming over different passages as she went. The part of her hungry for hot sex wanted to believe. The analytical half of her brain still had doubts. Compelled to learn more, Ericka continued to read.

With the help of her husband's clan, Akira hid them. Seven brothers scattered throughout the countryside on the slim hope that she would someday find a way to set them free. Ericka's heart thumped, her breath stilled. If the curse truly existed…and her family was torn apart…it had to have been devastating.

The riddle was a clue. But to what? Was it a way to set them free or the location of one of the brothers?

Tucking the diary in the waistband of her jeans, Ericka's feet hit the floor before she thought it through, knowing that if she did, logical reasoning would stop her. If her perspective of the first two lines were correct, then one of the brothers was hidden in the castle.

'Tis for all and none to see

The king within his castle center

She galloped down the stairs, taking them two at a time. An urgent need to find the castle's center coursed through her veins. Running out the front door, she skid to a halt in the driveway, spun around on her heels and faced the castle. Like a dead tree in a forest of green, the tallest tower captured her gaze. Crumbled stone slipped free and rolled down from the slender remnants of a window ledge. Ericka's heart skipped a beat. Was her fantasy man hidden within those tired walls? From the condition of the stone, she decided climbing to the closest window was not an option.

The king within his castle center. The line haunted her thoughts as if she should have known the castle held a mystery and the ancient tower was the key to unraveling the tale.

Where was its entrance? There had to be some sort of door.

Returning to the main hallway, she opened every door and searched each room for the tower's elusive entryway. As she passed the MacKinnon tapestry, an image of a grand archway opening into a long corridor flashed into her mind's eye. Stopped by the sudden vivid detail, Ericka turned to face the tapestry. Every nerve ending stood on edge, her breath hitched and her lips slightly parted as if to speak but no words escaped. An invisible band seemed wrapped around her shoulders, tugging her closer to the painted still of the MacKinnons. As if blinders were placed on her face, her focus limited to one figure, the others failed to exist.

Fantasy man, the one from her dream, stood in the center of the scene and now she knew his name. Aunt May called him

Gavin. Was it because of seeing his image on this wall hanging that she dreamt of him? She couldn't be sure as her gaze raked along his form.

Tall and strong, he stood. His broad chest and thick arm muscles made her gut clench. The phantom feel of his dark hair in her hands absently twitched her fingers, making her rub her palms on her thighs. Staring into his motionless eyes increased her pulse by a beat or two. The full curve of his sensuous lips made her mouth water for a real taste and not a dream sample. Tightening her thighs, she tried to quell the sudden ache of her clit for his tongue to tickle her intimate spot. She shivered, trying to rein in the overactive libido his image jump-started to life, but couldn't succeed in calming her body's reaction.

Damn, she reprimanded herself. He wasn't real, or was he? That little smidgeon of hope made a tingle trip along her spine, warming her from the inside out.

Was he trapped in stone and hidden in the castle? Ericka lifted her finger and gingerly caressed his cheek. Warmth zapped her fingertip, shot up her arm, down her spine and pooled in the pit of her sex, making her jump back. Clutching her hand to her chest, she stared wide-eyed at the image. Had she really felt heat sizzle through her fingertip? She couldn't be sure.

One thing she did know…she needed answers to this obscure riddle before she slipped any further into the insanity that threatened her normally secure world. Taking a deep breath, she forced her hand to move and brushed her fingers across the tapestry but did not touch Gavin's image. Nothing. No heat, not even a shimmer of warmth brushed her skin.

Carefully, she inched her fingers toward the image of fantasy man. Trembling, she brushed them across the painted replicas of his lips, aching for a true kiss. Heat spread from her fingertips, slowly burning up her arm to her neck, then warming her mouth as if the painted image had read her mind and sent her a kiss via pure heat. Ericka gasped, but couldn't pull back.

The heat inched a degree higher and traveled throughout her being with each movement of her fingertips. If a touch of his lips garnished her with an invisible hot kiss... Her heartbeat increased threefold, she swallowed hard and let her fingers travel where they may. Slowly, she caressed his torso, down to his kilt. What would happen if she touched where kilt met muscled thigh? In her dream, she experienced his magnificent cock, and secretly she hungered to fuck him for real, even though she had her doubt about his true existence. But a girl could dream, couldn't she? The thought entered her mind, making her smile.

Gathering her courage, she traced the lower edge of his kilt. The memory of his thighs brushing against the back of hers, his chest pressed to her back and his cock buried inside her pussy with his hands kneading her breasts as he fucked her from behind, made her knees weak as the dream flashed in her head and the sensation of heated breath tickled her ear.

Ericka jerked her hand to her chest, grappling for control over the surge of need rushing through her veins. Her heart pounded, blood raced through her system and she gasped for air as if she'd just run a race. What was wrong with her? she snapped in her thoughts.

She stepped back until she stood on the other side of the hall opposite the tapestry, leaning against the cool stone wall. As she steadied her nerves, she thought about the current exchange of heat with an inanimate object. His very essence seemed to have exuded through the silken strands of the tapestry, soaking into her soul and commanding her attention. His essence!

Ericka jerked the diary from her waistband and flipped it open to the riddle.

His essence captured by thy brush

Her gaze flicked from the diary to the tapestry and back again. It was a clue. Was the tapestry the entrance to the center tower? If so, why hadn't anyone found it before? Taking a deep breath, she tried to quell the rise of excitement rippling thorough her system as she studied the fourth line.

Bold 'n strong forged for the master

She closed the book with her finger holding the place and paced a circle in front of the tapestry. Bold 'n strong. Bold 'n strong. Pausing, Ericka studied the entire tapestry, gazing from one image to the other, searching every aspect of the picture for the simplest of overlooked detail. The answer was staring back at her, she just knew it, could feel it in her bones.

"Ericka, are you all right? Should you be out of bed?" Aunt May's concerned tone shattered her concentration.

She spun around to face her aunt. How had she not heard the jingle of the bracelets?

"Where'd you come from?" she snapped, aggravation clear in her tone. The surprised gasp of Aunt May startled Ericka's senses, making her realize just how mean she sounded.

"I'm sorry. I didn't mean that the way it sounded." She licked her lips and shook herself to gain composure. Aunt May's arm slipped across her shoulders, tugging her into a much-needed hug.

"It's all right, dear. You didn't hear me come down the hall, that's all. I frightened you. Lord knows you've been frightened enough today." Aunt May's gaze turned toward the ceiling as if looking for something or someone.

Ericka managed a weak smile. "Still, it doesn't give me just cause to snap at you."

As if on cue, her stomach rumbled and Aunt May guided her toward the kitchen door. "Come, dear. It sounds to me like you're hungry and to tell you the truth, I could use something too."

Once settled on the patio outside the kitchen with a bowl of stew, a slice of fresh bread and a tall glass of milk, Ericka relaxed. The diary passage played over and over in her head. The riddle was the key. But what did the fourth line mean?

Her aunt believed the curse was real. Would Aunt May understand the riddle? If Aunt May was connected with Akira as she claimed, would the ghost give her the answer? Was it hunger, exhaustion or the deep-seated desire for a man that didn't exist making her think the impossible?

Curses and ghosts don't exist.

Dipping the bread into her stew, Ericka managed a hearty bite. The diary sat on the table between her and her aunt. This trip to Scotland tired her thoughts and battered her sense of reality.

The man on the tapestry visited her dream. Was he the star of her exciting sex dream because she stared at him when she first saw the tapestry? A shudder ran down her spine and she almost missed her mouth with the spoon. Things like this didn't happen. Not to her. If she could touch it, see it, feel it and taste it, *it* was real.

Invisible sensations of his touch lingered on her skin making her shiver. His essence haunted her memory keeping her senses on edge. Closing her eyes for a moment, she reveled in faint remnants of the dream of how his body felt so warm wrapped around her and his cock was so hard as he plunged… Her eyes snapped open. Though she tried to convince herself it wasn't real, *he* wasn't real, her body reacted anyway, dampening her panties and pebbling her nipples. Though she forced the spoon into her mouth, she hungered for his taste and his alone.

The stew wasn't cutting it.

Chapter Four

ꟾ

While eating, Ericka explained what she found in the diary to her aunt. After they finished eating, Ericka and Aunt May returned to the tapestry. Together, they dissected the fourth line of the riddle. Ericka read aloud the first few lines.

"'Tis for all and none to see, the king within his castle center, his essence captured by thy brush. This made me think that there's something—"

"Or someone," Aunt May cut in.

Ericka cleared her throat as her heart skipped a beat at the prospect of fantasy man being real. "Or *someone* hidden in the center tower and this tapestry had something to do with it. Is there a way in?"

"I haven't found one. The couple I bought the castle from didn't know of an existing entrance. The people they bought it from never found an entrance either, so it was assumed that the passageway was sealed many years ago. And with this castle being so ancient, there isn't an existing original blueprint."

"Most of the outside and inner walls were refurbished. Why was one tower left untouched?" Ericka hesitated, but asked anyway, knowing what her aunt would answer and not sure if she was ready to accept it. "Why stop there?"

"Akira. She's haunted this castle, that tower in particular, for two hundred years. Every time any sort of renovation started on the outside of the tower walls, she ended it by scaring off the contractor or causing little catastrophes until they stopped and left it alone. I think she did it to protect her brother." Aunt May ran a hand lovingly across the tapestry.

She stood silent beside her aunt. A haunted castle, an ancient diary, a riddle and an aunt with an overactive imagination was a little too much for her to digest. Her aunt's face held a vivid glow to her skin and her eyes seemed to glimmer with delight as she studied the tapestry. This sort of stuff excited her aunt.

Suddenly, a veil of fog lifting from her brain, Ericka inhaled deeply. Aunt May read myths, fables and legends to her as a child. She believed in Bigfoot and the Loch Ness monster, even convinced Ericka that together they would find them when she grew up.

An unpreventable smile tugged at the corners of her lips. This was the Bigfoot and Loch Ness adventure she was promised as a child, except with a twist. It all clicked in place. The strange diary. The sudden acquisition of a supposedly haunted castle. And to top it all, she made Ericka travel into the highlands of Scotland.

This was Aunt May's way of keeping a childhood promise of the *big* adventure. She couldn't believe it took her so long to catch on and had to swallow hard not to audibly laugh at her own lack in perception. Somehow, Aunt May was behind all of this so they could have that great adventure they dreamt about when she was a kid.

As an adult, Ericka never was the one to jump at a spur-of-the-moment adventure. Everything had to be planned. This was the reason her last boyfriend dumped her four years ago, not spontaneous…too stoic, prim and proper.

Well, she'd show him. She'd do this without looking for a rational reason to back it. Careful not to touch Gavin, she ran her hand along the tapestry as she shot a sideways glance at her aunt. Besides, it'd make Aunt May happy if she played along with this little scenario.

"So." Ericka paused, took a breath then leveled her voice to sound normal, not wanting to let her aunt know she'd figured out the truth. "You really believe in this curse, don't you?"

"Yes, I do," Aunt May replied. "Read me the rest of the riddle and together we'll figure it out."

Ericka stifled the knowing laugh she felt rise to the back of her throat. If it was an adventure Aunt May wanted, Ericka wouldn't let her down. Once again, she read aloud from the diary.

"Bold 'n strong forged for the master, go forth 'n touch his claymore strength, 'tis giveth thine answer which ye seek."

As she spoke the words, the sensation of being watched skittered across her skin. Lifting her gaze, she met the dark stare of the oldest brother and her chest tightened. Gavin, his stance, bold and strong. She gasped. That was it. He was the answer. Was he the one supposedly hidden in the castle?

Her inner thigh muscles quivered at the prospect of him being real and a renewed ache lodged in her clit. But he didn't exist, she reprimanded herself silently. This was a game created by her aunt. A great big game of adventure. Her eyes widened the moment her gaze lowered to his hands.

Forged for the master! The cold steel of his sword…steel is forged to create different things, including swords, and the Scotsmen were known for their swords. Especially—she adjusted her glasses and leaned in closer to the tapestry—the Scottish Highlander's dual-edged, broadsword known as the claymore.

Why hadn't she thought of this sooner? Had she forgotten all that she studied about Scottish history in college? Or was it fogged by the jetlag she swore still plagued her system? It had to be the jetlag. A hearty victorious laugh verged on the edge of hysterical escaped as she stood up straight.

"You okay, dear?" Aunt May's hand touched Ericka's arm.

"Couldn't be better." She smiled at her aunt as she continued. "It's his sword."

"Whose sword? They all have swords."

Ericka pointed at Gavin. "His. He was the oldest. Was he not?"

"Yes, but—"

Ericka cut Aunt May off this time. "He ruled the clan after their father died so, that made him king of this castle."

"'Tis for all 'n none to see, the king within his castle center." The words crossed her lips on a whisper as her trembling fingertips brushed his cheek. As expected, warmth sizzled up her arm, igniting the excitement growing in her belly. Ericka licked her lips, then continued.

"Akira and her husband hid him where it was too obvious to look. Right here in his own home and I bet they're the ones that sealed its entrance to ensure his safety." Ericka stated as if hearing her reasoning out loud would convince her to believe her own conclusions.

"His essence captured by thy brush could only mean a painting such as this tapestry. Bold 'n strong forged for the master implicates a forged gift such as a sword for the master of the house. Go forth 'n touch his claymore strength could only mean..."

Slowly, she traced a path down his chest to his waist. Her hand shook, suspended in air millimeters above the masculine hands wrapped around the sword's large hilt. Was this the answer? Did it mean for her to touch his hands or rather the sword itself?

Oh, well, here goes nothing. With a shrug, she expelled the breath she hadn't realized she held as she pressed her finger against his hands.

A bump!

She felt a bump under the tapestry located behind his hands. The pressure from one finger wasn't enough so she pressed her palm against his hands. When that didn't work, she pressed both hands against his and leaned into it with every ounce of her body weight. Feeling a slight movement, she leaned in harder, refusing to buckle to the resistance from the unknown object.

Suddenly, her efforts paid off and the bump slid backward into the wall. Ericka fell against the heavy tapestry as Aunt May grasped the back of her shirt and helped her regain her balance.

The scrape of stone against stone and the grind of some sort of contraption reached their ears. Ericka's heart seemed to stop when a loud pop echoed from behind the tapestry. Then the noise stopped. Straining against the silence but unable to move, Ericka heard nothing.

What happened? Had she opened the entrance? A cool breeze fluttered the tapestry and made its fringed lower edges lift from the wall.

"'Tis giveth the answer which ye seek," Ericka whispered as she grasped the edge of the tapestry and lifted.

A dark hole appeared in the wall. Its size equaled that of one of the large stones in the castle walls, which were about four-feet wide by four-feet tall. Its depth was immeasurable due to the lack of light.

Ericka held the tapestry back with one hand and shoved her other into the darkness all the way to the shoulder, not certain what she expected to find. The end of the tunnel, a light source of some kind, but nothing brushed her fingertips. Where had the stone gone? She stuck her head inside, but nothing magically appeared.

Aunt May's bejeweled hand clasped her shoulder and pulled Ericka out. "I'll get a flashlight. Wait for me."

An incredible urge beckoned her to crawl inside the moment Aunt May was gone. Ericka slid a chair from the dining room and positioned it below the hole. With a sash from one of the dining room curtains, she rolled the tapestry back and tied it in place. This provided little light past the entrance of the hole, but that didn't stop her.

She stood on the chair and crawled into the tunnel. There wasn't enough space for her to stand, so she inched along on hands and knees. Several feet into the hole, a bright beam of light shot past her and lit the end of the tunnel. The length of the tunnel seemed to equal the width of about four of the large wall stones, approximately sixteen feet was her best guess.

"Couldn't wait for me, could you?" The light's beam jiggled as Aunt May quickly caught up and handed her the flashlight.

"Thanks."

Ericka focused the light on the end of the tunnel. It was blocked. Was there another secret door? Easing closer, she searched the floor and the walls for a trigger that would open the exit. When she reached the end, she examined the flat surface of the stone until she saw a bump.

Deciding it was the same bump that started the stone's movement, she pushed it again. Nothing happened. With the light in one hand she traced the edge with her finger and found thin cracks on either side. At the top and the bottom, the stone sat wedged tight.

"Anything," Aunt May whispered in her ear.

"Not sure, here, take this." She handed the flashlight to her aunt.

Ericka sat on her heels and put her shoulder against the stone blocking the exit. Digging her knees in, she leaned into the cold, hard surface. It inched forward but not enough to free it from its lodged position.

Aunt May set the flashlight down and squeezed in beside Ericka. Together, they leaned into the stone and pushed. It eased forward about another inch, then stopped.

They both inhaled deeply and wiped beads of perspiration from their brows as they sat back on their heels and rested. Ericka hadn't gone this far to be stopped by an inanimate object. It moved once and she was determined to make it move again. Grunting and teeth gritted, Ericka plowed into the stone with all the force that being on her knees allowed. The stone slid forward and toppled from the tunnel. The momentum of her adrenaline rush sent her tumbling out behind it.

Dust filled the air and coated her lungs. Coughing and gasping for breath, Ericka stood.

"You okay?" Aunt May's head popped out of the opening.

"Yeah. You?" Ericka helped her aunt from the tunnel.

"Yes!"

The excitement of her response made Ericka laugh as she retrieved the flashlight. "Glad to see you're having fun. Now to see where we've landed."

The large stone lay cracked on the floor. Looking up, she saw an early rendition of a pulley system. The bump on the stone was a trigger. Pressing it set the whole thing in motion, but the rope had broken. Years of deterioration caused it to snap before the job of removing the stone from the tunnel was complete.

Light from the flashlight fanned the massive room as she turned. A breeze filtered down a stairwell to her left and she shivered. A large collection of candles sat in the center of a table in the middle of the room. Gently, she shuffled through the books and parchment which lay stacked on the tabletop as if the owner would return to read them at any moment.

Aunt May moved to the table and pulled matches from her pocket.

"Always be prepared," she quipped, as she lit the candles one by one. As each flame flickered, then caught, the room became illuminated. Aunt May studied the papers as if she were a detective searching for a clue.

"Where do you think we are?" Cool air blew across Ericka's bare arms and an icy cold chill ran down her spine. She spun around, cascading the dark stairwell's entrance with light. Nothing appeared, though the sensation of being watched made her wary.

"This has to be the center tower," Aunt May replied without looking up from her task.

Ericka moved closer to the stairs and flicked the light up the cracked and crumbled staircase. They didn't look safe. At one time, they were probably a beautiful masterpiece of a craftsman's skill. A quiet sigh escaped as she turned to walk away. This tower was in dire need of repair and it broke her heart to see it in such ruins.

The moment her back faced the stairs, an icy cold sensation filled the room.

Déjà vu, it must be the wind. Ericka shook all the way to her toes.

"Looks like this was the master suite of the castle."

Ericka stepped on what once was a plush fur rug, which covered most of the floor. A thick pile of dusty pillows and furs were gathered near the fireplace. Visions of a romantic evening snuggled in a pair of strong arms traipsed through her thoughts and returned some of the heat to her veins.

Was this his room? Had he truly existed?

For a moment she stood lost in a daydream, longing for his touch, his kiss and a tumble in the pillows. A flush rose to her cheeks as the memory of fantasy man heated her from the inside out. Absently, her foot tangled in a fur and she stumbled into the darkest corner.

Ericka gasped as the air was knocked from her lungs when she abruptly stopped mid-fall. Colliding with something large, cold and hard kept her from hitting the floor. She sprang upright, spun around and stepped backward as she lifted the flashlight. Her jaw dropped. As she soaked in the magnificent stone statue of a man, her heart fluttered.

"Looks like the master's still in it." Aunt May gave a low whistle as she moved to stand beside Ericka.

Not just any man. Ericka swallowed deep with her eyes glued to the chiseled features of the stone god. The statue resembled her fantasy man. In her erotic dream, he dominated her body and gave her the best sex of her life. The sensation of his warm lips tasting her skin and his masterful fingers rolling her nipples, made moisture form in her sex, her heart raced and her clit throbbed.

How could this be? How was he the star in her wet dream? She glanced at her aunt. And more importantly…how had her aunt accomplished such a feat?

Standing within arm's reach of the statue, Ericka couldn't force herself to touch it. It wasn't real, it couldn't be. The strong features of Gavin were frozen in stone. She paced around him. His long hair was pulled back and tied with a simple strip of what she guessed to be leather. The square jaw, broad shoulders and chest hinted at his strength. On tiptoe, Ericka leaned in close as if she could read his thoughts through the pained expression which marred his otherwise handsome face. What had he seen? Pain? Treachery? What filled his thoughts at the time of his imprisonment in stone?

His right hand held the hilt of the sword partially drawn from the sheath on his left hip. *He never had a fighting chance.* Ericka bit her lower lip and touched the hand gripping the hilt of his trusted claymore. Warmth flashed through her fingertips and she stumbled backward.

Aunt May caught her before she hit the floor. "What happened?"

"Nothing," she stuttered, righting herself with her aunt's help.

That didn't happen, she reasoned, but chose not to touch it again. Rubbing her hand against her thigh, she tried to dissolve the warm sensation as she circled the statue. Ericka perused every inch of his masculine male being from his face to his knee-length kilt and stopping at the laced-up boots on his feet. Though her fingers itched to follow the tempting path of her eyes, she kept them wrapped tight around the flashlight, not willing to chance feeling the mystery heat again.

"What do you think that is?" Aunt May pointed to an oval-shaped, thin slate which lay at his feet.

Both knelt to examine it. Ericka brushed her fingertips across the Gaelic verse inscribed on its otherwise smooth surface. The words tumbled over in her head, yet their meaning sat poised on the edge of her gray matter just out of reach. In a feeble attempt at Gaelic, she recited the passage.

"That's all wrong!" An eerie female Scottish brogue echoed around the room as a cold sensation captured Ericka's body. Frozen to the bone, she shivered and her teeth chattered.

Without thought, she recited the passage again, but this time in perfect ancient Gaelic.

"Ceum saor de clach

Be ye biast air duine

'Tis gaol dara slighe

Ge ye be meinne

dh' oidhche mur

dh' la."

The coldness left her body as quickly as it had taken over. Ericka sank to her knees. Afraid of what Aunt May would say happened, Ericka didn't ask. Somehow, she spoke fluent Gaelic, something she otherwise wouldn't be able to do. Akira's presence must have entered her body, for not only had she spoken the passage, she could translate it into English.

The passage repeated in her head. It made no sense.

"Think we could get some tea?" Ericka rasped.

"Of course, dear, we can come back later."

Aunt May helped Ericka to the tunnel. After picking up the flashlight, Aunt May walked over and blew out the candles.

"Next time we'll bring more light and a space heater," Aunt May stated as if she spoke to someone else.

Ericka crawled into the tunnel. She needed a good stiff drink, but would settle for a hot cup of tea.

* * * * *

"Mind explaining what happened back there?" Aunt May said as she poured hot water from the kettle onto the tea bag in Ericka's cup.

"I can't. But I can translate what I said, though it doesn't make much sense." Ericka shrugged. She wasn't ready to admit that a paranormal event may have happened to her. It wasn't logical. Clearing her throat, she recited the words like they were a well-written poem.

"Step free of stone, be ye beast or man, 'tis love either way, though ye be mine by night, if not by day."

M'Gaol. My love. Chills fanned her skin and bulleted down her spine. He called her *M'Gaol* in her dream. Shaking her head, she swallowed hard. *He didn't exist. He lived in her imagination*. Silently, she reprimanded herself.

"Let's break it down like we did the riddle. It's sure to mean something, especially since we found it at Gavin's feet." A wide grin spread across her aunt's face.

"Oh, Aunt May," Ericka snapped on an exasperated breath. Regret washed over her the moment she saw the sparkle diminish from her aunt's eyes.

She shouldn't have spoken so harshly. This woman practically raised her when her parents were off on some archeological dig, leaving her in the States. Aunt May gave her life excitement when she was a child. What happened? Had she grown so analytical as an adult that she had no imagination left for the fantastical realm of her aunt? If Aunt May wanted to continue the charade, then so would she. Reaching across the table, she patted her aunt's hand.

"I'm sorry. I'm just a little tired. But if you want, we can break it down." She stood and picked up her tea.

Ericka sipped her tea while she paced the inside of the ivy-covered, three-foot high wall, which separated the patio from the side garden. The scene which greeted her tired eyes soothed her overactive senses.

Belvedere ran as if hot on the trail of something through the wildflowers, which grew scattered amongst the hills, rocks and trees. The sun sat poised on the edge of the horizon daring her to blink, for if she did, she'd miss its nightly disappearing act.

The ancient passage tumbled from her lips and whispered across the rim of the cup she held poised millimeters from her mouth.

"Step free of stone, be ye beast or man, 'tis love either way, though ye be mine by night, if not by day."

The sun disappeared as if it waited for her to speak those words and send it off to bed. The saying scrolled through her brain like it was imprinted on a ticker tape that revolved over and over.

"Step free of stone," Ericka repeated on a whisper. In the distance, Belvedere sprang from behind a boulder, chasing something obscured by the early evening light. Her eyebrow hitched as a vivid image flashed in her head. One minute he was hidden, the next he was free of the stone and visible. Beast or man, she mulled over the idea. Step free, beast or man…

"It's possible that what we found might be an anti-curse," she stated as she spun around to face her aunt.

May sat upright, her mouth dropped open as stuttered excitement shook her words. "You mean we've found the way to save him?"

Returning to her seat, she glanced up at the last lingering rays of sunlight. She hated what she was about to say because she knew the response she would receive.

"We didn't find the way to release her brother. It was placed there for us to find. But by whom?"

"Akira." The word floated out of her aunt's mouth just like she knew it would.

The older woman sat across the table from her with a smug grin on her lips, a gleam in her eyes and arms folded in a matter-of-fact way across her chest. This was more than just a game of wits with her aunt. It was the big adventure, so Ericka played along.

"Why didn't she free him herself if she knew the anti-curse?" Ericka leaned back and folded her arms across her chest. Two could play this game. She couldn't wait to hear this answer.

"'Tis only half a freedom."

Ericka jumped, dropping her arms to her side. Aunt May's lips hadn't moved. That voice! Her heart thundered and her stomach clenched. She'd heard that voice before.

"Akira, I asked you not to do that." This time, her aunt did speak. She watched her lips move.

Ericka grabbed the table's edge. Her knuckles whitened. A bright green-eyed, redheaded woman materialized behind Aunt May. It was the specter she thought she saw in the field earlier. It wasn't a dream. She wanted to believe it was a dream. How was her aunt doing this? Glancing from side to side, she searched. Where were the trick cameras? Where were the mirrors? Weren't these things necessary to complete a trick like this?

"'Tis not a trick." The thing her aunt referred to as Akira spoke, its lips moved.

Wait! Ericka covered the sides of her head and put pressure on her temples. *It reads minds*. She forced her focus to Aunt May's face. *How's she doing this*?

"She's not doing anything."

Ericka felt her eyes widen to a point she wasn't sure she'd ever gain the ability to close them again. The womanly shape glided to a position directly beside her and extended a transparent hand to her arm. Jerking from its icy cold touch, she stood, toppling her chair.

"You're not real!" Ericka screeched.

She had to stop the insanity. Her aunt had gone too far. Ghosts weren't real. She refused to believe it.

"This whole thing's not real! How're you doing this? Enough's enough!"

The glass door to the kitchen shattered when a giant man sprang through and landed in a crouched position, one hand on the ground for support. The other hand held the largest double-edged sword she'd ever seen pointed at her throat. Dark as coal eyes glared at her through one section of long dark hair that had escaped from his ponytail. Nostrils flared in the extremely masculine face. His jaw flexed tight. His lips were pulled into a thin, menacing scowl.

His gaze held her captive. Two steps of his long muscular legs closed the distance between them. The sword was held dangerously close to the pulse point on her neck. A quick shake of his head and glass particles from the door fell from his hair and shoulders.

"Who shall ye be?" rasped from his thinned lips in a thick Scottish brogue.

She swallowed shallowly, afraid that any more would allow the sword's sharp tip to pierce her skin. Strong arms held the sword firm. It did not even quiver in his grip, but remained steady and unwavering. With her chin tilted up, she stared into the darkest eyes she'd ever seen. He towered over her. She estimated his height to be over six feet. Nervously, her tongue darted across her dry lips as she forced her voice to activate and pushed words from her throat.

Ericka darted a sideways glance at her aunt, who sat frozen in her chair. At least as long as this nutcase's sword was pointed at her, Aunt May appeared to be safe. Inhaling, she took in his scent of earth with a hint of heather. Gathering her strength, she tried the act of speech again.

"I think the question is who are you?"

She thought she saw a flicker of a smile dare to pull at the corner of his lips before the fierce scowl returned, held glued in place by this man's angry resolve.

His eyes darted for a split second, taking in a quick perusal of his surroundings as if unsure of his location. Even if he wasn't sure, his sword never wavered from her throat. He stood with his other hand placed on his hip, his chest thrust forward and chin lifted. The stance reminded her of a male peacock when it strutted for a mate.

"'Tis I, the master of this castle, Gavin MacKinnon. 'Tis I and I alone who has the right to question." His deep voice resonated. Lowering to within inches of her face, his warm breath touched her skin as he spoke. "I ask once more and once more only, who shall ye be?"

Uncontrollable laughter rose from deep inside Ericka. Her aunt had outdone herself, from the portrait on the tapestry, the replica of the man in stone and now to the very model she used who stood with an antique sword in hand and clothed as an ancient Scotsman. Unfortunately, Aunt May overlooked one thing.

When Ericka stepped away from his sword, his jaw dropped in disbelief.

"Oh, get over it," she quipped between gasps for air in an attempt to control her laughter. "Aunt May, this is fabulous. But you forgot something."

She moved to stand beside her aunt's chair, placing a hand on her shoulder.

May stumbled over her words. Her hand clasped over Ericka's. "I don't understand what you mean."

Ericka pulled her hand away and pointed at the bewildered-looking Scotsman who stood poised as if ready to strike. "The jig's up. He should be speaking Gaelic if he's supposed to be the late, great, frozen-in-stone Gavin MacKinnon."

Aunt May stood, concern written on her face. She grabbed Ericka's arms above the elbows as if she were going to shake her. "He is. I don't understand a word that's coming out of his or your mouth. You answered him in *his* native tongue."

"Ah, come on!" Ericka jerked from the tender grasp of Aunt May. If she'd spoken Gaelic, she would have known it. Though she had studied the language to an extent, she did not know it well enough to speak it fluently.

She stomped around the table toward the actor playing the part of Gavin MacKinnon. When he lifted the sword to her chest, she stopped short and yelled. "Can't you see? I've figured it all out."

She spun around and stepped toward her aunt.

"You're behind all of this. The mysterious purchase of this castle and the desperate need for me to join you. The diary of a dead woman containing the greatest myth you ever heard."

Shooting a glance over her shoulder, she added, "You even acquired a gorgeous hunk to add to the air of adventure."

"Ericka!" Aunt May's shout rattled the cockles of her brain. Aunt May never raised her voice. As if he heard the harsh tone of his mistress's voice, six-month-old Belvedere jumped the garden wall, with snarling lips and pointed teeth aimed straight for the buttocks of the kilted man.

A flash of icy cold whooshed between Ericka and her aunt as the transparent woman reappeared. Her faint hand flew into a stop position and the protective English Springer froze in air. Ericka could see Aunt May through the woman's presence until icy cold surrounded her and fogged her glasses. Pure cold sensations rode into her lungs making it impossible to catch a full breath.

"Your aunt 'tisn't behind this. I am. And Gavin…" The woman drifted through Ericka's body. Ice chilled her veins as she spun around to follow the image. "Gavin 'tis my *brathair*. You spoke thy words. You set him free. 'Tis I which is the reason you understand his speech. 'Tis I which gave you thy knowledge of our mother tongue. Centuries of lingering hath taught me several tongues including your English."

Akira hovered face-to-face with Ericka. Cold flushed her cheeks and goose bumps covered her flesh but she stiffened her spine and held her ground. She removed her fogged glasses. At this close distance, seeing wasn't a problem.

"Upon thy rise of thy sun ye shall see thy reason thy words never passed my lips."

In a flash of bright light and a strong gust of ice-cold air, she disappeared right before Ericka's eyes. Belvedere landed with a thud on all fours and changed direction. Instead of sinking his teeth in Gavin's flesh, he leapt under Aunt May's chair and chose to guard her with rapid-fire barks and snapping jaws from that position.

"Akira," the bewildered Scotsman shouted. Akira didn't return.

Turning, Ericka saw her aunt fold into the chair. Aunt May pulled Belvedere from his place of embattlement and into a hug on her lap. Ericka had hurt her. This whole thing had gotten out of her control. She meant to protect her aunt, not destroy her fantasies. Ericka knelt at her aunt's feet.

"I'm sorry." She placed her hand over Aunt May's as it continually stroked Belvedere's liver-and-white-colored coat. "I'm sorry. I know you went to great trouble to set this up for our big adventure."

"I didn't do this." A weak smile touched her aunt's lips. "I asked you to believe in the impossible."

Aunt May cupped Ericka's chin and tilted her head so she could see the confused Scotsman. Though his hand still grasped its hilt, his sword no longer pointed at them.

"Some things have no explanation. Look at him, Ericka. He has no clue what's happened." Aunt May leaned closer to her ear as she spoke, "No clue what century this is."

She grabbed Ericka by the elbow, adjusted her other arm under Belvedere's tummy and stood, bringing Ericka to her feet at the same time. She urged Ericka toward him.

"Think of this as your life challenge, your Tarzan so to speak. Teach him. Mold him. If I were twenty years younger." She paused as an audible sigh left her lips and she released Ericka's arm. "Lord knows I would."

"Come, Belvedere," she spoke as she walked through the broken glass door with her precious pet clutched tight to her chest. "Let's go lay down. Mommy needs a nap."

Chapter Five

ꙮ

Was her aunt behind this?

If she was, she played the part of the hurt aunt perfectly. Ericka swallowed hard and kept her eyes glued to the supposedly ancient Scotsman. He seemed lost. But was that the script he'd been given to play? When she stepped in his direction, he shifted his stance as if wary of her movements. Strong hands gripped the hilt of the sword, though he kept it lowered. Bands of taut muscles rippled his arms, giving the impression that swift movement would follow if he felt endangered.

As she took another step, he lifted to full height. He was definitely over six feet tall, she noted, adjusting her glasses. Should she speak? Would it come out in Gaelic as her aunt suggested? A slim smile tugged at her lips.

"How…" She paused, hearing exactly what she thought she'd hear, English. "How much is my aunt paying you?"

The same look Belvedere gave her every time she spoke to him crossed the giant man's face, one eyebrow cocked, head tilted sideways as if he didn't understand. Had he taken lessons from the dog? The puppy-dog look made him seem almost vulnerable…almost. She shook her head slightly then stepped closer.

"*Stad*," rumbled from his lips as he shifted to a combat-ready stance with sword lifted in one hand. His other hand was held in the stop position within inches of her face. The dark pupils of his eyes glared directly at her. The sight of his tongue darting across his lips kindled a spark in the apex between her thighs.

Gaelic words reached her ears in a rich Scottish brogue as he spoke, sending a shiver down her spine.

"'Tis iongantach rud's nach hath tachair. Caite 'tis m' teaghlach?"

Surprised and confused by the fact that she understood his speech, Ericka hesitated then replied slowly in his native tongue.

"True, strange things have happened. Unfortunately, I don't know the location of your family." She answered his question then added, "Or your origin, as a matter of fact."

Taking a chance, she touched the point of his sword with her fingertip. It had to be a replica. The sword was unexpectedly sharp, she jerked, causing a tiny drop of blood to form.

Swift movements wrapped the man's large hand around her wrist. Though it swallowed hers, his touch was gentle. He sheathed his sword without releasing her hand.

"Never hath the blood of a woman been shed by my sword." When he lifted the injured finger to his lips, she froze. His kiss burned her flesh. His tongue flicked the wound, shooting fire from the injured fingertip, up her arm. The sensation of his tender touch rocketed throughout her bloodstream, sending waves of warmth in its wake. The moment he released her hand, the warmth of his gentle embrace was replaced by sudden coldness.

Never had her body responded with such force to just a touch. Was it his Gaelic tongue, the Scottish brogue or simply the essence of this gorgeous hunk turning her on? Her gaze glued to the ripple of his biceps as he tore a strip from the tablecloth, shredded it to fit then wrapped it around the small cut, tying it in place.

"Thank you," whispered from her lips as if she were a small child with a boo-boo.

His hand held hers as she met his gaze. A hint of dark green swirled in the depths of his eyes, though confusion still edged his irises. A crooked smile touched his lips, causing her stare to linger on their fullness. *His kissable lips* danced through her thoughts before she shivered, pulling her hand free.

Don't you go there. This is all an act. Silently, she chastised her overactive libido. She dared to look him in the eye. Though bewilderment shone clear in his gaze, he played the part well.

Ericka cleared her throat. "Why'd you point your sword at me if you've never used it on a woman before?"

Needing space, she stepped out of his reach and turned her back to him, breaking the hold his strong masculine aura held over her logical thinking. A chance to catch her breath was impossible if she continued to study the cut of his physique instead of asking pertinent questions to learn the truth of his employment.

When he didn't answer, she glanced over her shoulder, then spun around to face his back. Those protective broad shoulders were slouched and the aura about him seemed to darken to shades of gray. His aura! She snorted. When did she start believing in such nonsense? Impulsively, she reached to touch him, but halted.

Was this still part of the act? His hands were braced against the top of the patio wall as he stared into the dark.

"'Tis this Castle MacKinnon?" His voice was a mere whisper and Ericka had to strain to hear it.

Ericka stepped closer, but stopped short of touching him. Akira's ghostly image floated opposite the wall in front of him. He hadn't spoken to her at all. His words were for Akira. They spoke as though Ericka was no longer in their presence and she had to bite her tongue to keep from butting in on the act.

"Aye, *brathair*. 'Tis our home."

When he attempted to touch his sister's cheek, his fingertips passed through her. Jerking back, he flexed his hand as if it had lost all feeling.

"'Tis true! Thy spirit walks this world though thy body has lain to rest." He spun on his heels. Though he now faced

Ericka, his gaze seemed distant, like he was trying to gather his thoughts.

When he shoved a loose strand of hair back from his face, Ericka's fingers twitched and she wondered at its texture…soft and silky or coarse and knotted? Then his hand slid down his neck, stopping at the curve where shoulder and neck meet as if the muscles bunched tight at that point. The need to massage his pains away spiked through her system. It took tremendous resolve to keep her arms at her sides and not touch him. Instead, she stood still and watched his continued performance.

"'Tis all my fault. Thy spirit must seek rest."

Ericka gulped at the knot in her throat as heat radiated from his massive bulk. Somehow, she knew his pain. The feeling of loss for a sibling stabbed at her gut. Man, his acting was good, she thought, as she blinked back the tears, refusing to let them fall.

Akira disappeared, then reappeared in front of him. "'Tis my choice, Gavin. I vowed to protect my *brathairs* as they would have should I hath been the one cursed."

Slowly, he knelt on one knee.

"How can I help you? You hath set me free. Tell me how I repay this debt? Thy spirit shall rest. 'Tis my solemn oath." His hand covered his heart as he spoke, chin lifted and gaze focused on the shimmering figure's face.

Akira's faint hand lifted to his brow as her body grew brighter.

"Do not worry, my *brathair*." A thin smile tugged at her lips. "Rest comes soon. My time is limited now that you're free. Now 'tis your turn to protect our *brathairs* as I hath protected you."

"Our *brathairs*," he whispered. Ericka stood close enough to see his eyes widen as if it finally dawned on him that he wasn't the only one cursed. "Are they in the castle? Where are they?"

Akira's ghost drifted upward as he stood and stepped forward in an attempt to follow the fading figure. Akira pointed and he turned in the guided direction.

"She holds the key to each of our fallen *brathairs*. Seek and ye shall find the answers. Find them. Guard them well. *M'Gaol,* Gavin."

In a flash of brilliant light, Akira disappeared. Ericka's mouth dropped open as she stared into the sky. Akira was gone. But had she even existed? She wasn't given the chance to think this through before two large hands grabbed her just above the elbows.

"If you're the key, where's my *brathairs*?" A harsh Scottish brogue of ancient Gaelic seethed between clenched teeth.

"I don't know," she snapped, wiggling unsuccessfully in his grip. "Take your hands off me!"

He stared at her as if she had three heads, so she repeated the words, concentrating on voicing them in Gaelic.

"Nay, woman," he spat as his voice rose to a shout. "Not until ye answer me. Where's my family? Where's my *brathairs*?"

On tiptoe, she leaned in close with her chin tilted up and met his glare. His eyes had darkened and she took the shade change as a sign of his anger.

"And I tell you again, I don't know where they are!" She returned his shout, then did the first thing that came to mind. She kicked him full force in the shin.

"Agh!" His grip relaxed.

She twisted free and sprinted for the broken glass door. Before she reached it, his arm wrapped around her waist, jerking her against him. He held her off the ground perched on his hip with one arm. She fought, wiggling and kicking, pinching and scratching, but his banded arm of pure muscle held her tight without even a flinch. Her hair tumbled loose from the bun, spilling long locks of deep auburn hair around her face. His other hand fisted in the strands.

"Hold still, you fiery-headed wench!"

Motion and time suspended. Ericka froze as did he. Vivid visions of the dream reappeared as if it were a movie played on a big screen in her brain. Memories of his hands, lips, taste, scent and feel rose to the surface of her over-sensitized skin. The moment he released her and placed her on her feet, coldness replaced the warmth where his hands had touched her. Shivers riveted down her spine as she stiffened and scooped her hair from her face while staring at the hulking man.

With each breath, his chest heaved, wild eyes capturing hers while his hands balled at his sides. He knew. But how? He wasn't there, yet the words…they were the same. He called her a fiery-headed wench with his fingers laced in her hair in the dream just before he…

Ericka dared to hold his heated glare. Deep swirls of green replaced the dark as the remembrance of passion shared electrified the air between them. Warmth crept into her cheeks as she dragged a timid gaze down his body's length, halting at a prominent bulge in his kilt. In a coward's move, she snapped her blatant investigation downward to stare at her feet.

Gentle fingers lifted her chin, forcing her eyes to meet his ardent gaze. He closed the gap between them and Ericka swore the air around them dissipated. His head tilted as his expression switched to curious puppy, similar to the face that Belvedere sported constantly. Slipping the round-rimmed glasses from her face, he tossed them without looking onto the table. A strong arm encircled her waist and snugly fit her shivering body against his hardened form of pure male hunger. Ericka struggled to breathe, overwhelmed by his masculine scent of heated arousal, leather and a subtle hint of heather.

For decency's sake, she should stop his advances. But she couldn't—no, wouldn't—even if she wanted. He commanded her body with an aggressive sexual confidence she'd never known. The hard pressure of his growing cock twitched impatiently against her belly, igniting liquid heat to soak her sex not to mention the cotton granny panties she regretted wearing at this moment.

His fingers laced in her hair. Full kissable lips lowered to hers. A timid tongue licked her lower lip then, teased her mouth to open. A hot tongue experienced in the ways of kissing plunged deep, tangling with hers. She'd been kissed before, but never like this, with the exception of her dreams. It was as if he'd invented the kiss and she was his apt student, hungry to learn, taste and feel every aspect of his mouth.

Her palms splayed flat against his chest, while her inept fingers fumbled to release the opening of his shirt. The moment muscled flesh touched her fingertips, a pure jolt of electricity shot up trembling arms, progressed the length of her spine, then radiated down both legs to the tips of her toes. Thick dark curls covered his broad chest. A rampant craving to lay her cheek upon the solid wall of muscle and lie comfortable and secure within his strength reared to life in her soul.

Ericka's world as she knew it tilted. This wasn't happening. Forcibly, she ripped her lips from his delicious mouth and gasped for air. Unsuccessfully, she wiggled against his chest, trying to place some space between them. Instead, he backed her into a corner, hindering her escape. The taste of his mouth lingered on her thoroughly kissed lips. The visible rise and fall of his chest hinted that he was suffering the same difficulty in breathing as she. There was no stopping this, not now.

The moment he stooped and pulled a hidden dagger from his boot, she froze. Did he plan to force her? Deft movements slit her t-shirt and bra straight down the middle. Any efforts to clasp the cut material together were useless. He stepped within millimeters of her body. Though heat radiated from his being, Ericka trembled. She knew it wasn't out of fear, but her body's highly stimulated reaction to his closeness. He placed one hand flat on the wall beside her head. The fingertips of his other hand traced her neckline, then lowered to her hands. Every nerve ending tingled when his skilled lips hovered near her earlobe.

"Move thy hands."

His warm breath toasted her skin and pebbled her nipples. In slow motion, she lowered her hands. Forcing her chin to lift, she met the hooded gaze of deep green swirls in his eyes. He wanted her and not one ounce of her wanted to fight him. Hell, she wanted him so bad it hurt.

When the tip of his tongue flicked her nipple, she gasped. A smile tugged his lips as he nibbled tenderly, then moved to the perfect match and administered equal care. He massaged the orphaned nipple with thumb and forefinger while his lips, mouth and teeth teased the other. Unable to control it, a sigh escaped her lips as his hand glided down her abdomen.

Sliding his hand down the silky skin of her belly, he enjoyed her softness. When the tip of his finger slipped along the waistband of her manly pants, her moan stirred his shaft to full attention. Her strange clothes made him ache to rip them from her body.

The taste of her breasts increased his desire to cover every inch of her with his mouth. This avid need, he knew, could not be sated while she remained dressed. He suckled the hardened nipple and lavished the tender mound into his mouth. Slowly, he soaked in the warmth and smoothness of her skin as he caressed beneath the remnants of her shirt, trailing the length of her torso and sneaking at a snail's pace to her back. He lingered at the small of her back, ministering soft circular motions with his fingertips before exploring lower to her full round bottom.

Cuddling her rump in his palms urged his hunger to new heights as he lifted her effortlessly, pinning her between the wall and the painful thickness of his erection. With her legs wrapped around his waist, he rubbed against the warmth of her clothed mound in shallow movements, bringing his cock to total engorgement. A low groan rumbled from his lips, which were still wrapped around a nipple.

Her scent, her feel, her taste was better than any dream he ever imagined. Desire barreled through his bloodstream, urging him to lavish from breast to breast. He wanted to be inside this wanton vixen at any cost. Reluctantly, he lowered her to her feet.

Ericka twisted to strip in his arms. She hungered to have him buried deep inside. Every inch of her body burned for his touch. Immediately sneakers, socks, jeans and panties slid to the floor along with the remnants of her bra and t-shirt. With only her hands as a shield, she stood naked in the night air.

This man had brought her to near orgasm, suckling her breasts and rocking his hard cock against her aching pussy, while holding her pinned against a wall. Though she shouldn't feel shy, she did. As a heated flush rose to her cheeks, she slowly lifted her eyes to meet his ardent gaze. The sexual intensity which flashed within his irises rocked her senses. Her knees weakened as moisture flooded the apex between her thighs and sizzling need washed over her.

Ericka leaned against the wall for support. His sword and sheath tumbled from lean hips. He covered her hands with his and warmth singed her skin but she didn't pull away.

"Never shield thyself from me." The words rasped on a throaty growl as he pulled her from the wall, wrapped his arms around her and hugged their bodies tight.

With each breath he took, his chest rubbed against the oversensitive nubbins of her breasts and transferred into erotic synergy down her spine. She lifted her chin as he lowered his lips to hers. The fierceness of his kiss felt as if he'd devour the life right out of her, but she couldn't stop. She wanted more. More of his taste, more of his tongue, his mouth, his… Her hands shook as she raised his kilt. The long thick cock filled her palms and throbbed with the same need humming between her thighs.

He cupped her buttocks and lifted her onto the patio wall. Ericka wrapped her legs around his waist as her arms encircled his neck. This was wrong and she knew it. She didn't even know him. But she couldn't stop. Hunger for his massive size ravished her body and ceased all logical thought. As he nuzzled her neck, his fingers spread her lower lips. The moment a thick finger plunged inside, Ericka gasped.

"*M'Gaol*, you're ready for me," he whispered against the tender skin of her neck as he slid another finger into her sex.

Unable to restrain a whimper, she shivered. He had her on the edge of orgasm. Without thought, her body responded to the rhythm of his movements. Her hips shifted to and fro as his fingers delved deeper and his thumb massaged the tender hidden bud of her clit. A cry caught in her throat when he removed his fingers and replaced them with the plump head of his shaft. His ragged breath rushed against her ear.

"'Tis been too long, *M'Gaol*. I cannae wait."

One swift push and he was buried to the hilt. Ericka bit back a scream. It felt as if he ripped her open with his massive size. She wasn't a virgin but she'd never been with a man who held claim to such a healthy portion of cock. In her dream, he'd been gentler.

Her tight warmth gloved him. As he breathed in deep against her hair, her scent filled his nostrils. Her legs wrapped around him in a sensual erotic hug made his heart thunder. She felt so good, so tight clasping around his shaft, holding him captive within her sheath. He held dead still within her, willing himself not to move for if he did, he feared the moment would not last. Feeling her face burrow against his shoulder, he thought he heard a muffled cry followed by the warm wetness of possible tears.

Lifting her chin with his fingertip, he forced her to look at him. Placing featherlike nibbles along her cheeks, he caught each tear. Tenderly, he traveled to her lips, leaving a trail of butterfly caresses with his kisses upon her skin. He suckled her tongue, while massaging a nipple with minuscule circles of his thumb.

A flood of moisture and spasms coated his buried cock as she granted him his reward for patience. He slid slowly from the warmth until only the head of his shaft remained perched in the entrance of her heavenly sheath. Clasping her chin in both hands, he held her face turned up.

"Look at me," he commanded. "I want to see your eyes."

Automatically, she followed his request. His eyes turned deeper green with each plunge into her body. Caressing his chest, the beat of his heart increased with the tempo their bodies set. The faster she rocked, the deeper his shaft delved, bringing her closer to erotic orgasm heaven. Never had she wanted to sexually explode as she did now. Was it his size? His skill? At the moment, she wasn't certain and truly didn't care as long as he didn't stop.

Though each thrust threatened to split her insides, she couldn't stop. Teetering on the edge of the wall with her legs wrapped tight around the waist of the devastating Scotsman, she wanted more. She dug her heels into his taut bottom with each upward thrust of her pelvis, forcing him to maximum depth.

He released her face and grasped her hips. He latched onto one of her nipples, suckling, sending waves upon waves of moisture between her thighs. The rhythmic pound of flesh against flesh sent her spiraling into a depth of ecstasy she'd never known. On the brink of release, she buried her head against his and pressed her lips into his hair to muffle the sound of pure joy as it ripped from her throat.

Her warm folds clenching around him were enough to melt the last strand of his resolve. It amazed him that he lasted as long as he had with such a magnificent vixen in his grasp. A flood of his seed released from his shaft at the last deep plunge into her. He massaged her hips and kept her pressed firm against him, not wanting to be released from the tight warmth of her sheath. Her arms hung loose around his neck. Her breath was heavy and steady against his hair. The scent of their union filled every intake he took and brought a renewed hunger to his shaft. Lifting his head, he smiled.

The deep green shade of passion in his eyes sent chills across her exposed skin. He kissed her lips, her cheek, and her eyes, then eased from her body as his strong hands lowered her from the wall. Coldness coated her body immediately when he released her. Ericka couldn't move. Her legs shook and every other muscle ached to be touched by him again. She leaned against the patio wall and crossed her arms over her breasts as he straightened his kilt, replaced the sheath and sword across his chest, then gathered her clothes. After handing her the tattered remnants of her clothes, he swept her from her feet into his arms and pressed her close to his chiseled body.

"'Tis been a long time for me." A sheepish grin crossed his face. "Lead me to thy room, *M'Gaol*. The night 'tis young."

Ericka blinked, unable to believe what he was suggesting. Could he possibly want her again? Wiggling against his kilt, hard evidence led her to believe in miracles. She grabbed her glasses off the table as he spun and headed for the broken doorway.

She guided Gavin to her room, grateful that they didn't run into anyone along the way. It would have been difficult explaining why she was naked in the arms of a gorgeous hunk. He pulled back the covers and placed her on the bed. Turning his back to her, he removed his sword, setting it next to the bed.

As he sat on the edge of the bed unlacing his boots, she scooted up behind him and pressed her chest against his back. The warmth of his skin against her breasts shot an arrow of wet need to her pussy. A boldness she never knew before coursed through her veins as she playfully brushed her swollen nipples up and down his spine. When her tongue outlined his ear, his movements froze and a deep growl escaped his throat.

"Lass," he spoke on a ragged breath. "If ye continues, I'll be taking ya in my kilt again."

He whipped around and pinned her to the bed. Wild, unkempt, dark hair cascaded around his face and tickled her skin as he nuzzled each breast, then suckled a tender nipple harshly between his teeth. Banded arms of muscle released her as suddenly as he had pinned her and pushed up off the bed to stand facing her.

The front of his kilt showed amazing evidence he was ready to take her again. A wicked smile plastered her lips as she boldly watched him remove his clothing. No shame showed in his face. Why should there be? she thought. With a body so well formed, so well proportioned as his… Her blatant perusal lowered to his engorged cock and she bit the edge of her lower lip. This might be the only chance in her lifetime to enjoy the expertise of such male perfection. Even if it were all an act, a simply play orchestrated by her aunt. But Ericka doubted her aunt expected the actor to go this far…to include her sexual pleasure. On a deep breath, she gathered her courage. This was her night and she planned to make the most of it.

Ericka crawled toward him. When she reached the edge of the bed, she sat on her knees, quickly trailed her fingers up the inside of his thigh, grasped the thick shaft, then teased the tip with her tongue. She heard his deep inhalation. The spasm of the taut muscles of his cock tickled her palm. Smiling up at him, she saw his chest heave as if he took his last breath and his lips hovered, slightly parted. The deepest shade of green she'd ever seen swirled in his eyes. She held his full, unguarded attention.

His hands tangled in her hair as he bent at the waist and captured her lips. She liked the feel of his tongue in her mouth as she tenderly caressed his cock. Up and down, lower and lower until she fondled his balls in a tender massaging foreplay. The moment his hands encircled her wrist, she stopped. Startled, she disengaged their kiss. Had she hurt him? She met his hooded gaze as he lifted her hands to his lips and placed tender kisses in her palms.

"*M'Gaol*, if I had not stopped you," he spoke in a raspy voice as he eased her back onto the bed and covered her with his body. "I would have been spent in your hands."

"Oh." Ericka sighed. It thrilled her to know she had this man on the edge. When he nudged her thighs, she parted them.

"I see we both want the same." He smiled as he settled between her legs.

Pressing the head of his shaft into her tight opening, her muscles contracted, then released, giving him full access to her sheath. Her back arched off the bed, welcoming him into the warmth of her heaven. As he pushed forward, her sex consumed him inch by inch. Her pussy fit perfectly around his cock as if she was made solely for him.

Fisting her hair, he stretched her neck taut and trailed kisses along the delicate skin. The taste of her mixed with the alluring scent of her arousal increased his need to pump faster and harder into her tender sheath, but he fought the urge. He wanted to savor the taking of her this time.

Slowly, he licked and kissed his way down her neck to her chest until he encompassed the taut nipple of one plump breast with his mouth. The feel of her hardened pebble against his tongue enticed him into a hungered frenzy, sucking from breast to breast.

When her pussy contracted and moisture coated his cock, he knew that she was ready. Plowing deeper and deeper, he couldn't get enough. He wanted more. He needed more.

Releasing her nipple with a pop, he commanded her mouth. Her tongue met his plunge for plunge. The tight grip of her legs around his waist encouraged him in farther, giving him more depth for his expanded need. He suckled her mouth, taking all that she gave and responding to her desires.

Needing to be at the deepest depth possible when he reached orgasm, he slid an arm underneath her slender frame. In one swift movement, he lifted them both upright with her legs wrapped tight around his waist and his legs bent underneath him as he rested on his knees. He gripped her bottom and held her poised, hovered partially lowered on his shaft. Her body size being much smaller than his, he worried this would hurt her.

Sensing his hesitation, Ericka gave him no chance to change his mind. She realized the method of this new position and relaxed the death grip she held around his waist. This time she captured *his* mouth as he pressed her lower and lower on his rigid shaft.

Repositioning her legs to either side of his hips, she took over. She rode him in slow motion. Using her inner muscles, she gripped his cock with every up-and-down glide. Her juices flowed, easing the slickness of their movements. His stiff cock, the magnificent feel of fullness within her vagina and the ripples of adrenaline pulsating through her system prompted her to ride him more fervently than she ever imagined. Her breasts bounced as she increased their sexual tempo.

Her inner muscles tightening around his cock was pure torture, but one he'd never resist the pain of sampling over and over again. Each attempt to lower her all the way to the hilt was resisted by the nymph upon his shaft.

She controlled their pleasure, not he.

His eyes met hers and were held, lost in the vivid passion flashing in her irises. Sliding his hands up her body, he watched the flicker of her pupils when his thumb and forefinger pinched the swollen nipples. The wetness lathering his cock as the pace quickened was his reward. Her body responded well to his touch.

Lowering his mouth, he latched onto one of her nipples and her body increased its tempo, up and down, faster and faster until neither could restrain any further. She grasped his shoulders, digging her nails into his flesh as he grabbed her hips, embedding to the furthest reaches possible inside her pussy.

Their bodies jerked in unison. His seed filled her tight wet sheath which vibrated around his shaft, accepting every ounce. The spasms of her inner muscles massaged his swollen cock into a state of complete submission.

As he lowered her to the bed, he knew he didn't want to leave the warmth between her thighs, but held no choice in the matter. The beautiful woman in his arms was spent. A radiant glow covered her skin along with the glorious scent of a woman well satisfied. He laid back and snuggled her close. She curled up beside him with her head on his chest. Her hair spread across his arm and shoulder in a tangled mess.

Within moments of lying cuddled in the afterglow, the woman in his arms drifted to sleep. The steady rhythm of her breath feathered across his chest and stirred a faint hunger to life in his groin. He brushed a kiss across her brow and knew that she needed rest when her body shifted closer, but she didn't wake. He lay with one arm wrapped around her. The other was tucked behind his head as he surveyed his surroundings.

Strange things were in the room. He felt certain this was once Akira's room. The desk in the room looked like Akira's and the portrait of their mother still hung on the wall. Shifting his massive weight on the mattress, the box spring squeaked at his effort. The bed beneath him was different, softer, more comfortable...but different. The bedding and the material hanging around the bed from the four-corner posts, all were unusual to him.

He glanced across Ericka's head at the source of light glowing from the table on the opposite side of the bed. Light shone from an odd object in some form of magic. No flicker of a candle caused this. Every muscle stiffened. *Must be magic. 'Tis she a witch*? Returning his gaze to her face, the softness of her features quelled the rise of nervousness in his gut.

It was she who had visited his dream. Closing his eyes, he soaked in the sensations of the woman in his arms. The deep auburn hair, her taste, her scent, the roundness of her breasts and the fullness of her bottom engulfed his senses. The splendor of her mouth upon his shaft had nearly ended him. No other woman had ever touched him like that, not even...*Tavia*! His eyes sprang open.

Free for hours, not once had he thought of her. His heart seemed to stop. Instead, he fell from grace in the arms of another. As gently as possible, he slipped from Ericka's bed. The breath caught in his chest when she rolled onto her back. Intently, he watched her angelic face, but she didn't wake. Releasing his breath on a heart-heavy sigh, shame riddled his body. His shoulders sagged and his knees almost buckled. He betrayed the woman who carried his seed, the mother of his child...

Tavia! *Where was Tavia*? *Was she cursed too*? *Where was his child*? *Was it boy or girl*?

Gathering his clothes, he dressed without thought. As he turned to leave, he met the eyes of his mother in the portrait above the bureau. *Shame*! He thought he saw shame exude from the depths of her stilled eyes. He shamed the name of MacKinnon. He betrayed his wife and his family. And all for...

Pausing in the doorway, he stared at the motionless beauty in the bed. A fist of pain clenched tighter around his heart as his body betrayed him. His shaft stirred to life at the sight of a pouting nipple, peeking out from beneath the tousled auburn hair spread across her chest. Teeth gritted, a distraught growl rumbled low in his throat. Both fists flexed open and shut at his sides as he fought the urge to touch her again.

He closed his eyes so tight that stars shot behind his lids as if doing so would wash the perfect vision of her naked beauty from his sight. He broke his vows of matrimony. Without looking at her or the picture of his mother, he left the room, closed the door and disappeared down the hall.

Chapter Six

ꙮ

Ericka woke to the first rays of sunlight streaming through her bedroom window. Stretching, she rolled onto her side expecting to be greeted by a solid chunk of male anatomy. Totally naked, she sat up and realized she was alone. Where was the gorgeous hunk? Where was Gavin? The sheet smelled of the man. His scent made her mouth water and she craved his touch. Every muscle ached and her legs were numb as she slid from the bed. Her lips, though tender, hungered for another round of excellent kissing from the master.

On shaky legs and wrapped in a sheet, she walked to the window. The rub of the soft material against her breasts reminded her of him. His tongue and teeth had teased the tender nipples and enticed her sensuality. The memory of his talented mouth sent chills down her spine as she basked in the morning sun.

Was he in another room? Why had he not wakened her? A sigh escaped as she leaned her head against the windowpane. Maybe last night was a one-night stand. *Her first.* She bit the edge of her lower lip, but still couldn't stop the satisfied smile. A just-been-thoroughly satisfied glow warmed her from the inside out.

Turning to gather fresh clothes from the bureau, the eyes of the portrait caught her attention. Were they sad? Had they changed? Were they like that before? She shuddered, but refused to acknowledge the tug at her conscience. *No.* She glared up at the portrait. *There won't be regrets for the best night of my life.*

She gathered her things, slammed the drawer shut and stomped to the doorway. One last glance at the portrait assured her that she was seeing things. Portraits don't project guilt, they're inanimate objects.

A chill shot across her skin. She jerked the door closed. *There must be a draft, castles are known for drafts.* And *ghosts*! The word echoed in her head as she darted down the hall for a hot shower.

* * * * *

"Morning, Aunt May," Ericka stated cheerfully as she entered the patio for breakfast. A twinge of disappoint misted her spirits when the sight of Gavin did not greet her eyes. Throughout her shower, she hoped he would be at breakfast. *If he's even still in the castle.* She sighed across the rim of her coffee cup as she sat beside her aunt.

"Good morning, Ericka, dear," Aunt May replied with a bright smile on her face.

Her aunt seemed happy, so Ericka decided not to mention the fight they had the night before. Instead, she'd wait to see her aunt's next move in this game of hers.

Leaning toward Ericka, Aunt May asked, "How's our man of stone doing this morning?"

Ericka choked, nearly snorting coffee through her nose. Her aunt's expression showed no surprises. Somehow, her aunt knew that she and Gavin…

Laughter pealed from her aunt as she pulled something from her pocket and tossed it on the table in front of Ericka. "Belvedere brought those to me first thing this morning. Good thing for you he gave them to me and not Ned when he was out here measuring the door for new glass."

Mortified, Ericka grabbed the panties from the table and tucked them under the edge of her t-shirt. Shakily, she placed her elbows on the table and hid her face in her hands. Heat filled her palms as embarrassment soaked her cheeks.

"Ah, Ericka, don't worry. Like I said, if I were only twenty years younger." Aunt May didn't need to finish her sentence. The sparkle in her eyes said it all.

Sitting back in her chair, Ericka simply shook her head. Aunt May amazed her. Here she thought—even though she was a grown adult—her aunt would be appalled at her jumping into bed with a stranger. Instead, she wished she could trade places.

Then, it hit her. She asked how *he* was doing. Ericka accepted the plate of food her aunt handed her. Concentrating on salting her food, she asked, "Have you seen him this morning?"

"Who? Ned or Gavin?" Ericka heard the tease in her voice.

"Gavin." Ericka looked across the top of her glasses at her aunt.

"No, I thought he was with you."

"Maybe he's in his room," Ericka replied, keeping her voice steady. Last night's ghostly theatrics may have kept her from thinking straight at the time. But today, her head was clear thanks to the solid sleep she got after Gavin—or whatever his name was—completely wore her out. She wanted to get to the bottom of this. Was her aunt behind it all? Was he a paid player in her big adventure? "Which room did you give him?"

"Room? Ericka, I haven't given him anything." Aunt May stood. Her eyes widened as if an idea inflamed her brain. "Maybe he's back in the room where we found him."

Without giving Ericka a chance to reply, Aunt May walked toward the broken door. After last night's fiasco, she refused to hurt her aunt again. Keeping her thoughts to herself, she decided to play along. She grabbed a muffin, since finishing her breakfast was obviously not happening and followed her aunt.

Belvedere's bark, echoing across the meadow, stopped them before they entered the kitchen. The rapid barks sounded fierce, but scared and far away.

Not sure what was wrong with the puppy, Ericka and Aunt May ran through the patio gate. Ericka led the way, following his trail marked by an uneven pattern of trounced wildflowers. Aunt May called to the puppy, but he failed to acknowledge her through his onslaught of barks and growls.

As they reached a hill, his barks grew louder. At the top of the hill, they saw him racing around inside the tattered fence of a burial ground. From their position, they saw the majority of the graveyard. Ericka scanned the area, but couldn't figure out what had the dog so spooked. He ran to the open door of what appeared to be a small building, barked, then turned and ran around the graveyard before repeating the process.

What had him worked into such a frenzy? Did he have a wild animal cornered in that building?

When they reached the gate, Ericka grasped it gently, since it hung partially open on fragile hinges. An audible squeak echoed as rusted metal ground against rusted metal as she opened it wider. Its eerie echo stopped Belvedere's barks long enough for him to realize he was no longer alone in his quest. He bounded toward them, nearly knocking Aunt May to the ground when he leapt on her legs. Ericka moved closer to the building as Aunt May stooped to calm her pet.

The design of a Celtic cross was carved in the top of a large stone archway a few feet in front of the run-down building. The MacKinnon family name, though worn by the elements and time, was also etched in the archway. As she got closer, Ericka noticed the thick rotted door of the building was open and hanging on what was left of one hinge. Someone had plundered the family tomb. *Vandals*!

She froze. What if they were still there? Maybe that's what the dog was going nuts over. Before she could think, Belvedere bulleted through her legs and entered the building.

She cut Aunt May off and ran in first. If someone was in there, they'd have to deal with her before she'd let them hurt her aunt. Not that she would be able to stop them, but at least it would give her aunt the chance to run for help.

Skidding to an abrupt halt, she almost fell over the puppy, who stopped short at her feet. Aunt May hurtled in behind her, scolding Belvedere for his misbehavior. As Aunt May scolded and simultaneously comforted her puppy, Ericka scoured the room.

Candlelight illuminated the one-room building. The candles sat in a circular pattern at the front of the room. It appeared to be a makeshift altar of some sort, but who lit the candles and why? As she neared the glowing altar, she saw a cracked oval-shaped slate in the center of the circle. Picking up the slate, she read the one word etched crudely in its smooth surface, *Tavia*.

What did it mean? Was it a person, place or thing? She put it back where she found it. Obviously it meant something important, but what? Searching the room provided no answers to its meaning.

Since it was unsafe to leave candles unattended, Aunt May blew them out while Ericka examined the door. The door showed signs of damage from being forced open. It appeared to her that the door had once been rotted shut or sealed. Whoever did this must have thought there was something of value hidden inside. But why light all those candles, place that slate in the center and leave?

What was the significance of the word *Tavia* in conjunction with all of this?

Pausing in the doorway, she scanned the graveyard. Headstones and crosses were scattered in random patterns amongst renegade trees, which grew wild in the untended family resting place. Monuments both large and small made of stone or wood were the only remnants of a long-forgotten clan. Ericka's head shook as a sad sigh escaped. What seemed to be an entire clan lay at rest here. And yet, she was unable to locate any documentation of their existence in her research.

Belvedere scooted out the door, then skid to a stop. He stared at her, stamping the ground with his front paws and barking as if she should understand his tirade of noise.

"He wants us to follow him," Aunt May stated, moving toward the bouncing puppy. He swung around and bounded off between the tombstones.

Ericka didn't like the idea. What if the person who broke into the building was still out here? Were they armed and dangerous? Picking up the largest stick she could find, she followed her aunt.

Weaving between the grave markers, each step took them farther from the building and deeper into the trees. An eerie sensation settled beneath her skin and Ericka was uncertain if it was from the cool breeze or the fact that they were wandering in a forgotten graveyard with only an overzealous puppy and a rotted piece of wood as protection. As Ericka stepped around the tallest and widest of the stone markers, she ran face first into the back of her aunt.

"What the—" Ericka gasped as the reason her aunt stopped short filled her line of sight.

The back of a stone statue of a man faced her. In unison, she and her aunt stepped closer to the statue as Belvedere barked and ran in circles around it. The massive kilted figure gave the appearance of praying. One knee placed upon the ground, the other bent with both hands folded upon it and his head lowered. Portrayed in stone, his long hair strayed from a loose ponytail at the nape of his neck and shielded his face.

Ericka's knees grew weak with each step closer to the solid mass. She swallowed, but couldn't remove the dry lump in her throat. Even before she knelt to see his face, she knew. Though frozen in stone, his essence filled her senses. His eyes were closed and pain riddled his expression.

Gavin.

She touched his solid cheek and warmth shot through her fingertips. Stumbling, she scooted away from the inanimate object. *She hadn't felt it. Not again.* Ericka sprang to her feet and ran as fast as she could toward the castle with Belvedere hot on her trail. Aunt May's shouts didn't stop her. She had to see if there were two. If there were, then the jig was up. There couldn't be two for the story to be true.

When she reached the castle, she didn't stop though her lungs begged for a rest. Belvedere raced past her, jumped through the broken door and stood barking as if he won the race. Out of habit, she opened the door even though she could have easily stepped through it.

Belvedere rejoined the race at her heels. He ran past her when she stopped at the tapestry, then slid on his butt as he halted his overactive puppy paws, flipped his body around and hustled back to sit at her feet. His tongue lolled heartily in and out of his mouth and she swore he was laughing at her as she bent over gasping for air.

As soon as she was able, Ericka dragged a chair over, then lifted the edge of the tapestry. Though her chest heaved from overexertion, she stood on the chair and crawled into the tunnel. Knowing where she was going, she didn't need a light. Instinct guided her. He had to be there. He just had to be.

After jumping up onto the chair and climbing into the tunnel, Belvedere joined her quest. Hot puppy breath tickled the exposed skin of her ankles.

A dim light shone from the tunnel's other end. She scooted through as fast as she could on hands and knees, then hopped to the ground when she reached the end. She leaned against the cold stone wall and took a deep breath, hoping to quell the blood roaring through her ears. This was the most strenuous exercise she'd done in months—with the exception of her sexually driven night with Gavin.

Belvedere bounced in behind her and took off exploring his newfound surroundings. The sunlight seeping in through the boarded windows was enough to show Ericka what she needed to see. Staring at the darkest corner, she crossed the room.

It was gone!

The stone statue of Gavin MacKinnon no longer stood by the fireplace. The only evidence of its existence was a few crumbles of rock in its place. The oval slate with the anti-curse still lay on the floor.

Ericka's knees buckled and she landed in the dirty pile of pillows and furs. Disbelief washed over her. This couldn't be. She picked up a remnant of stone from the place where Gavin had once stood. How had her aunt done this? Men don't turn to stone. And stone statues don't turn to men.

Or do they?

* * * * *

Aunt May sat in the chair at the tunnel entrance when Ericka crawled out with Belvedere in tow.

"What was that about?" Aunt May asked as she stood to let Ericka step down.

"Nothing."

"Don't tell me nothing," Aunt May snapped and clasped Ericka's wrist. "Something happened when you touched that statue, didn't it?"

Ericka jerked from Aunt May's grip. Needing to think, she turned her back on her. Something tugged at the edge of her gray matter, but she wasn't sure what. Maybe it was a piece to the puzzle or a way to figure out just how her aunt was doing this. But it wouldn't come to her. It sat on the outskirts of her mind, teasing her intellect.

Aunt May broke in on her thoughts as she stood behind Ericka. "He wasn't in there, was he? Had to see for yourself, didn't you? You still think I'm behind this?"

Ericka spun around to face her. Her aunt's cold stare met her dead-on and any smart reply she planned never left her lips. Aunt May stood eye to eye with her. The scent of her perfume filled Ericka's nostrils.

"I've never lied to you. I didn't do this. This isn't some *big* adventure like you seem to think." Aunt May's hands lifted and shook in the air around her head, sending her numerous bracelets into a symphony of jingles. "I asked you to believe in the unbelievable."

Her finger lowered to within millimeters of Ericka's nose. "You believed enough for a roll in the hay, but now that he needs you…"

Ericka swore she saw steam rise from her aunt's ears as she turned and walked away with Belvedere right behind. She'd never seen her aunt this mad.

"And it wasn't just a roll in the hay," Ericka mumbled low, not wanting her aunt to hear, but needing to reply.

If it wasn't a simple one-night stand, then what was it? She slumped into the chair. Her body ached. A tingle grew in her palm. Lifting her hand, she stared at it as if it were a foreign object.

Was what she experienced real? Had there truly been a sensation of heat? She stood, rubbing her palms together. How could a man be a man, then a statue of stone at the same time? A statue of stone at the same time…

The curse! What had she read about the curse? What had Akira called it?

Something nudged at her subconscious. She didn't believe in the curse, or ghosts, or even a man of stone—though his cock reminded her of stone last night. An unstoppable smile teased her lips and a twinge of need surged between her thighs.

Ericka hurried to her room, retrieved the diary from her bag and positioned the desk chair beside the window. The warmth of the sun heated her skin as she adjusted her glasses and smoothed back a few loose strands of hair from her bun. She eased open the fragile, yellowed pages and scanned, searching for the one word which eluded her grasp. Though she wasn't sure what she searched for, she felt certain that when she saw it she would know. Her fingers glided across the lines of perfectly written Gaelic. Each interpretation she knew almost by heart.

The story of the destruction of a family and an entire clan caused by one man unfolded. Captivated by their story, Ericka stopped skimming the ancient pages and soaked in each detailed line.

A lost clansman returned to the clan after years of separation with a vengeance unknown to the MacKinnon brothers. He's accepted back by all but one, who does not trust him and with just cause. She felt an evil in him, a dark and horrid desire, but she held no proof that he planned them harm. Her eldest brother tried to calm her fears and suggested it were an overactive imagination.

Day after day, Akira's fear grew. She felt his anger, though he hid it beneath the surface until he got his chance. In the dawn of the day before the rise of the full moon, he set his plan in motion. He confronted each MacKinnon brother while they were alone and cast his horrid spell. None were given the chance to protect themselves or even draw their swords. The twins he wielded no mercy on their youngest souls. He froze them as they still slept and Gavin's wife…

Ericka paused. He was married. The other woman in the portrait was Gavin's wife. She needed to know more. What happened? Where was she? She continued reading Akira's desperate journey.

And Gavin's wife, heavy with their first child, he took no chance that she'd birth a boy to one day seek revenge. He ran her through with a sword as she gathered fresh heather for their bedchamber. His feat accomplished in the swiftness of a day, he rode out on his horse before the evil he exuded came to light.

Ericka gasped. *Don't tell me he got away.* She flipped to the next page, hoping to read that someone had killed this monster.

Her family, her brothers all turned to stone and she was helpless to protect them. She should have known. Should have persisted that Gavin heeded her plea, that evil lived in Hugh MacGillivray's soul. Now, how that mistake had cost them.

The sense that he would return filled her soul. A knowledge deep inside her whispered that he may return and finish the deed of which he'd done. Their bodies hindered by stone, the simple pound of a club to their tombs and they would crumble, never to return.

It took two weeks, but the deed was done. Her brothers were safe. With the help of her husband's clan, they hid the brothers. Their bodies frozen in stone were scattered for none to see and only those with the key could find them.

By the grace of her Lord, Akira promised to find the way to set them free of the curse placed upon them by Hugh MacGillivray. She vowed to send his soul to the fires of hell where he belonged for the wrath of evil he placed upon her kin.

May his voice never speak those words again…the words of the curse of the gargoyle.

She found it! The word she searched for within the confines of Akira's diary. Gargoyle! Akira called it the curse of the gargoyle.

Ericka saved the page with a bookmark, closed the book and laid it on her nightstand. Gargoyles…gargoyles, the word rolled around in her brain as she stood to stare out the window. Her knowledge of the creatures was limited.

Visions of two hideous, winged creatures seeped from some long-forgotten memory. Ericka rubbed her temples as bits and pieces of something Aunt May told her in her youth resurfaced. While on a visit to a museum, she noticed a strange pair of statues above the entrance and pointed them out to her aunt. The explanation amazed and scared her as a young child of eight. The legend Aunt May shared was one where people of ancient times believed the creatures protected them at night, then turned to stone by day for rest.

But could it be true, could gargoyles have actually existed and what about this supposed curse of the gargoyle? Ericka bit her lower lip and stared in the direction of the graveyard. Had it truly turned a man to stone? Unanswered questions buzzed within her gray matter to the point she felt her brain had swollen and her skull would crack.

If it truly was a curse and he was turned to stone, what if like the gargoyle…

Ericka brushed back a loose strand of hair then adjusted her glasses. Was the idea that sprang to life in her thoughts wrong? What did she have to lose? Her aunt asked one thing of her since her arrival. To believe. But in what? She wasn't sure, but she had an idea how to find out.

* * * * *

Late afternoon, Ericka packed a basket with a pad, a pen, a blanket, a flashlight, sandwiches, several bottles of water, a bottle of wine, an opener, and, just in case—she threw in two wineglasses instead of one, along with Akira's diary. She snorted at the sad sight of the glasses tucked safe within the blanket.

"He's not going to show. It was all an act. He's probably returned home by now." Ericka stated under her breath as she secured the basket lid. With an audible huff, she grabbed the handles. If nothing else, she'd get a chance to finish Akira's story.

Since Aunt May went to the village with Margaret to shop, she wouldn't have to explain this trip back to the graveyard. Exiting the gate, she whistled and Belvedere scurried to her side. It was the least she could do so he would leave Ned alone to fix the door.

"Just let Aunt May know he's with me," she called. A muffled grunt from Ned was the only reply she received that he even acknowledged her comment.

Belvedere barked and ran ahead, stopping every few feet to run back in her direction as if to make sure she was there, then turning and taking the lead again. Ericka laughed at his antics, especially when a colorful butterfly distracted him from his duty as guide. Since the day was warm and beautiful, they took their time. And besides, the basket was heavier than she had anticipated when she started this little adventure.

"Next time I pack a lunch, remind me not to bring enough for an army." Ericka set the basket on the ground and knelt to ruffle Belvedere's ears. She stretched her neck from side to side, releasing the taut muscles and rolled her shoulders several times. Determined to make it to the graveyard, she adjusted her grip on the handles and continued.

At the top of the hill, Belvedere skid to a stop and tilted his head to look up at her. His tongue lolled from his mouth and his expression was one of puppy confusion as if to say *why are we here*? Putting the basket down, she knelt to pet his head.

"It's okay, Belvedere. We're here on a covert mission." When he put his paws on her knees and licked her chin, she smiled.

"As long as we're together, we'll be fine." She stood and picked up the basket.

He kept close beside her as if he understood the part about them sticking together. Ericka walked through the broken gate and weaved through the family plots, stopping now and then to read the headstones.

So many MacKinnons, young and old, were laid to rest on this hallowed ground. Her head shook in dismay. How had their clan escaped the documents of history? Were there other lost clans out there without any historical reminder of their existence? A sadness wound around her heart with the realization that history was incomplete. She continued drifting from grave to grave, reading and writing down what she learned from each. If she could help it, at least this clan would be acknowledged.

When she walked around the largest of the tombstones, she shivered. The statue sat in the same spot as earlier. But what had she expected? She chided herself. *This is stupid, but might as well make the best of it.*

She placed the basket beside the tree closest to the statue. Pulling out the blanket, she carefully removed the glasses tucked inside for safekeeping, put them back in the basket and spread the blanket on the ground. She grabbed a bottle of water, took a sip then poured some in her palm to share with Belvedere. After the puppy lapped her palm clean, she took out Akira's diary and settled on the blanket with her back against the tree. Belvedere snuggled beside her. With the stone statue in full view, if he even flinched, she'd see it. Contemplating her situation, she wondered if her aunt had the statue inside the castle removed and this one placed here. Was Aunt May going to such extremes?

Ericka wanted to relax and believe her aunt wasn't behind this. Who else had the money and the means to create such a fantasy? Certainly not her parents. They were good parents but they were always off chasing their dream of finding the next archeological breakthrough. That was their dream.

Their dream. Ericka leaned her head back against the tree trunk. Her parents were dreamers. Her aunt was the biggest dreamer of all. Why couldn't she be like them? Why couldn't Ericka believe in the afterlife or ghosts? Or even believe in a curse. Automatically, her chin dropped and her gaze fell on the kneeling, stone god of a man. *No.* She shook her head. *This wasn't real.*

She opened the book and read for several hours. Page after page, Akira's story grew more interesting. Six different riddles were written. If one led to the supposed elder brother, she dropped the book in her lap and stared at the statue, then maybe the rest of the riddles would lead to the other brothers. Ericka stretched, then stood.

Without waking the snoring puppy, she moved closer to the man of stone. The sun hung low in the sky and she guesstimated that there wasn't much time left before it set. Ericka eased around the statue without touching him. Whether the heat that filled her when she touched it earlier was real or not, she wasn't taking any chances.

Where would you go if you woke up from a two-hundred-year-long nap? she wondered. Who had he come to see? A suspicion gnawed at her gut. She wanted to know whose grave he knelt in front of with such a look of sheer grief and despair upon his face.

Was it Akira's? Perhaps his mother's or his father's? Did she truly need to know? What difference would it make? He wasn't real anyway, she silently chided herself. Taking a deep breath, she gathered her resolve. *It's just a tombstone.* Her hands shook as she lifted the low-lying tree branch covering the inscription. The words were faded in its crumbed face, but she was able to read it.

Tavia, wife of Gavin MacKinnon, and their unborn child, laid to rest 1740.

Ericka stumbled backward. The last rays of sunlight filtered from the sky as if they'd only lingered long enough for her to learn the truth.

His wife!

He visited his wife's grave.

A low rumble emanated from deep within the statue. It trembled and vibrated. Belvedere sprung from a dead sleep to a protective stance at her side, barking. The rumble increased to the sound of a roll of thunder. The statue changed shape. Her mouth gaped and her eyelids opened wide, unable to focus on anything other than the metamorphosis occurring within arm's distance from her.

In the gray light of evening dusk, the stone shattered and crumbled. When the dust cleared, she couldn't believe her eyes as the anti-curse replayed in her head.

Step free of stone, be ye beast or man, 'tis love either way, though ye be mine by night if not by day.

Gavin shook, sending remnants of stone from his body, then stood. He spun on his heels with sword drawn. Ericka stared up at him from its tip, held within millimeters of her face. His eyes the deep, dark color of night glared down at her. The muscles of his face were taut and drawn lips thinned into a threatening scowl.

"Lass, 'tis only you." He relaxed and sheathed his sword. He held his hand out to her, but didn't look directly at her. When she hesitated, he snapped at the dog.

"*Samhaich*," he commanded and the dog stopped barking.

"*Suidh*," he spoke in a deep Scottish brogue filled with authority and the dog sat. This time when he extended his hand to Ericka, she accepted his help.

His touch warmed her hand to the point that she thought she'd been burned. As soon as she reached her feet, she pulled her hand from his.

"How'd you do that?" she asked, trying to comprehend the vision she'd just seen.

"Dogs need to know who's the master. 'Tis not the words spoken, but how the animal hears them," he stated as he stooped to pet Belvedere, who reacted as if Gavin's touch was reward enough for good behavior.

"No! That! How did you do that?" Frantically, she pointed at the pile of dust and rock from which he'd just broke free.

Gavin gathered a piece of the broken stone, rolling it over in his hand as he stood. Handing her the stone, pure anger danced in his pupils and sent a shiver down her spine. "Lass, 'tis an answer I do not have."

Once again, he knelt at the tombstone with his head bowed as if in prayer. Ericka swallowed the lump in her throat. Seeing him in this position touched her soul. It was as if these were truly his people, his family. In slow motion, she knelt beside him and willed her hand to move. Prepared to suffer the enticing heat touching him seemed to produce, she laid her hand upon his shoulder. Warmth radiated through her body and pooled in her feminine core. Was he aware of the power he wielded over her senses? One glance at his bowed head and she felt that he didn't. *Get a grip*. She shuddered inwardly, trying to tamp down her oversensitive reaction to this man.

"'Tis my fault," he whispered. "'Tis all my fault."

"You shouldn't blame yourself for this," Ericka tried to soothe him. He jerked from her touch and stood, turning away from the grave.

"Should never have married." He spun to face Ericka as she stood. "He wanted her for his. Can't you see?" His voice cracked as he spoke.

Unshed tears didn't dare fall to his cheeks, though she thought she saw them shimmering in his eyes. Lifting to full height, his fist balled at his side. "'Tis I alone who knew how much he loved her, but I couldn't resist temptation."

She saw his Adam's apple flicker as he swallowed hard, then continued. "Her spirit and her beauty captivated me. I had to have her. I stole her heart from him. 'Tis the one true reason he did this. I brought this curse upon my family."

Slumping beside the tombstone, he laid his head to rest upon its jagged edge. "'Tis the reason he killed her. She carried my seed, my child. 'Tis my punishment to walk this world without them."

Ericka stood behind him, unsure of what she should do. Should she touch him? Should she speak? What part should she play here? She stepped closer. Shakily, she stroked his ponytail, praying for the right words to say. On a heavy sigh, she licked her lips and spoke softly in Gaelic.

"Gavin, this happened so long ago. There's nothing you could've done. Hume MacGillivray—" She didn't get to finish. He leapt to his feet and grabbed her by her shoulders.

"Don't ever speak his name again." The words seethed between his clenched teeth. His eyes deepened to dark black and fire laced his pupils. Hot air flowed from his nostrils against her brow. His grip tightened and his strength hinted of his ability to snap her in two if he wanted.

"My mistake," she whispered, biting back the pain. A tear she couldn't prevent slid down her cheek.

Releasing her, his mouth opened, then shut without speaking a word. He turned and marched toward the run-down building. Dumbfounded, Ericka stared after him. The moment he was out of sight, she decided to leave, not caring what happened to him. Stone. Man. It didn't matter which. In her opinion, either way he was a testosterone-riddled actor overplaying his part. She gathered the blanket, Akira's book and the basket. After pulling out the flashlight and turning it on, she whispered. "Come, Belvedere, let's go."

It surprised her when the puppy listened. He kept close to her heels as they weaved through the tombstones. The path she chose brought her within several feet of the building. On a silent command, she got Belvedere to sit and guard the basket. A nagging need to know forced her forward. She knew better than to spy, but hid in the shadows beside the door anyway, leaning just enough to peek inside without being seen.

He stood, relighting each candle. A haunting verse of an ancient Gaelic chant floated from the building.

He asked for forgiveness.

Ericka froze. This giant of a man chanted beautiful words in ancient Gaelic, begging for forgiveness in the deaths of his family and clan. He asked for the knowledge to save his *brathairs* from the curse. Though she knew she intruded, she couldn't force herself to move. Mesmerized, she strained to soak in every syllable. His voice, an awesome timbre, filled her eardrums with a haunting rendition of a forgotten era. Chills scurried up and down her spine. His sorrow dripped from every note. With the back of her hand, Ericka brushed the tears away. Fighting the urge to sniffle, she refused to make a sound that might interrupt this cleansing of his soul.

The chant continued until each candle was lit. He fell to his knees and resumed the stance of prayer. Silence filled the air. Feeling guilty for snooping, Ericka turned to leave, but his words stopped her as if they were a brick wall. If her translation was right, he asked for the strength to avenge their deaths. Holy sanctity or not, he couldn't avenge their deaths. Uncertain if this was part of his act, she chose not to take a chance.

"Gavin!" she snapped as she sprang through the door.

"Leave me be, lass," he spoke without looking up.

"No." Wrapping her hand in his ponytail, she jerked his head back. The moment her fist tightened in his silken strands, she realized she had made a crucial mistake.

His action was swift. Twisting, he clipped her in the ankles with a sweep of one long leg, snatching her feet out from under her. Stubbornly, Ericka refused to relinquish her hold. If she was going down, so was he. She fell flat on her back, landing him full force on her stomach. His massive bulk shot the air out of her lungs. After her head hit the floor, her grip released his ponytail and his face blurred before everything went black.

Chapter Seven

ℬ

"Lass."

A heavily accented male voice speaking a foreign language drifted from somewhere far off. A rough, warm tongue licked her cheek. Sharp barks next to her ear made the pain inside her head reverberate around her skull. Without opening her eyes, she dug her palms into her temples in an attempt to thwart the blinding pain. Strong hands helped her into a seated position as the faint memory of where she was tap-danced to the front of her muddled thoughts. Opening her eyes was difficult, but she managed. Everything spun. Massaging the sides of her head only slowed the motion from turbo-spin to gentle cycle.

"Lass, are you all right?"

"Except for the pounding in my head." She paused. Gavin's confused look reminded her to speak in Gaelic. "Fine, I'm fine."

With as little movement of her head as possible, she searched for her missing glasses.

"'Tis this strange thing for which you seek." Gavin held out her glasses.

"Yes, thank you." She took them and placed them on her face.

"What do they do?" His head tilted to the side just like Belvedere. The honesty in his question surprised her. Without warning, he took her glasses and held them backward to his eyes. Jerking them away, he handed them back to her as his other hand wiped his eyes.

"They're called glasses. They help me see things more clearly."

She repositioned them correctly on her face. Even the sound of the low laugh from her throat hurt. Rubbing her temples, she hoped to relieve the pound of the drum in her head.

"Huh," he said as if he understood, but from the guarded look on his face, she knew he didn't.

When she attempted to stand, she swayed, but wasn't given the chance to fall. Gavin swept her into his arms and carried her. Outside the door, he stopped as if uncertain of what to do next.

Strong arms hugged her close to his chest. His steady heartbeat against her arm matched the pace of her own as heat flooded her senses. Moisture formed between her thighs as her clit throbbed with an intense ache to have him touch her there. Ericka ran a dry tongue across her lips. Was he feeling the same sexual heat as she? Or was this just her overreaction to the touch of a gorgeous hunk?

What would a man built for sex want with someone like her? Unable to look at him while her thoughts were on his gorgeous build, she stared up at the darkening clouds and tried to focus on anything other than his touch, his scent or the feel of him close.

Last night was a fluke, she silently chided herself. *If it was true and he was frozen in stone for over two hundred years, then you were the first female in his path.*

What better way to vent that much pent-up frustration? Or was this some sort of act performed by a talented and extremely sexily built magician? Ericka wasn't completely convinced. Had she really seen him emerge from stone? The pounding of the invisible drum in her head shot pinprick-sized darts to the backs of her eyes. Though pain lanced her brain, visions of Gavin naked, massaging her aches both inside and out, sporadically appeared in the fog of her thoughts. Being in his arms wasn't helping her gain control of her raging hormones.

"Put me down, please," she whispered from her trembling lips. She needed to breathe and clear her head, but as long as he held her, she didn't stand a chance of thinking clearly.

Helped by his gentle grasp, Ericka slid, slowly to a standing position, brushing every inch of his muscled form as she stood. Stretching her legs to the ground, a stiff cock thumped her hip. An astonished gasp escaped her lips. This couldn't be happening. He couldn't want someone like her. Though she didn't want to leave the safety of his arms, she leaned back, placing a gap between them.

Deep swirls of green clouded his eyes. Without releasing her completely, he shifted his stance, increasing the space between them. As he straightened to full height, his eyes never left hers. The slow motion of his tongue across his lower lip made her salivate for another taste of his kissable mouth.

Coldness replaced the warmth of his hands the moment he released her arms. Still weak and a bit dizzy, Ericka tilted her chin. On a deep breath, she steadied her resolve and refused to lower her eyes from his hooded gaze. Chills skittered down her spine when he brushed a loose strand of her hair from her brow and twined it between his fingers in excruciatingly slow motion. The irises of his eyes flickered with a deep-seeded flame of need, causing the breath to stutter in her lungs. A low throaty growl emanated from him as he jerked his hand free and stepped around her. His head shook and she swore she saw him shiver.

"This canna be between us," he whispered.

He tripped over the picnic basket and sent the flashlight flying off the top of it. The moment it hit the ground, it switched on, sending a beam of light across the darkened graveyard. Gavin sprang into combat position, crouched low with sword in hand. In search of the light's mysterious origin, his head snapped from side to side.

Ericka walked over to the flashlight. Kneeling slowly so her head wouldn't spin, she lifted the bright beam directly into his eyes, which held that animal caught in the headlights expression. Immediately, he guarded his vision with his arm.

"What manner of witch do ye be?" he gasped, with his sword thrust out and held firm in one hand.

Lowering the light, his wild, confused expression was unbelievable and the fact he called her a witch simply made her angry. He either was one heck of a good actor or he truly was a seventeenth-century Scotsman who'd been frozen in stone. Ericka bit back her disbelief and swallowed the spike of anger his "witch" statement caused and decided to play along.

"It's a flashlight." She held the handle out to him with the beam pointed to the ground. When he didn't move, she stepped toward him. When the sword leveled with her neck, Ericka lifted her finger to remind him of the fact she knew he wouldn't hurt her. Lowering his sword, he grabbed her finger with his other hand.

"What's this?" He pinched at the covering on her finger. She replaced the cloth bandage he made the night before with a Band-Aid after her shower.

"It's called a bandage." Focusing the light on her fingertip, she flexed it.

Brushing his finger across it, he lifted the edge, curled it up just a little then pressed it back in place. He took the flashlight from her and rolled it around in his hand. Ericka read his expression as true bewilderment, but she could be wrong.

"This button turns it on and off." Covering his hand, she slid the button up and down by making his fingers do the work with minimal pressure from hers. It took determination to stifle the laughter at the childlike expression of wonder on his face as he flicked it on and off several times. It was as if he was truly seeing this for the first time. An Oscar-rated performance, if she said so herself.

A low rumble came from his stomach and Ericka realized she'd forgotten something. She leaned over to pick up the picnic basket. Wrong move. Dizziness overwhelmed her and she stumbled. Belvedere barked and hopped up and down as if to warn of her impending fall. A warm, strong grip encircled her elbow and helped steady her on her feet.

The dark clouds burst, dousing the area in rain. Before the onslaught of water could soak her, Gavin lifted her into a cradled position against his chest. He carried her back into the run-down building with Belvedere close on his heels. Once he settled her near the lit candles, he retrieved the picnic basket and the flashlight.

Though the pain subsided, sudden movements made her dizzy. She sat cross-legged on the floor and opened the basket. Gavin stood in the doorway with his back to her, surveying the rainstorm. A gust of wind rushed in, extinguishing half of the candles.

Not wanting to set her brain into another revolution, Ericka moved gingerly on bended knees to relight the candles. Gavin pulled the door closed as much as its broken frame allowed.

He knelt beside Ericka, perusing her shape. A lean frame accented by a firm round bottom that held the ability to fill his hands nicely. Her plump breasts were perfect for a man to taste. He licked his lips. Inhaling her scent, his mouth watered and his hunger for her grew. Easing closer, his cock shifted and he knew she was a temptation he was too weak to resist. Her luscious neck, elegant jawline, high cheekbones and straight nose were all signs of beauty to him. But it was her hair that drew his attention.

A few strands from the bun-shaped knot at the nape of her neck enticed his fingers to twitch at his sides. He wanted to loosen the rest from their bondage and ease the ache to wrap his fingers in their silk. Instead, he resisted the urge to plumage her hair and wrapped his hand over hers, guiding its movement from candle to candle.

The warmth of her skin against his palm sent heat waves to the pit of his stomach and stirred the growing need beneath his kilt. Whispered words of Gaelic tumbled from his lips before he could restrain them.

Chills danced on her skin. According to her translation, each candle they lit represented something. A loved one, be they family or clan member, battles conquered or battles lost, and journeys yet to take.

She followed his guidance in an erotic dance of hands from candle to candle until only three remained. At these, their motion stuttered before his grip tightened and he lifted her hand toward the three tallest candles in the center. She wanted to ask the symbolism of these center candles, but the intense darkness of his eyes locked the words in her throat.

It was as if their bodies became one, connected through their touch. The air stilled around them and Ericka's heart skipped a beat. What was he thinking? She was given no chance to ask and couldn't judge from the shielded expression on his face. Unable to pull her eyes away, she saw his jaw tense and his shoulders straighten as he continued the ritual.

Together, their hands flowed in unison to the candle on the far right.

"*Dochas,*" he spoke the word she translated to mean hope, then guided their hands to the candle on the left.

"*Sonas,*" he spoke the word of happiness.

Their hands lingered in midair above the middle candle's wick. Ericka's stomach tightened. Why had he stopped? What was the significance of this last one? She saw the flicker of the flames dance in his irises as he stared.

A long time ago, he performed this ritual with Tavia. He spoke the words and lit the candles. Swallowing hard, he tried to remove the knot of bitterness within his throat. The sacred words meant nothing to him now. As if a band of steel tightened around his heart, he gritted his teeth. He loved his wife, Tavia, and look what that had gotten him…his family cursed…his clan destroyed. And he…he was locked in a stone prison for how long?

Without her seeing, he shot a sideways glance at her. She would know. Akira called her the key. Reluctantly, his gaze lowered to the woman, who knelt beside him and he dared to look upon her face.

The sight of her tongue licking, nervously, across her bottom lip flicked to life an urge he fought desperately to control. Her taste haunted his mouth and enticed his tongue. Sexual need roared through his veins and desire burned in his soul, hardening his cock to a point of pure pain.

Just one more round. The thought shot through his brain as the devil in his kilt twitched as if begging to be between her thighs once again. *Nay*. He shifted his kneeling stance, straightened his back and lifted his shoulders. *Canna happen again*.

When she met his gaze, hesitation and indecisiveness haunted his features. A muscle in his chin twitched as the flame lingered, teasing the candle's tip. Hot wax dripped from the candles beside the unlit middle pillar. It seemed as if this candle meant so much more than all the others. But what?

What was its significance in this little game of his? Though his silence made her uncomfortable, she didn't falter. She held her hand steady and her gaze leveled on his. The patter of rain on the roof and the sound of her heartbeat echoed in her ears. Suddenly, he released her hand and cupped her cheek. Heat warmed her skin and sent sparks down her spine. Ericka's lips parted slightly, expectant of his kiss.

"*Stad,*" Gavin roared and jerked her from the enchanted state her mind had drifted into. He lunged past her and grabbed Belvedere by the collar. A sandwich wrapper hung from his mouth.

Uncontrollable laughter almost brought her to tears. One moment, this giant of a man held her captive in a romantic fog and next he looked as if he would skin the dog over food. The two stared at her with similar looks of confusion upon their faces. Both held their heads tilted sideways. Belvedere's tongue lolled from his mouth. Gavin's eyebrow cocked. She moved beside him and took the dog from his grasp.

"It's all right, there's plenty," Ericka said as she released Belvedere and handed him the sandwich he stole from the basket. The puppy scooted with his prize as far from Gavin as room allowed.

The sudden movement had her head doing spins, but it only lasted for a moment. When she pulled out the blanket, Gavin grabbed an edge and helped her spread it on the floor. Ericka lowered to her knees beside the basket, took out a sandwich and held it out to Gavin.

For a moment, he stood silent as her hand lingered in air, then he removed his sheath and sword and sat beside her. Taking the sandwich, he turned it over in his hands, then sniffed it. While he stared, Ericka took the sandwich, unwrapped it and pushed it to his lips. He leaned back.

"Eat." Ericka knew he was hungry. The low rumble of an empty stomach echoed from his side of the blanket. A thin smile tugged at her lips. She took a bite, then held it up to him. As if she proved it wasn't poisoned, he took a huge chunk in one big bite.

Ericka handed him the rest of the sandwich, then pulled out the bottle of wine, the opener and the two glasses. Out of the corner of her eye, she noticed she held a captive audience in Gavin. He watched her every move. When the cork popped, she poured two glasses and handed him one.

"Cheers." She touched her glass to his, then took a sip.

Unable to pull his eyes away, he watched her lips graze the rim of the glass. Watching her lick a stray drop from her luscious lips, his gut clenched and his throat tightened. She was testing his resolve. The hunger to taste her mouth made him salivate. Inwardly he shuddered, then forced his gaze from her wanton mouth.

Straining to concentrate on anything but her, he swirled the red liquid around in the glass then lifted it to his nose. An unfamiliar fragrance filled his nostrils. *But wasn't everything unfamiliar, including the food she shared?*

For a moment, his gaze locked on hers across the rim of his glass. A warm glow heated his gut. Though her eyes were sheltered by those things she called glasses, he reveled in her gaze. The witch was making it difficult for him to maintain his promise.

Raising the glass, he gulped the substance. It warmed his throat and chest as it traveled to his stomach. *Not as good or as strong as mead, but it would do, for now.* He wiped his sleeve across his mouth. Maybe if he drank enough of it, his thirst for her would dissipate. But he doubted it, even as the liquid warmed his insides.

Ericka choked on a sip of her wine. After chugging the whole glass, he held it out for more. She filled it to the brim. *Maybe if she got him drunk, he'd tell the truth.* Was he a paid actor working for her aunt or was this truly a fantastical event occurring in her reality? Though she'd witnessed him burst from stone, it could still have been some sort of magical trick. She sighed. Magicians accomplished tricks all the time without her figuring them out.

Careful not to drink her glass too fast, Ericka paced her sips. She split the last sandwich in two and gave Gavin half. Deciding to play along with his game while they ate, she chose words in Gaelic as close to her meaning as possible.

"This is a sandwich. It's made with ham and cheese, lettuce and tomato with a little dab of mayo." Though he gave no sign that he understood, he continued to eat.

Lifting her glass, she continued. "This is wine." She paused and took a small sip. "Ummmm, my favorite."

"Ummm." He mimicked then took another gulp.

"Who are you?" Ericka poured more wine into his glass.

A glazed look filled his eyes as he leaned against the wall.

"I." Lifting his glass as if in a mock toast, he continued. "I am Gavin MacKinnon, leader of Clan MacKinnon or whatever there is left of it." After he tossed half the glass of wine down his throat, Ericka filled his glass again.

"Where and when were you born?"

"Lass." He paused as he gazed upon her face. The soft skin, the supple shape of her lips, the taste of her mouth, her mouth wrapped on the sensitive skin of his... Clearing his throat, he tried to shake visions of her naked body from his thoughts as he repositioned his kilt in an effort to hide the stiffness between his thighs.

"I was born here at Castle MacKinnon, the first of five boys and one daughter born to Farlan and Grizel MacKinnon."

"But there were seven brothers." Ericka's eyebrow cocked. Had he made his first mistake?

"Aye, lass, that there were." He smiled.

After taking another gulp from his glass, he continued. "Me mum died when Akira was a wee one of three. Me da needed help with the baby and with us all being boys, none of us knew how to care for a young'un, especially a girl. So, he married Siusan."

A heavy sigh escaped as he paused. A dark sadness gleamed in his irises just before he swallowed another mouthful of wine. "Now there was a beautiful lass if ever I seen one and good for me da and us wee ones." He tilted his head back against the wall and closed his eyes.

"So, Siusan was the mother of the other two boys?"

"Aye, twins, Donell and Dour, born a few years after Siusan came to live with us."

As a sensation of warmth spread through his system, his defenses unwillingly relaxed. Opening his eyes, the sight of auburn-colored hair caught his attention. Vivid memories flooded his thoughts…her scent…the feel of her beneath him. Before he could stop his mouth, the words slipped passed his lips on a whisper.

"Hair the color of pure fire."

As if in slow motion, he inched closer to Ericka. Gathering a loose strand of her hair, he lifted it to his nose. The scent of heather filled his senses and sent him on a journey to the past. The desire to taste her heightened his need. Wrapping his arms around her, he pulled her close.

The softness of her skin, the scent of her arousal, the touch of her beaded nipples pressed against his chest increased his need to be inside of her tenfold. This woman had his cock hard and he hadn't even tasted her mouth. Instinct took over. He had to have her beneath him with her legs around his waist and his shaft buried deep.

He wanted her wrapped around him with his cock nestled in her warmth until his seed spilled inside her sheath. A sheath he swore was made just for him and him alone. Urged on by raging need coursing through his veins, he had to taste her.

Before she could protest, he crushed her mouth in a bruising kiss. Just as quick, he eased back, tracing her lips with the tip of his tongue before he plunged inward again.

Unable to think, Ericka responded. She delved into the deliciousness of the man and suckled his wine-flavored tongue as if she were thirsting to death. *Oh man, could he kiss.*

A twinge of guilt sparked at the base of her brain, but was extinguished the moment his hand slid up the back of her neck, sending spirals of heat skittering down her spine. Swift fingers wiggled her hair free of its bun, then balled tight in the strands. He tugged her head back and she reluctantly broke from their kiss.

A trail of fire followed his lips as he littered kisses from her chin, down the length of her neck, then back up to the lobe of her ear. When his teeth nibbled the soft lobe, she gasped. The moment he traced the rim with the tip of his tongue, her nipples shot to full attention, begging to be the next victims of his sensual assault.

Ericka fought to gain control over her raging need, but floundered at the sensual master's touch. When his warm palm skittered up the inside of her t-shirt to cup her breasts, she melted. Her resistance weakened no matter how hard she tried to maintain some level of control. The masterful way he teased her breasts had her aching for skin-to-skin contact.

"What nature of clothing 'tis this?" he whispered as he fingered her bra.

The warmth of his breath upon her skin sent chills racing down her spine and moisture soaked her panties. He pulled her shirt up above her bra. When his finger lifted the nipple free of the cup, Ericka gave up the inner fight. There was no denying it…she wanted him.

Lacing her hands behind his head, she tugged him to her breast. His mouth found its home and suckled the pouting bud into the depths of its warm wetness. Arching her back, she thrust her nipple deeper into the suction of his mouth. Eagerly, he engulfed her nipple and areola as if it provided nourishment to a dying man.

The harder he suckled her breast and tugged upon her nipple, the wetter she became between her thighs. He commanded her senses. Though she knew better than to give in—again—her mind became mush and her body his playground. Every ounce of her burned to be kissed by him, to feel his mouth on her skin.

Forcing her hands to release his head, she reached over her head then jerked the t-shirt up and over. The well-practiced angle of her arms behind her back released the bra within seconds.

Desperately, she wanted skin-to-skin contact as she tugged at his tunic. Without hesitating, he released her breast long enough to discard the tunic, then switched to the other breast, whose nipple stood proud and pouting for his touch.

Plowing her hands through his hair, she undid his ponytail. Thick strands flowed through her fingers. With each tug and nibble of his teeth to her nipple, hunger racked her body. Her panties were soaked and her pussy throbbed. She wanted him so badly it hurt. Pushing back, she tugged her nipple from his mouth with a pop. On shaky legs, she stood. As sexily as possible, she kicked off her shoes and wriggled her jeans down at record speed, then flung them across the room with her foot.

Slowly, she sank to the ground. His hooded gaze mesmerized her. Warmth caressed her sides as his hands caressed her taut abdomen, then slid up to cradle her breasts. The breath hitched in her throat when he circled a nipple with the tip of his tongue. Pure need arrowed from the nipple held captive by his teeth to her clit as if the two were connected. Grasping his shoulders, Ericka gently led him down until she was on her back and he lay nestled between her thighs.

As he rose to his knees, the heat of his gaze caressed her skin from face, to pouting nipples, to the smooth plane of her abdomen, then dropped to the silk of her panties. Why had she left those on? she chided herself.

As she grabbed her panties, he stopped her. A hazed glazed-over appearance filled his eyes when she met his gaze. The smell of wine heavy on his breath stilled her actions. Was she taking advantage of him?

"Let me," he whispered. Kisses feathered her body from neck to nipple.

Who was taking advantage of whom here? The plunder of her body by his mouth melted any thought of resistance. He suckled her nipples, then lapped at the sensitive valley between both breasts. His tongue continued its torturous route, lavishing a hot wet trail to her navel. The expert tip of his tongue laved the rim of her navel and a jolt of pure lightning bolted to her pussy, causing her inner muscles to spasm. Need pounded in her clit and it was all she could do not to force his head down and hold him captive with her thighs.

As he inched his way, every muscle quivered at his slow, sensual perusal. The heat of his breath and the touch of his tongue and mouth seemed to tattoo her skin as his. When he nudged her thighs apart, she spread them wide. Every ounce of her hungered for his expertly skilled tongue to work its magic on her oversensitive clit.

When he slid down between her legs, more wetness pooled between her folds. *God, he hadn't touched her pussy and she was wet for him.* Ericka sighed.

With his teeth, he grasped the waistband of her panties and Ericka gasped at the gentle brush of his upper lip against the sensitive skin of her lower abdomen. Clasping the sides of her panties with his hands, he stared up at her and held her gaze captive. His eyes seemed to glow brilliant green as he shredded her panties with his hands and teeth. Jerking the tattered remnants from underneath her bottom, he tossed them to the side.

Frantic for his touch, Ericka arched, lifting her bottom and spreading her knees apart, presenting her pussy close to his face. Though she couldn't believe she held herself open for his inspection, she couldn't move. The beat of her heart thudded in her chest as she waited for his approval.

She held her precious treasure within inches of his face. Her thighs spread wide, opened its pinkness for him to enjoy. The scent of her arousal filled each intake of air, increasing his hunger. The unique signature of her scent thundered through his senses. It was different. Different from what? He shook his head slightly. Something wasn't right, but at the moment he couldn't think straight. Was it the wine muddling his head or the beauty of the woman spread before him? On a deep inhalation, a smile tugged at the corner of his lip. Right now, it didn't matter what was different. All that mattered was she wanted him and he liked the way she responded to his touch.

Plump nipples had tickled his tongue and filled his mouth perfectly when he suckled from them. And now…her juices dripped for him and he hadn't so much as touched his prize.

Soft, curly hairs brushed his cheek as he nuzzled her mound and parted the way with his fingers. Licking the length of her ripe opening, a gasp reached his ears, urging him on. A hint of her taste tempted his mouth and increased his hunger. He dove into her moist folds until the swollen bud he sought touched the tip of his tongue.

When her legs hitched across his shoulders, he took it as a sign that he was welcome to feast upon her bounty. No other invitation was needed. He suckled on the hardened bud as her juices dampened his face. Her flavor was exotic to his tongue, intoxicating his senses. Unable to get enough, he lapped and dipped his tongue inside her pussy again and again until her legs tightened about his neck.

The rush of her womanly pleasure was close. Clamping possessively onto her sensitive clit, he tugged it deeper into his mouth and lavished it with strong flicks of his tongue. A flash flood of her intoxicating juices was his reward. He lapped and suckled, not wanting to miss a drop. The liquid heat upon his tongue was pure addition.

This man—ancient or not—knew ways to bring her pleasure that she had never before experienced. His greedy mouth and masterful tongue drained her body of jolt after jolt of pure wet heat until her legs shook and she gasped for air.

"Gavin," she rasped on a hoarse breath. Ericka's fingers twisted in his hair and reluctantly lifted his face. Having his mouth on her pussy was fantastic, but now she wanted his cock and she intended to have it.

A wicked smile and glazed deep green eyes met and held hers as he traveled slowly up the length of her. His tongue teased the sensitive skin of her abdomen all the way to her breasts, making her unable to catch a full breath. But breathing wasn't important, he was. The look of a sexually charged hunk crept up her body, teasing every ounce until his face was level with hers.

Without warning, he latched onto her mouth and took her tongue captive in a rough kiss heightened by passion. Instead of fighting the abusive kiss, she reacted hungrily. Pressure for pressure, she engaged their mouths tight in a tongue-fest of heat. She reveled in the knowledge that it was her flavor upon his tongue.

Abruptly, he broke their kiss as he cupped her face. Butterfly soft, he placed kisses on her cheeks, her eyes and her brow. A shift of his hips placed the thick head of his cock hovering, nudging at her opening and her heart skipped a beat. It took sheer will-power not to rush the moment and enjoy the gentle rub of his cock against the tender sensitive flesh of her clit.

Chills skittered up her abdomen. Blood rushed to her core and still she forced control. Wait for him to make the next move. Hold still, don't push up and take him in before he's ready. She bit her lower lip as electric jolts shot from her clit straight to her nipples when he brushed the thick head of his cock against it. He was killing her. Did he realize that? She stared at his face, but his eyes were closed. What was he thinking? How much more teasing could she take?

Though he wanted to bury himself deep inside her sex, he hesitated. The exotic flavor of her taste watered his mouth. Her unique scent filled his senses and heightened his need to sheathe himself within her. And yet he yielded, savoring the wonder of her beneath him.

Her breasts were heavier than he remembered. That magnificent rump seemed fuller and more capable of handling a man of his size and weight. Her hips held his in a sturdy, controlled fashion. A way that swelled his heart with the prospect of future heirs born on a woman of such a fine build.

This woman held his heart in her hands and between her thighs. The thought made him smile, though he held his eyes closed, enjoying the perfect beauty of her face in his mind's eye.

Without any effort on her part, she had him ravished with need to the point he would never get full of her bountiful graces. He wanted his auburn-haired beauty. He wanted his…

"Tavia."

The word rushed upon warm breath across the sensitive, thoroughly kissed skin of her lips. Ericka's eyes snapped open. Fast as lightning, she slapped his cheek. An invisible fist tightened around her heart.

He called her Tavia.

Needing to be away from him, she bucked and squirmed beneath his heavy weight. He called her by his wife's name. How stupid could she be? Heat flushed her skin and she couldn't look at his face. Pushing with all her might, she tried to get him off her, but failed. The lumbering giant stayed put. Tears welled in her eyes, but she refused to let them fall.

He wanted his wife, not her!

The skin upon his cheek sizzled. Shaking his head, he attempted to clear the cobwebs from his thoughts. The wine muddled his brain. *Must be stronger than mead.* Tavia had never slapped him, no matter how drunk he had gotten.

Staring down at her, his thoughts were fuzzy and unclear as he forced his eyes to focus. The beauty beneath him was not Tavia. *That* was what was different. She wasn't his wife. What had he done? Rolling off her, he lunged to his feet.

For the first time since he'd been a young lad, the room spun and he lost his balance from being too far into his cups. *What had she done to him? Had the witch somehow poisoned him? Had she hexed him into being unfaithful, again?*

Heavy-headed, the room blurred. One step in her direction and his knees gave way as a haze wrapped around his thoughts. Would she forgive him? was the last clear thought before darkness overcame him.

When he crumbled to his knees, she tried to scurry out of the way but wasn't fast enough. The man slithered to the floor like a limp noodle then toppled, face first, into her lap.

Tears streaked Ericka's cheeks as the last shred of her control slipped away. Gavin's face lay nestled in her lap. The warmth of his deep breaths scorched her thighs. This time his touch burned her and not in a good way. It wasn't her he wanted. It was his wife.

The sensation of being dirty scored her system and fried her nerve endings as guilt riddled her soul. In desperate need of a shower, she had to move. Maybe, if she scrubbed hard enough, she could scour his touch from her skin and ease her conscience somehow.

Ericka struggled against the dead weight of his shoulders and wriggled her legs out from underneath him. His head bounced in her lap, then between her thighs and down her legs until she was free. Unintentionally, she let his face land with a thud on the blanket.

Had she hurt him? She nudged his side with her foot. He was out cold. She shouldn't care if she did hurt him. His words had more than hurt her. They'd torn her heart apart. It ached with each labored beat it took. Ericka sniffled against the onslaught of more tears.

He thought she was his wife.

Frantically, she gathered her clothes. Where were her panties? A tattered edge of cotton teased her from underneath the ancient hypocrite—or actor—the desperate doubt fleeted thorough her thoughts. At the moment, she didn't care which he was. He could keep her panties. She wasn't about to touch him in order to get them.

Belvedere was curled up next to him. *Traitor.* She huffed, hopping on one foot trying to slip on her jeans. With the grace of a drunk getting dressed, she tugged on her shirt and shoes.

Grabbing the flashlight and the basket, she hurried to the door and shoved it open. A flash of lightning and a rumble of thunder ripped across the sky right in front of the building. High wind rocked the trees and howled past her through the open door.

"Just great, an all-out storm," she mumbled, dropping the basket and struggling to close the door. It wasn't her best option, but it was her only option for now. Ericka's shoulders sagged as she turned around. She was stuck here alone with Gavin.

He lay sprawled facedown across the blanket, Belvedere curled at his side. Rain pelted the fragile roof above their heads. Ericka inspected the roof for leaks. So far there were none, but that could change at any given minute. She glanced over at the half-naked Gavin. Considering her luck, the roof would probably collapse.

Careful not to touch him, she sat on the blanket's edge. *This is what happens when you act like a sexual deviant,* Ericka reprimanded herself as she snorted, leaning back, trying to get comfortable against the wall.

Should've stuck with those good ole gut instincts. Guys that look like him don't want the girls with intellect. She sighed, scanning his broad shoulders, the narrow waist at the junction of his kilt, his firm bottom, then down the length of his long legs.

Nope. Guys like him want them built like models, but with bubbleheads for brains.

The consistent rhythmic beat of the rain upon the roof brought heaviness to her eyelids. Blinking, she shook her head, attempting to stay awake. But eventually, she lost. Sliding down the wall, she curled up, keeping Belvedere between her and Gavin. She may have to sleep near him, but at least she wasn't going to touch him.

* * * * *

It took tremendous effort to sit up with a pounding head. He ground his palm into his temple in slow, circular motions. No matter how hard he pressed, the pain persisted. Grasping the empty bottle at his side, he glared through slender slits at the foreign brew. *Wine*! he scoffed. *Rather have mead.* A rough tongue scraped across his dry mouth and he knew he needed a drink if he was to regain any form of moisture in his throat.

Shakily, he stood and moved to the door. When he pushed it open, Belvedere scurried out. The rain had stopped and signs of it nearing sunrise were close upon him. He stepped around the building's edge to relieve himself and noticed Belvedere doing the same at a nearby tree. When he was done, he gave a sharp whistle that almost cracked his aching skull and the dog returned to his side.

Quietly, he slipped back into the building, closing the door behind him. Ericka lay on her side. He crouched at the basket in hope of finding a flask of water. The round clear bottle he lifted from the basket held a liquid, and as parched as his throat felt, it would be better than nothing. After several tries, he couldn't figure out how it opened. The frustrated growl from his throat only irritated the desert situation of his mouth. He pulled the *sgian dhy* from the sheath in his boot, and with one swift move, sliced the top from the bottle.

Relieved to find that it was water, he took several large gulps, then slid over to Ericka. Auburn hair scattered about her face and shoulders reminded him of Tavia. Automatically, he touched his cheek. Mistakenly, he called her Tavia. How could he have been so blind? Her taste, her smell and the feel of her body, each were different to Tavia's. Only the hair…

His fingers trailed through the tangled strands. The hair was similar in color.

Jerking her hair from his hand, she sprang upright. Her eyes opened wide as she plastered herself against the wall in an attempt to get as far as she could away from him. Falling asleep was not part of the plan, leaving before he woke had been the number one idea, but now, she was trapped.

"Lass," he spoke.

"The name's not lass," she snapped. "It's Ericka."

With her back pressed tight against the wall, she worked her way into a standing position, though her head ached. Chin lifted, she stared at Gavin. The need to escape rifled through her system, but she couldn't break free from his gaze.

He looked lost. Dark circles decorated underneath his eyes. His long hair was a tangled mess pushed back from his face. A day's growth of dark stubble etched his chin. With his shoulders slumped and his chest bare, he sat upon his knees facing her.

"Lass, I…" He ran a hand through his disheveled hair.

"What's the matter? *Tavia* the only name you know?" Ericka growled as she pushed past him. When she shoved the door open, the first rays of early morning sunlight slithered into the room.

"Ericka!"

Pure pain laced his voice as the air crackled with a sharp sizzling sound. She spun around just in time to watch his body react to the new dawn. An outstretched hand reached for her. On bended knees, he leaned in her direction. The distraught look upon his handsome face turned to stone right before her eyes with her name frozen on his lips. Belvedere barked frantically at his side.

Ericka's jaw dropped. No tricks. How could this be? Each step wavered as she moved toward him. Snagging her foot on something, she lifted it and shook it out. His tunic hadn't changed to stone. It wasn't on his body. Clutching the rough cloth to her chest, his scent filled her nostrils.

Before the sun captured his spirit in rock, he had spoken her name. She touched his frozen cheek and traced his unshaven face with her fingertips. Warmth spread through her hand, but this time she didn't pull back. Shakily, she trailed his muscled outline until her palm splayed across the middle of his chest. A tender rhythm vibrated against her palm.

In slow motion she knelt, holding her hand firmly in place against his chest. It couldn't be. Pressing her cheek against his chest, heat rushed from the stone across her cheek, then warmed her chilled body. Falling backward, Ericka's heart beat jackrabbit fast. She swallowed hard, tamping down the urge to run.

On a deep breath, she brushed the hair from over her ear and readied her system for the heat the stone produced at her touch. She pressed her ear, cheek and palm firmly to the center of his chest. A steady rhythm echoed faint and consistent against the inside of the stone. She scrambled backward from his frozen figure.

It couldn't be. But she knew, deep in her soul, that she heard his heart beat within his stone prison.

Chapter Eight

ᘓ

Every muscle ached and a bone-deep tiredness controlled her slow movements when Ericka finally returned to the castle. Belvedere pounced onto Aunt May's lap the instant they entered the garden gate.

"About time you two got home," Aunt May laughed between slobbery puppy kisses.

Ericka forced a weak smile, dropped the almost empty picnic basket on the ground and slumped into the closest chair. The look of pure joy danced across Aunt May's face with each swipe of Belvedere's tongue. Uncertainty bounced around her thoughts. *Should she interrupt? Should she tell her aunt what she saw?* Most of all, was *she* certain that Gavin had changed to stone in front of her eyes? The event was unbelievable, but still it happened as she watched. There was no denying it. She searched in a last-ditch effort to disprove the curse, but failed. There were no trick cameras or other paraphernalia in or around the building.

After pouring a cup of coffee, Ericka rested her elbows on the table, holding the cup in both hands. If she admitted a curse existed, would her credibility as a researcher be crushed in the sane world? It was a tough decision, but how else did she explain this?

Carefully, she listed the events of her morning in her head. First, she woke stiff, tired and cold with Gavin's hand in her hair. Second, he turned to stone as she watched. Third, the beat of his heart reverberated through the stone. Fourth, she wrapped him in the blanket, blew out the candles and closed the door as best as possible. And now, she sat with coffee cup in hand trying to distinguish between reality and fantasy.

The coffee aroma teased her senses. Licking her lips, the taste of stale wine and Gavin's flavor watered her mouth, renewing the unrequited hunger for him. Her gut clenched as she forced a swallow of coffee. She needed to figure this out before this man's sexual pull drove her nuts. Was he real or was he not?

As Ericka sat quietly trying to sort her thoughts, Margaret served breakfast. The scent of bacon and eggs rose from her plate and commanded her attention. *Food*! All he had were sandwiches and wine…too much wine because of her untrusting need to know. Ericka tried to swallow the lump of guilt fixed firm in her throat. Gavin passed out drunk because she tried to ply him for information.

Aunt May interrupted her thoughts. "What happened? You went back out to the cemetery, didn't you?"

"Yes." She couldn't look at her aunt. Instead, she stared at the eggs on her plate. *Wonder how he likes them…fried or scrambled? What does it matter? He doesn't want you, he wants his dead wife*. Ericka sat her cup down with a thump, sloshing coffee over the rim.

"You all right, dear?"

"I'm just tired." Ericka never thought she'd say this, but the words spilled from her lips before she could think better of them. "I saw him turn to stone."

Aunt May choked on a swallow of coffee. "He what?" She leaned forward, excitement shone in her eyes. Ericka simply nodded. "He turned to stone in front of you. How? What happened?"

"Belvedere and I went to the cemetery. I wanted to see for myself." She paused, not certain how much she should say. The true intention of her excursion to the cemetery had been to prove her aunt was behind this farce. Telling Aunt May that would break her aunt's heart. So, she didn't. Ericka rose from her chair and paced the length of the patio wall.

"I think the curse has something to do with the legend behind the gargoyle. Though ye be mine by night, if not by day." The words whispered from her lips as she stared across the horizon toward the cemetery.

"You mean to tell me, he's a man by night and a stone statue by day. Just like the creatures of the gargoyle, a protector by night." Aunt May's voice exuded with enthusiasm.

Margaret interrupted before Ericka could answer. "Mistress, you have a visitor. I took the liberty of placing him in the parlor."

"I'm not expecting anyone," Aunt May stated then turned to Ericka. "Are you?"

Ericka shook her head no. Aunt May, Belvedere, Margaret and Ned were the only ones she knew here.

"Did you get a name?" Aunt May asked.

"Said his name was Brother Leod from some brotherhood. More n' likely he's one of the monks from the monastery over in Oykel. Been there more n' a hundred years or so that one has. Strange lot..." Her voice trailed off as she turned and walked away.

"Brotherhood?" Ericka's eyebrow lifted.

"It's the first I've heard of it. Better go see what he wants." Aunt May stood and turned to leave.

Unsure of whom this guy was or what he wanted, Ericka decided not to let her aunt deal with this person alone. With a stiff gulp of coffee, a swift run of her fingers through her hair and an adjustment to her glasses, Ericka hustled to catch up with her aunt. Hovering outside the parlor, the sight of the man with her aunt caught her completely off-guard. Monks weren't supposed to look like this. Tall, with wavy brown hair, broad shoulders and when he turned to greet her, a smile that rivaled most male models. Maybe he wasn't a monk. He wasn't dressed like a monk with his formfitting jeans, boots and a baby blue, button-down dress shirt. Not what she expected at all. Her mouth went dry the moment he extended his hand. His eyes, the color of a field of ripe golden wheat, snagged her focus from anything else in the room.

"Hello, I'm Brother Leod from the Brotherhood of Our Sons of the Servant of Judgment." A deep Scottish brogue rolled from his lips.

A surge of electrified current raced through the touch of their hands and warmed her body, hardening her nipples. When his tongue darted across his lips, hers automatically did the same as if she could taste him there if she tried really hard.

"I'm Ericka Russell," she rasped, a little more sultrily than intended. Surely, she was going straight to hell for the illicit thoughts tainting her brain.

"Pleased to meet you." The words sounded husky as Brother Leod spoke. His eyes held hers and she swore she saw a devilish glint sparkle in his pupils.

"Ericka's my niece," Aunt May interjected as she motioned for them all to sit.

Ericka sat beside her aunt on the sofa and Brother Leod chose the overstuffed chair across from them. A lingering sensation tingled in the palm of her hand and she rubbed it against the leg of her jeans, trying to soothe it, but the itch didn't ease. She folded her hands together in her lap. The skin, muscle and tendons of her hand simmered into an intense heat as if scalded by boiling water. Silently sucking in deeply through clenched teeth, she attempted to swallow the pain. Stoically, she willed control over her facial features and held a thin polite smile on her lips.

Odd, this happened after the touch of Brother Leod's hand. Chin lifted, fist knotted tight in her lap, she sat rigid, determined to focus on the supposed man of the cloth.

"What brings you here for a visit?" Aunt May smiled.

"Our brotherhood is a self-sufficient organization. We require little from the outside world But…" he paused. His gaze shifted from Ericka to Aunt May and then returned to her. Hands folded in his lap, legs crossed as he leaned back into a more relaxed position, killer smile in place, Ericka half expected him to whip out a boom box, jump up on the coffee table and start to strip. He looked that good.

Stop! Ericka jerked her gaze away and stared anywhere but in his direction for a moment in an attempt to refocus. Where had that come from? He's a monk or was he? She dared a glance at his face and met a challenge in the reflection of the golden, wheat-colored eyes as if he read her mind. Refusing to back down, she held her chin tilted up and her gaze fixated on him.

"Our monastery is well over one hundred years old and each year repairs have grown more costly," he continued.

"So, you're here for a donation," Ericka replied, keeping her voice cool and collected even though the pain in her hand increased. The motive for his visit was clear. He was here to take advantage of a wealthy widow. Well, she wasn't going to let him.

"Ericka," Aunt May admonished.

Brother Leod cleared his throat. "I'm not here for a donation."

Leaning over the arm of the chair, he pulled a large book from his attaché and handed it to Aunt May.

"Each year, my fellow brothers and I compile historical information concerning different castles in the form of a book. It includes the origin, the structural architecture, the changes made throughout the years and of course…" His gaze fell once again on Ericka. His smile seemed deliberate and calculated as he spoke. "We do a thorough investigation into the ownership of the castle, right down to the original clan."

His pupils dilated and Ericka couldn't pull her eyes away. Those eyes seemed to suck her in. Pulsating golden waves appeared to flow in his irises in a weird sort of light show and she wondered if the scene was only visible to her.

Visions of him naked flashed in her head. His face millimeters from hers, lips close enough to touch as his hands cupped both breasts, kneading them to perfection. The burn in her palm intensified to a full-fledged forest fire. Ericka's eyes widened as she bit her lower lip in an attempt to lessen the pain in her hand. She swore a bolt of energy shot from him and coursed through her body, landing in the pit of her stomach, gouging the inner lining to shreds. Her mouth opened, then closed in a rush to keep the acid reflux from spewing onto the book of castles on the coffee table in front of her.

Needing to gain control, she had to break this invisible connection. But over what? Was he actually doing this to her or was she coming down with something? Forcing her eyelids to obey, she closed them tight. His naked form dissipated, the heat cooled in her palm and her stomach settled to a disgruntled bubble of agitated assault.

"This book is marvelous," Aunt May exclaimed as she flipped through the pages.

Ericka leaned forward, hoping to quell the need to spew. The pictures were precise and included the most intricate of details of all aspects of a castle, including complete coverage of its grounds.

Without looking up from the book, Ericka swallowed hard then spoke. "What does this have to do with us?"

"Each year we choose a different location for our book and this year we would like to study your castle." The sensation of his gaze boring into the top of her skull rippled through her system as he spoke. Something was wrong, but what? She couldn't be sure and as long as she suffered from these peculiar ailments, she couldn't think straight.

Aunt May's hand covered Ericka's as they leaned back into a more comfortable position on the couch. Hesitantly, she leveled her gaze to his, but felt nothing, no surge of energy, no fire bolt in her hand, no waves of nausea in her belly. The breath she hadn't realized she held eased from her chest. This burning feeling had to be a bug, a cold or something.

"At what cost to me?" Aunt May surprised Ericka with the sensible question.

"Absolutely none. We provide you with an original copy, free of charge, of course."

His brilliant smile returned as he eased back into his chair, hands rested on the arms. As Ericka studied his face, his gaze remained on Aunt May. Confidence exuded from his charms.

"We sell the rest. Since my brothers and I do all the work, from the pictures, to the writing and editing, to the finished bound copy in the monastery, the cost is minimal and the profit is enough to compensate for the repairs."

"The offer sounds interesting." Aunt May paused. "But would you mind if we gave it a few days to think it over?"

Ericka caught the taut subtle twitch in his chin. The confident air about him seemed to shift to a warm hint of anger that went unnoticed by Aunt May. But for some reason, Ericka thought she sensed a change in him.

"Of course."

Standing, he reached for the book, but Aunt May was quick. Her hand landed on the book lying on the coffee table before he could grab it.

"Mind if we keep this to look over? I promise to return it along with our decision in a few days." The smile that crossed her face dripped with pure sugar and sweet old woman innocence.

The hand he held lingering above the book swiftly tucked into his shirt pocket and pulled out a rectangular-shaped piece of paper. "Sure. Here's my card. I can be reached at the number listed on the bottom. Just leave a message and I'll get back to you within twenty-four hours." He stooped, picked up his attaché and followed Aunt May's lead out of the parlor into the main hallway.

"Ladies." He nodded. "I do thank you for your time this morning."

"And I thank you for dropping by. You'll be hearing from us." Aunt May pulled the front door open to escort him out.

"What was that all about?" Ericka whispered out of the side of her mouth as they waved goodbye.

"Not sure," Aunt May whispered back.

When he was clearly on his way to the roadway in his car, they shut the door. Ericka turned to face her aunt. "I caught the look you gave him."

The raised eyebrows in response made her chuckle. "Don't give me that look. You know what I mean." Placing a hand in front of her face, fluttering it fanlike and the other over her brow, Ericka pretended to be a damsel in distress.

"My kind sir, may I keep this book and mull over your precious offer?" Ericka batted her eyelashes.

They burst out laughing at the absurd reenactment.

"I never realized I could look so desperate." Aunt May sniffed back a tear of laughter.

"Only when you want something." Ericka adjusted her glasses and coughed back a laugh. "You don't believe him, do you?"

"Not for one minute." The serious expression on her face sobered Ericka instantly. Any remaining laughter died in her chest and she fell into step beside her aunt as she went back to the parlor.

"What do you think he's up to? Do you think he's running some kind of scam to part rich widows from their money?" She settled on the couch close to her aunt.

The soft, comfy couch seemed to cradle Ericka. Tiredness oozed through her muscles and her head dropped back against the couch. The night had been long and the events of the morning hadn't allowed her a moment to rest. Their strange visitor and the sudden onset of pain had taxed the last of her limited energy.

Odd. Her hand no longer hurt. She examined her palm for burns, but there were none. Her stomach had settled as well.

"Nope. I think he's after something bigger than that." Aunt May lifted the book and placed it open in her lap.

"What makes you think that?"

"This book for starters. Notice that several pages in the front have been slipped out and replaced with different ones." Aunt May ran her finger down the barely visible seam. "These are the pages that give credit where credit is due, like the copyright, the editor, the publishing house and so forth."

"I get the gist." Ericka sat up and took the book from her aunt. "These first two pages aren't the same class or weight as the rest of the pages either."

Aunt May smiled. "Good job! Besides all that, I have this book in my collection and it wasn't put together at a monastery by some brotherhood. It's one of a series I own on the castles of England, Ireland and Scotland. He made a mistake bringing this book here."

"Then what's he after?" Ericka sighed.

"I don't know." Aunt May shrugged as she continued to examine the book. "I just don't know."

* * * * *

On her aunt's advice, Ericka went upstairs to soak in a warm bath. The huge claw-footed tub filled to the brim with hot water and lavender-scented bubbles was just the ticket she needed to ease the tired ache. With her head rested on an inflatable bath cushion, she lifted a suds-covered hand to her face. The pain had been so intense she was certain the skin would have been marred in some way. But not a mark was visible.

Had the good Brother Leod inflicted that pain mentally? Was he some sort of telepathic individual with some sort of mind control ability? *God,* she huffed as water splashed over the tub's edge when she dropped her arm back in its warm. Had this trip gone off the deep end of reality? What was reality? She watched a man switch from stone to man and back to stone. Was it a well performed trick or was it truly a curse?

Ericka's tongue darted across her lips, igniting the memory of Gavin's taste to flood her senses. The thought of how his tongue brought her to the edge of the universe in wave upon wave of sexual release made her clit ache and she hungered to feel him buried to the hilt deep inside. She balled up in the tub. He wasn't hers to touch or feel.

He wanted Tavia, not her.

Chapter Nine

ꕤ

"Brother, I sense that we were right in our belief that one has arisen. I felt an unexplained presence in the young woman," he spoke into the cell phone headset.

"You have served the brotherhood well. Are they responsive to our plan?" a gruff Scottish brogue replied.

"The older woman requested a few days to think it over."

"We don't have a few days. We must strike now."

"I understand the necessity to move quickly." He paused, keeping his voice and attitude in check. To raise one's voice with an elder of the council would bring disgrace to one's family and dishonor to thy name.

"The brotherhood has waited over two hundred years for this. To rush the matter now may only bring defeat and the opportunity may be lost. I shall visit the ladies again and persuade them to accept our offer."

"Let us hope that patience will suit us well. I shall report your progress to the council."

When they disconnected, a vindictive chuckle escaped his lips. The old geezer had no clue to the strength of his abilities. The younger woman, the one named Ericka, she was responsive all right. He shifted in the driver's seat as his cock thickened at the thought of her.

Take those glasses off, let that hair down from that ridiculous bun, get rid of those loose-fitting clothes and put her in a tight, low-cut sweater and a miniskirt and he bet he could make her beg for more than just a daydream fantasy of his touch. He ran a hungry tongue across his lips. The reaction on her face to his illicit mind play had made it difficult for him to remain seated and not lunge over the coffee table to act on the vision he placed in her brain.

No, he chuckled. The council truly held no knowledge to the extent of his abilities. As a child, he placed thoughts in other children's heads to take the blame for his misdoings. His father was the only member of the brotherhood who knew the strength of his power and he took that secret to his grave. Telepathy and mind control were his specialties.

The council wasted the book and would not train the younger members of the brotherhood in the ways. *The old fools.* They refused to use the book's dark magic. But he held no such reservations about using at least one of its passages.

Leod snickered as he massaged the key in his pocket. His powers had gained him access to the book. But only for a few moments. Though his powers were strong, he didn't want to arouse suspicion from the council. *They'd know soon enough of his true plan.*

The Brotherhood of the Sons of the Servant of Judgment was in his blood. His father believed Leod was the direct descendent of the Servant of Judgment. The one ordained to fulfill the ancient prophecy.

Leod smiled. *His time had finally come.* He would claim his place as the rightful heir and command the book of shadows. The council wouldn't have the power to stop him, no one would.

He parked in front of the cottage in the village he rented for this mission. Once inside, he locked the front door behind him. At the first bedroom to the right, he unlocked the door and entered the dark room.

Though it was morning, no light shone through the tightly closed black drapes. He lit several candles scattered around a makeshift altar in the center of the room, then knelt. An easel sat on either side of a large wooden trunk in front of him. Portraits of the two men he worshiped and respected seemed to return his stare.

"Father, the time has come for our prophecy to be fulfilled. One has risen, his presence I have felt." He gazed to the portrait on the left easel of his father. "You were right. A woman shall be his downfall."

Licking his lips, the image of Ericka naked flickered through his brain and tightened his groin. Turning to the portrait on the easel to the right, he continued.

"Oh, holy one, I hath risen to thy challenge and I've accepted. My distant ancestor by thine own decree for the one who vanquishes the blood of thy enemy from this earth forever shall be decreed the rightful predecessor of thy precious book."

Leod slipped a key from his pocket and unlocked the trunk centered between the two portraits. He removed a slender black notebook from a hidden compartment in the bottom of the trunk. Closing the lid, he laid the notebook opened on top of it as he flipped through his scribbled notations.

"Ah," he sighed. "Here it is." He steepled his fingers and smiled at his ancient ancestor's face.

"Forgive this one transgression, your holiness. Thy book I could not resist. Several of its spells I found enlightening, so I took it upon myself to copy them in a black book of my own. That is, until you deem me worthy of thy book." A lopsided smile tugged at the corner of his lip.

He laid his hands upon the open page. "I feel the need is great and this passage of valued use in our efforts to subdue thy enemy."

Ancient words of a society long forgotten echoed from his lips. Thrice, he repeated the passage. When he reached the end, he bowed his head and folded his hands in a moment of silence.

"The book of shadows shall be mine," he whispered. A wicked sideways grin twisted his face as he still held it bowed.

"And the wench." He paused, then licked his lips as if he could pull in a taste of her. "In the end, she shall be the vessel for our future."

* * * * *

After a bath and a nap, Ericka met her aunt for a late afternoon lunch on the patio. No sign of last night's storm remained. Vibrant sunshine coated the hills and a cool breeze coasted through the warm summer air.

"You look rested," Aunt May stated as Ericka took her place at the table.

"The nap helped." A weak smile touched her lips as she told a little white lie. She hated not telling her aunt everything that was happening. Truthfully, the nap had been restless and Ericka was more confused than ever.

She lifted the silver kettle from the center of the table and poured a hot cup of tea. In its steam, she envisioned a replay of the dreams that kept her fitful. Each time, it started with Gavin, who held her in a warm tender embrace, then blundered the moment by calling her Tavia. Then in flashed Brother Leod, which frightened her more than aroused her. Restful sleep had been impossible. She huffed across the rim of her teacup.

A supposed man of the cloth naked with her in her dreams made no sense. *Was she that sexually deprived that she dreamt about leading a monk astray?*

Ericka sipped her tea and allowed its warmth to soothe her nerves, which quickly turned to molten-hot memories of Gavin's sensual skills. She definitely couldn't consider herself sexually deprived anymore. Not after sharing the greatest, hottest sexual experiences of her life with Gavin.

Boy, would the ex-boyfriend who called her stoic and un-spontaneous be shocked to know she had sex on a patio wall and in a graveyard. An uncontrollable smile tugged at the corner of her lips as she forced herself to refocus to the problem of the present.

"Given any thought as to what that man wanted this morning?"

"Not sure what he wants. But it might be in our best interest to find out."

"How?" Ericka didn't like the tone her aunt's voice implied.

"Ever heard that old saying about keeping your friends close and your enemies even closer?"

"Yeah, but what's that got to do—"

Aunt May cut her off. "Don't think I don't know that something was going on between you two."

Ericka's mouth dropped open. "How'd you know?"

"I've spent the last several months with a ghost named Akira. Don't you think I should be able to feel a change in the air around me by now? Right, Akira?" She nodded over her shoulder and the essence of Akira appeared.

"One should hope," Akira's Scottish brogue whispered in the air around them.

Ericka gagged and almost spit tea back into her cup. No matter how many times Akira's presence appeared, she didn't think she'd ever get used to it.

"Morning, Ericka." Akira floated toward her. "Or should it be good afternoon? Either way, it doesn't matter." She flicked her transparent hand in air. "How does your hand feel?"

Ericka tucked her hand into her lap. "My hand?"

Akira laughed. "Don't play. Let me see. Your aunt sensed the strong presence of heat in the air around you this morning. 'Tis why she summoned me."

"She summoned you? How?" Pursing her eyebrows, she stared across the table at her aunt.

Akira's gaze turned to Aunt May, then back to Ericka.

"She needed me. 'Tis a special bond between thy aunt and I." She stretched her hands out to Ericka. "Let me see thy hand."

Reluctantly, Ericka lifted her hand palm up. Though Akira didn't actually hold it, the sensation of cold air surrounded her hand and chilled her to the bone. Ericka shivered in her seat. Akira's transparent hands covered hers and the pain of fire burning flesh ignited once again in her palm. For a split second, the vision of a burning Celtic cross with a sword pierced through it appeared etched in her skin. Akira released her hand and the symbol and the pain disappeared.

"MacGillivray," she hissed in a thicker than normal Scottish brogue. "'Tis the symbol of pure evil. The book of shadows..." The words trailed off as her sentence died on her thinned transparent lips.

"MacGillivray?" Ericka rubbed her palm. Nothing appeared, no charred flesh, no residual pain, and yet she witnessed a flaming scene in her palm.

The figure of Akira paced franticly to and fro along the top of the patio wall, while Belvedere sat, eyes glued up to her. His puppy head looked as if he watched a tennis match, moving side to side, following the ball. But in this case he watched Akira.

"What should we do?" Aunt May asked. Akira stopped pacing.

"'Til we know his motives, Gavin must be protected at all times. Unfortunately, 'tis not I who hath that power. 'Tis a strong disturbance on the wind. I must go. 'Tis up to you." She glared at Ericka, then in a brilliant flash of light she was gone.

"She was positively no help," Ericka snapped.

Tea sloshed over the rim of her cup as she whipped the cup from its saucer and tilted it to her lips. *MacGillivray, evil on the wind, utter nonsense*, she scoffed, then gulped down a large swallow of tea.

"I think she was. Think about it. When Akira's presence is near, how do you feel?" Aunt May sat up straight, arms crossed over her chest.

"What do you mean?" Ericka's head tilted to the side. She started to state that she wasn't even sure that Akira was real, but the sight across the table stilled the words in her throat. Her aunt's eyes were focused directly on her. No anger, no joking around shone in her irises, only sincere intuitiveness sparkled there.

"How does the air around you feel?"

Ericka swallowed, then breathed in deep with her eyes closed and allowed her senses to work. How did she feel each time Akira was near? Shivering, she opened her eyes.

"Cold," she whispered. "I feel cold air all around me."

"Good." Aunt May clapped. "It feels like an iceberg has encased your soul, doesn't it?"

"Yeah." Ericka smiled, nodding her head. "It sort of does."

"But there's no pain when she visits."

"How'd—" Aunt May's hand shot into the stop position and cut her off again.

"I felt heat in the air. I've learned that a strong surge of heat in the air can mean evil lurks. The sensation of evil set the hair on the back of my neck to stand on end." She leaned toward Ericka and grasped the hand in which Brother Leod's touch started the whole fire scenario.

"And no matter how hard you tried to hide it, I knew you were in pain."

Ericka opened her palm. Had she imagined the fire and the pain? No. She flexed her hand open and shut. The pain was real and so was what she saw. Akira was a ghost. Though it bothered her to admit it, she accepted it as fact.

Akira called the burning cross a sign of MacGillivray, the sign of evil. But hadn't he died along with all the others of that time? What about Gavin? She shot a glance across her shoulder in the direction of the graveyard. What if something evil truly lurked nearby?

"What's our next step?" Ericka asked, as she turned to face her aunt.

"First, we make sure Gavin is safe. Then, we invite the good Brother Leod here. He doesn't know that we're on to him, which makes him vulnerable. With that information in our court, we can find out what he's up to." Two eyes twinkled full of mischief and a broad smile covered the face of her aunt, but Ericka didn't feel the same exuberance. Instead, a twinge of something she couldn't explain gnawed at her gut.

* * * * *

Standing at a window in the library, Ericka watched as Aunt May and Belvedere hiked to the graveyard to check on Gavin. The plan was for one of them to sit with him until dark, then bring him back to the castle. Relief washed over her when Aunt May volunteered. As it was, she wasn't sure how she was going to face him when he returned.

She glanced up at the sun, grateful that problem wouldn't arise for several more hours. Turning, she faced a mountainous task. Aunt May volunteered to protect Gavin while she handled the venture that she was skilled in best…research.

Three of the four walls of the library were covered from ceiling to floor with shelves filled with books, some of which belonged to the castle since its beginnings. Others were added throughout the castle's history. Ericka knew half of one wall of shelves contained some of her Aunt May's personal collection. Somewhere amongst this vast array of antiques and new, she hoped to find answers.

Double French glass doors set in the middle of a wall of windows acted as an inlet of pure sunlight for the library. The library had been refurbished to include a six-foot leather couch with two matching leather chairs. A large oval, glass-topped coffee table, with a massive set of antlers as its base, sat in the center of the couch and chairs. The chandelier that hung over the table was also made with the antler motif in mind and matched the table precisely.

When she found a book on the churches of Scotland, she thought for certain there would be a listing. Several reputable monasteries were noted, but not the brotherhood. If it were as old as Brother Leod claimed, there should be some record of its existence. Ericka browsed for over an hour before she came across any mention of Hume MacGillivray or the Brotherhood of Our Sons of the Servant of Judgment.

In a thin paperback containing odd events and weird occurrences throughout the highlands of Scotland, she found the first mention that Hume MacGillivray truly existed other than within the pages of Akira's diary. It accredited him with the creation of an occult monastery deep in the highlands and sheltered from the prying eye of public scrutiny. Only descendents of its disciples were admitted into the tight-knit alliance. No church recognized them. The monastery was named the Brotherhood of Our Sons of the Servant of Judgment.

The article gave her no specific information about the man or what the monastery represented. Ericka huffed and tossed the book on the table. She continued searching for something more substantial. In a book on ancient clans of Scotland, the MacGillivrays were mentioned, but only as an unimportant asset to society. They kept to themselves and lived in a monastery in the hills.

She laid the book on the table, increasing her slim collection to two which mentioned MacGillivray. Both books pointed to the monastery. Why would Hume MacGillivray drag his family into the walls of a ruined monastery to live? Had the curse made him insane? Ericka kept searching. There had to be something. Hours passed and the sun dropped behind the hills.

Chapter Ten

ꟾ

A beautiful vision greeted his eyes as he stared through the French doors. His hand quivered on the handle, uncertain if he should enter. She sat reading a book, the things called glasses perched on her nose and her hair trapped in a bun. Sweat beaded upon his brow. *Och,* how he wanted her forgiveness, hungered to taste her, to mold her breasts in his hands and bury his shaft in the warmth of her heavenly sheath. But he knew he didn't deserve even one of her favors, not after the mistake he made.

While entombed in stone for the day, his thoughts ran rampant. Unrest filled his soul and the desperate desire to make things right burned in his gut. He hadn't meant to hurt Ericka, but his careless mistake in calling her Tavia during a moment of passion wounded her deeply. Her pain penetrated his daytime prison and ruled his every thought.

Scrubbing a hand down his face, he gathered his resolve and forced his hand to ease open the door. On each intake of air, her scent filled his senses, making his blood warm and the increasing hunger to taste her watered his mouth. He shifted his stance, took a deep breath and tried to tamp down his growing need for her. Now was not the time for this. Earning her forgiveness was not going to happen if he didn't gain control over his lust.

Gavin rolled his eyes to the heavens and issued a silent prayer for strength. Nearly knocking Gavin to the ground, Belvedere raced between his legs and into the room. Belvedere pounced onto the couch and landed in Ericka's lap. *Lucky dog,* he thought as a smile tugged at his lips.

"Belvedere," Ericka snapped, grasping the puppy by the collar. Attempts to thwart his slobbery kisses failed. He slapped a sloppy tongue across her face and knocked the book to the floor. Mission accomplished, he jumped down, then returned promptly to sit at Gavin's feet.

He heard her sharp intake of breath. The sight of her hands trembling as one adjusted her glasses and the other retrieved the book tightened his gut. He sensed the pain he'd caused her simmering just beneath the surface of her skin. Soaking in her essence, he waited, not wanting to say the wrong thing. As if in slow motion, she lifted the book to her lap, her back straightened, her shoulders held taut and her eyes glued on the open pages. After several moments, he noticed she hadn't turned the page, but he hadn't moved either.

On legs more shaky than he'd ever known, he stepped toward the couch and sat beside her. When she didn't look at him, he leaned forward, chin tilted, trying to see her face. She twisted, turning away from him.

This was harder than anything he had ever done. A fight where he was outnumbered ten to one would have been more easily handled. He sighed heavily. Never had he needed to speak the words of sorrow for something done while seeking pleasure with a woman.

He dared to touch the knot of auburn hair trapped at the nape of her neck. Her shoulders stiffened and her chin lifted, but she didn't turn his way. With meticulous effort, he released each pin from her hair until the last strand fell free. Caressingly, he stroked the silken tresses and lifted them to his nose. The scent of heather and lavender teased his senses and filled his heart. She was so much like… His hand froze with her hair tangled in his fingers.

He swallowed hard, but the lump held firm in his throat. Forced words rasped in a thick Scottish brogue across dry lips. He traced her neck to the edge of her collar.

"Ericka, I canna tell ya, lass, just how sorry I feel."

Ericka couldn't look at him, knowing what she would see if she did. A massive chest of muscle and arms of pure banded steel. Why hadn't she given Aunt May his tunic so he could put it on before coming in? It was clean. Uncertain of the shirt material, she had hand washed it and hung it out to dry.

The moment she laid eyes on him in the doorway, hot moisture flooded her panties and when his tongue slid across his lips, she shivered with the knowledge of what that tongue was capable of accomplishing. The memory of his head buried between her thighs caused her breath to stutter. But she couldn't let him see the way he affected her. When he sat beside her and tried to look her in the face, she had to turn away, afraid he would read her thoughts.

She wanted him so badly that every muscle burned to be massaged by Gavin inside and out. Closing her eyes, she willed control over her desires. It wasn't she that he wanted. It was Tavia. No matter what, she had to remember that simple fact. But he was making it difficult.

His warm breath against her hair sent chills down her spine. The way he spoke her name was sweeter than any love song she'd ever heard. The moment his fingertips brushed her skin, her clit ached for his touch to trail lower, much lower. She wanted nothing more than to lean against him and taste the mouth that enticed her senses with the simple sound of her name upon his lips. His words of sorrow reached her ears and snapped her from the sexual trance the lure of his masculine essence caused. Shivering, she fought a battle for control over her rampant sex drive.

"I'm not her." Choking back the tears that threatened to fall, her voice shook as she continued. "I'm not Tavia."

"Aye, lass." He paused. "Ye are not."

He stood, walked to the windows and glared out into the darkness.

"Tavia is gone. 'Tis what I must accept."

Ericka couldn't breathe at the sight. The gentle giant stood, shoulders slumped with his back to her. Obviously, he was a man in pain. *Think how you'd feel if you woke up two hundred years later with no family, no friends and all you knew was lost.* She sighed.

Taking a deep breath, she stood on shaky legs and walked to stand beside him. Her hand hovered millimeters above the muscled flesh of his back as she silently reprimanded herself. *Be his friend, he needs someone to help him through this.*

She closed her eyes tight and mustered the inner strength she'd need to do this. *Be his friend, not his sex toy. Teach him to survive in today's world. What did Aunt May say? Oh yeah.* She touched his shoulder. *He's your Tarzan, mold him.*

At the incredible feel of his skin against her palm, heat and moisture flourished throughout her system. *Think friend*! she mentally chanted, then cleared her throat.

"Gavin, we need to talk."

He turned to face her. Vivid green eyes locked with his. The woman before him was shorter and more pronounced in her womanly features than his beloved wife. Her breasts were plumper, filling his mouth nicely and her rump was perfect for a man his size, more flesh to knead and hold on to as he buried into her mound. Swallowing hard, he reveled in the warmth her body emanated from their closeness. The scent of her arousal, though she tried to hide it, taunted his soul.

The traitor between his legs stirred. *Mercy, how this woman ignited his blood. He shouldn't be feeling this way. He should be mourning the loss of his wife and searching for his* brathairs.

"Aye, lass, we should." The words rasped from his throat as he tried to focus on anything other than her beauty.

Akira said she held the key to his brathairs. *Focus on that and not your cock,* he silently chided himself. When he followed her to the couch, he sat beside her, leaving a gap between them.

Belvedere leapt up and snuggled into the space between them. Gavin tousled his ears, grateful for the puppy's insight and the momentary distraction.

"I have your shirt," Aunt May called. As she entered the library, she handed it to him. "I gave your sword to Ned to clean. It desperately needed the dirt removed from it."

With a nod at Aunt May, Gavin rose and pulled on the tunic. He ran his hands across the familiar material, but something felt different. Lifting the sleeve to his nose, his eyebrows shot upward as he gasped.

"'Tis soft and smells of flowers."

"Your tunic felt rough after I washed it, so I rinsed it in fabric softener. It makes clothes soft and comfortable. I didn't think about the smell," Ericka stated without meeting his gaze.

If it were possible, her back seemed even straighter and her shoulders more taut than when he first entered the room. Gavin sighed. He needed her on his side if he were to find and free his *brathairs*. And at the same time, he needed to gain control over his growing lust. He returned to his seat on the couch.

"Aye, feels nice against the skin." He smoothed his tunic and smiled, hoping to ease the tension between them.

"Gavin," Aunt May started the conversation. "I've asked my housekeeper, Margaret, to prepare some of her specialties for dinner in honor of your presence. I hope you're hungry."

"How'd you do that?" Ericka interjected before Gavin could react.

"How'd I do what?" Aunt May asked nonchalantly.

"You spoke perfect Gaelic." Ericka regretted the words the moment she spoke them. She knew what the answer would be. It was the only explanation for how she spoke the ancient language and now so did her aunt. But it still bothered her logical mind to admit the truth.

"Akira, dear. I asked her to refresh my memory so we both could help Gavin."

"You speak Akira's name. You know of her?" Gavin leaned toward Aunt May.

"Yes, she's the reason we are here to help you." Aunt May smiled brightly.

Gavin rubbed his forehead. Easing into the comfort of the couch, he studied the situation. He knew his sister's spirit walked without rest. It was his fault that she did and in his gut he knew he needed to make it right.

He glanced from Aunt May to Ericka. How were two wee women such as these supposed to help him? One was an older woman with a spirited force within her soul. But what good would that do him should a battle arise with McGillivray during his search? Women were weak.

The other… He dared to look at Ericka. The other held the ability to heat his blood and harden his cock without so much as a touch from her hand. Though every ounce of him wanted her, she was a distraction he did not need. Not at a time when clear thought and a strong tactical plan were needed if he were to succeed.

Uneasily, he shifted in his seat. In his gut, he knew he couldn't risk the life of another in his quest to free his *brathairs*, especially that of a woman. Standing, he paced to the window, paused, then turned to face them.

"Akira sent two women to help me? I dunno how ye are to help me with this matter. Where are thy men? Who art in charge of the castle?"

He may be ancient, but she didn't have to take his egotistical attitude. Ericka shot to her feet, barely able to contain her anger as she snapped. "Oh, get over yourself. We women are in charge of the castle. Take a look around. Take a real good look. Do you realize what year this is?"

Gavin stepped back, squared those broad shoulders of his and glared down at her. Heat rippled from his essence and filled her space. But she held her chin tilted up and her gaze locked on his.

"Nay, 'tis not important," he stated.

They stood glaring at one another for a split second before he lifted his eyes from hers. Regret washed over her at the sight of confusion flickering in his irises. Swallowing hard, she wished she could take back her angry words, uncertain if it was his chauvinistic attitude or her uncontrollable attraction to him making her temperature rise. Though she worked hard to gain recognition in a field that was predominantly male, he didn't know that.

He was from another era. From her studies, she knew that men of his time protected, provided for and cherished their women as possessions. She sighed. It was up to her to change his views.

Never had any woman other than his sister stood up to him before. This woman contained a strong will similar to Akira's. He read it in the way she held her stance steady, unwavering in his presence.

Och, how he liked a challenge in a woman. Yet, he married Tavia, a gentle woman who obeyed his every wish. Now was not the time to think of women, he chided himself as Ericka's words sunk in and he tried to make sense of them.

The year...what did that matter? Gazing across her head, he realized that it did. Things were different. In a quick perusal of the room, he took in his surroundings.

Though the grounds and the outside of the castle were similar to how he remembered his home, the room in which he stood had changed. Instead of one case of books, the walls were lined with them. The seat upon which he had sat was completely different than anything he remembered. Strange light glowed above his head. Instead of candles, magic oozed in the form of some sort of fireless way.

"What sort of witches do ye be?" He stumbled backward a few steps and grabbed aimlessly for the sword no longer at his hip.

"We're not witches," Aunt May stated.

Ericka sensed his confusion and fear. This place had been his home and now…now it was his prison. She took a step toward him.

"Gavin, we're not witches and this is no longer 1740." She paused, licked her lips then continued. She thought it best to lay it out straight with him. "It's the year 2005. You've been encased in stone by a curse for over two hundred years."

Slowly, she took a step without releasing his gaze and then another until she could reach his arm. Her hand shook as she stroked his biceps. As she attempted to soothe Gavin, the simple caress sent heat waves to her core and reignited the need to have him buried deep between her thighs. Shifting her stance, she swallowed hard, trying to force her libido to back down and her muscles to stop quivering. How could just touching him turn her on so much?

He needs a friend, someone to help him, she silently reminded herself. *Help him, not hump him.*

"Come sit with us and together we'll sort this out."

She tugged lightly at the sleeve of his tunic. When he didn't budge, she tried a different angle. Tilting her chin up, she batted her eyelashes innocently, with a smile plastered upon her face.

"We wee women need your strong warrior mind and skilled tactics to help figure out how to make things right."

"*Aye,*" he rasped harshly. Her touch had him hard to the point of pain. What he needed was a dive in a pool of ice-cold water to cool his raging lust.

As if his joints were rusted, he walked stiffly back to the couch. Because of his condition, he lifted Belvedere onto his lap and used him as a shield. No need for the lass to see his need for her.

"There's so much we need to teach you," Aunt May stated. "First, we must work on your English and get you acclimated to your surroundings."

Ericka couldn't remember ever seeing such a glow in her aunt's eyes.

"'Tis still Scotland, 'tis it not?" Gavin sat straight, confusion clouding his eyes as he looked at Ericka,

Ericka grasped his forearm which flexed and tensed under her touch. "Yes, it is, but Gaelic isn't—"

The finger of his other hand shushed her lips and stilled the words in her throat.

"Lass, with many English lords have I dealt." His Scottish brogue struggled in English.

His eyes, focused solely on her, made her confidence falter. Helping him as a friend was going to be the hardest thing she'd ever done. Nervously, she wet her lips with her tongue.

Gavin's stare lowered to Ericka's mouth. When her tongue traced her lips, his throat went dry and he hungered for a taste. Her hand on his arm warmed the skin through the thin cloth of his sleeve and made it even more difficult for him to concentrate. Cooling his loins wasn't happening, instead his shaft stiffened to the hardness of steel.

Grateful the puppy was content to sleep on his lap, he ran a hand through Belvedere's coat. Though he'd much rather have Ericka planted firmly on his lap, her legs wrapped around his waist, one luscious nipple suckled in his mouth and his shaft burrowed to the hilt in her sweet sheath. Momentarily, he closed his eyes and willed the vision away. It wouldn't do to think of her in those terms. It only made his situation more tense and painful.

"You understand English," Ericka asked.

"*Aye*, but only a wee bit." Opening his eyes, he returned to the ease of Gaelic and shifted the puppy, adding to the pain of his hidden engorgement. "My father felt it wise that each of his sons know enough to help protect the clan from English control."

"Then we should use English as much as possible. This will be fun." Aunt May clapped.

Together, they spent several hours discussing the differences of today's world compared to Gavin's of 1740. Ericka was astounded at how quickly he caught on. Though confusion shone in his eyes, he listened to everything they told him. They answered his questions as best as they could and used several of the books in the library to teach him some of the changes throughout Scotland.

Gavin was grateful for the distraction and the opportunity for his shaft to lessen, though her closeness kept him semi-hard at all times. There were many changes in his world, and with the help of these two women, he intended to learn.

When Margaret called them to dinner, Gavin's head throbbed. The smells enticing his nostrils as they entered the dining room made his mouth water. His world and its people may have changed, but food still smelled the same.

After dinner, Ned asked Gavin to meet him in the parlor. When they were alone, he presented Gavin with his sword, shined and sharpened to perfection. The elderly man's grip on the handle shook from the sheer weight of the ancient piece of weaponry.

Gavin accepted his sword. The man's precision to detail was a gift of mastery. He could not have done as well if he'd deemed it done himself.

"'Tis a fine job," he boasted with the sword held straight out from his hand and his words spoken in English, keeping the promise he made to Ericka and her aunt that he would practice. He smiled at Ned. "'Tis a fine job, indeed."

A slender smile twisted Ned's otherwise surly lips. He sauntered to the liquor cabinet and pulled a large, green bottle capped with the old-style, replaceable plug and snap.

"Don't blame's ya for not wantin' ta taint yer palate with wine at dinner. Not when there's homemade mead awaitin' ya." He winked as he poured two cups of the hearty substance.

Gavin forced a smile, not daring to tell the reason he chose not to drink the wine at dinner. Just the scent of the red liquid made his stomach knot with the knowledge of what he'd done to Ericka. Wine was a substance with which he held no control, though he knew in his gut the wine wasn't to blame for his stupidity. The lack of control over his lust was his undoing with Ericka.

When handed the cup, he took it warily. After touching his cup to Gavin's, Ned gulped a swallow down. Gavin sniffed the substance. A spark of recognition fired up forgotten memory cells. *Mead.* Now this was a liquid he could handle. He tossed back the first cup, then belched. Holding out his cup, Ned refilled it. Times may have changed, but the drink in his hand hadn't.

Chapter Eleven

ꕥ

With Gavin in Ned's care, Ericka snuck upstairs for a quick shower. Even though she had soaked in a hot bubble bath earlier, she wanted a chance to refresh and maybe even reenergize before tackling Akira's diary with Gavin. Before dinner, he was adamant about finding his brothers and she felt certain Akira's diary was the key to their locations. Tomorrow, while he slept encased in stone, she planned to continue researching the mysterious Brotherhood of Our Sons of the Servant of Judgment and that shady Brother Leod. She didn't trust that man. Just the thought of him made her palm twinge in phantom pain.

She stepped into the shower and closed the curtain. The hot water flowing over her sore muscles eased some of the tension. Sleeping on the ground in a graveyard wasn't the most comfortable thing she'd done in her life. If she hadn't gotten Gavin drunk, it could've been better. Remembering what ended their sexual foreplay made her wince. The sound of Tavia's name spilling from his lips reverberated in her ears, renewing the sadness in her soul, but didn't ease the want between her thighs.

As she lathered her body with the lavender-scented soap, eyes closed, she thought of Gavin. She imagined his broad shoulders, strong arms and washboard abs being caressed by her hands. The memory of the sensational pressure of his pelvis rubbing against hers as his heavy cock teased her sensitive clit sent a pure shiver of need shimmering down her spine and spirals of chills across her skin.

She hungered to have him touch her, to be the one coating her body with the suds. As she slowly circled her aching nipples with the soap, the memory of his hands on her skin took over. Cupping her breasts, she tweaked the pouty points until her clit tightened and her pussy spasmed. Lowering her hand, she massaged the wanting nub. A gargled whimper escaped as she bit her lower lip. A need for something or someone she knew she couldn't have burned in her veins, adding to the building pressure of her impending orgasm. God, how she wished it were Gavin's hand instead of her own.

After a bout of mead with Ned, he went in search of Ericka. She had promised to help him find his *brathairs*. He followed the unfamiliar sound of running water in the castle. It wasn't natural, this magic these women performed, even though they claimed they were not witches. Could he believe them? They'd shown him so much before dinner. If what they said was true, he had much still to learn.

Stopping at the door where the sound was the loudest, he grasped the handle and found it unlocked. The scent of lavender and Ericka taunted his senses. He knew he should leave and go back downstairs to wait for her, but he couldn't. His mouth salivated at the scent of her arousal. The air was thick with it.

Clothes lay scattered on the floor. Her shadow danced upon a curtain from which the sound of the running water radiated. Her shadow's hands slid over her body, a place where his hands ached desperately to be. Without a sound, he removed his clothing and slipped in behind her.

Her legs weakened and she leaned back, anticipating the cool sensation of tile. Instead, heat and a solid wall of muscle collided with her back. The scream drowned in her throat as thick arms wrapped around her waist. Spinning around, the level at which her eyes looked at his body was a pure vision from a romance novel cover. His chest, complete with tiny curls, glistened. Every muscle seemed to ripple and flex under her close scrutiny. Forcing her eyes to meet his, it hit her. He had caught her masturbating while thinking of him. She dropped her gaze to the floor as heat scorched her cheeks.

Warm fingers cupped her chin and tilted her face upward. Unable to look at him, she wanted out of the shower, but his arm tightened around her waist and held her firmly locked in place.

"Look at me." The commanding tone of his Scottish brogue compelled her to lift her gaze to his.

The sight of his eyes hooded with desire made her heart skip a beat. His chest heaved as he grabbed her by the elbows and pulled her against his naked form. She gasped when his cock brushed the tender skin of her belly, shooting sparks directly to her clit.

Oh god! How was she supposed to think *friend* when he did things like this to her?

Shock waves quaked her core when he shifted, slipping his cock between her lower lips, caressing the oversensitive swollen nub hidden there. It was obvious he wanted her. But Ericka knew it shouldn't happen. No matter how bad she wanted him inside her. She had to stop this, though her body begged to differ. Drawing on her last shred of decency, she opened her mouth to speak, but his lips covered hers in a soul-searching exploration.

If he had thought he was hard before, it was nothing compared to the painful erection thrusting at the sight of her pleasuring herself under the mystical rain from a round object above her head. Her subtle whimper tugged at his resolve. When she leaned back against his chest, the scent of her sweet juices turned him into a ravishing beast.

The sight of her flustered and water-soaked sent shivers through his body. Her nipples stood out, begging for a touch. The tickle of her nether curls along his shaft tightened his balls. And when he brushed the head of his cock against the swollen nub hidden in the flesh he hungered to taste, he almost lost it.

As if he was a condemned man and she was his last meal, he captured her lips. He had to taste her, he needed to fill her mouth, her body, her soul with him. No matter how he tried to refuse his feelings, he wanted her. She haunted his thoughts while imprisoned in stone during the day. But now…now he was all man and she was all woman.

The need to know every aspect of her body took control as he trailed his hands down her back in slow tumultuous torture. He massaged the small of her back, then grasped the luscious rump he dreamt of kneading all day long, pressing her tighter to his hardened shaft.

He lavished nips, kisses and nibbles from her lips, along her neck and down to the pouting rosebud peaks of her breasts. With the tip of his tongue, he laved first one, then the other. Her hushed gasp only urged him on further until he suckled each into a swollen, reddened mound. Greedily, he lapped a trail down her body and traced the sensitive navel of her belly.

On his knees, he wasted no time. Her hands plowed through his hair, massaging his scalp as his eager fingers parted her lower lips and his tongue sought his prize. He licked her clit and lapped his tongue within her sweet release, suckling her juices until her knees went weak and her hands squeezed his shoulders for support.

In one swift movement, he stood, lifting her body, wrapping her legs around his waist and burying himself deep within her heavenly sheath. Her muffled cry against his neck and the tender nip of her teeth along his skin tightened his balls. The heat of her lips as they trailed up to his ear sent chills along his spine.

"Gavin." The heated whisper of his name coursed through his veins.

Her back arched and her shoulders pressed against the wall, cascading water over their bodies as he urgently pounded in and out of her tight wet canal. He couldn't stop. The sensations of Ericka wrapped around him, touching him, caressing him and the musky scent of their combined lovemaking, overloaded his ability to maintain control and urged him close to release.

Her inner muscles contracted, gripping his shaft. The excruciating surge of tightness surrounding him relaxed long enough for him to bury to the hilt and explode his seed deep within Ericka. As her inner muscles grasped him, sucking every ounce of seed from his sac, he commanded her mouth. He couldn't get enough of her as he deepened the kiss.

In her mind, she honestly tried to stop. But when he commando-raided her mouth, she forgot what she was going to say. Something about being his friend hovered in the fog of his erotic foreplay. He was a master and she was his pupil. Nothing could have stopped him. Not that she wanted to.

His lips were everywhere at once, thrilling her soul and setting her skin on fire. He teased her nipples until she thought they would burst. And when he suckled them into his mouth, she melted.

The moment he lowered to his knees, anticipation of his tongue caused her pussy to flood and her clit pearled. Feeling him drink from her over and over weakened her knees. Never had anyone cherished her body the way Gavin did.

When he stood, wrapping her legs around his waist and impaling her on his cock, any thought of stopping vanished. Tightening her grip around his waist, she relished his thick rod pounding her pussy. Deeper and deeper he drove as her climax soared. The cool of the tile against her back, mixed with the heat of their bodies slamming together, pushed her over the edge. As ecstasy washed over her, her pussy clenched his cock, coaxing him to match her orgasm. Warm wetness filled her as their releases combined.

Moments ticked by as she gasped for air with her face nestled against his neck. Her heartbeat slowed to almost normal. The muscles in her legs relaxed around his waist. The blood had just stopped thrumming through her veins when she felt his cock twitch, still buried deep within her.

His stamina surprised Ericka. Neither of the men she once called lovers had ever been ready again so quickly. She knew she should stop this. *Be his friend* flashed behind her lids, but disappeared the moment he moved his cock in long, slow, tortuous motions within her already aching walls of flesh.

Goose bumps shot down her spine as he nibbled her lip, then lowered to her nipple. She gasped as he suckled from one breast to the other, while his strong hands kneaded her bottom. His exquisite technique of deliberate slow pumps sent waves of tremors through her body and a flash flood to her pussy as she climaxed. Tightening her legs around his waist, she rode wave upon wave of electric pulsations coursing through her pelvis. The hot burst of erotic sensations shot up her abdomen to the tips of her nipples, then consumed all rational thought in a ball of sensational orgasmic fire, pushing her to the edge of completion. She buried her face against his neck to stifle the scream of pure erotic pleasure. But it wasn't enough. She thrust her head back and his warm wet kiss covered her mouth.

When her lips pressed against the flesh of his neck, his shaft painfully thickened once more. The sensation of her muted sounds of pleasure against his skin stirred him on as he increased his tempo. Grasping her luscious bottom, he pressed her back against the shower wall. He nibbled her ear as her head lay nestled against his neck.

The need to fill her overwhelmed him. He wanted to bring her to her joy once more before he found his own. With the tip of his tongue, he outlined the tender skin of her ear. Her legs tightened around his waist, urging him deeper and deeper, harder and faster, until her body shook in his arms and he knew she was on the verge once again.

When she lifted her face from his shoulder, he captured her lips and swallowed the sound of her ecstasy. The power of her release soaked him as he clutched her perfect rump tight, and buried to the hilt, added his seed to their sweet mixture. Never had he taken a woman twice in so little time. He should be sated and yet his arousal renewed as he lowered her to stand on shaky legs. Even the cold water splaying across his back didn't dampen his growing need to bury himself deep inside the woman wrapped in his arms.

"What sort of witch do ye be to control me as you do?" he whispered against her forehead as he held her.

Ericka stiffened. Chin lifted and jaw held taut, she met his hooded gaze.

"I'm not a witch."

Reaching around him, she turned the shower control off and stopped the flow of water. She jerked open the curtain, stepped out, wrapped a towel around her body and grabbed her clothes from the floor.

Gavin stood speechless as she left him standing there, cold and wet in the claw-footed tub as she marched from the bathroom.

What had he done? He hadn't meant to hurt her feelings. He just wanted answers to what was happening. Stepping from the shower, he grabbed a towel from the rack, dried off, then dressed. The image that stared back at him in the mirror was his own, but somehow different. Both hands raked through his hair as he stared at his reflection.

Should be mourning Tavia. Instead, ye are plowing the voluptuous body of Ericka as if ye were a young buck in heat. He snorted harshly as he continued to stare.

A shudder rippled beneath his skin as he tried to still the growing need beneath his kilt. No decent man would fail to mourn. Yet, he failed. Was he himself not a decent man? A frustrated growl emanated from his chest, hands planted on the cool surface of the rim of the sink, head hung low. He swung his head up and glared at his reflection.

This canna happen again. No matter how tempted.

"This canna happen again," he whispered between clenched teeth to the cold image staring back at him.

* * * * *

With her eyes closed, Ericka leaned against the inside of her bedroom door. Even swallowing hard and taking deep breaths couldn't soften the rapid rhythm of her heart beating in her throat. Shoving off from the door, she quickly dried off. Each swipe of the towel reminded her of his caress.

Naked, she stood in front of the mirror. The vision of a ravished woman stared back at her. Nipples swollen and red rose to full attention as if waiting for his warm mouth. Brushing her fingertips across her puffy, thoroughly kissed lips, a soft sigh escaped. When she shifted her stance, the tenderness between her thighs reiterated the fantastic feel of his cock buried between them. Just thinking about him made her pussy throb and moisten, ready for another round with Gavin. The intensity of how much she wanted him scared her and she shivered all the way to her toes.

Be his friend. Grabbing the brush, she tugged it through her hair.

This shouldn't be happening. Control yourself. Be his friend. As she pulled her hair into a bun, she glared at the reflection she no longer trusted. The brush held firm in her hand, she pointed it at the person in the mirror and chided. "You're an educated woman. Control your urges. This can not happen again."

Ericka dressed, then walked to the door. Her grip froze on the knob as his words reverberated in her head. He hadn't called her a witch. He asked her how she controlled him. The breath hitched in her throat. How she controlled him? Did he suffer the same uncontrollable urges that she did when they were together? No. She shook her head and yanked the door open. Not possible.

The air stilled in her lungs at the sight of him, wet hair pulled into a ponytail and tunic clinging to his chest as he stood waiting for her at the top of the stairs. Green eyes so dark they were almost black met hers in an unreadable stare.

Ericka took a deep breath, stiffened her spine, then forced a step forward. *Be his friend* repeated through her thoughts as she walked to his side.

Be his friend echoed as she held her chin tilted high and her eyes fixated on his hard glare. The closer she got, the angrier he seemed to be. Was he angry at her? Did he blame her for what happened between them? She swallowed hard.

Then so be it, she sighed. *Let him lay the blame wherever he deems necessary.*

As she neared, he shifted his stance. The scent of lavender and pure woman encapsulated his space and his heart skipped a beat, but he refused to waver in his new resolve. It had to be this way. He was a decent man. He would mourn the loss of his wife.

When she reached his side, it hurt to hold his hard-edged attitude and not reach for her. Sheer will forced his hands to remain at his sides. His insides quaked and his shaft twitched, but he would not be controlled by desire. Sweat beaded upon his brow as he warred within himself.

Heat burned his gut, need filled his cock and still he held firm in his decision to resist the raw hunger gnawing at his insides for Ericka. Holding his back straight, his gaze level and his shoulders taut, he was determined. *Think only of Tavia.* He swallowed hard.

When she took the first step down the stairs, he leaned forward and his mouth went dry. His jaw tightened and words he meant to whisper instead escaped in a gruff Scottish brogue.

"This canna happen again, lass."

Ericka paused in mid-step. Chin lifted, she met his gaze, their faces close enough to touch. His breath against her cheek, she raked her tongue across her lips, but no moisture would form from the desert of her mouth.

"No, it cannot," she rasped in a whisper. She turned and hustled down the stairs. At the bottom, she allowed her lids to blink for the first time in what seemed like an eternity. She refused to cry. It was for the best.

Be his friend. She sniffed back the unshed tears and replayed her silent mantra.

Be his friend, screamed through her head as she marched toward the library. Without looking, she sensed his presence behind her and knew he followed at a distance.

Chapter Twelve

ஐ

"Where did you find me?"

After hours of total silence, Gavin's voice startled Ericka. The strained silence had frayed her nerves as they reviewed Akira's diary. True to her word, she sat with him in the library, studying the verses and trying to figure out where the next brother could be found. It was well after midnight and her eyes, mind and resolve had grown weary.

"Here in the castle," Ericka stated, lifting her glasses and rubbing her tired eyes.

"Where in the castle?" Gavin stood and stretched with his back to her. The scent of her hair and skin wreaked havoc on his senses. Concentration on anything other than her was increasingly becoming impossible. Needing to move, he walked around the couch until he stood directly behind her.

"You were in the center tower. It's the only one that hasn't been renovated." Ericka leaned back into the couch and stretched her legs out in front of her.

Gavin turned, leaned on his elbows against the back of the couch and quickly wished he hadn't. The sight of her breasts pressed taut against the front of her shirt as she stretched caused an immediate response from the hungry shaft between his thighs. On a heavier breath than intended, he whispered against her ear.

"Why's that? And why you?"

For hours sitting next to him, researching Akira's diary, she fought the urge to touch him. But now, with his lips so close to her ear, the heat of his breath upon her skin, she faltered. Chills covered every aspect of her skin and set her nipples to full attention. Shooting upright, Ericka stood, crossed her arms over her chest and grasped her elbows. Nervously, she circled the coffee table as his words stumbled through her brain.

"Why me what? I don't understand your question," she gasped as she attempted to smother the defiant reaction of her breasts to his warm breath upon her skin.

Gavin swallowed the smile that taunted his lips. Hopping over the back of the couch, he landed in the warm spot she left behind. Her body's reaction was a dead giveaway that she was having the same difficulty as he. She wanted him. He could smell it, but refused to allow himself to act on it.

"That was my tower. The master of this castle. Why not repair it?"

"You were hidden there. Akira protected you from outside intrusion. She scared anyone who got near you away."

Leaning forward, he rested both arms on his knees. Ericka's essence filled his senses. He struggled against the sudden spike of need for her rumbling in his gut as he contemplated what she said. There had to be some reason behind the events that happened. Why now, after so many years? *And why Ericka*?

Before his shaft could turn to raging hard, he focused on his dead wife and the reason the woman across from him could not be his. He would bring no further shame to the memory of Tavia. Desperately, he tried not to inhale Ericka's scent or admire her womanly attributes. Though his eyes seemed determined to fixate on the subtle rise and fall of her breasts with each breath she took. If it killed him, he would mourn Tavia's loss. And refusing himself the pleasure of Ericka just might accomplish that feat.

Swallowing hard, he forced his eyes to lift to her face and asked. "How did you get past my headstrong sister's spirit when everyone else failed?"

Ericka stared at Gavin. Though he attempted to be relaxed, the tightness of his shoulders suggested otherwise.

His eyes were no longer guarded and dark. The irises swirled with a hint of the passionate shade of green she saw each time they… She closed her eyes and bit the lower edge of her lip.

Concentrate. Be his friend. She took a deep breath, opened her eyes and forced her focus on a book on a shelf behind his head.

Exhaling, she held her voice in a professional manner, though there was nothing professional about the twist of emotions knotted in her stomach. If he had jumped a little higher over the back of that couch, the reason her inner thighs ached would have been in full view, giving her a glimpse of the most perfect cock she'd ever experienced. She swallowed hard and tried to railroad her thoughts away from that exquisite vision of male dominance.

"Your sister led me to you. She felt it was time you were set free."

"Why you?"

"I don't know," tumbled from her lips. Honestly, she didn't know. *Why had Akira chosen her*? Until now, she hadn't realized that Akira had chosen her.

For over two hundred years, Akira protected Gavin, but did nothing to stop her from finding him. Instead, Akira helped. She gave Ericka the ability to understand and speak Gaelic with ease. Ericka lowered her gaze to the diary. There had to be a reason, but asking Akira was out of the question. At dinner, Aunt May told them Akira was no longer in contact with her. Though she tried, Akira had not responded. Aunt May believed Akira's spirit finally crossed over to heaven since Gavin was released.

A nagging sensation burning at the base of her brain made Ericka think otherwise. Akira's sudden disappearance wasn't right. Something was wrong, but she couldn't be sure as to what. Shoulders straight, Ericka took a deep breath, then looked directly at Gavin.

"What do you remember? Were you asleep all these years? Did you hear anything that could help us find your brothers?"

Leaning back, Gavin laid an arm along the back of the couch. A wicked smile tugged at the edge of his lips.

"The first thing I remember," he paused, "is a hearty run through a field of heather and the tight, warm, wet feel of the prize at the end of the chase."

He heard the soft intake of breath at Ericka's gasp and watched the flicker of her irises as the memory of the dream resurfaced. It was a memory neither would ever forget. Jerking his gaze from hers, he stared out through the windows.

At least in his dream, he was a faithful man. He thought she was Tavia, even though the feel of Ericka was more enticing. Shifting his position on the couch, he straightened his kilt to hide the hardened traitor between his thighs. Eyes closed, he forced the memory of Tavia's face to hover beneath his lids. Maybe if he kept her image embedded in his thoughts, then the overpowering need to plunder Ericka would cease.

Ericka watched as his eyes darkened right before he turned to look out the window. Was he ashamed of what happened between them? It didn't matter, she decided. What did was helping him. *Think friend.*

Her mouth went dry as she forced words into coherent questions. "What else do you remember? Anything before that?"

As soon as they exited her lips, she hoped for a reprieve from discussing the dream. Just the mention of it had her wet and wanting him to the fill that void once again.

"Nay, nothing before the dream. Akira's voice spoke to me once, after that."

Suddenly, he stood and glared down at her. She saw the indecision on his face. Heat radiated from his body even though he stood on the opposite side of the coffee table from her. God, she wished she knew what to say. No way was she prepared to handle the feelings he must have felt while trapped within walls of stone. She wasn't a psychologist. Her job was research.

But the darkness that filtered in his eyes she read as deep-seated anger. No need for a degree to understand that. She swallowed hard, frozen in place, waiting for some sign that he had control over the rage which filled his aura.

"Somehow you awakened me after years of sleep. Before, I knew nothing of my surroundings and slept in peace. After..."

The need for her grew more painful. Instead of acting upon his desire, he concentrated on the hallowed walls of his stone cell and the curse which placed him there. Anger boiled to the surface as the face of his captor flashed through his thoughts.

Hume McGillivrey cursed his family and ended the way of life he had known. Everything was gone. His life...his family...his clan...

All he had left was in this room. A castle and lands, but nothing else. Why waken him? Why not leave him as he was, imprisoned without knowledge, asleep without feelings or desire? He spun on his heels and marched to the window. Nothing made sense as he stared out into the night with his hands laced behind his back, his shoulders taut and his legs spread wide in a rigid stance. He needed to think this through.

Silently, Ericka moved to stand next to him and ticked off what she knew in her head. Somehow, they shared a dream of great sex which triggered his subconscious into activity, but neither knew how that happened. Before her arrival, he slept without knowledge of his existence or his entrapment. Now he lay awake in his stone-encased tomb. Were his brothers in a similar predicament? Did they sleep or did they know they were trapped?

How awful, she thought as she stared at the stars. The need to help him burned in her gut. She couldn't leave him cursed to live this sort of dual existence. A heavy sigh escaped as she lowered her head.

'Tis only half a freedom. Now she understood the reason Akira never said the words. Shaking her head, she regretted speaking the words that gave him half his freedom. Cursed? Had she accepted the fact that he was cursed? She shot a sideways glance at the Scottish god of a man beside her. Was his awakening her fault? Had everything that happened between them been because she was some sort of horny loser unable to control her sex drive?

The workings of a witch. His words echoed from somewhere in her brain. The edge of her lips twitched at the thought, but she held her smile in check. Maybe she was a witch and just didn't know it. Maybe curses did exist. She turned to face him. As far as she knew, this one did. She touched his sleeve. Darkened eyes with the hint of green swirling in his irises looked down at her. No matter what he thought, she intended to help him break it.

"Would you like to see the place where we found you?"

Heat seethed through her palm and warmed her entire body, but she relished the feel of his arm. This heat was good, she decided. It was not like the fire that burned her skin at Brother Leod's touch. The thought of the strange monk made her shiver and drop her hand back to her side.

Without looking, he knew the moment she moved to his side. No matter how hard he tried to deny it, he was tuned to her essence. Her scent filled the air around him and seemed to calm his thoughts.

Coldness replaced the warmth of her hand and he missed the pressure of her touch. He knew he shouldn't want it. It wasn't right to desire the touch of another. He took a deep breath in an attempt to quell the spark which flickered to life in his balls.

"*Aye*, to see me chambers would be a sight of good for the eyes."

Silence fell between them as she led him to the ancient tapestry of the MacKinnons. He stood tall, chest puffed as he gazed upon the members of his family. One by one he touched each brother and spoke their names, then lowered to the ladies in the front row.

The woman to the left she knew to be Akira. But she liked hearing the way he spoke the name. The woman in the middle, he told her, was his father's second wife, Suisan. That left the last woman in the row. His wife.

Staring at the portrait, the air stuck in her throat. Until now, she had never truly looked at the other woman. Their hair was almost exactly the same shade of auburn. His hesitation in speaking his dead wife's name tugged at her heart. Was it guilt? Had he mistaken her for his wife?

M'Gaol...a term of endearment. One look at the shadowed face of the silent man beside her and she knew the truth. The word hadn't been meant for her ears. Unable to look at the woman any longer, Ericka grasped the tapestry and rolled it back. She tied the tapestry in place with the sash she used earlier from the dining room window.

She swallowed hard. Sucking on the inside of her cheeks, she acquired enough saliva to speak. This was going to be tough, but she was determined to help him. No matter what the cost to her sanity and dignity.

"Akira's diary led us to the tapestry, which was the key to the hidden tunnel to the center tower."

Gavin ran his hand around the tunnel's edge, stepped back, then glanced from one end of the hallway to the other. "Someone sealed this. The door to my chambers was once here."

Ericka slid the chair in place, stepped up and crawled on all fours into the tunnel. Chin tilted, she glanced across her shoulder and caught his eyes glued to her bottom. Heat rose to her cheeks. Snapping her gaze forward, she repeated the silent mantra in her head.

Don't think about him. It's his wife he sees, not you. She grabbed the flashlight that she and Aunt May left in the tunnel for their next trip to the tower and switched it on.

"You coming?" echoed as she called out to him. She didn't dare glance to see if he still watched as she crawled. Sensing the heat of his gaze upon her tush, she knew that he was.

On all fours, Ericka's bottom arched up, tempting his shaft to pulsate and harden. He took her like this in a dream. To feel her tight, wet canal wrapped around him in this position could only be… A low growl emanated in his chest, fists balled tight at his sides. He could not. He would not succumb to desire. A decent man should mourn.

He grasped the edge of the tunnel, placed a foot on the chair and hoisted his large frame up. Flashes of his first awakening reverberated in his brain. Through this narrow passage he escaped the shadowed walls of the former tower, once home to his private chambers. When he first broke free of the stone, he was dazed, confused and stood alone in the shattered hull of his home. The only way out was through a hole he found in the wall. Closing his eyes, he willed the remnants of that day from his brain.

Her strong feminine scent urged him closer. The gentle sway of her hips as she crawled mere inches in front of him increased the rate his heart pounded. A sudden stop and he was upon her.

His arms landed, one on either side of her waist, and his chest pressed against her bottom. Without thought, he shifted position. His chest hovered against her shoulders and his lips touched the tender skin of her ear. Her round bottom fit snug against the solid form of his growing shaft. He wanted her here and now.

But he couldn't have her…*think of Tavia*!

A rumble rippled from his chest along her back before the low growl reached her ear. He was angry with her, but why? It wasn't her fault he ran into her. She stopped because her hand landed on a sharp edge.

But that didn't matter now. What did matter was his body hovering over hers in the close space. The throb of his thick cock against her bottom beckoned moisture to flood her pussy and dampened her panties. She wanted him and didn't care if it were in this position like a dog in heat.

The muscles tingled between her thighs when he moved in tight. Warm lips brushed her neck, pebbling her nipples. Then heated words shot down all hope of easing the horny ache thrumming within the walls of her vagina.

"Move or lie flat and let me pass," he rasped in a graveled grumble.

Ericka's first thought was to drop flat and cower so he would not see the pain he inflicted. But instead, she dragged the length of her body slowly out from under his powerful bulk. She shuddered at the coldness which replaced the heat his frame generated while wrapped around her in their momentary stall. Anger surged her forward.

If he doesn't want me, then why is he hard? Because of the similarities to his wife, chortled silently in her head.

Because of his wife. She clenched her eyelids tight to prevent the flow of tears. She refused to let him see her cry. Increasing her doggy strut, she scooted toward the end of the tunnel. The quicker she got out of this hole, the better.

Och! How he ached to grasp her by the waist, bury himself to the hilt and repeatedly pound into her until his every need was sated. He missed her touch the moment she moved. As she crawled out from beneath him, he shuddered from the sudden cold that filled the void she left behind. He could have taken her just one more time. What would have been the harm?

Tavia's memory would have been disgraced once again.

He fell flat against the cold stone in hope that it would cool his distended shaft. Facedown, he held his head in his hands and contemplated his fate.

What spell hath this witch placed upon me that maketh me dishonor thy name so?

He lay still for several moments as he attempted to gain control over his renegade shaft. Visions of Ericka naked beneath him filled his thoughts, no matter how hard he tried to think of something or someone else.

This woman, be she witch or simply mortal woman?

"AAAAgh!" Ericka's scream echoed down the tunnel along with the sound of crashing rock.

Gavin shot from his position of self-proclaimed misery, scurried to the end of the tunnel, landed with a thud and sprang to his feet, sword drawn, combat-ready. Ericka was nowhere to be seen. The flashlight beam shone toward the entrance of the stairs that once led to his master bedchamber.

He crept to the base of the stairwell. Ericka's body lay tangled in a mass of rotted board and stone, which was once a grand stairway. Gavin sheathed his sword.

"Ericka." His voice escaped in a thin whisper as he brushed her brow. When her eyelids fluttered open, he released the breath he hadn't realized he held. She stirred and tried to sit up.

"Nay, lass. Let me help." Gavin lifted her from the dirt and debris.

He carried her to the pillows left gathered in front of the fireplace and lowered her as gently as if she were made of glass. "What happened?"

Pushing up on one elbow, Ericka rubbed her brow with her other hand.

"I thought I heard something upstairs. I made it up about three steps when the next one crumbled out from under me. Stupid of me, huh?"

Ericka brushed a lump on the side of her head and squinted. Gavin pushed her hand away and took over the inspection of the tender spot.

"Nay, lass, 'tis not your fault the stairs gave way."

Cupping her chin, he tilted it up and smiled at her. Absently, his thumb glided across her lower lip, sending a shiver up his arm. He glided his tongue across his lips as if doing so would grant him a taste of her. Their eyes locked in a momentary stare. Ericka's involuntary shiver broke the trance.

"You're cold," he rasped as his hand reluctantly dropped to his side.

Gavin swung about on his knees, grabbed a fur, then laid it over her body. Once he tucked her in, he stood and moved to the fireplace. Rotted wood lay piled beside the fireplace and several logs sat poised inside the hearth as if ready and waiting for the master to return. Sifting through the dust on the mantel, he found an ancient flint, then lit a piece of kindling and tossed it into the fireplace. The wood caught without a hitch and he could only hope the chimney wasn't clogged or filled with some sort of nest after all these years. When the smoke rose instead of filling the room, he breathed more easily and returned to Ericka's side.

"How do you feel? Anything broken?"

"No, I'm just a bit bruised, but otherwise..." Ericka's voice trailed off as her entire body shuddered.

The look upon her face scared Gavin. It was wild, pain-stricken and paled before his eyes. Sensing pure fear, he wrapped an arm around her shoulders and pulled her close.

"Ericka, are you all right?" he whispered against the top of her head.

Her answer of "I don't know" sounded strained. When she looked up at him, tears sat poised, ready to fall as sweat beaded upon her brow.

Intensive heat grew and pooled in one location. Her body trembled even though Gavin's massive form wrapped around her. Every muscle burned. Confusion flashed through her thoughts. What caused this? Was she hurt worse than she thought?

No. She swallowed hard but the burning still rose up her throat. Her gut clenched and she felt as if she would spit flames if she coughed. Then the liquid heat sensation changed direction. It shifted from the pit of her stomach, up her throat then whipped down the length of her arm. It took a tremendous effort to lift her hand, but she had to see. She flexed her palm open. Her eyes glassed over before she was able to make them focus. What she saw made her wish she'd kept them closed.

"Look," she stammered on a ragged breath.

Gavin's eyes widened. The sign of a burning Celtic cross with a sword pierced through it appeared red-hot in Ericka's hand. What act of the devil was this?

His first reaction was to slice the afflicted hand from her arm. But he wasn't given the chance to act. Ericka shook violently in his arms. Instead of relinquishing the devil from her, he grasped her tight against him with one arm, while the other kept the afflicted limb extended away from them.

Did the devil live within her? How could Akira have chosen someone in league with a MacGillivray to free him? Was she also sent to destroy him?

His heart raced. As much as he wanted to remove himself from her closeness, he also wanted to protect her from this madness. Should he dip her in cold water? Would that kill the devil within her soul? How did one exorcise such a demon?

'Tis a strong disturbance on the wind, echoed through her head. Akira's words!

As fast as the flame appeared in her hand, it disappeared right before their eyes. Ericka buried her face against Gavin's chest. The molten heat flushed from her system, replaced by a cold chill. Trembling, she snuggled tighter against him, as if nothing but his touch could warm her.

What happened? Had she been possessed by something evil? Ericka couldn't be sure. But something purely evil touched her soul and left an unwanted invisible mark inside her system. A faint tug at the edge of her subconscious made her aware that something was wrong. Akira was in trouble. But how could that be? What could happen to a ghost? She was already dead. What could be worse?

The last of her brainwaves seemed to sizzle and continued thought was painful. She needed to rest. In his arms, she was safe. Nothing could reach her as long as he was there. If she could only catch her breath and stop the tears that fell uncontrollably, she would be all right. Every ounce of energy drained from her body. The warmth of his arms and the comfort of his shoulder underneath her head gave her a haven of safety. A heavy sensation attacked her eyelids and she could no longer keep them open, no matter how hard she tried.

Gavin pressed the afflicted hand to his lips. It was the strangest thing he'd ever seen. The sign of the devil danced in flames in the palm of a woman. A true sign she was some sort of witch, should he fear her or strike her down for the act of heresy? The sound of her muffled crying against his chest answered his questions. Nay, a witch wouldn't cry. She's but a mortal woman, her face had shown fear.

"Gavin," she whispered. A ragged cough shook her body as he lifted her into his lap, hugging her tighter. He brushed his lips against her brow.

"It's Akira. She needs us." She drew a shaky tongue across her lips.

"What do you mean, lass?" Gavin rocked gently back and forth with her in his arms as if she were a small child. He sensed her fear with the flame and now he felt the tiredness consuming her body.

"I'm not sure."

Ericka's warm breath spread across his neck. Absently, her tongue wet her lips and darted ever so slightly along his skin as she snuggled deeper against him. His spine stiffened, even though he knew the touch of her tongue to be unintentional.

As he shifted her on his lap, she fell asleep. The steady rise and fall of her breasts against his chest and the warmth of her breath on his neck tested his resolve. He wanted nothing more than to lay her back amongst the ancient pillows and fill her sheath with his stiff shaft. Though he hungered for her taste, he fought the urge to plunder her mouth and cup her breasts as he sat with her in his arms. When he was certain she slept soundly, he laid her on the pillows and tucked the furs around her.

After feeding the fire in the hearth, he sat at the table and laid his sword upon it, near his hand should there be a need of his protection. His gaze never left her face as he watched over his sleeping beauty. The last fading hours of night gave way to the early rays of morning light and still he kept watch.

Chapter Thirteen

Fur fluttered against her face and pillows shifted as she sat upright. She ran a hand across her hair and adjusted the glasses which had slipped sideways on her face. The glow of embers from the fire illuminated the unfamiliar room. Shadows danced in the flickering light. The night's events resurfaced as she flexed her palm open. There were no scars, no mark from the flame and no residue of the emblem. Had she truly seen it?

Ericka crawled from the warm makeshift bed and stood. Gavin sat at the table, arms crossed over his chest, feet propped up on one of the other chairs, and sword laid, hilt at the ready, facing his stone still form. He must have sat watch over her the rest of the night. On shaky legs, she walked to him, brushed her fingertips across his face, then lowered her lips to his ear.

"Thank you," she whispered, then pressed a kiss upon his hardened cheek. A spark of warmth ignited the tender skin of her lips. This time the sudden jolt brought forth no fear. She lingered against his cheek. His essence coated her soul with a warm inner glow.

The creak of unsteady wood crept to her ears. Fear pierced her soul and the need to protect him during the day jabbed at her gut. The chair looked like it might break at any moment. Considering the sheer size of the man when he was all flesh, his body must be twice as heavy in this stone persona.

Would he shatter if the chair broke and he fell to the hard floor? She didn't want to find out, but she knew she couldn't lift him. Rushing to the other side of the room, she gathered every pillow she could carry, then stuffed them under and around the chair. She raced back and forth until every pillow was placed and all but one of the furs was tucked in around him. If the chair broke, at least his fall would be cushioned somewhat. Hopefully, it would be enough to save him. Ericka whispered a silent prayer that the chair would hold and they wouldn't have to depend on the haphazard safety net she concocted.

Chills skittered up her arms and down her spine. Furiously, she rubbed her arms, but the cold wouldn't dissipate. Something in the air didn't feel right. Her gut instinct told her Akira was in trouble, but she didn't know how, why or where to start. How did one help a ghost and how could she prove that Akira was in trouble? All she had to go on was a sensation of fear, the strange image that appeared in her hand last night and the echo of Akira's words in her head. Who would believe her?

Aunt May would.

She took the last fur and hung it as best as she could over the opening to prevent a breeze from escaping to the inside wall of the castle. She couldn't risk anyone other than her and Aunt May knowing of its existence. After hoisting herself up into the tunnel, she turned to tuck the fur down over the opening and soaked in one last quick perusal of her job. Gavin was safe here for over two hundred years. On a heavy sigh, she closed the fur. Hopefully, he'd be safe here again. At the other end, the slobbery tongue of Belvedere kissed her face as he stood with front paws on the edge of the tunnel's mouth, hind paws braced in the chair.

"Woof," he greeted her with doggy breath.

"Good morning, Belvedere. Mind getting out of the chair so I can get down?" Ericka laughed and tousled his ears. Belvedere leapt from the chair and landed at Aunt May's feet.

"Good morning, Ericka. Wasn't quite sure how I was going to get through there without spilling these." Aunt May stood with two coffee cups in hand and a broad smile upon her face.

The moment her feet touched the chair, Ericka took a sip from the cup she was handed. Once she settled on the ground, she turned and released the sash holding the tapestry rolled back.

"We have to protect Gavin. He's in the tower for now," she explained, brushing the fabric with her palm to remove any wrinkles.

"I take it you two spent the night together again." A knowing smile peeked across the rim of Aunt May's coffee cup. Ericka rolled her eyes.

"Not in the way you think." *Much to my disappointment*, she wanted to add, but didn't. "He wanted to know where we found him, so I showed him, then something strange happened."

She told her aunt about the appearance of the burning cross in her hand and her fears about Akira. "Any idea what it means?"

"I'm not sure. We'll have to look into this," Aunt May stated in a hushed voice. The unexpected chime of the doorbell echoed down the hall and they both jumped.

"Wonder who that is this early in the day? I'm not expecting anyone," Aunt May asked.

"Then we'd better not take any chances." Ericka took a large gulp of coffee, handed the cup to Aunt May, lifted the chair and headed for the dining room with her aunt close on her heels. "We can't let anyone find the entrance, at least not until we figure out what's going on," she whispered to her aunt.

Peeking around the dining room door's edge, Ericka felt like a child in trouble. Her heart pounded in her throat. As Margaret answered the front door, it seemed like time stopped while she strained to catch a glimpse of the visitor. When Margaret stepped back, he entered.

Brother Leod! She stumbled backward, almost knocking down her aunt and Belvedere.

"Brother Leod. He's got to be behind this," Ericka whispered, absently rubbing her palm against her jeans. Aunt May grabbed her hand and pressed it firmly in hers.

"We'll find out. He doesn't know we suspect him of anything and let's keep it that way. Now you go get cleaned up." She shooed Ericka through the door that led to the kitchen and the back staircase.

"And where will you be?" Ericka asked, not sure she should leave her aunt alone with the strange monk.

"Why me? I'll be the doting old woman having breakfast on the patio with the handsome young monk." Aunt May batted her lashes and fanned her face with her hand in an overly exaggerated motion while heading for the patio. She stopped at the door and winked at Ericka.

"Come join the fun, won't you?" she added, then disappeared.

Ericka's stomach churned. She didn't like the idea of leaving her aunt alone even for one minute with that man. Something about him gave her the creeps. The burning in her hand started after the first time he touched her. Somehow, he was behind it. She just knew it. Taking the stairs two at a time, this would be the quickest change she'd ever done.

* * * * *

She didn't know where she was, but she knew she didn't like it. A thin film surrounded her essence, preventing her escape. Repeatedly, she tried to penetrate the transparent cell, but failed. Nothing she did aided her cause. In this floating tomb, her power to move objects was nonexistent.

Where was she? Why was she here? And better yet, who had done this to her? Had the heavenly spirits imprisoned her for refusing to join them? Was she being punished for protecting her *brathairs*? This couldn't be. The heavenly spirits wouldn't do this. Never in two hundred years had they used force. They were kind and good.

Nay, someone or something else was behind this. Akira shivered as heat radiated around her.

Nay, this wasn't of good intent. This was pure evil. Eyes closed, she concentrated with all her ethereal power.

"Gavin, be safe. 'Tis my fear that I can no longer protect thee."

* * * * *

When Margaret escorted him to the patio, Aunt May smiled. The game was on.

"Why, Brother Leod! What a pleasant surprise. I was going to call you today, but I see you've beaten me to it."

"I hope my visit isn't too early." He returned her smile as he shook her hand.

"Should've thought 'bout that afore ya came..." mumbled Margaret as she strolled back into the kitchen.

Brother Leod shot a glare over his shoulder at Margaret's back before quickly dousing it and returning his attention to Aunt May. "Your planned phone call," he paused, licked his lips then continued. "It was to tell me good news, I hope."

"Ericka and I have given your proposition some thought. Please, won't you join me?" Aunt May motioned to the chair across from her.

"Allow me." He grinned like a Cheshire cat, grabbing the silver coffee carafe before Aunt May could reach it.

With one of the obstacles in his path contained, he chose to strike more quickly than he led the council to believe. His need to conquer another obstacle fueled his desires.

Visions of her naked tormented his dreams. Though a woman would not be his downfall, she would be the vessel in which to vent his needs. He swallowed the wicked grin which tempted his lips and forced his cock to still, though it hardened instantly at the thought of being inside Ericka.

If this meeting went the way he hoped, he would have access to search the castle for the MacKinnon scum. *Find and destroy thy enemy and ye shall conquer the book.* His father's words echoed in his head. He was born to be the one, the master of the book. And he refused to fail.

He breathed deep, quelling the rising rush for power racing through his veins. His time was now. One old woman and her niece were not going to stand in his way. Lifting the carafe, he poured their cups, smiled his best smile and shielded his dark soul with the false persona of humble monk.

"Your niece, will she be joining us this morning?"

"Of course, she should be down any moment." Aunt May stirred cream into her coffee. Pressing a long, red fingernail to her lips, she continued. "Now where were we? Oh, yes. Ericka and I discussed your offer of our castle being a feature in your brotherhood's book."

She lifted a plate laden with food. "Muffin?"

"No, thank you." He shook his head. It was a strain, but he held his voice calm. The old woman was dragging this out. Was she waiting for her niece? Should he strike while they were separated? *One alone was weak, two together…* He huffed lightly under his breath. The need to gain full access to the castle burned in his gut. The hint that one had arisen nagged at his soul. He read the ancient one's story and knew of the curse. It was the very reason the book was kept locked away in the hidden burial chambers of the ancient one.

He wanted that book and the MacKinnon was in his way. And so was this old woman. A wry smile touched his lips. *Use your mind control powers, strike while they are separated.* Before he could place a controlled thought in Aunt May's head, Ericka stepped through the door.

Dressed in jeans and a short-sleeved green shirt, she looked plain. He scoured her body with his gaze. Her hair pulled into a tight bun at the nape of her neck and the glasses perched on her nose gave the appearance of a spinster librarian. But she couldn't hide the secret beauty of her body from him. He sensed that with the proper guidance—*his guidance*—she could be a true sexual adventurer. At the thought of her hidden attributes, his pants tightened.

"Good morning, Ericka," he spoke, extending his hand.

Hesitant at first, Ericka cautiously accepted his hand. So no heat touched her skin, she made sure their contact was brief. "Good morning, Brother Leod. We hadn't expected to see you again so soon."

As she took the seat he held for her, she tried to force the tremors in her stomach to relax. Being this close to him was a challenge. Just his essence seemed to keep her on edge. Or was it the fact that she knew he was up to no good. She couldn't decide. Never had she not trusted someone as much as she didn't trust this man and she barely knew him. He—a man of the cloth—was supposed to be considered trustworthy. She cast a quick glance in his direction as he settled into his chair.

Oh my god! *Did he have a hard-on*? She tore her eyes away from the front of his pants. This wasn't right. Now she really felt ill at ease. An untrustworthy monk with a hard-on, a ghost that's in trouble and a Scottish god of a man trapped by a curse, what else could go wrong?

"I do apologize for coming unannounced. When I informed the others of your desire for a few days to think it over, one of my fellow brothers suggested that this year's book center on a different castle." He paused and smiled from one woman to the other. *Easy targets* flashed through his thoughts as he continued. "I'd hate for you to lose this opportunity."

"Why the rush?" Ericka settled back with a full cup of coffee in hand.

Even though his eyes were the most gorgeous color of golden wheat she'd ever seen, she didn't like the way Brother Leod stared at her. The obvious hard-on only added to the sensation that he was undressing her with his eyes.

She took a sip of coffee, hoping its warmth would quell the chills racing upon her skin. Though it surprised her, she sensed a flux in his aura. Somehow, she was tuning into a spiritual aspect of her own being. It had to be something in the Scottish air making her feel these strange things.

It had to be the high level of suspicion flowing through her veins, she thought. Nothing else. She couldn't put her finger on it. But the burning in her gut told her he was definitely up to something and it had more to do with than just this castle.

"We're getting an unusually late start this year. And as in every market, the best period for a retail product is around the holidays. We'd like to have the book available for press before then so our margin of profit is increased."

He liked the way her lips touched the cup's rim. The image of her mouth wrapped around his cock teased his thoughts. Should he send her that vision? Share his erotic thoughts? He sighed, but resisted.

Soon he would share his thoughts with her. Her body, mind and soul would be his. But for now, he needed to control his urges. He took a deep breath and focused on the reason he was there in the first place.

Gain access. Search for the MacKinnon. Destroy the enemy.

Then he would have the power of the darkest known magic in his hands. With that sort of power, she would not be able to resist any of his commands. No one would. His cock twitched and he allowed his gaze to rake across Ericka's body once more before he reined in total control of his desires. She would be his to do with as he liked.

As she spoke, determination filled his soul and quenched his rampant need for sex. *One goal at a time,* he thought to himself. *One goal at a time.*

"So you need an answer right away in order for my aunt's castle to be included or else another location will be chosen," Ericka stated.

"Another castle has already been chosen. Fortunately, I was able to delay that decision until after I spoke with you this morning."

"Ericka, as you know, I'm enchanted with the idea of having my castle in a book. I think it's a fabulous idea." Her aunt smiled and her bracelets jingled as her hands clasped together.

Silently, Ericka wished they had more time to research this suspicious brotherhood. Instead, he was here pressuring them into a decision. She shot a sideways glance at Aunt May. Though she wanted to tell him no, their plan didn't leave her that option. Turning to look at Brother Leod, his eyes seemed to shine. A heat that was almost palpable radiated in the air around her. Dread settled in the pit of her stomach and an acrid taste coated her tongue. Going along with her aunt on this one may have been a mistake. One she hoped they didn't end up regretting. Or dead, she sighed.

"Then I guess it's decided. When will you start?" Ericka said, keeping her voice level and her thoughts at bay.

"I'd like to start today, if that's possible?"

The sight of his tongue sliding across his lips sent the sensation of being licked down her neck. Uncertain if he somehow caused this effect, she fought the urge to touch the spot. Instead she twisted the napkin in her lap and hoped he would soon leave. The next words out of his mouth made her jaw drop.

"In order to expedite the process, would it be possible for me to stay at the castle?"

"What?" Ericka sputtered. She couldn't believe the gall of this guy. Not only did he want access to the castle for reasons unbeknownst to her, now he wanted to live here too. This wasn't good. What about Gavin? They had to protect him.

Before she could react, Aunt May interrupted. A thin smile appeared on Aunt May's lips and her aunt's hand clasped hers under the table.

"Brother Leod, I don't think it would be proper even for a man of the cloth to stay here with two unmarried woman such as we. Even though I am old enough to be your mother."

The look upon Brother Leod's face was priceless and Ericka had to stifle a laugh. To her, it seemed as if he couldn't believe her aunt insinuated that he had an interest in them as women. Didn't he realize a hard-on was a dead giveaway? She bit the inside of her lip and waited for her aunt's next move.

"I assure you the only reason for my request was to hasten the research process. With me staying at the castle, work could carry on around the clock and the book could be completed in a more timely fashion."

The timid smile on his face and his attitude seemed strained to Ericka. What did he really want? With each word he spoke, it was as if he were fighting for control over his anger. Didn't monks take a vow of some sort that didn't allow them to become angry? Ericka watched him closely, scrutinizing his every move. Something wasn't right with this man and she was determined to figure out what.

"We at the brotherhood have taken many vows. One of which protects your virtue, if that is your fear."

Heat from the gaze he raked down her body gave Ericka a case of the willies. *Virtue, my ass. That look was pure sex-oriented.* Instinctively, her back stiffened and she held her chin lifted defiantly. She'd give him no reason to believe he had any effect at all on her.

The moment her gaze met his, Ericka sensed his mood shift. The palm of her hand tingled with the essence of heat. She watched subtle changes occur on his face. Those golden eyes narrowed and his lips seemed to thin, though they portrayed what appeared as a friendly smile. Ericka didn't like this and hoped her aunt held her ground.

"Nevertheless, this is a business arrangement. We are granting you and the brotherhood guided access to the castle anytime during the day for as long as it takes to complete the research for your book. Are the terms agreeable to you?"

Releasing the breath she held, Ericka's aunt squeezed her hand under the table. Silence fell between her aunt and Brother Leod. Each studied the other. Ericka had never witnessed this business side of her aunt's many façades. She always thought of Aunt May as kooky and helpless. To hide the smile that tugged at her lips, she sipped her coffee. But now, she had a whole new venue of respect for the woman.

Brother Leod stood. She read the obvious dislike for her aunt's decision in the tenseness of his rigid stance. Would he agree? Part of her hoped that he wouldn't. Maybe if he couldn't get near the castle, he'd go away. She hadn't thought of that. But a bad feeling in her gut told her that nothing said or done was going to stand between this man and whatever it was that he was after.

"My lady, you drive a hard bargain, but I accept your terms. I shall notify the brotherhood of our agreement. May I start today?" He shook Aunt May's hand when she stood.

"Of course, I see no reason why you can't start today. Do you, dear?" she stated, turning to Ericka.

Standing beside her aunt, Ericka pretended not to see his outstretched hand. No way was she touching him and chancing that the slow burn in her palm would increase to incineration level. She wasn't sure how he was doing it, but she knew he was behind it.

"I think around lunchtime would be sufficient."

"What a wonderful idea! Won't you join us for lunch today, Brother Leod? Afterward, we'll tour the castle." Aunt May clapped, setting her many bracelets into a tirade of noise. She rang a little bell which sat on the sideboard table,

Ericka saw the Adam's apple bob as he swallowed hard. His unhappiness filled the air and encased her in a bubble of tension.

"Of course." He nodded and turned on his heel to leave, only to almost run face first into Ned.

"Ned, would you please see Brother Leod out?" When he nodded his reply and held the door for Brother Leod, she added, "Thank you."

As soon as he was out of sight, Ericka wrapped Aunt May in a bear hug. "I'm so proud of you. For a moment there, I thought you were going to let him stay here. I've never seen you negotiate like that before."

"My dear, you don't marry and outlive two of the world's most powerful businessmen and not learn how to handle a deal. Besides, vow or no vow, I saw the way he reacted when you walked in. From the size of his vow, I'd say it wasn't one of abstinence."

Ericka laughed, but it didn't ease the knot in her stomach. She saw his desire, sensed his mood change, felt the heat in the air and the tingle of it pooled in the palm of her hand. Dislike and pure suspicion nagged at the base of her skull which made her certain he had something to do with Akira's disappearance.

How and why would he be after a ghost? Was he after Gavin? It made no sense. He had to be after something else, but what?

Chapter Fourteen

ꟃ

Though he wanted to argue the "guided access" part of her conditions, he thought better of it. *They can't watch you all the time.* Sliding into the driver's side of his car, he muttered *old bat* under his breath. *How could she possibly think that I'd want her?*

He jammed the key in the ignition and started the engine. *Who in their right mind would want her?* Shifting the car into gear, it jerked forward and spurted down the driveway. A twisted grin dragged across his lips.

Ericka. She was a perfect pearl hidden in an oyster, just waiting for the right diver to bring her to the surface. And he planned to bring her erotic pleasures to the surface repeatedly until she gasped for air and begged for more. Yes, she was going to be his. As soon as he found the hidden MacKinnon, he intended to wipe him from existence forever. With that task completed, the council would have no choice but to grant him ownership of the book, for he would have fulfilled the prophecy and claimed his destiny.

He proclaimed out loud to no one as he adjusted his hard-on. "Wipe the blood of thy enemy from the face of the earth. Once the deed is done…I shall be king. The wench shall be my queen and the vessel of my seed."

Laughing, he sped along the country road leading into the village. There he would gather the items he needed from his cottage and begin his triumphant journey for supreme leadership over the brotherhood and the book of shadows.

* * * * *

The pain in Ericka's hand disappeared the moment Brother Leod exited the castle. This further cemented the idea in her head that he was behind these deep-seated sensations of heat. She ran the brush through her hair and pulled the freshly washed mane back into its common bun.

Akira brought forth the sensation of cold and her intentions were only meant for the good of others. She stared at her reflection in the mirror. Each time Brother Leod was around, he set her hand on fire with intense heat. This time, she even felt heat in the air around her. Was this a sign that he was bad news? What was he after? Ericka huffed as she tossed her clothes and wet towel into the hamper.

Though she didn't have much time, she needed a shower. The way Brother Leod looked at her left her with a crusty layered sensation of filth. No amount of scrubbing could remove the synthetic layer of nastiness his gaze seared to her skin. Even as she dressed, the thought of his golden, wheat-colored eyes blazing over her body sent an electric sizzle down her spine. And it wasn't a good sizzle either. He may be one good-looking hunk of male monk, but his aura was pure evil.

His aura. She shrugged at the thought. *First ghosts, then curses, now auras! Who would have thought you'd ever believe in such nonsense.* Laughing, she shut the door behind her. Finally, she admitted that she did believe.

Diary in hand, Ericka met Aunt May in the library. Together, they foraged through books looking for any morsel of information about the obscure Brotherhood of the Sons of the Servant of Judgment. They found nothing helpful.

"It's as if they don't exist," Aunt May conceded.

"I feel naked without the use of my computer. Shouldn't have bothered even bringing my laptop with me on this trip," Ericka huffed, slamming the book in front of her shut. Lifting her glasses, she pinched the bridge of her nose with her forefinger and thumb. The castle was in an Internet dead zone.

"Why didn't I think of this before! There's one of those Internet cafés in town. You can take your laptop there and hook up a connection." Aunt May's bracelets jingled as she sat beside Ericka on the couch.

"I'll get Ned to drive you down," she paused, "that is, if you think you can handle the ride."

A ripple of queasiness coated the inside of Ericka's stomach at the thought of another car trip. Glancing at the clock on the wall, she got a reprieve. "It's almost lunchtime and I'm not leaving you here to deal with Brother Leod alone."

"I think I can handle him, dear."

"After this morning's demonstration, I'm sure that you can. It's just…" she paused.

Aunt May's comforting touch soothed Ericka's arm. "I know, I've felt it too. His aura's laced with darkness and evil."

Ericka covered her aunt's hand with her own. "Then you understand why I won't leave you alone with him. It has nothing to do with the car ride."

"I know, dear." Aunt May smiled.

"I don't trust him." Ericka held her aunt's knowing gaze.

Secretly, the car trip did bother her, but that wasn't the reason she wouldn't go and she wanted her aunt to know it. Besides, she had managed to travel by plane and car to get here and survived. If it took a short ride to gain access to the Internet, she knew she could do it. Of course, motion sickness pills would have to come along for the ride.

"I don't either. But at least this way, he's under our careful watch and maybe he'll slip up and we'll find out what he really wants from this castle. At this point, I don't think there even is a brotherhood. I'm beginning to think he made it all up," Aunt May stated.

"If I hadn't found a reference to it in two of these books, I'd tend to agree with you." Ericka sighed.

"Well, there may be one, but I doubt he's a part of it," Aunt May huffed.

The sound of the doorbell echoed through the castle.

"If nothing else, he's punctual," Ericka said with a shrug.

* * * * *

In the first rays of morning light, he sensed her presence with the touch of warm lips upon his cheek. Whispered words of "thank you" seeped through to stone-cold ears. Though he took no breath, her essence filled his senses. Her taste lingered on his lips, the silk of her skin taunted his memory and the shape of her rump fitting perfectly against him fueled thoughts of tight warmth and sweet wetness, which teased his stilled shaft.

Every muscle in his body refused to respond. His mind was in full gear, trapped in this wall of silence. He couldn't move, couldn't speak, while avid thoughts flowed freely without interruption, moment after moment, hour after hour.

Was she in the room with him? He sensed that she wasn't. Was anyone else there? He couldn't be sure. What if she were the only person he could sense if they were around? Were there others near him and he didn't know it? Panic flashed through the only active part of his being…his mind.

Desperately, he wanted to scream, but no words formed in his throat. Instead, his mind bellowed in the confines of his skull.

Akira! Where are you? Once you spoke to me within the walls of this prison, speak to me again!

Silence. An eternity of silence fluttered and crashed down around his soul. *Is this what it's like to fall into madness?*

No muscles moved, yet he knew his heart ached and his body hungered for freedom. He prayed for the fall of night and the freedom of a limited escape.

Dusk would be his salvation. The shadows of darkness brought him release and the beauty of Ericka. Her image floated behind stilled lids and chased away the flood of anxiety. The vision of her naked lushness eased his troubled mind and brought forth anticipation for her taste. Subtle memories of her helped calm his overactive rush to escape a cell that was impenetrable.

Yet guilt ran close like a rabid dog on the heels of his pleasurable thoughts. Memories of Tavia should be the vision from which his soul sought ease. But *nay*, it was the beauty of another that weakened his vows of holy wedlock, faithful to one, seeking comfort in no other.

He was a devoted husband. What had become of him now? *A decent man should mourn* screamed through his brain as Tavia's beautiful face intertwined with the clouded muddle of images from years past. A home they built together, held strong by family and clan, set in the highlands of Scotland in a time long forgotten. If tears could have fallen, he would have drowned in the onslaught as haunting images of his past paraded through his brain in an unstoppable march.

When he neared the last strand of his sanity, an auburn-haired beauty stepped from the shadows of the farthest reaches of thought and vanquished the ancient visions from his aching head.

Och! How his head did pound and he without the ability to relieve the pain. It felt as if he had spent the night knee-deep in a draught full of mead. But then she appeared again.

Don't fight the thoughts, his soul soothed his mind. *Relax and have faith that she shall protect you as you protected her through the night. The past cannot be changed. It is what it is, pleasant memories of a time that no longer exists. Dream of her beauty, her taste and the nature of her passion, for these shall ease your passage of time until the last rays of light leave the sky. Nightfall brings a temporary freedom. But for now, rest, dream of the woman who taunts your soul, for in this dream she is yours to claim.*

*****

Lunch seemed to last forever. Ericka concluded that Aunt May deliberately drew it out. For some reason, that seemed to bother the benevolent Brother Leod. Was he in that much of a hurry that he couldn't humor an eccentric old woman? Who, in her special way, managed to ask him everything from what his favorite color was to who his parents were.

Of course, there were the occasional questions about the brotherhood. Aunt May managed to ease those in amongst the other useless nonsense. A wry smile tugged at the corner of Ericka's lips as she walked with him around the outside of the castle. Aunt May definitely was a convoluted woman.

Though he answered all of her questions, his answers were vague and unhelpful in their attempt to learn more about their wayward monk. She shot a sideways glance at the mystery man. He didn't act like a man who'd taken any religious vows. Who was he really and what did he want?

At lunch, he stated repeatedly how much he wanted to tour the inside of the castle. She immediately noted his displeasure when she chose to escort him around the grounds instead. What was inside that he wanted so badly? His sudden grasp of her elbow brought her to a halt and roused her from her thoughts.

"Ericka, I've noticed that most of the outside walls have been refurbished. Why not the center tower?" While pointing with the fingers of one hand, the other hand was kneading her elbow like a mound of clay. When he lowered his gaze to hers, a spark ignited in her palm. She had to break the connection and quick.

"And I've noticed that you haven't taken one picture the whole time we've been out here," she snapped, pulling her arm free of his unwanted caress. "For someone in such a hurry to get started..." A sudden flash blinded her.

"There, I've taken one." He released the camera hanging from a strap around his neck, letting it drop carelessly to his chest.

Ericka blinked until she regained full focus and realized he stood with only inches separating them. The sensation of heat suddenly slithered from her palm and spread across the surface of her skin.

"Brother Leod, you're quite the character, aren't you?" Stepping back, she bit her tongue in an effort to quench the rising anger in her gut. She wanted to slap the smug look off his face, but she needed to know what he was up to.

Clearing her throat, she forced a level of control into her voice and held a tight smile upon her lips. "The final tower will be renovated as soon as my aunt decides upon the proper contractor. As far as we were able to discern, the prior owners over the years just never got around to that one."

Quickly, she turned and continued their stroll around the castle perimeter.

"Any particular reason?" He fell into step with her.

Over the years, he had heard the rumors that the castle was haunted, that tower in particular. It was top on his list to search. But his agenda had been squashed by the astute *Miss Ericka*. His gaze fell to the sway of her bottom.

Its gentle rhythm teased his hunger. Would it hurt to explore her curves as well as the castles? The thought hardened him instantly. Never had he been so tempted. He glanced up at the tower and grinned. Was it because he was close to his goal?

How connected was she to the MacKinnon curse? Did she know of its existence?

In time, he hoped for a chance to sample her assets. But now, he needed to ease farther into her mind, not to mention her body, and search for any trace of the MacKinnon scum. He scanned the gardens for a place he could guide her for a private session on the wonders of a man of the brotherhood.

"Lack of funds, I guess," Ericka said with a shrug.

She had no intention of telling him the truth. Gavin was hidden there and his sister had haunted the tower to protect him. She gazed up at the sun. It was afternoon.

When she caught a glimpse of his gaze, she shivered. She didn't have to be a mind reader to know what he was thinking. The size of his cock said it all. Though they were outside, being alone with him suddenly felt constrictive. She needed to move and keep a reasonable distant between them.

Increasing her pace, she urged them forward on their tour. Hopefully, he would get the hint. Ericka stiffened her spine and held her gaze straight. But the flux of heat skittering down her back let her know he was staying close.

"What else can I show you today?" She forced the words to sound normal.

Besides you, the words whispered through his wicked thoughts. He should be focused on his mission. But he sensed something about the woman within his grasp. Was it because she was not of his kind and thus forbidden fruit? Or was it the possibility she could lead him to his goal? Deciding it was the latter, he inhaled deep. Her scent filled his senses and he had to command his libido to back down. Licking his lips, he sensed her resistance. Now was not the time. But soon…

"The outside is fine for now. You're right, though. I do need to take a few pictures." He forced his focus from her, lifted the camera and shot off a few frames in a row.

They spent the rest of the day walking the grounds. While Brother Leod seemed enthusiastically enthralled with taking pictures, Ericka avoided any further contact with him. Though the heat sensation passed she wasn't taking any chances.

Several times she swore he was taking pictures of her, but he acted like he wasn't. It gave her the creeps. What was he truly after? Why would he want pictures of her? She tried to shrug off the eerie feeling at the base of her brain. Something wasn't right with this whole scenario. Each time she spoke of the brotherhood, he managed to redirect the conversation to the castle or to her. It seemed like he wanted to avoid any mention of them at all.

By the time they reached the front of the castle, the sun was low on the horizon and she wanted him gone. The need to greet a sleeping giant strummed at the strings of her heart.

"Well, I see it's time for you to go." She stood next to his car and turned to face him for the first time in several hours.

"What? We just got started." Lifting the camera over his head, he tossed it onto the backseat through the open window.

Without skipping a beat, he pinned Ericka's back to the driver's side door. He hovered over her, his hands placed on the car roof on either side of her head, which allowed no easy escape. "I'd hoped to get a few shots inside before we called it quits for the day."

The brush of his pelvis against her lower abdomen left nothing to the imagination. A solid cock twitched with each rub. His innuendo turned her stomach. What was wrong with him?

Ericka shoved against his chest. Wrong move. Fire roared through her system. Visions of them naked scorched her synapses and crackled through her gray matter. Though she tried to fight it, her gaze was pulled to his by some unseen force. Golden fields of wheat swayed in his irises, mesmerizing her senses and hammering away at the last strands of her restraint.

The feel of him traipsing around inside her head turned her to mush. Thoughts of them together soared through some invisible connection that she wanted desperately to sever, or at least change the channel to something less pornographic. If only she could. Every muscle in her body refused to follow any command of hers to move.

The hard extension of his cock pressed against her lower region. His face lowered to within millimeters of hers. Her vision blurred. Her glasses were mashed against the bridge of her nose while his eyes never allowed her to break their hold. A hungry tongue danced across her lips, then plunged into her mouth and she wanted to gag.

Deepening the stolen kiss, it seemed as if he controlled her body. His hands slid from the roof of the car, down the sides of her body until they clutched her bottom. Pure fire ignited in the trail he left behind. Unwanted moisture formed within her pussy when he grabbed her butt and pressed his body tight against hers. The cold metal of the car door along her back was her only salvation against the raging heat radiating through every fiber of her being. His lips and tongue engaged in a military assault on her mouth. Her hands were held pinned between his chest and her breasts.

She knew for certain the thoughts flashing within her mind were not her own. She had to break his hold, but how? How was he doing this? Somehow he commanded her body. *Hell*! She couldn't even close her eyes. They were glued to the swirling irises of his.

The swirling irises, she decided, that was how he was controlling her. Somehow, he was sending the unwanted visions into her head through this mystical gaze of his. If she could just focus on something other than his eyes and not the triple X-rated show going on in her head, then maybe she could turn the tables and get free.

The slow creep of his hand up her body sent flame-laced shock waves through her system and all thought of escape ceased. He maneuvered under the tight fit of her arm pinned between them. Renegade nipples responded to the rough probe through the material of her shirt and bra. Ragged breath raked across her skin when he lowered to her neck. Wet lips and teeth along with an anxious tongue lathered the tender skin with a tirade of nibbles, sloppy kisses and unduly warranted suction.

With eye contact broken, the fog lifted, though the forest fire raged on in the tiny cage of her skull. Overly heavy, her eyelids slammed shut. The visions of what he wanted to do to her went from triple X to extreme hard-core.

Think! Her deep inhalation only brought forth a full hand groping of her breasts.

"Ericka." The melodious sound of Aunt May's voice echoed from somewhere around the side of the castle. His body went rigid. Both hands clasped the sides of her face and forced her to tilt it up.

"Look at me," he commanded.

His thick Scottish brogue rasped through clenched teeth. Though she tried to fight it, her eyes opened and her gaze glued to his. The swirls of golden wheat increased to what seemed to be tornado-speed spins. "You won't remember any of this."

With one last quick slip of his tongue along her lips, he stood upright and took several strides, placing a gap between them. By the time Aunt May came around the corner, it looked like nothing had happened.

"Good evening, ladies. Thank you for your time today, Ericka," Brother Leod quipped with a smile as he nodded in her direction.

On autopilot, she stepped away from the car, allowing him to get into the driver's seat. After starting the car, he called through the window. "I'll see you both tomorrow, say, around breakfast." Then he waved and added, "'Til then."

'Til then, he chuckled to himself, drawing in the flavor of Ericka with a sweep of his tongue across his lips. *You will be mine*, he thought as his glare shot to the rearview mirror and Ericka's shrinking image. The sight of her rubbing her arms renewed the pain of unrequited need in the stiffness of his groin.

Should be me rubbing your body. He had to keep his thoughts in check before he ran off the road. *I knew she'd respond well.*

The taste of her fueled his quest to find the MacKinnon. He sensed she was the one who'd lead him directly to the ancient stone statue. The elders were right…one had risen.

He felt certain the vision of the man he saw in her thoughts was that of the MacKinnon. Just as the MacKinnon had destroyed his ancestor's love for a woman, he would destroy the MacKinnon. A woman shall be his downfall. *And an extra reward for me, along with the book,* he laughed.

Until tomorrow or maybe even sooner if the pictures proved to be of any help, just needed to get those developed. With the castle out of sight, he slammed the gas pedal to the floor and surged the car into overdrive. His need to examine those pictures and find a way into the castle undetected at night intensified along with the raging hard-on in his jeans.

* * * * *

Ericka's brain burned, chills racing across her skin. She shuddered uncontrollably from the lack of something, but what? Something happened but, try as she might, nothing surfaced from the shuffled deck of her memory other than the two of them standing by the car.

"You okay, dear?" Aunt May asked.

"I'm not sure." She stared at her aunt. A black void lingered along the furthest recesses of her brain. Something dark lurked there and held her memory at bay.

"I know something's wrong. I felt it in the air. That's why I came looking for you." Aunt May laid a comforting arm across Ericka's shoulders and guided her toward the front door of the castle.

"Heat, I remember a fierce sensation of heat and then…" Ericka stopped on the top step.

Aunt May's grip around her shoulders tightened. Concern rippled through her words. "Ericka, what are you saying, dear? Did you black out? Did he do something to you?"

"I'm not sure," she said hesitantly.

Clear thought was impossible. Something didn't feel right. A strong suspicion that Brother Leod committed some offense to her body seeped along the edges of her gray matter. But try as she might, she couldn't force it to the forefront of her thoughts. A bolt of fire racked her brain. Both palms dug at her temples, but couldn't stop the blinding pain. Her knees buckled and she felt Aunt May's arm wrap around her waist.

Out of the corner of her eye, the last rays of sunlight turned the sky wondrous shades of red, gray and pink. *Nightfall*! Her brain sizzled. *Gavin*!

"I've got her."

His brogue warmed her ears. Strong arms lifted her against his chest. Though the effort sent pinpricks to every nerve in her eyes, she forced her lids open. The deep green beauty of his shone through the muddled fog of her brain like a beacon of light leading her to safety and she relaxed.

Chapter Fifteen

ꕥ

When Gavin broke free of the stone, the sensation of extreme pain slapped his senses. The pain was not his own. Ericka needed him. He scrambled through the tunnel and rushed to her side. At the front door, he found her leaning on her aunt for support and his heart sank with a thud into his stomach.

Now, with her in his arms, he wanted desperately to protect her. The scent of her hair filled his nostrils as he pressed a gentle kiss against her forehead. As she snuggled closer, his chest expanded and blood rushed through his veins. This frail creature needed him as much as he needed her. With a heart-heavy sigh, he laid her on the bed. He wanted nothing more than to join her but…

Aunt May's hand on his arm drew his attention from his sleeping beauty. "Come. We need to talk and Ericka needs to rest."

Though he didn't want to leave her, he followed Aunt May out of the room and down the stairs. When they were settled in the library, she filled him in on their visitor.

"And that's when you woke up."

The entire time she spoke, he paced. He paused at the door and listened for movement upstairs.

"What do you know of this Brother Leod?" He shot a glance over his shoulder at the older woman perched comfortably on the couch.

She shrugged. "Not much. All we know is that he's supposedly from a monastery called the Brotherhood of the Sons of the Servant of Judgment."

Gavin stopped dead in his tracks. "The servant of judgment, did ya say?"

"Yes. Does that mean something to you?" She stared up at him.

"MacGillivray, 'tis the surname meaning for the servant of judgment." An audible growl escaped as he glared out at the night sky.

Taking a deep breath, he tried to calm the churn of heat in his gut. A descendent of Hume MacGillivray had harmed Ericka somehow. It was his fault that she was involved with the devil himself. The need to strike made his hands fist at his sides. He knew what he needed to do.

"Where can I find this Leod?"

"We don't know."

The sound of her voice made him spin around to face her. Even from across the room, her scent engulfed him. Ericka leaned heavily against the doorframe. Several long strides and he embraced her trembling body.

"Lass, ye shouldn't be outta bed."

"I'm fine." The words came out on a weak whisper.

She forced a timid smile. With her chin tilted up, she met his worried look. Holding on to him for support, his warmth radiated through his clothes, filtered through her palms, flowed into her bloodstream and traveled throughout her body. The strength he exuded filled her senses and kept her safe. She sighed. Wrapped in his arms forever was where she'd like to be.

But she knew he wished she were someone else. Before the fantasy of being his lover took root, she stiffened. Though every ounce of her wanted to stay in his arms, she attempted to step back. Weak legs trembled and threatened to give way as she felt his grip tighten around her waist.

Knowing she needed to separate from his touch, she forced her legs to obey and held herself upright, captured in his arms. With Gavin wrapped around her, she had difficulty thinking straight. His essence made her cravings for him stay hovering just beneath the surface of her skin, making clear thought impossible.

Maybe it wasn't his closeness that had her brain buzzing. She shook her head slightly. A burning sensation at the base of her brain hinted that something bad had happened. Trying to focus on anything other than Gavin, she fought to sort through the fuzziness in her head. Why was she so weak? What happened? She couldn't be sure, but she had an idea who was behind it…Brother Leod.

"I need to sit down," she stated, staring up at Gavin. He helped her to the couch. The instant he let go, she felt chilled.

Aunt May smiled, patting Ericka's hand. "Your timing couldn't be better. Margaret should have dinner just about ready."

As Ericka settled back against the couch, her stomach rumbled. Was it because she hadn't eaten that her thoughts seemed so scrambled? Without looking at him, she knew his gaze was upon her. *He stares at you because he needs your help. Nothing more,* she thought. The need to find answers forced her to focus. There was one thing she knew she needed to do and there was only one place in the area where she could do it.

"After dinner, I want to go to that Internet café. There has to be some record of the monastery somewhere."

"I'll go with ya," Gavin pronounced.

He had no idea where it was she wished to go, but he intended to be at her side. No telling what the MacGillivray's next move would be. The thought that his enemy would harm Ericka gnawed at his gut.

MacGillivray had no heart, no conscience and a deep-seated desire to cause harm against his clan. If the

MacGillivray's descendent was sworn to uphold the hatred, then he may act against anyone he deemed close to a MacKinnon. This Gavin felt to be true.

Trapped in stone, he had plenty of time to think when visions of Ericka weren't playing with his mind. A slight smile tugged at his lips. The thoughts he had of her kept him sane in his captivity. The smile faded. He wouldn't be imprisoned if it weren't for the devil. And now the devil had struck again. He felt it all the way to his core. When he came out of the stone and Ericka's pain filled his senses, he knew a MacGillivray was at work. It was time he found this person and ended the unwanted feud between clans forever.

"That's not a good idea." Ericka met his concerned gaze.

"Why not?" He stood, shoulders taut, jaw set firm. She could see his determination setting in as if it were a veil he pulled down around him.

"It's not safe for you out there." Standing to face him, her legs felt like gelatin, but she forced them to work.

As he held his arms straight out from his sides, his laughter roared around the room. "Not safe for me, lass? From what does a man my size have to fear? 'Tis not safe for you." Pointing at her, he continued, his tone turning even more arrogant. "No lady should go anywhere unescorted, especially at night. 'Tis not proper."

When his arms folded in a matter-of-fact way across his chest, his stance reminded her of an egotistical Neanderthal and she wasn't about to take it. She was supposed to be protecting him, not the other way around. There was no way she could let him wander around town. He wasn't ready for that.

"I can take care of myself," she snapped.

"*Aye*, I saw how well ya took care of yourself today, lass and 'tisn't gonna happen again. Not on my watch." He glared down at her.

"Your watch," she sputtered. Fire flowed through her veins, but this time it was different, these flames were fueled by anger.

Aunt May slipped in between them, placing a hand on each of their arms. "Gavin. Ericka. Let's not fight."

"There's no fight. I go with her or no one goes." Gavin's gaze fixed on Ericka's.

"I think that's a good idea." Aunt May's response surprised Ericka as she spun to face her.

"What? He's not ready for the outside world. Look at him. He won't fit in even if I took him with me." She motioned, pointing out his clothing.

How could she take him dressed like a seventeenth-century Scotsman into the town? But it was Scotland. Would anyone notice? She scoffed. It didn't matter. He wasn't ready. Better yet, the outside world wasn't ready for him, she thought, raking a gaze up and down his massive form.

"Trust me, dear. I've taken care of that. Ned went into town earlier and did some shopping for me." Aunt May chuckled.

The dinner bell chimed and Aunt May moved toward the doorway, adding over her shoulder. "After dinner, you get the honors of explaining his new clothing to him."

* * * * *

Snaps, zippers, buttons and laces were common items for her. To an ancient Scotsman, it was confusing. She held each item up for his inspection. Explained each article of clothing in detail, laid everything out according to usage and which went on the body first. When she thought he understood, she left the room, giving him privacy to dress. As the thought of physically dressing him shot through her brain, a spark ignited in her pussy. That would definitely test her vow not to have sex with him again.

She rolled her eyes to the ceiling and said a silent prayer. *Oh, please let him figure this out.* After what seemed like an eternity, he opened the bedroom door and stepped into the hall.

The snug fit of the faded jeans enhanced the muscles of his thighs and the delectable curve of his rump, sending shock waves of moisture through her already damp vagina. His choice of the white crew neck t-shirt accented his chest and conformed to every muscle of his being, halting her ability to breathe evenly. She was grateful he hadn't tucked it in or his washboard abs would most definitely be obvious through the second skin nature of the shirt. As it was, the short length of the sleeves showed off his massive arms and made her ache to be held.

"Well, how do I look?" He held his arms out for inspection.

The need to show him how good he looked barreled through her system. If it were up to her, she'd push him back into the room, throw him down on the bed and strip the clothes from his glorious body shred by shred. Ericka swallowed hard. It wasn't up to her. Jerking her gaze to the floor, she found a moment of salvation.

"You look fine, but you didn't tie your shoes." She forced a steadiness to her voice that she didn't feel inside as she knelt.

A sheepish grin touched his lips as he shrugged. "You didn't show me that part."

When she stood, their bodies lingered close to one another, each lost in the other's essence. She wanted to touch him, but didn't. The deep sea of green she saw during each time of shared passion flickered in his irises. Knowing his desire wasn't for her, Ericka sighed, forcing a step back.

"You sure you want to do this? The area won't be the same as you remember."

The need to touch her face and brush the loose strand of hair from her eyes twitched his fingertips. But he sensed the invisible wall she placed between them. Forcibly, he kept his hands to himself as he spoke. "I'm sure."

A knot clenched in his gut. He truly wasn't sure. All he knew of this new world was the changes made to his castle. Would the village be so different? Had his people changed? At one time, the village depended on his clan for protection and support. Did they depend on the masters of the castle in the same manner now?

These were things he needed to know. If he were to regain his title as master of his castle, he needed to understand how this world worked. Coming to terms with his decision to adapt to his new life, he stood tall. This was where fate had placed him…a new world, a different time and—his gaze fell to Ericka's face—a second chance.

"If I am to survive in this world of yours, I need to learn everything. The places, the people, and who my enemies are." He swallowed the words "*and you*" before they could pass his lips.

Absently, he flexed his biceps, making the t-shirt arms stretch to capacity. The instant urge to stroke those muscles made her palms itch. Balling her fists tight at her sides, she resisted. Not touching him was harder than anything she'd ever done.

"We have an idea who the enemy is. Now we just have to find out more about him and what he wants with this castle."

Think friend, Ericka silently reminded herself. With one last long look, she turned away from the gorgeous view of male anatomy and headed down the stairs. God, what was wrong with her? She wasn't a virgin and Lord knows she had more sex with Gavin in the last forty-eight hours than she had in the last few years.

Rolling her eyes, she forced herself to focus on the matter at hand. Something bad happened to her while alone with Brother Leod. Somehow, the event was blocked from her memory. Each time she tried to unlock that thought, blinding pain shot through her brain. So, she chose not to think about it. Hopefully, the memory would resurface on its own.

At least that was what she and Aunt May decided earlier. Could they wait that long? Ericka doubted it. Tonight, she was determined to uncover the truth behind the mysterious Brother Leod and his creepy little brotherhood.

Stiffening her spine, she refused to glance across her shoulder. She could do this. She could work with him and not hump him. Just the thought of Gavin naked sent goose bumps racing along her arms. Oh boy, she sighed. This was going to be a long night.

When she turned and started downstairs, he followed. His gaze found the curve of her bottom and glued to it. The vision of her pressed against him in the tunnel flashed through his thoughts and hardened his shaft. These things she called jeans tightened and made it more difficult to move. Stopping midway down the stairs, he adjusted his problem.

How a man could wear such confining clothing was confusing to him. He liked his kilt. Nothing binding. No zippers or snaps. Just the free flow of air and man as God intended. He shifted uncomfortably as he continued downstairs.

Though the clothing felt foreign, it was the sway of her bottom that bothered him most. The gentle motion as she descended in front of him teased his shaft and made him hunger for her touch.

Och, how this woman controlled his desires. When he reached the last step, he tugged at the front of the t-shirt and hoped it was long enough to hide his hardened shaft. The last thing he needed right now was Ericka aware of how much he desired her. Freeing his *brathairs* and seeking revenge against the MacGillivray came first.

His desires came last. Forcing his gaze to lift from Ericka's rump, he took a calming breath and followed her into the parlor.

"Why, Gavin, you look positively wonderful. Does everything fit?" Aunt May circled him as if inspecting for any flaws.

"It feels strange. 'Tis not what I'm accustomed to. But 'twill do, milady." He flashed a timid smile as he tugged at the shirt collar.

"Good. Ned did his best to get the sizes I gave him. I suggested the church's secondhand store so you wouldn't stand out as much as you would in all new clothing. He even raided his son's closet since he's away at college right now and doesn't need them." Aunt May poured and served them each a brandy as she spoke.

Without missing a beat, she raised her glass in Gavin's direction and gave a toast. "Here's to your first trip out into the new world."

Gavin nodded and downed his glass. Though the taste of the brandy was smooth, it couldn't ease his hunger for a taste of Ericka. He doubted anything ever would replace her flavor. Swiping the back of his hand across his lips, he set his glass on the table.

Watching her sip from her glass shot an arrow of need directly into his balls. Her luscious lips on the rim made his mouth go dry. Visions of her mouth wrapped around his… Gavin had to turn away before his body's traitorous reaction became too obvious to all in the room.

He walked to the window and stared out into the night. *Think of ye* brathairs *'n nothing else. Nay, think of MacGillivray.*

If that didn't shrink his problem, nothing would. Taking a deep breath, he was determined to find this man and end at least one of the problems on his list of many. Returning to Ericka's side, he extended his hand to her.

"Shall we go?"

She hesitated, then took his proffered hand and stood. The brandy she had only sipped sat wasted in the glass beside his empty one. Picking up the satchel containing her laptop, she led him out the door. An unsettling feeling churned in her stomach, but she couldn't determine if it were concern over taking him into the village or the touch of his hand that caused it.

When they stepped outside, the car came into view. Instantly, she decided it was the trip that stirred the massive churn of queasiness in her stomach. How was she going to do this? His first time in a car had to be with her…a woman who feared even the simplest mode of transportation and depended on a pill to ease her nerves.

Ericka swallowed hard and took a deep breath. She could do this. After all, she lived through her journey here. A short trip into town was a piece of cake. The thought of icing and sugar added to the swirling mixture brewing in her gut and she fought the urge to gag.

His hand tightened around hers and made her drag her gaze from the car. His infectious smile eased her anxiety, if only for a split second. But it didn't last. As if she were a bug drawn to a light at night, her gaze returned to the car.

"'Tis all right, lass."

The moment they stepped outside, he sensed her emotional distress. The beat of her heart raced through her palm and he felt her fear increase its rhythm. What held his beauty's interest and scared her so?

Following her gaze, a shiny metallic beast rose from the mist. What sort of creature was this? A horse! He needed a horse if he were to be on even ground. Yet no matter which direction he looked, not a horse nor a carriage could be seen. How could this be? A woman of such obvious stature as

Ericka's aunt must own at least one horse, but none could he see.

An audible gasp escaped when the thing opened, its insides lit up and Ned stepped out. *Have mercy*! *This beast had disliked his taste and spit him out.*

Automatically, he grasped at his side for a sword that wasn't there. Upon Ericka's insistence, he left it inside. Her claim that weapons were no longer necessary was obviously a misjudgment on her part. He snorted. Now he needed it if they were to have a chance against this beast. Lunging at the older man, he shoved him sideways and positioned himself between the beast and Ned.

"Ye are safe. Fetch me my sword whilst I keep it distracted." He screamed the order over his shoulder.

His warrior stance, and the way he circled the car as if it had a life of its own, almost brought Ericka to a fit of uncontrollable laughter. But she stifled it, though the expression on Ned's usually bland face was priceless. It was obvious he thought Gavin had lost his mind. She walked over, opened the backseat passenger door and had just enough time to set her satchel inside.

With catlike reflexes, Gavin wrapped his arm around her waist and jerked her away from the car. "Ericka! 'Tis not safe."

Grasping his arm, she tried to wriggle free. "Gavin, put me down. It's our ride into town."

Though his grip relaxed, he continued to hold her close. Ericka leaned her head back against his chest and tilted her chin up until she met his gaze. His eyes were fierce and dark as the night around them. This dark color, she knew, appeared when he was angry, or scared.

The thought filtered through her brain. The heavy rapid beat of his heart pounded against her back, beating a ferocious rhythm. This giant of a man was scared, and why shouldn't he be? Though she knew what it was, the car scared her too.

Closing her eyes, she regrouped her thoughts. Though having him pressed tight against her wasn't helping. The simple feel of him was a distraction. She tried to douse her own fears in order to soothe his.

"It's called a car. You ride in it to go places."

"It has no horse. How does it take anyone anywhere?" Confusion shaded his face as he released her.

His stance emanated warrior abilities and his stare remained fixed upon the car. Though his breathing remained heavy, she felt the tension in his aura ease. Ericka led him to the front of the car and asked Ned to open the hood. The older man obliged, but never took his eyes off Gavin or turned his back toward him in the process. She pointed to the humming engine.

"This is how it works. It's called an engine. I'm sure if you apologize to Ned for knocking him down, he'd teach you more about it than I can." She shut the hood, went to the open backseat passenger door and crawled inside.

"You coming?" she called, waving him in.

Gavin took a deep breath. This car thing moved by the force of some style of magic called an engine. Men wore pants which confined their cocks. He shifted, flexing his thigh muscles in an attempt to stretch the material clinging to him like new skin.

No weapon at his side made him feel even more vulnerable than his awkward appearance. He raked a hand through his disheveled ponytail. It was all too new, but he refused to let her out of his sight, not with a MacGillivray out there somewhere.

Standing at the open door, he peered in. Ericka sat quietly inside the metal beast. *If she could do this, than so could he.*

He eased onto the backseat beside Ericka. Ned shut the door behind him, mumbling something inaudible under his breath. Stiffening his spine, he felt confined in the belly of the beast. With a glance at Ericka, he tried to force himself to relax.

This was new. He could do this. When the car lurched forward, he jerked. *Rather have a horse,* he thought. The lack of control made his gut knot and he stared straight ahead. *Wish I were riding a horse. At least I'd be the master.* He huffed.

Fifty miles to the village trapped in the backseat of a car. Ericka rolled the window down and sucked in two lungsful of crisp night air. It didn't ease the pounding beat of her heart or the continuous roil of nausea in her stomach. With his thigh touching hers, the heat in the car increased by tenfold.

Bad enough she had to ride in a car, he had to be there. His massive toned body, inadvertently close, pushed her senses to full alert even if he didn't notice her. The desire to show him what she heard was the best use for a car's backseat niggled at her subconscious.

Like that was going to happen. She rolled her eyes up at the night sky and gulped back another wave of nauseous misery. When was the motion sickness pill going to kick in? Next to the airplane flight, this was going to be the worst trip of her life.

Craning her head out of the window like a puppy, she caught a glimpse of Ned's reflection in the side mirror. He shot sneak peeks at the interior rearview mirror in Gavin's direction. In the pitch blackness, she knew he could only see a large dark shadow of the man sitting silent. Granted, the ancient Scotsman had thrown him like a rag doll across the lawn, but in Gavin's eyes it had been a noble gesture to protect an elder.

The car hit a pothole and bounced its passengers around in their seats. Gavin gripped her thigh. Ericka's attention snapped to the large hand splayed on her leg. The sight of his other hand gripping the armrest of the car door made her realize it was just an impulsive reaction to the unfamiliar situation. His gaze was not directed at her. It was focused out into the night, as if he watched for some unforeseen danger.

She couldn't bring herself to make him move his hand. His touch seemed to help ease her anxiety. Taking off her glasses, she placed them in a side pocket of her satchel and relaxed back against the headrest.

When his hand nestled in between her thighs, Ericka didn't try to stop him, though she knew that she should. Her body reacted to his touch, moisture pooling in her vagina. Ericka bit her lip in an attempt not to gasp as his fingers nudged her legs apart. With her eyes held closed tight, she shifted in her seat. She couldn't look at him, afraid of what might greet her. His hand became more insistent and she spread her legs, giving him access to the crotch of her jeans.

His weight shifted on the seat next to her as he slipped across the narrow span that separated them. Hip to hip, side to side, the hand in her lap worked her body into a frenzy even without skin-to-skin contact. Never had she experienced such pleasure before in her life. If she didn't stop him, she knew she would climax and cream in her jeans, something she hadn't done since her first boyfriend in high school. Reluctantly, she grabbed his wrist, stopping his precise ministrations. Though she tugged, his hand didn't budge.

A chill skittered down her spine when his other hand lifted to her chin and turned her face toward his. She sat mesmerized, watching the event unfold in slow motion. Warm lips lowered to hers and placed a tender kiss upon them. As he gently trailed kisses up her cheek, she automatically closed her eyes. Then he traveled to her eyelids and kissed each, featherlight. Pure shock waves flooded her system.

When his lips brushed the curve of her ear, she thought she would melt. But it was his whispered words on a hot ragged breath that shot arrows of heated need into her pussy.

"I want to touch you."

Every fiber of her being knew it was wrong, yet she couldn't muster the strength to deny him. Releasing his wrist, she spread her legs wider. He grasped one leg and rested it across his, so her leg dangled in between his muscled thighs. One quick glimpse and she knew it was too dark for Ned to see in the backseat. Could he hear their muffled movements?

"Ned, could you please turn on the radio?" she croaked, while Gavin's fingers worked magic against the jean material between her thighs.

Static filled the air, followed by music flowing from the speakers. Gavin jerked up from the warmth of the spot he had created nestled against her neck.

"What," spewed from his lips just before she captured his mouth.

Grasping his face, she suckled his lips in a momentary kiss before she whispered, "It's okay. Trust me."

His fingers slipped to the top of her zipper. In one swift movement, her jeans were undone. The caress of his palm against her silk panties made her clit throb for his touch. The moment he slid his hand underneath the waistband and flesh touched flesh, she burned. Fingers nestled in the hidden patch of her curls for a second before parting her lower lips and exploring her aching folds. The breath hitched in her throat when he wasted no time and buried a finger deep inside.

Quickly, he caught her barely audible gasp as he captured her mouth. His tongue plundered her sweetness. Her flavor filled his senses. Though he ravished her mouth, he couldn't get enough. Each taste made his hunger increase. Passionately, he kissed her, delving deeper with his tongue, gathering every aspect of her mouth's bounty.

Was it her intoxicating taste, driving him to such a fevered hunger? Or was it the fear in his gut of being inside the beast? At the moment, he didn't care. He preferred to think it was Ericka and not fear surging through his veins.

Repeatedly, he plunged his finger knuckle-deep, in and out of the warm wet spot where his distended shaft longed to be. Uncomfortably, he shifted in his seat. There was no give in the tightness of his jeans. The confining material had reached the level of maximum discomfort. He wanted nothing more than to free himself and slide deep inside Ericka.

As if she read his thoughts, her hands gripped his jeans. One snap, a zip and the pain of confinement ended. His swollen cock sprang free and into the hands of the nimble female who released it. Her fingers wrapped tight nearly brought his need to immediate eruption. Shaken by his body's heated response to her touch, he jerked free of their kiss.

"Easy, lass," he rasped in a graveled whisper against her ear.

Turning her head, she ran the tip of her tongue across his lips, then whispered one word with the shake of her head. "*Nay*," then rested her head against his chest.

Ericka slid one hand farther into his jeans until she reached the hidden sac for which she searched. His forehead fell against the top of her head. The rise and fall of his chest against her cheek increased. Warm air escaped from his lips to caress her hair.

Though she massaged his cock, his fingers never skipped a beat in their meticulous rhythm within her pussy. It took every ounce of concentration she had not to fall back against the seat and buck in tune with his thick talented fingers.

Without clear thought, her hand fell into pace with the repetitive motion of his fingers. Up and down she massaged his shaft. In and out his fingers slipped in the ever-growing moisture of her folds.

When his thumb ground into her clit in hard circular motions while his fingers continued their plunge, she lost control. Spasms quaked through her pussy. Every inner muscle contracted and soaked his fingers with her juices. She wanted to scream in ecstasy, but didn't. Instead she leaned over, licking and suckling the thick head of his penis.

Pinned by her body, his fingers were buried in her warmth. Explosion nearly occurred the moment her mouth wrapped its softness around his shaft. His free hand plowed into her hair, knocking loose several of the bobby pins and releasing a few of the silken auburn strands. While he massaged her scalp, she lavished his shaft with kisses and suction along its entire length.

Fondling fingers found his swollen sac and his balls tightened. His body tensed at the pleasurable grip of her other hand in its ever-increasing pace up and down his mounting climax. Rapid forced air escaped through his nostrils, his heart pounded and he knew he couldn't last much longer.

His fingers entwined in her hair, attempting to pull her free. She refused to stop, her pace increased and the intoxicating suction she applied to the throbbing engorged head cost him his last measure of restraint. The fingers buried inside her warm wet treasure plunged deeper, gripping the insides of her sheath, coating his skin with more of her pleasure juices while simultaneously his seed flash-flooded Ericka's skilled mouth.

To his surprise, she didn't gag. Instead, she suckled and drained his shaft while her fingers continued to massage his tender sac.

When she licked his shaft clean, she sat up, but didn't look at him. Slowly, he pulled his fingers, damp with her release, free. Wrapping an arm around her shoulder, he used that hand to lift her chin. Her eyes were closed. With each light kiss upon her closed eyelids, he whispered.

"Ericka. Watch as I taste you." When she didn't comply, he tightened his grip around her shoulders. He slid first one and then the other finger of the hand dripping with her flavor into his mouth.

His cheek was pressed firmly against hers. She felt him suckle each of the fingers that had given her merciless pleasure. The feel of his subtle sucking motion against her skin and the scent of her on his fingers made her sizzle inside. But she couldn't make herself watch him taste her.

When she bit the edge of her lip, his flavor lingered there. The sensation of his powerful release remained a vibrant tingle on her tongue. And still she couldn't look at him. *This shouldn't have happened* flashed behind her lids.

His lips brushed against her ear and his tongue ran around its sensitive rim, halting the breath within her chest.

"Uhm… Sweet. 'Tis a taste for which I shall always hunger," he whispered, sending chills racing across every aspect of her skin.

Had he meant such sincere words for her or was he captured in the moment? She wanted to look into his eyes, see into his heart, but her eyelids seemed welded shut. It wouldn't be she that he wanted. In her heart, she knew it would be another reflected in his pupils.

The music lowered and Ned interrupted. "Coming up on the village, lass." Ned turned the music up and seemed content to ignore the two of them.

Ericka pushed from Gavin's chest, fumbling with her zipper and snap. Without looking at him, she whispered, "We must get dressed."

His grip lessened, his arm lingered across the back of her shoulders. With his free hand, he lifted her chin. He placed a gentle kiss upon her stiff lips, but no gaze from her eyes met his. She held them closed as though the sight of him pained her somehow.

What had he done? He sensed her tension. The scent of her arousal had set his soul on fire and tested the strength of the material of his jeans.

Together, they managed to ease each other's need for some sort of release, be it of the fear of the metal beast or just simply the need for each other. Had he been wrong in touching her? Tasting her? Inadvertently, his tongue ran across his lips, drawing in a haunting taste of her sweet juices. He sighed heavily, then eased his arm from around her, settled back to his side of the car and snapped and zipped his pants.

While confined in his tomb, he dreamt only of her. Since his evening release from his prison, he hungered for her touch. During his daylight sleep, his rapid thoughts rationalized that two hundred years of entombment were enough for any man to mourn. It convinced him to accept the death of his wife.

Was what he wanted now wrong?

He glanced at the woman who sat silent, staring out the window. Something wasn't right between them. The urge to hold her grew, but he held his fist balled tight in his lap and fought the desire.

This canna be flickered through his thoughts. Snapping his gaze in her direction, he realized the problem. He told her this could not happen again. That they should not be and then he…

His head fell listless against the headrest as he stared. *'Tis be a rocky road ahead,* his thoughts ran silent through his head. *But ye must make her see that 'tis her that ye want and not the memory of Tavia.*

Chapter Sixteen

ꟃ

Gavin stood silent behind Ericka outside the pub where Ned dropped them off. More of the metal beasts sat along the street. Others scurried past with glowing bright, round eyes leading their way. How could these things not be considered beasts?

As he studied his surroundings, he shook his head. Not one hovel did he recognize on their ride into the village's center. Its size seemed several times larger than what he remembered. The village had grown.

He followed Ericka into the building with a bright red sign in its window, flashing "Internet Pub". Several people sat on stools along the bar in the front. Others were seated at different tables in the middle of the room and at private booths along the back wall. All seemed dressed in similar clothing. He noticed everyone wore some sort of leggings such as the ones he wore. How did one tell the men from the women?

Finally, a woman—or at least what he thought was a woman—approached and escorted them to a booth. He couldn't help but stare.

Her hair was a bright white color and stood in short spikes. A thick black collar wrapped around her neck and he wondered if she had been imprisoned by an angry overlord at one time. A tight black t-shirt barely hid her breasts from view and left her middle bare. Heavy black boots covered her feet and stopped at her knees. She was one of the few people in the place wearing some sort of plaid, though it was much too short to be considered a kilt. To which clan did she belong? The plaid's colors were unfamiliar. The rough drag of her brogue drew his attention from her dress.

"What'll you have?" She stood with her hand on her hip, glaring up at him through dark black-outlined eyes.

Ericka grasped his arm and nudged him toward one side of the booth. "Do you have any mead?"

"Only the finest in all of Lochsbury." She snorted as if it were a worldwide fact.

"He'll have mead and I'll have a diet soda." Ericka shot her a courteous smile while she scooted into the booth and sat across from Gavin.

As soon as the waitress flounced away, Ericka pulled her laptop from her satchel and began the process of accessing the Internet connection provided at the table. Gavin scanned the room. People sat staring at odd boxes and tapping on some sort of board.

"Where have ye brought me ta, lass?" Gavin leaned toward her and whispered, though his gaze never left his pertinent scan of the room.

"It's a place where people with limited Internet access go to get on the web," she answered without looking up from her screen. Though the connection was slow, she logged on without a problem.

"Get on the what?"

She dared a glance in his direction across the top of her laptop screen. There it was again…that lost and confused puppy-dog look, just like the one Belvedere sported. Pure innocence of the world around him exuded from his aura. The thin layer of invisible shielding she placed around her personal space toppled. Adjusting her glasses, she reprimanded herself.

She could do this. She could teach him. He's your Tarzan, remember. Teach him.

"Why don't you move to this side of the table and I'll show you what this is all about." She slid over. Before he moved, she added, "You have to promise to keep your hands to yourself."

A smile tugged at his lips when he caught her eyes for the first time since they were expelled from the belly of the beast. He thought he saw a flicker of desire lace her irises, then dance away as quickly as it appeared. The wayward waitress slapped the mug down in front of him, breaking their momentary eye contact.

"Here's your mead and here's your diet soda. If you've got any questions about the Internet service, just ask. Otherwise, all access is rounded to the half hour from the moment you log on."

"Thanks." Ericka gave her a thin smile before the waitress left.

Gavin slid in beside Ericka and the lesson began. The images flashing before him on the screen were pure magic. He watched her tap the thing she explained as the keyboard. Different pictures and words appeared. They traveled the Internet, yet they didn't move from their seats. After an hour, his head spun, it was all too confusing. He reached for the mead which stood untouched behind the laptop screen and downed it.

"Ah, 'tis a fine mead indeed." He exhaled and nodded with the empty glass in his hand at the waitress. Leaning back into a more comfortable position in the seat, his arm draped around her shoulders.

As the waitress delivered another round, Ericka bit her bottom lip. She wanted to chastise him for going back on his word, but his arm around her shoulders seemed natural. She drew from his warmth and ached for his touch, yet in her heart she knew it was wrong.

It had to be the mead, she thought.

"You promised," she whispered, wiggling forward, leaving his arm dangling.

Instantly, she missed his touch, but she chose to ignore it. They had to keep this friendly. He needed her to be his teacher of current world events and not a guru of the kama sutra.

It took every ounce of her resolve to focus on the screen. If a web site with pertinent information hadn't popped up, she wasn't sure how much longer she would've been able to resist her growing urges.

Unable to deny her subtle challenge, he leaned forward, resting his chin on her shoulder and whispered deliberately close to her ear. "No such words hath I spoken."

Lazily, he laid his hand on her thigh. The flicker of the irises in her eyes was the only sign that she acknowledged his touch. Without hesitation, he slid his hand along her thigh, landing on her knee. Her back stiffened and he grinned.

Teasing her was pleasant. In a slow grazing motion, he trailed his fingertips up the inside of her thigh to the inner uppermost section. After twirling them in a tender circle near her junction, he stopped.

He heard her breath hitch when he wiggled his pinkie finger dangerously close to the warm sanctuary where he longed to be nestled. As her chest rose and fell in a stilted manner, her irises darkened and he knew she was affected by him. No matter how hard she tried not to show it, he knew she wanted him almost as badly as he wanted her.

"That's..." Her voice trailed off as she swallowed hard. Remembrance of the power of his majestic fingers shot chills down her spine. She wanted his touch, but... Clearing her throat, she wet her lips then forced the words to exit. "That's a mere technicality."

His closeness was becoming a problem, so she pressed a key and sent the information to a download file in her computer. It was impossible for her to concentrate on it now. If she were to get any work done, it would have to be without him sitting on top of her.

She coughed as an image of Gavin on top of her flashed in her thoughts. Well, on top of her would be nice. Shivering, she reined in the heated sex thoughts and tried desperately to change the direction this evening was continually taking.

It is your fault, she chided herself. *You did give him a blowjob in the backseat. No wonder he keeps hinting at sex. Think friend! Think Tarzan's teacher! Think anything but sex.*

Unfortunately, he kept making that difficult.

"I know not of what this word technicality means, but..."

He slid his hand in a slow tortuous route from her inner thigh, up the side of her abdomen, brushing the base of her breasts before running the tip of his finger along her lower lip.

"Your body speaks differently from your mind. Why's that?" He lowered his fingers to her chin, tilted her face toward his and held her eyes locked with his brilliant green gaze.

* * * * *

Unable to believe his good fortune, he grinned. After developing the pictures in the self-made darkroom in the bathroom of his rental home, he dropped in for a beer and some computer access time. The moment he stepped through the door, his senses were greeted with a pleasant surprise.

Easing onto a corner barstool out of her line of sight, he watched her sitting with some oversized oaf in a booth. Had traces of the incident earlier somehow lingered in the back of her mind? Was she here seeking sexual release because of him? A wicked happiness gripped his soul and his cock grew.

The instant he spotted the giant's arm settle around her shoulders, heat engaged in his being. From this distance, he wouldn't be able to penetrate her thoughts. Without eye contact, her will was her own. The scene had to be stopped. No way was some local going to reap the benefits of his inventive mind play.

He downed half his beer in one swallow, then stalked across the room. The closer he got, the more he saw. A hand rubbed between her thighs, then trailed up her body to her chin. The sound of a whispered deep brogue fanned the flames until the internal fire almost consumed him. He grappled for control over his anger. The woman would be his and no one else's.

Modern words mixed with a twist of a few ancient Gaelic semblances froze him within a strained earshot and the big oaf's position kept him out of her view. Molten pinpricks shot through every fiber of his being. Years of lessons had him tuned for just this moment. The feeling couldn't be wrong. Could it be? Electrified sparks flowed through his veins with each step.

"Ericka." He interrupted the huddled couple.

Ericka went rigid as her head snapped in his direction. Reflexively, she lowered the laptop screen from view. He was the last person she expected to see. Not that she expected to see anyone.

"Brother Leod, what a surprise." She feigned a pleasantness to her voice that she did not feel.

His presence made her uneasy. How long had he been there? Was he following her? Had he seen Gavin touching her, caressing her? Granted, the booths were more private than the tables, but what had he seen?

And better yet…why was he here?

The air around her filled with heat. Instinctively, her hand balled tight in her lap, anticipating the flame of a fire to pool in its palm. A forced smile tainted her lips. Something at the base of her brain nagged that she shouldn't look into the fields of wheat, so she avoided direct contact with his eyes.

Did he have the power of mind control? Was that what happened to her earlier? She couldn't be sure, but she didn't want to take any chances.

Gavin sensed her mood change and knew it was because of this man standing beside them. How dare he interrupt? Couldn't he see that they were involved?

The sound of the other man's name upon her lips set Gavin to his feet. Squaring his shoulders, he stood several inches taller than his opponent. No matter. In battle, height did not matter. Skill did.

Out of habit, his hand slid to his side in search of the heavy hilt no longer on his hip. *No sword*! His hands flexed by his side. If he made one wrong move against Ericka, then hand-to-hand combat it would be.

"Who's your friend?" Brother Leod quipped, peeking at Ericka around Gavin's massive shoulders. Each of the MacKinnon brothers' names was etched in his brain.

If the burning sensation in his gut were a true indication, this oversized hulk was a member of the clan. His chance to claim his rightful place stood before him in all his ancient glory.

Come now, Ericka, he thought. *Tell me which brother stands before me. Tell me which I shall send to the gates of hell and claim the book and my throne over the brotherhood.* He licked his lips in anticipation.

Ericka inched out of the booth, which wasn't easy since Gavin blocked her way. Squeezing in beside him, she held his arm. The air thickened and swirled around her, making each breath she took difficult. Odd, the palm of her hand remained cool.

The smirk upon his lips made her wish she could slap it, mouth and all, completely from his face. She refused to let his aura scare her. Not if she were to protect Gavin.

"He's a friend of mine." She smiled up at Gavin. Automatically, his other hand covered the one she held on his biceps. But she noticed his focus never left Brother Leod. Turning back to Brother Leod, she started to speak his name, but the word stalled on her lips. "Ga…"

Was that a twitch at the corner of Brother Leod's eye? Was he anticipating her words? *Think fast.* A nervous tongue darted across her lips, then she started again.

"Gaylord. Gaylord Guinness."

Immediately, she felt Gavin's gaze switch to her, but didn't look up. Instead, she gave his arm a squeeze and hoped he understood. The good brother wanted something and she suddenly had the distinct impression it had nothing to do with the castle and everything to do with the man at her side.

"It's a pleasure to meet you." Brother Leod extended his hand to Gavin.

Though his action was hesitant, Gavin accepted the gesture, studying the person attached to the usual friendly greeting. He grasped the other man's hand and held it firm. The return was not one of strength, it read of a character, which he would not trust.

The eyes of the other man were colored of wheat and grain. They held no truth within them and shifted each time he tried to focus deeply on them. His gut response was not to trust the good Brother Leod.

"Of which clan do ye belong?" The question rumbled in modern words on Gavin's brogue as he held his Gaelic tongue in check.

Ericka had not wanted this man to know of his true nature and had spoken falsely of his given name. For now, he would follow her guide in this matter. Later would be the time to question her judgment.

"Of which clan?" Brother Leod's eyebrows rose and a mocking tone laced his words. His gaze shot to Ericka, who continued to avoid his eyes. *Smart little minx, you can't resist me forever.*

"He meant your last name," Ericka quickly asserted, placing a faked, friendly smile on her lips. Leveling her gaze to his chin, she added. "Come to think of it, I don't remember ever hearing it."

"I don't recall ever giving it." He tilted his head, trying to catch a glimpse of her pupils, but she kept darting them in any direction but his.

A knowing smile tugged at his lips, but he held it in check. No need to let her think she's not in control at the moment. His time would come. Eventually, she would slip and meet his gaze. Then, she would be his to control and do with as he pleased.

Lifting his chin, he stared directly at the man beside Ericka. Even at his full height, the MacKinnon was taller than he, but that didn't matter. The ancient Scotsman was no match for one of the gifted.

As if to test his opponent, he kept his voice level and allowed his arrogance to taint his words as he spoke. "My given name is Hume Leod MacGillivray."

Gavin's back stiffened, his chest expanded, every ounce of him wanting to pounce on the descendant of his enemy. The need for revenge roared through his system. Ericka's arm shifted from his arm to around his waist and he held his anger at bay. For some reason she didn't want him to attack. He sensed it in her touch. Since this was her world, her time, he would respect her wishes. For now…

Even though giving Brother Leod a thorough beating would provide a smidgeon of revenge, Gavin held firm his position by her side.

Ericka pretended to catch a glimpse of the clock. "Oh. It's getting late."

Looking up, she saw the dark color his eyes had changed to and knew his anger brewed. She wasn't certain how long he would remain in control and not follow the ways of his ancient clansman, an eye for an eye, so to speak. When she touched his chin, he lowered his gaze to hers.

"We have to meet Ned," she said.

Gavin stood on guard as she disconnected her laptop and gathered her belongings. Nostrils flared, his eyes leveled on Brother Leod's. The two glared at one another. He didn't like the scent of the air around him. The man's presence brought a distasteful flavor to his mouth.

There was a reason to distrust this man. His eyes were not normal. The grip of his handshake was weak. And his stench could curdle milk, Gavin decided.

A man of the cloth he was not. A MacGillivray he was. Gavin felt it in his bones. This man was evil and it was his job to protect Ericka from him.

Ericka squeezed into the narrow space between the two testosterone-ravaged males. Before something drastically went wrong, she needed to get him out of here. She didn't like the heavy static in the air around her. Not only was it laced with heat, it was charged with unknown sensations which terrified her to the core. Something about Brother Leod was truly evil and she didn't care to find out what. Not now. Not ever.

"It's time to go," she stated, grasping Gavin's hand as tight as she possibly could. "Sorry to have to skip out so soon. But we've got a ride to catch." She nodded in Brother Leod's direction as she tugged Gavin's hand. Hopefully, he wouldn't make this difficult. If she had to, she would drag him from the place, but it wasn't necessary.

Gavin detected the desperation in Ericka's grip. Fear surged through her hand and raced up his arm. She wanted out of here. The need to get her to safety overrode his desire to pummel the descendent of his enemy. His time would come, this he knew to be true.

As he stepped in her direction, he made sure his shoulder collided with Brother Leod's in passing. The force of the blow toppled Brother Leod onto the table behind him, sending a computer screen crashing to the floor.

A small sense of justice brought a smile to Gavin's lips. This would have to do until they met again. Then, it would all come to an end.

Ericka hustled Gavin through the chaos. Screams from startled customers followed them to the door. The sound of chairs grating on the floor and mumbled curses filled the air.

She stopped long enough to shove a wad of crumpled American money into the Goth-styled waitress's hand.

"This should cover the damages and any other charges," she stated, pushing open the door and leading Gavin out into the cool night air.

When they reached the outside, she didn't stop. She wasn't certain what type of crowd hung out at the Internet Pub and she wasn't about to find out if it were an angry drunken sort with an itch to fight. Several blocks away and certain no one followed them, she slowed her pace. Gavin snatched her arm and brought them to a halt.

"Mind telling me what ye were thinking back there?" He nodded over his shoulder.

"Mind telling me what *you* were?" she snapped back at him.

"'Tis not in me nature to run from a fight." He glared down at her, releasing her hand. With his back held straight, his arms crossed over his chest, his shoulders squared and his jaw tight, his stance was saturated with pure male arrogance.

"Aggh! You're unbelievable. We went in there to gain information. Not to have to bail you out of jail after a bar fight." She spun around and marched away from him.

He stood for a moment basking in the beauty of her anger. Her bottom swayed in a nice even sexy keel with each pronounced step. The sleeping shaft within the slim confinements of his jeans awoke. Though he didn't understand her reason for anger, he liked the results it caused. Within a few long strides, he was by her side. He glimpsed a vision of her breasts, bouncing with each heated step.

Aye, he liked it when she was angry.

* * * * *

Brother Leod stood outside the Internet Pub, sucking in her fading essence. He knew Ericka lied. Her slip of the tongue dared him to believe it was the eldest MacKinnon son, Gavin, broken free. But he couldn't be sure.

One thing he knew, there was no Gaylord amongst the siblings. He wasn't able to obtain a reading through their momentary handshake, nor had he been able to penetrate his mind. Some men were tough. He was only able to manipulate the weak or unsuspecting through thought persuasion. At first, he wasn't certain the giant of a man was one of the MacKinnons until he spoke. The man's choice of words reinforced his gut feeling.

Which clan? Brother Leod snorted. His mastery of the modern language was completely lacking in grace or style.

Shoving his hands in his pockets, he walked down the street. At the corner he stopped short, she said they had a ride to catch. Did this mean the MacKinnon was at the castle? Had he been there all this time? How had he been freed? Was Ericka behind it?

His father was right. A woman would be the downfall of the MacKinnon just as it caused the collapse of his ancestor. In the morning, he'd visit the castle again.

And Ericka…she was his key to the MacKinnon. Laughter rolled from his lips and echoed in the empty street. It all would be his soon…the MacKinnon, the book of shadows and the woman, Ericka.

There was just one thing left he needed to take care of first.

Chapter Seventeen

ꟼ

Though the pictures showed him no easy way into the castle, they did provide him with something he found of great interest. The center tower, the one not renovated, appeared in almost every shot. It had to be the place. Why hadn't anyone thought of this before? Because they stopped looking after Hume MacGillivray died of what the brotherhood considered madness. He snorted loudly as he pasted his favorite photographs on the walls of his altar room.

Fools! The book itself had not caused madness in his ancestor. All of them were fools to fear the power of the book, but not he. He was the one of the prophecy…the one his ancestor predicted would be born with the knowledge and strength to command and wield the power of the book of shadows.

Leod pasted another picture to the wall. Groomed by his father to be the one. He was the true descendent of Hume MacGillivray. The brotherhood should never have stopped the quest for the stone statues of the brothers. Heat grew in his belly. But if they hadn't, there wouldn't be this golden opportunity.

Childhood stories surfaced in his thoughts. Ghost tales. One in particular stood out…the tale of the haunted tower. For as long as anyone could remember, the ghost of a long-dead Scotswoman haunted the great tower of a castle in the Grampian Mountains.

Some versions of the tale claimed she died a horrible death and that was why she walked its halls. Others said she was locked inside and left to die because of infidelities to her husband. But the one that he liked best was the one where they swore she lingered as a guard, some sort of protector of the tower, and allowed no one near.

In his gut, he knew the ghost he held captive was that guard. The only MacKinnon physically untouched by the curse had haunted the tower and now he knew why. She protected a stone statue of one of her brothers. Wicked laughter rolled from his throat as he jerked open the closet door. A brilliant flood of luminescent red light filled the room.

"Come," he commanded. The essence of pure energy followed him to the center of the self-made altar.

"Clear." He waved his hand at the floating bubble and the cloudy murk inside dispersed. A transparent figure with vibrant red hair and bright green eyes appeared.

For the first time since her entrapment, Akira saw her surroundings. Her prison moved, but she knew not where it went. The room she did not recognize. A man she did not know knelt before two portraits with his back to her. The portraits of two men sat on either side of a large trunk in the middle of the room. Lit candles formed a circle surrounding the shrine.

She turned inside her bubble, but could not make it move. It hovered frozen to the spot directly behind her silent captor. Pictures on the wall caught her avid attention.

Ericka! Her face covered the walls. *Ericka*! *Oh no*! Something was wrong. It didn't make sense.

"Don't panic, Akira."

She spun around. A wicked grin stretched the mouth of the male face held pressed within millimeters of her aura-encased bubble.

"It will all be over soon."

Heat permeated the thin barrier between her and freedom. His arms lifted and encircled the floating capsule, but did not touch it. She jerked back as far as she could. Extreme heat flowed from his being and filled every molecule of her cell. The substance of her prison rose to boiling temperature. A strange sensation sparked within her transparent being. Fire, heat, burning, melting, his thoughts melded with those of her own. It was as if he wanted to fry the remnants of her essence and disintegrate her soul.

Desperately, she tried to call upon her ethereal powers. Nothing came. As the heat intensified, she thought of her *brathairs*. Their freedom shall be obtained. Gavin shall see it done.

Transparent eyelids closed and thoughts of all their good flowed. Memories of their childhood together danced around a ring of fire, mocking the magnitude of the heat around her weakened soul. The power of her love created a veil around her spirit. Locked out were the waves of intense heat and coolness soothed her transparent shell.

No matter how hard he tried, he couldn't burn through to the fragile soul encased in ice in the middle of his heated cell of black magic. Not a drop of water fell. The harder he tried, the thicker the layer of ice became. Exhausted, he snapped.

"Aggh!" His arms slammed down to his sides. His face flushed bright red, perspiration dripped from his forehead and brow, and still the spirit survived.

An "A" student in exorcism at the brotherhood, he knew he could do it. Of course, he added his own twist to the procedure by utilizing his ability to manipulate heat. It failed. Now how would he rid her from his path?

He circled the cell. That creation worked. He captured her without a problem. The spell he cast pulled her in and trapped her within its impenetrable layer of evil. She couldn't escape. Stopping dead in his tracks, a face-splitting grin stretched his lips to capacity.

"That'll just have to do."

"Return!" he shouted. The bubble lurched toward the closet and floated inside.

"Don't you fear, Akira. Ericka shall be in good hands once I rid the world of your brother, Gavin."

His words penetrated her iced capsule. Akira screeched. "*No*!" Ice shards fell as she threw her transparent being against the outer shell of her prison. Her actions were useless. The bubble failed to move.

"*Gavin*! *Ericka*!" she cried as she curled into a ball of ethereal energy. Her pleas landed on deaf ears.

He grasped the door and slammed it shut.

"You may be able to resist me now, but just you wait. With Gavin dead, your reason to be shall be gone and so too shall your weakened spirit."

* * * * *

Grant's Tavern was more like the proper drinking establishment of which he was accustomed. If his memory was correct, it stood in the same spot as the tavern he and his *brathairs* frequented. With its wooden door and stone-faced front, it resembled the prior establishment remarkably. The small single-roomed pub held a few round tables with chairs where several older men sat huddled already knee-deep in their mugs. A large antique bar ran the length of the back wall. That was where the bulk of the crowd stood gripped in a heated debate.

Ericka was surprised to find Ned situated in the center of the crowd. Apparently from the shouts, he had bet on a favored to win the dart tournament, but there was a dispute over whether the man stepped over the line during his final toss of the dart. A hush fell over the crowd the moment Gavin's hulking frame stood next to the bar.

Suddenly, she realized the Internet Pub wasn't the place she should've been concerned over a fight breaking out. It was here. Men of varied ages stared at Gavin. She slid closer to

Gavin's side. Maybe she should've left him outside while she came in to find Ned.

"Canna a man spot a round fer the house?" Gavin proclaimed, tossing a solid gold coin at the barkeeper.

The breath hitched in Ericka's throat while the man behind the bar examined the coin. Where'd he get that? She didn't know he had any sort of money. Was that still considered money in this day and age? Before she could move, the barkeeper spoke.

"Are ye sure ye wants ta part with such a prize, lad? It's more 'n a couple hundred years old and worth a lot more 'n a round." A grin sprouted on his unshaven face as a thick Scottish brogue flowed from his lips.

"Aye, then 'twill be more 'n a round." Gavin nodded.

Hands patted Gavin's back and welcomed him. Mugs and glasses slammed on the bar. Ericka was bumped and shoved from Gavin's side as every man in the place pushed close to greet him.

What had he done? Never had she seen such sudden camaraderie. *Men*, she huffed. One moment they're ready to pounce, yet offer them a drink and they act as if you've just returned to the pride after years of absence.

After every mug was filled, a glass of something she assumed was ale was shoved in her hand. Ned raised his mug in the air and led the first round of cheers to their newfound companion. One sip and the taste of the drink stung her tongue. Gavin, she noticed, downed his mug in one hearty gulp, slamming it on the bar where the barkeeper refilled it with haste.

A tournament of darts started with Gavin at the lead as the ale flowed. *This could be a long wait*, she huffed. Amongst the ongoing revelry, Ericka slipped to an unoccupied table. No one noticed the only woman in the pub, no one except for Gavin.

With every toast of a drink and toss of a dart, he cast a glance her way. The beauty sat in the corner. The thing she called a laptop cast a pale light upon her face as she seemed lost to the pub noise. Her attention was drawn into the magical world which danced upon the screen.

After his seventh consecutive win, he bowed out of the tournament. He gave Ned a nod to wrap up his bets, then headed for the secluded table in the corner.

"'Twill ye be waste'n such a fine ale 'tis this, lass?" He raised her untouched glass.

"You can have it," she answered without looking up.

"Bless ye," he stated, then downed the lukewarm brew. With a swipe of the back of his hand across his lips, he sat beside her and set the empty glass on the table. Resting his chin on her shoulder, he peered at the blurred words on the screen. "Find anything?"

Ale-soaked breath warmed her cheek and tickled her nose. Her leg twitched when his hand splayed possessively on her thigh. She liked the feel of his touch and though the scent of ale was thick, she ached to taste his lips.

While he played, stolen glances across the laptop screen filled her mind with visions. His biceps flexing with each toss of the dart fueled a growing need in her chest to have those strong arms wrapped around her. The expanse of his chest seemed to broaden with each win and her desire to cuddle against it expanded as well. When she turned her chin slightly, their lips brushed, igniting a spark in her core. The deep swirl of his passionate green eyes locked on hers and she knew—he wanted her.

"Ahem." Ned cleared his throat. "I'll be in the car when yer ready."

Ericka shot upright. Her look of dismay followed Ned's retreat out the door. Ned had certainly shown a side she never expected to see. Obviously he'd forgiven the earlier incident outside the castle when he brokered Gavin's bets and won a few of his own as a result of Gavin's natural talent at the game of darts. The chime of the clock on the wall caught her attention. It couldn't be two in the morning already.

"We need to go. This wouldn't exactly be the best place for us to be when the sun comes up," she whispered as she gathered her things and shoved them into her satchel. Before she could stand, he caught her arm.

His mouth found hers with ease as he took what he wanted. A kiss, a taste of the beauty he hungered for all night. With each throw of the dart, he thought of plunging into her as the dart did the corkboard. Deep and penetrating, that was how he wished to be, but he'd settle for a taste of her lips, her tongue and her mouth. He pulled back and stared at the glazed look of her glasses covered eyes. She wanted him. Her arousal couldn't escape his heightened senses, even when dulled by ale.

"Aye, 'tis time to go." He smiled.

He stood, took her hand and carrying her satchel, led her out the door. When they reached Ned and the car, Ericka froze.

"I forgot to take…" She shuffled through an outer pocket on the satchel in Gavin's hands.

Covering her hand with his, he stopped her frantic search. A tear-filled gaze darted up to his. He brushed away one renegade drop from her cheek, then placed a gentle kiss upon her brow.

"Ye won't be needin' it, lass. Trust me."

Unable to speak, she nodded and swallowed against the first wave of fear. *Trust him*. She wasn't sure why, but she knew that she did. Ericka slid into the backseat with Gavin close behind. After placing her satchel on the floorboard, he pulled her against his chest. The rhythm of his heartbeat filled her soul. The feel of his arms around her chased away the nausea from her stomach. Strength seemed to ooze from him and into her by the simple contact of his hug.

As the car surged along the dark roadway, Gavin stretched, managing to place his legs on the seat with his back against the door. He lifted Ericka, laying her with her back against his chest, her bottom in his lap and her legs nestled between his. Cradling her head against his shoulder, he liked having her in his arms. With tiny circular motions of his fingertips on her abdomen, he worked to soothe her discomfort. True, the metal beast scared him at first, but for some reason it terrified the tender creature in his care.

"Tired?" he whispered into her hair. Though laced with the stench of tobacco the other men at the pub smoked, the faint scent of lavender lingered.

"Uhm, a little," she whispered. She snuggled closer, trying to slip deeper under the warm shield of his skin. Loving the way his fingertips soothed the massive roar of the overactive monster in her belly. She couldn't believe how safe his touches made her feel. Though she wanted to roll over and show him just how hot and bothered he was making her, she didn't dare break the spell.

What if the nausea returned the moment his fingers stopped? Shifting slightly in his lap, the hardness of his cock nestled against the small of her back. A hidden smile tugged at her lips, he wanted her too.

"Rest, 'twill be time for that later."

* * * * *

Ericka woke with a start to a vibrant cascade of jingles and the shake of a red nail-tipped hand on her shoulder. Flipping on her side, she craned to see the assailant. Gavin's heavy arms braced tighter around her waist. His head rolled to the side in the open window and a hefty yawn escaped his lips. Ericka's nose scrunched. The smell of stale ale was unattractive. Aunt May's face came into focus.

"Gavin. Ericka. You have to get up. It's almost time for the sun to rise." Her voice sounded frantic. For a moment,

Ericka couldn't understand why her aunt was waking her at such an early hour. The sun wasn't even up yet.

The sun! Ericka scurried from his lap and opened the opposite car door. Shaking her hand in a frenzied motion, she beckoned him to take it. Gavin sat up, bumping his head in the window. "*Och,*" bellowed from his lips as he rubbed the tender spot.

"Come on. We've got to get you into the tower before the sun comes up," she commanded.

With a heavy head, Gavin slid across the seat. The night of drinking and gaming flashed behind his lids. He paused, digging his palms into his welded-shut lids. The urgent tug on his arm forced him into action.

Sunrise was bad for him, but why? The thought escaped him for the moment as he found his footing and placed an arm around her shoulders. Though sparks of pain lashed through his brain, he fought to gain control over his laden lids.

"Gavin!" Ericka snapped. She hated to do it, but she had no choice. She slapped his cheek.

His head snapped up and his eyes sprang open wide. Brushing the back of his hand across the inflamed skin of his cheek, he growled. "Lass, ye better be havin' a good reason fer that."

"Now that I've got your attention, we've got to move." She grasped his chin and held it steady. Red laced the whites of his eyes. The pupils, though hazed, glowed dark. She had angered him. But that wasn't her biggest concern right now, the sun was.

Cupping his chin, she turned his head in the direction of the slow sneak of the sunrise. "Once that's up, you're stone and I can't move you."

"*Aye*, lass." Though his head ached, he grabbed her hand and led her in long strides toward the castle.

When they reached the tunnel, he hustled through first with her close behind. Gently lifting her from the tunnel, he nuzzled her ear with his lips. "Sleep t'was not that for which I wished last night."

Chills raced down her spine. Nervously, she met his gaze. Were his words honest? He wanted her. The moment her tongue wet her lips, his mouth captured it, sucking her into a hungry kiss. His taste was addicting. She plundered his mouth, returning his kiss pressure for pressure, taste for taste. Morning shadows slithered into her peripheral vision and she pushed from their embrace.

Turning, she ran and gathered the pillows bunched under the chairs for his protection earlier. She laid them in a neat pile. Before she could get more, he was behind her with the rest.

"Please lie down. I want to know that you're comfortable and safe." Pressing against his chest, she urged him to lay back.

Immediately, he grasped her hand. "Lie with me. 'Tis your face I wish to see last before the curse befalls me."

Ericka lay facing him. His hand caressed her cheek, her hands wrapped around his other one. Their eyes fixated on one another's as the first rays of morning light penetrated their private sanctuary. A sizzle she knew well crackled in the air as this gorgeous man transformed to stone in front of her eyes. His hand weighed heavy on her cheek.

The warmth of his touch was lost. Though his eyes were solid, she believed that he could still see her. She pressed her lips to the cool ones etched in the stone of his face. With her palm flat against his chest, she felt the rhythm of his heart pound through the frozen chamber of his curse.

His curse was now her curse. Sighing, she realized she'd fallen in love with him. She had to save him. Even if it meant accepting the fact his dead wife, Tavia, held claim to his heart.

After lying with him for over an hour, she wiggled from his embrace. She stuffed a pillow between his arms to take her place and pulled a blanket of ancient fur over his body. With one last kiss upon his brow, she hurried to the tunnel and scurried through to the other side.

While lying with Gavin, the adventures of the night replayed in her head. A vague theory formed, one she needed to discuss with the person who could help her sort out the details. She smoothed the tapestry. When she was certain the entrance was secure, she went to retrieve her satchel from the car and find Aunt May.

Ericka tapped on the bedroom door. "Aunt May, can I come in?"

"Of course, dear," Aunt May replied.

Aunt May sat on the bed, towel-drying her hair, wearing a multicolored silk robe and fluffy pink slippers. With his tail wagging, Belvedere greeted Ericka as she sat on the bed next to her aunt.

"He's after Gavin."

Just saying it made her stomach knot, but she knew she was right. She detected a change in Brother Leod in the air around her last night at the café. Until now, she wasn't certain what that change was about. Brother Leod wasn't after the castle. He wanted a MacKinnon. Did he know that Gavin was one? Deep inside, she hoped that he didn't. But a burning sensation at the base of her brain hinted that he did.

"Who is?" The towel stopped in mid-drying motion as she peered from beneath it at Ericka.

"Brother Leod. We ran into him last night in the village." A heavy sigh escaped as she dragged her laptop from the satchel.

"What happened?" Aunt May gasped.

"Gavin knocked him on his arrogant ass." A slight smile tugged at her lips as the memory of Brother Leod falling feet over head flashed through her brain. Ericka flipped open the screen, turned on the power and logged on to her files.

"Wish I could've been there to see it. You wouldn't happen to have that on video?" Aunt May laughed.

"Only in my head," Ericka quipped, then turned the conversation to the reason she looked for her aunt in the first place. They needed answers and they needed them before he arrived for his next scheduled tour.

"Did the good Brother Leod ever mention his last name to you?"

Aunt May's brows bunched as if in deep thought before she spoke. "Can't say that I recall him ever giving a last name."

As she continued scrolling through the file, she stated. "And for good reason, he's a MacGillivray. His full name is Hume Leod MacGillivray."

"Why, the little sneak! No wonder he wanted access to this castle. He's searching for a MacKinnon. Wait 'til I get my hands on him. I bet he isn't associated with any brotherhood either," she snapped, pointing her finger wildly in air.

Ericka sighed, turned the screen so she and her aunt could share it and continued.

"Unfortunately, he is. But it's not like a normal monastery based on religious beliefs and filled with monks. From what I've read, it's more like a cult that was formed by the original Hume MacGillivray. He brought together his kinsmen and bound them into this brotherhood. According to this web site, he became their leader and drove them to find the MacKinnon brothers. After his death, they ceased the search. For unknown reasons, the brotherhood remained together."

"You'd think they'd disband once the leader was dead. Why'd they stay together?" Aunt May asked.

"The information is sketchy. It hints at the use of dark elements, black magic and a sort of devil worship. But there's never been any proof." She shrugged.

"The heat that fills his aura is proof enough," Aunt May stated.

A faint burn shivered down her spine. If his heat were a true sign of evil, then they were in trouble, Ericka thought.

Somehow she had to get to the bottom of this, protect her aunt, keep Gavin safe and—she swallowed hard—keep from burning to a crisp in the process. Trying to focus on the screen, she continued.

"I'm not sure how significant this is, but before now, no one from the outside was admitted into their close-knit society. I found an application for admittance on this web site."

"Wonder why, after all these years, they changed the rules?" Aunt May asked with her eyes glued to the screen.

"Maybe most of the lineage died off and they're in need of new recruits," Ericka replied without looking up. Adjusting her glasses, she focused on the last section of the form.

"How'd I miss this last night?" The phantom sensation of Gavin's hand on her thigh jarred her memory with the reason she didn't finish reading the file. Leaning in closer to the screen, unsure she read it right, she spoke the last few lines out loud.

"It requests that no one without the true desire for diabolism need apply. Those with natural *gifts* and the ability for devout loyalty shall be rewarded." She shot a raised eyebrow glance at Aunt May.

"Ericka, you know what this means." Ericka had a bad feeling that whatever was about to come out of her aunt's mouth wasn't something she was going to enjoy hearing. "They're recruiting new forces and I'm certain it's not the entertaining magician kind. They're looking for people with magical muses."

"You're not saying..." Ericka's voice stalled, refusing to express her thoughts. First a ghost and a haunted castle, then a curse and a man of stone, Aunt May couldn't expect her to believe in the forces of magic as well.

"Wizards, warlocks, witches and maybe even those with telekinetic abilities." Aunt May's head nodded with the enunciation of each word. Her red nail pointing to the word diabolism forced Ericka's gaze to glue to it as she continued.

"It's not the good ones like you they want. It's the ones with the gut-driven force of black magic and evil."

"What do you mean, good ones like me?" Ericka braced herself. She knew her Aunt May believed in a lot of things most normal people didn't. But this was the first time her aunt ever mentioned sorcery of any sort being a part of their family.

Her aunt's arm wrapped around her shoulders. "Think about it. You felt the heat of evil that surrounds Brother Leod's dark-colored aura. Like me, you connected with a good spirit, Akira. Thus, you felt the cool sensations acquainted with good. I won't deny I experienced a form of inner revelation since Akira awakened it."

The squeeze she gave Ericka's shoulders did nothing for the newly formed knot in between them. "I know I've asked you to believe in a lot of things you normally wouldn't, but please give this a chance. You've been given a gift. It may not be any more than the ability to feel the sensations between good and evil. But it's still a gift. How far you take it is up to you."

Why hadn't she felt these sensations before? Had Akira truly awakened some sort of magical ability in her? She couldn't be certain. Everything was bundled in a tangled web of mixed emotions. What was real? What wasn't? She swallowed at the lump in her throat.

"And what of Akira? I don't think she passed over like you thought," Ericka rasped.

"I know, I experienced her pain in a dream last night." Sadness clouded her aunt's words.

"I didn't know ghosts felt anything." Ericka's brain spun. This whole concept was new to her. What were the rules when dealing with ghosts? Before now, she thought dead meant dead, not feeling, talking or existing in the real world. She snorted. What was the real world? Her perception of reality had definitely taken a blow.

"I don't know if all spirits do. But I know what I felt. Pure heat tortured her soul and we both know who generates an aura of heat."

Ericka met her aunt's unwavering stare. She did know, but how did they prove he held Akira? They couldn't take this matter to the local law enforcement. No one would believe their story. A ghost captured by a member of an occult brotherhood wasn't exactly normal thinking to the average person. It would probably lead to the two of them being locked up in Scotland's equivalent of an insane asylum instead of Brother Leod.

Returning her gaze to the computer screen, she continued scrolling through the online application. Her heart stopped for a beat or two. The name of the contact person seemed to reach out and slap her. Proof was at her fingertips. But was it enough?

"Aunt May…" Ericka's voice trailed off as she pointed to the culprit's name. Her mind clicked a mile a minute. He was behind it. But was he alone?

"You think the brotherhood knows about this?" Aunt May asked.

"Has anyone other than Brother Leod been in touch with you?" Ericka tilted her chin and met her aunt's gaze.

"No."

"Then there's a possibility they don't know and he's the only one behind this."

"Or…" Ericka didn't like the tone of her aunt's voice and had the distinct feeling she wasn't going to like what was about to follow that "or". "He's united an entirely new MacGillivray following and from the looks of this application, it's not good."

Chapter Eighteen

ᔓ

What were they up against? reiterated over and over in her head. Why were they still after the MacKinnons after so many years? It didn't make sense. Was it some sort of ongoing feud between two warring families? As it was, the MacKinnons were nonexistent in this battle for the past two hundred years. Why continue?

There had to be more to the story, something else that fueled the brotherhood's actions, but what? Were there many or just the one? She thought she could handle Brother Leod, but an army of Brother Leods she wasn't so sure about. How would she protect Gavin if they stormed the castle?

Storm the castle? She almost laughed at the thought. What century did she think this was anyway? No one attacked castles anymore. At least, she hoped they didn't. As she stepped from the warmth of the shower, she heard the distinctive ring of the doorbell.

He's here! Wasn't he ever late? Wrapped in a towel, she scurried across the hall to her room, leaving a trail of foot-shaped puddles. The rapid beat of her heart felt like it would pound its way up her throat and out her mouth.

Relax. She glared at her reflection in the mirror. *He doesn't know you're on to him*. Taking a deep breath, she attempted to quell her nerves. As she dried off, her hands shook.

Think of Gavin screamed through her thoughts. *You must protect him*. She dressed, brushed her hair and pulled it into its normal bun.

Protect Gavin flashed through her thoughts as she adjusted her glasses and took another deep breath. *If Akira is in trouble, then you're all he's got. Don't let him down.* She jerked open the door with a newfound determination.

As far as she knew, she held the upper hand in this deadly game. Though she didn't understand her new abilities to sense good and evil, she knew she could use it against him. His aura gave him away. No matter what, she planned to keep him from finding Gavin.

* * * * *

"Good morning, Ericka," Aunt May greeted her cheerily when she entered the patio. Belvedere lifted his head and yipped from his position safe in Aunt May's lap.

"Morning, Aunt May, Belvedere." She smiled, ran her hand through the puppy's coat, then nodded toward Brother Leod. "Morning, Brother Leod."

"Good morning, Ericka." Brother Leod stood and pulled out her chair. When she moved to take her seat, he quipped low in her ear. "Rough night?"

"Not anywhere near as rough as yours. How's your backside?" Ericka smiled over her shoulder at him. She caught the audible chuckle that escaped from her aunt. The moment her gaze connected with his, a sensation of heat poured through her veins and pooled in her stomach.

Wrong move! Forcibly, she pulled her gaze away and focused on her cup. *Something with his eyes, don't look at him directly.*

Aunt May laid a pair of dark shaded clip-ons on the table in front of her. Ericka noted she had put on a pair of dark sunglasses. "Here, dear. The sun's awfully bright this morning. I thought you could use these." Her gaze turned to Brother Leod as she added. "Sorry, I don't have an extra pair for you."

Somehow, her aunt knew. Without hesitating, she snapped the shaded covers onto her glasses. Hope this works, she prayed.

Glancing from one to the other, he plastered a broad smile to his face. *Those dark shades may help you for now.* He held his gaze fixated on Ericka's eyes. *But you won't have them on forever.*

"Thank you for your consideration. But as you can see, the sun is behind me so I truly have no need for them." He forced a friendly tone to his speech.

Had they figured out his abilities? He doubted it as he sat in the chair across from Ericka. Or were the glasses simply to block out the sun, as the old bat suggested? He couldn't be sure. Ericka avoided looking at him directly last night.

Maybe that was because when she looked at him, thoughts of sex filled her brain. Crossing his legs, he attempted to hide the sudden growth of his cock the thought of Ericka naked caused.

Soon enough their eyes would connect unshielded and he would make her his. Right now, he needed to focus on his mission. *Find the enemy, then take your prize.* He raked a gaze down her body as he cleared his throat.

"Ericka, we could trade places, then you won't need those dark shades."

"No, thank you, I'm comfortable right here."

"Will your friend be joining us this morning?" He stared at his reflection in her shaded lenses. Though he couldn't see her eyes, he knew they were scrutinizing every inch of him. Just the thought that her gaze touched him made him shift in his chair to adjust for the growing strain in his jeans.

"My friend?" She chose to play dumb. Even though they sat in the sun, the way he looked at her gave her the chills.

"I think his name was Gaylord."

"Oh, him. He's a local I met last night. I doubt we'll see him again." The breath hitched in her chest as she held her voice steady and hoped he bought her story. Lying wasn't something she was good at, so it took tremendous concentration to pull it off.

"I hope it wasn't something I said."

The words were laced with heat, causing a wave of nausea in Ericka's stomach. Suddenly, she realized that it wasn't just his eyes he used to project heat, his entire aura glowed with it. Taking a deep breath, she forced the bile to back down.

Though she knew he couldn't see, she glared at him. Last night, everything he said made her on edge. His aura made her aware of who he truly was and what he really wanted…Gavin. She had to protect him. Licking her lips, she stated as point blank as she could. "Trust me. It was nothing *you* said that ended our time together."

It was your ancestor, flashed through her brain, though it never passed through her lips.

"Well then, now that that's settled…" He let his voice trail off as he stood and moved to the serving table. For a moment, he forced his focus on a spot on the wall. The little vixen had his blood running hot and his cock hard. Now was not the time for her.

Relax, take your time. You've got all day. You need her in your confidence in order to find the MacKinnon or the door to the tower, whichever comes first.

Biting back a grin, he spun around on his heels with the silver coffee carafe in hand. These two were simple women. Nothing a MacGillivray as strong as he couldn't handle.

"Ladies, may I serve you?"

* * * * *

After breakfast, the ladies escorted him to the front door so he could retrieve the items he needed from his car.

"How did you know about his eyes?" Ericka whispered. They both stood in the open doorway watching his every move from behind dark shades.

"What about his eyes?" Aunt May whispered out of the side of her mouth.

"I'm not sure. Why the sunglasses?" Keeping her voice low, she turned to look at her aunt.

"Thought they'd piss him off and a pissed-off man can't think straight," she stated in a matter-of-fact way as she tilted her head toward Ericka's and continued to whisper. "What are you not sure about?"

Ericka almost laughed at the comical look of her aunt in a brightly colored kimono, a feather in her hair and dark sunglasses. Glancing toward the car, she saw Brother Leod walking their way. "It's just a feeling I have. Don't look directly at his eyes."

Aunt May quipped low so no one else could hear. "Not a problem. Do you think its okay to focus on the bulge in his jeans?"

Ericka's mouth fell open, but closed without speaking a word. Her aunt never failed to amaze her. Though they knew he was the enemy, she chose to check out his package anyway. With those dark glasses on, he wouldn't be able to tell what she was doing.

"Ready for your tour of the inside of the castle?" Ericka said when he reached the doorway. She had no intention of letting him out of her sight or leading him anywhere near Gavin. This was going to be the longest day of her life.

"Of course." He reached for her elbow to guide her back inside, but Ericka sidestepped his move. The last thing she wanted was to connect with the heat of his touch. Bad enough she was smothered by it in the air.

Turning her back to him, she flipped up the clip-on shades. She sensed his glare upon her back and hoped he couldn't burn a hole in her. What type of magic did he control? Obviously, one of his abilities had something to do with severe heat.

Aunt May led the tour. As if he were her assistant, Belvedere was close on her heels. They started in the main entrance hall, but never made it as far as the family portrait tapestry. She led them into the front sitting room, then the parlor. The grand ballroom was her favorite. Aunt May's knowledge of the castle seemed endless.

Brother Leod wrote notes and took several rolls of film. Occasionally, Ericka swore he was focusing his camera on her. It had to be her imagination. She shivered, trying to shake the eerie feeling that he seemed as interested in her as he was in the castle.

"Brother Leod, are any of the others from the brotherhood going to come and help you with the research?" Ericka forced herself to join the conversation.

"Uhm," he sighed. Ericka's voice was a relief from the incessant chatter of the old woman. It was the first she had spoken since the start of the tour. Looking up from the camera's lens, he hoped to catch her eyes, but she conveniently held them averted. *You can't avoid me forever.*

With a shake of his head, he stated. "There seems to have been an outbreak of an illness at the monastery and they won't be able to join me." *Not that I would let them.* He flashed her a smile.

"That's too bad," Aunt May stated with a knowing glance at Ericka.

Now they knew he was alone on this venture, but for how long? So far, he hadn't let anything useful slip. Were they really sick or just waiting for a signal from him?

Ericka wrung her hands and glanced at the clock on the wall. Only one o'clock. It felt like an eternity passed in his presence. How was she going to get through this? Shooting a sideways look his way, she saw Brother Leod busily taking pictures while Aunt May described the room and all its paraphernalia.

Think! How did the detectives on those TV shows draw out information from their suspects? She bit her lower lip. By asking questions, that's how, but what?

Treat him like a research project. A tiny smile tugged at the corner of her mouth. Research was her job. In her own way, she was a detective, a detective of research. She took a deep breath. *Here goes.*

Forcing a friendly smile, she turned to face him, making certain she kept her gaze either on one of his ears or his chin, but never his eyes. She took a deep breath and tried hard to sound sincere. "Brother Leod, it was a pleasant surprise running into you in the village last night. I didn't know monks were allowed out of the monastery at night."

"The brotherhood isn't like that. We're allowed *privileges* many others are not." The way his eyes scoured her body and his tongue wet his lips made Ericka cringe inwardly. The "privileges" he implied, she decided, weren't permitted by a monastery.

Chills shimmered down Ericka's spine and the heat in the air increased by several degrees. A strange sensation prickled her nerve endings and she knew he wanted her, but not in a good way. She sensed it in every fiber of her being, but refused to back down. Gavin needed her. It was the only reason she stood her ground and continued with the friendly charade. Though it nearly made her gag, she added a hint of flirtation to her voice.

"So, you have a place of your own?"

"We own no personal property, but I rented a small place for my time here."

A quick glance over his shoulder told him the old woman sat with that horrid mutt in her lap in a chair, looking out the window. Both were quiet for the first time all day. He leaned near Ericka and whispered. "I'd love to show it to you."

His lips were close to her ear. Breathing in deep, he inhaled her scent. Ah, he thought, the scent of the woman who he planned to use to defeat a MacKinnon. If he could get rid of the crone and her mutt, he could work much faster. Getting Ericka alone would give him the chance he needed.

When her back stiffened, he sensed her fear. *Good, fear me. A mind afraid is easier to control.* Tilting his chin, he tried to focus on her gaze, but she resisted. *Not ready, little one. It's okay. You will be.* He stepped closer.

The need for space barreled through her system when he inched closer, but she willed herself still. Heat flushed Ericka's cheeks. Instantly, she knew his place wasn't the only thing he wanted to show her and the obvious bulge in his jeans backed her suspicions. Her throat went dry and she wasn't sure what to ask next, but didn't have to. Aunt May came to her rescue.

"Are you staying at that lovely little bed-and-breakfast in the village?" Aunt May asked without leaving her seat.

He eased back, giving Ericka the space she desperately needed. With his back to her aunt, he answered.

"No, I've acquired something more private." As he stared directly at her, his enunciation of the word private made Ericka's gut knot and she took the opportunity to step back.

"Oh, I wasn't aware there were other options," Aunt May stated.

"Yes, several." The chime of a bell filled the air and he didn't elaborate on his rental situation.

"It's time for lunch." Aunt May stood, helping Belvedere to the floor and extending her hand to Ericka. "Shall we head out onto the patio? I'm sure Margaret has prepared something wonderful as always."

When he didn't move to follow, Ericka called over her shoulder. "Coming, Brother Leod?"

Not yet, my sweet, he thought as he fell in sync behind them, *but later…*

*****

Ericka filled his thoughts. She made him comfortable and wanted him to be safe. As the curse befell him, he knew she lay beside him and sensed she stayed long past his imprisonment. Her taste lingered on his lips. Her scent was permanently etched in his mind so much so he swore he could smell her wrapped around him.

Her essence surrounded his immobile body and electrified his soul. The memory of her touch, the silk of her skin and the shape of her luscious body drove his vividly active imagination to the brink of frenzied hunger. He wanted her. He needed her. He loved her?

How could that be? How could he have allowed that to happen? Tavia was dead. He accepted that fact. But to love another so quickly, was that morally right? Was it really love?

This woman was different, as was this strange new world to which he awakened. Many things he still needed to learn. His *brathairs* were out there somewhere and he vowed to find them.

But was it right to find love first? Should he be allowed such luxury, since it was because of him and his love of Tavia that the MacKinnons were cursed in the first place?

He wanted to scream, but no voice would form in his stilled throat. Ericka's face floated across the inside of his closed lids. The simple vision soothed his ravaged brain. *Rest* echoed somewhere deep inside his thoughts on the sound of her voice, but he refused to succumb to the need to sleep. His body may rest, but his thoughts continued to battle with his conscience.

Was it right to love again?

Was it fair to his *brathairs*?

Was it really love that warmed his heart?

He knew he wanted to bury himself deep inside her body and nestle within her warmth. But was it love? Her taste singed his lips, her mouth he ached to kiss. The nipples of her breasts fit perfectly in his mouth and he hungered for the chance to suckle from them. Though his body did not physically respond to his thoughts, he wanted her. He wanted in her and on her and her on him.

But was it love?

The question haunted him. He needed to find out the truth, but how? Until nightfall, he was trapped. He wanted to talk to her, to hold her, to taste her lips upon his own, but he could not. Not until the death of the daily sun and the rise of his savior, the moon, would he be released.

'Tis an eternity! He felt as if it were an eternity between the light of day and the fall of night. *'Tis a strange creature to which I hath become.*

* * * * *

Lunch nearly killed him. The old woman prattled on and on about the castle as if he truly cared. Though his patience was wearing thin, he nodded and made the occasional comment. He wanted to be shown the tower and nothing else. Nothing else except Ericka, spread naked before him, waiting anxiously for him to fuck her repeatedly. He bit back the grin his vision provoked.

Finally, they continued the tour and he followed them from room to room, secretly looking for the tower's entrance. No door was obvious. It had to be hidden. Or they hadn't taken him into the room which led to the main tower. He decided that at the rate they were going, it would take too long. When they reached the top of one of the other five towers, he took a chance.

"Will we be getting to that tower today?" he asked politely, pointing to the un-renovated center tower of the castle.

"No," escaped from Ericka in an unwanted rush. She cleared her throat, then tried again in a calmer manner. "No. That tower was sealed off years ago because of its run-down condition. Until Aunt May has the opportunity to have it rebuilt, no one is allowed inside."

"That's a shame. Just think, what fun it would be to explore something that old?" He turned his back to them and took a few pictures of the tower from the window. Glancing over his shoulder at Ericka, he added. "Imagine what ancient *things* we might find hidden there."

She shot a split second daggered glare at him. It was the first eye contact from her without the dark shades over her glasses. It was too quick for him to take control of her thoughts. Though he hadn't controlled her, she gave him an answer without knowing it. He bit back a laugh. A MacKinnon was hidden there. Was it the big boy who was with her last night? It didn't really matter. Though in his gut, he knew it was.

That was the reason they hadn't led him there. They were protecting him. Did they know he was after the MacKinnon? No, he smiled slightly as he adjusted his camera. He'd given them no cause to mistrust him. Besides, they thought he was a monk.

Focusing his telescopic lens on the tower, he snapped a few pictures as the wheels in his mind turned. It would take days to find a way into that tower. Time was something he didn't want to waste.

"We need to go. The sun is going down and without it the light isn't good in these towers. It makes it difficult to see to descend the stairs."

He heard the tinge of nervousness in her voice and knew that he was right. The MacKinnon couldn't come out until dark. It was the way of the curse. Every aspect of the curse was embedded in his brain. Somehow, she set him free of the stone to walk the world as a man condemned. She must have found an anti-curse. But it wasn't complete. Ideas rolled at a such rapid pace that his mind barely kept up.

Visions of the night before flashed through his thoughts. A grin spread his lips. Why hadn't he thought of this before? *Too busy thinking like the older generation of the brotherhood,* he chided himself as he followed the women and the annoying mutt. He hated dogs and fought the urge to boot it down the stairs. That wouldn't look good. His eyes glued to Ericka's juicy bottom, he licked his lips and his cock stiffened and twitched.

As far as the brotherhood was concerned, he felt it was time for the old to be gone and the new to claim the rightful ownership of the book. *His rightful ownership of the book,* he snickered to himself. A new twist to his wicked plan brewed in his skull.

Chapter Nineteen

ꟷ

Ericka walked Brother Leod to his car. Aunt May took Belvedere to the kitchen to prepare his dinner. *Good,* he sighed. *Finally, I have her alone.*

Brother Leod opened the small trunk of his beat-up car. If she wouldn't lead him to the MacKinnon, then he would make sure the MacKinnon came to him. Quietly, he gathered a roll of masking tape from the tool kit he kept there.

"Would you care to see some of the pictures I took yesterday?" he shouted around the edge of the trunk lid to conceal the rip of tape from her ears.

"Of course," she lied with a thin smile on her lips. Anything to get rid of him.

Absently, she checked the clip-ons, making sure they were in place. She wasn't taking any chances. One glance over her shoulder and she knew sunset was near. An urgent need to get rid of Brother Leod surged through her veins.

Gavin would rise soon. Her heart skipped a beat. The thought of seeing him gave her the confidence to face Brother Leod for a few more moments. She took a deep breath. Not long and this would be over for the day. Tomorrow it would start again, she thought with a shiver.

"Come here. I have a box full of wonderful shots you might enjoy."

His voice made her skin crawl. Was he up to something? A warning flashed inside her skull. *Make him come to you with the pictures.* But she wanted him gone, so she failed to heed the signals that something wasn't right. Time was short, Gavin would soon be here and she had had enough of Brother Leod for one day. Forcing her legs to obey, she stepped toward the trunk.

As she got closer, the air thickened with heat. The hairs on the back of her neck stood on end. A faint burn singed her palm. All were warning signs she chose to ignore. Whatever it took, she was determined to get him to leave.

A bright flash directly in her face blurred her vision. Temporarily blinded, she felt one of his hands clasp the back of her head. Fire shot through her brain at his touch. Its severity rendered her immobile. The other hand slapped a sticky substance across her mouth, muffling her screams.

Repeatedly, she blinked behind her shades, but still couldn't focus straight. Everything was a blur. Uncertain if it was from the camera's flash or the fiery heat of his touch, Ericka attempted to wiggle free of his grip. No matter how she tried, her body would not respond. Her limbs turned into dead weights. How was he doing this?

Using the same sticky substance she assumed to be tape, he bound her wrists behind her back. A massive fire roared through her system and pain riddled every aspect of her limbs when he lifted her. She fought the debilitating sensation of his touch, even though it threatened to consume her.

"You're mine now." The words seethed on his intensely heated breath against her ear. Possessively, he kissed her lips through the rough tape. The sensation of being scalded tortured her mouth. Pure liquid heat slithered down her throat. At no other time in her life had she ever been as thankful as she was now for a piece of tape. For without it, she thought her mouth would have melted if he made direct contact.

Belvedere's bark echoed. He jerked from the unwanted kiss and dropped her in the trunk. Twisting her ankles, he wound tape tightly around them. Suddenly the dark clip-on shades were grabbed from her glasses. Instinct took over and she shut her eyes against his powerful glare.

"You won't need these," he laughed, tossing them to the ground and slamming the trunk lid closed.

The sound of growls and snarls penetrated her tight-fit prison. Belvedere came to her rescue. Pants ripped and Brother Leod screamed. Ericka hoped Belvedere went for the balls as she silently urged him on in his attack. Within seconds, the crystal clear sound of a pain-filled yelp pierced her ears. Her heart stopped and the breath hitched in her throat. *What had that bastard done*?

Heavy footsteps ran to the driver's side and the car sputtered to a start. *Oh God*! *No*! She heard Aunt May's screams as the car surged forward. Was Belvedere all right? She strained to hear over the sound of flinging gravel from under the rear tires. Nothing. Not even a whimper. The noise of the car drowned everything out.

The car! *Ohmygod*! *I'm in a moving car.*

Nausea flooded her stomach. She was trapped. Sweat beaded upon her upper lip and brow. She couldn't catch her breath. The space was small and cramped. The sharp edge of a toolbox ground between her shoulder blades. There was no window for more air. Bouncing around, every bone being jarred, every muscle being bruised, her lungs couldn't work. Suffocation was bound to happen.

Think! *Think*! screamed through her brain. The taste of bile rose to the back of her throat. No matter how hard she swallowed, she couldn't make it go away. The horrid flavor tortured her tongue and threatened to gag her. If the ride didn't kill her, then asphyxiation probably would.

Where was he taking her?

What did he want?

Tears stung her eyes. *Gavin*! *I failed you.*

* * * * *

"Gavin! Gavin!"

Aunt May's desperate cries echoed through the tunnel. They were the first words to grace his ears upon awakening. Fear soaked his soul with the knowledge that something was wrong. Where was Ericka? She was supposed to be here. He rushed through the tunnel on hands and knees. The bellowed sound of his name nearly shattered his eardrums when he almost collided face-to-face with Aunt May, who stood screaming his name at the tunnel's entrance.

"Milady, 'tis enough." He landed on his feet in front of her and grasped her elbows. The sight of tears gushing down her face and a whimpering dog in her arms doubled the knot in his gut. Something was terribly wrong. "What happened? Where's Ericka?"

"Heeee," her voice cracked through the onslaught of tears. "He has her."

A weak, pain-filled howl from Belvedere emphasized her statement. The puppy was injured. Gently, he took the animal in his arms. Aunt May's hand shook as she stroked the puppy's coat.

"He tried to save her. That bastard kicked him. I think he may have broken his ribs." Aunt May dabbed at the tears with the corner of the long sleeve of her kimono.

Gavin held the puppy wrapped in the curve of one arm and checked his body with gentle motions of his fingertips. No bones seemed to be broken. But when he touched the animal's side, he yelped.

Aunt May cooed, patting his head. "It's okay, baby. Gavin didn't mean to hurt you. Belvedere tried to protect Ericka. He took a bite out of his pants leg. That's when the bastard kicked him."

Water-filled eyes met Gavin's and he asked, though he knew the answer. "Who has Ericka?"

"Brother Leod. We have to get her back," Aunt May replied.

"Don't ye worry, miss. We will." Gavin looked across Aunt May's head, following the voice and spotted Ned and Margaret in the dining room doorway.

Ned walked over to Gavin, then leaned around him, peeking at the hole in the wall. Gavin and Aunt May had forgotten to cover it. He then held his expressionless gaze leveled with Gavin's.

" A MacKinnon ye be?"

"*Aye*." Gavin stated the one-word reply as he handed the wounded puppy to Aunt May. He held his form to full height as the elderly man seemed to inspect him from head to foot.

"'Tis true the curse?" Ned spoke again with his chin tilted up and his unwavering gaze held firm to Gavin's.

"*Aye* 'tis true." Unsure of what would happen next, Gavin stood his ground. Ned circled him twice before extending his hand. Gavin clasped Ned's arm in the traditional grip, forearm to forearm, hand to elbow and elbow to hand, they shook.

"'Twill be me honor to help." Ned nodded at Gavin as they released their embrace.

"Thank you, *M'Caraid*." Gavin clasped his shoulder and called him his friend in the ancient language. He knew Ned understood, since many of the men of the tavern still conversed in a form of the ancient tongue. Gavin lifted his chin and caught Aunt May's gaze across the top of Ned's head.

"*Milady*, 'tis time ye returned me kilt. 'Twill be needin' to be me to face my enemy."

* * * * *

With Gavin dressed in his kilt, his plaid draped from left shoulder to right hip, the brooch of his ancestors fastened in place and his trusted claymore sheathed at his side, he lowered into the front seat of the metal beast beside Ned. Margaret helped Aunt May, with Belvedere in her arms, into the backseat. The plan was to drop them off at the closest person around to being an animal doctor, Ballock McNab's place. His was the last farm on the main road leading into the village. Then Ned would take Gavin to the tavern to find out where Brother Leod was staying.

"Ifn' anyone can help yer dog, it'll be old Ball," Margaret said, comforting Aunt May as they pulled up to the front of the McNab's farmhouse.

Torn between the need to take care of her baby, Belvedere, and the knowledge that Ericka was in danger, Aunt May froze, unable to move from the backseat. Gavin reached over the seat and touched her cheek. "*Milady*, know that Ericka 'twill be safe."

He lifted her chin and held her tearful gaze. "'Tis my solemn oath to ye."

Aunt May couldn't speak. She simply nodded as Margaret helped her from the car with Belvedere clasped tight against her chest.

After leaving the women, Ned continued his frantic driving pace. They made it to the tavern in record time. If there was a place to be rented in this village, it had to be from Angus MacDonell, the barkeeper. Not only did he own the tavern, he also owned several other businesses and the only two rental cottages in the village.

They stood huddled at the far corner of the bar as Angus answered. His eyes never left the sight of Gavin dressed in full ancient Scottish regalia.

"*Aye*, Ned. I rented the cottage o'er on the end o' Beacon Road ta a young fella. What's it ta ya? An why ya dressed to the hilt?" He nodded his chin at Gavin.

"'Tis be no one's business but me own," Gavin replied, tossing another of the ancient coins to Angus, who caught it. "'Twill do no good fer this to go any further."

"Should ye be needn' help…" The brawny man paused. Angus tossed the coin back at Gavin, who caught it without even a flinch. Angus raised his arms out wide from his body. "All ye needs ta do is ask."

Though the other men had no clue as to what was going on, shouts of "*Hear*! *Hear*!" echoed from behind raised mugs as Gavin and Ned exited the tavern. Gavin glanced over his shoulder at the tavern. When they got back into the belly of the metal beast, Ned must have seen his look of surprise.

"Ye has more friends than ye thinks," Ned stated with a shrug, then started the engine.

* * * * *

The horrendous movement stopped. With the slam of the door, she knew he was no longer in the car. She lay quiet, straining for a speck of audible sound of something she recognized. A dog barked in the distance and the rumble of other cars was faint, but clear. To her disappointment, no voices or sounds of people passed her prison. Where had he gone? Did he plan to leave her here? Was the oxygen going to last?

Constriction seized her throat, though she knew the last thought was ridiculous. Trunks were not airtight, especially this one. Being bounced around, she saw several rusted-through spots, where not only air came in, but dust and dirt as well. It was a small relief to know that air had a way in.

She shook uncontrollably in the cramped confinement. Her arms throbbed and her legs were numb. Though it was difficult, she tried to make noise. Knocking her feet against the trunk granted her a low thump. She tried to keep the limited action going, hoping someone would hear. Her efforts were not only tiring, but fruitless.

Relief washed over her when he finally opened the trunk. Fresh air. She breathed in deep. But her reprieve was short-lived. Before her eyesight adjusted, he flung a blanket over her head. In rough, swift movements, he wrapped her completely in the scratchy woolen garb. Lifting her, he tossed her limp form over his shoulder. Each step dug his shoulder into her stomach and she thought she'd throw up. It would serve him right if she puked down his back, but she couldn't. The tape was still firmly in place, not allowing any form of sound to escape, much less a spew of the limited contents of her stomach.

One, two, three steps up he stomped, then stopped. Hinges creaked as he opened a door. Was she at his place in the village? Where had he taken her? How was she going to escape? During her stomach-turning ride, she strained her brain to concentrate, though the waves of motion sickness made it difficult. If only she had her medicine or Gavin.

Oh, Gavin, please be safe, she prayed.

Slam! He closed the door behind them. Heavy footsteps clomped across the floor until he turned into another room. Her head banged against the doorframe. Stars shot behind clenched eyelids. It wouldn't do to scream. No one would hear through the tape. She winced and held her tears at bay.

After the uncaring way he carried her, she feared he would drop her, but instead he knelt, then lowered her to the floor as gentle as a newborn babe. Light filtered in as he unwrapped the blanket from her face. Repeatedly, she blinked, focusing.

"Welcome to my home," Brother Leod spouted proudly, sitting her up.

Though her glasses were smudged, the sight of the makeshift altar was clear. Two portraits sat, one on either side of a large trunk. A slender black spiral notebook lay open on top of the trunk. Her head nearly spun from her neck at the sight of the walls plastered with pictures of her.

"As you can see, I've been busy." He splayed his arm out wide in a sweeping motion.

His wicked laughter slithered through the portals that were her ears and she wished that she could close them. No matter how she tried, she couldn't help but watch him. With his back to her, he lit a candle, then used it to light all the others. Within moments, she was captive in a ring of fire. Once finished with his task, he turned to face her. The candle glow enhanced his evil aura and its dark essence shook her to the core.

Don't look him in the eye, whispered at the base of her brain as she followed his movements. He circled the ring several times and chanted in some language that she'd never heard before. The flames around her shot up toward the ceiling, but did not reach it. Her eyes sprang opened wide. He controlled the fire.

"Yes, Ericka, I do control the fire." His voice turned strangely deep and husky.

He read her thoughts! Was she imagining the sensation of someone traipsing around in her head? The low rumble of his wicked laugh gave her chills and she knew she wasn't. Somehow, he was in her head.

When he spun around and walked to a narrow door on the opposite side of the room, the sensation ceased.

"Not only do I control that…" He jerked the door open.

Brilliant, red light shone from a large, floating bubble inside the closet. Ericka had no clue as to what it was, but the color was magnificent and bright. He swept his hand in front of the object and the red cloudiness inside dissipated.

Akira!

"I control Akira."

In a flash, he spun around and stared down at her. Without thought, she glared up at him. *No,* shouted through her brain. Too late. He captured her eyes in his unrelenting gaze. She tried to pull away, but failed. It felt as if some sort of invisible vise held her gaze locked to his. The flames around her died down, allowing him to step into the circle. His eyes never released hers. They looked like flowing waves of grain, sucking her in deeper.

He lowered to his knees beside her and the air thickened, making it more difficult for her to breathe. His hand on her cheek ignited a flame to her skin. As he trailed his fingertips along her face, to the curve of her chin, down the length of her neck, then stopping at her collarbone, pure fire singed her skin. It felt as if he left his mark in a firebrand along the slender trail of his fingers. She grappled for air the moment his hand moved and grasped her breasts in a crushing hold.

As he leaned in closer, she couldn't help but focus on his eyes. Fields of waving wheat swirled, mesmerizing her. His other hand removed her glasses and tossed them across the room. "And now, I control you."

"Watch, Akira," he commanded without looking away from Ericka. "Watch as I remove the stench of your brother from her body."

Grabbing the front of her shirt, he ripped it open. Buttons flew and she was powerless to stop him. The touch of his hands on her flesh was like a lava bath. If she could look down, she knew she would see charred skin in his wake. Clasping her head, he traced the outline of her lips with his tongue while the tape was still intact.

Their noses touched, the closeness made her vision blur, but she could not even blink. Scorching breath burned through the tape to her lips as he spoke more words of some forgotten language or maybe he made it up. At the moment, she couldn't think straight. His nonsensical words echoed in her head and her body reacted.

Every ounce of her blood heated several degrees above normal. With a strength she wouldn't have guessed he possessed, he repositioned her onto her knees without releasing the vise-grip hold he had on her mind through their gaze. He left her ankles and wrists bound together.

With one swift movement, he snatched the tape from her mouth, causing a ripping pain which broke their eye contact. Her head snapped back and her mouth flew open. The scream was stalled in her throat by a fist to her stomach, leaving her gasping for air with her body balled forward. He grabbed the knot of hair at the base of her skull and stretched her neck back, forcing her to return to the prior kneeling position.

"Don't make me do that again, Ericka," he stated through clenched teeth against her ear.

Producing a large knife, he held it to her throat. "Now be a good little sex kitten and don't scream, or else this could get messy."

She couldn't imagine where he had hidden it, and truly didn't want know. But she knew where she wanted to stick it. She glared at his back when he stood and left the room. In a desperate search for Akira, she squinted into focus. Though she tried to muster enough saliva to speak, her mouth was dry and her voice scraped out on a raspy whisper. "Akira, can you hear me?"

The bright redhead bobbed yes. The bubble didn't move. Akira's mouth moved, but no sound reached Ericka's ears. This was useless. How was she going to get her out of that thing if she didn't even know what that thing was? She wasn't given the opportunity to think. Brother Leod returned with a bucket filled to the brim with soapy water.

Stepping into the ring of fire, he set the bucket beside her. One flick of the knife and her bra popped apart. The sight of his tongue licking his lips made the nauseous waves form a riptide in her bowels. He dipped the cloth into the steaming hot water with one hand, while he gripped the handle of the knife with the other.

"'Tis the stench of a MacKinnon I remove. 'Tisn't it, lass?" He wiped the dripping wet cloth across her chest.

She flinched from the sizzle of the sudsy hot cloth and felt it burn with the intensity of more than just water. *What was in that bucket*? She glared at him down the length of the knife held close to the tip of her chin. His eyes were swirls of wheat fields, swirls and swirls of flowing grains of golden wheat. Heat thickened the air around her, making it hard for her to breathe.

He pushed back the tattered bra and smoothed the cloth across each nipple in slow circular motions. Against her will, the wayward renegades stood to full attention. Smiling, he lowered the knife to her waist. The tip pressed into her flesh, but not hard enough to break the skin.

"Umm, now I can taste you."

The moment his lips touched her sensitive nipple, a forest fire roared to life beneath her skin and almost consumed her soul. His closeness, his dark aura collided with her own. Did he know what he was doing to her soul? Was he even aware of the firestorm within every cell of her skin? If he kept this up, he would destroy her with each suckle, with each nibble of his teeth. Why was her body reacting this way? Sure, she hated him. But why did it feel as if she'd melt like candle wax?

Each breath she inhaled scorched her lungs. She had to gain control, but how? He couldn't win. She refused to let him. Somehow, she would defeat him. Somehow, she'd turn this against him. Prying her eyes open, she turned her gaze to Akira's.

Though she spoke no words, pure strength exuded from the bright, green eyes of the transparent woman in the bubble. *Hold on! Help 'tis on the way,* flew through her thoughts like a banner attached to the back of a plane. Somehow she heard what Akira needed her to know.

He gripped her chin, forcing her gaze back to his. The quick lick of his lips was her only forewarning. But it wasn't enough for her to brace herself for his touch. His lips crushed hers. His tongue forced its way into her mouth, plundering deep, making her gag.

Gavin...screamed through Ericka's brain right before a fireball flashed behind her eyes and brought her teetering on the edge of destruction. Then all went black.

Chapter Twenty

ℵ

Beacon Road was a short drive from the tavern. It was a dead-end street and Angus' rental cottage was the last house on the left side of the road. Ned didn't turn down Beacon. Instead, he passed it and parked a street over, which ran parallel with it. Together, they got out of the car.

Ned led the way, followed by Gavin. They eased unseen through yards and across several fences until they were in the bushes across the street. The cottage appeared dark. Brother Leod's beat-up car was parked in front.

When Ned started to move from the bushes, Gavin grabbed his arm.

"*M'Caraid,* 'tis my journey from here." He stared down at the older man.

"Know that if ye needs me, jus' signal and I'll be right behind ye," he whispered, then resumed his position squatted down, taking over sentry duty behind the bushes.

Gavin eased out of cover, knowing someone he could trust watched his back. In any battle, this was important. He didn't know if this Brother Leod was alone or acted in a force of many. With Ned in the bushes, at least he'd be alerted should more of this clan MacGillivray called the brotherhood appear.

The metal beast Ned pointed out as belonging to MacGillivray sat in front of the cottage. He crossed the street, keeping the car between him and the cottage, using it as cover. Hunched down, he meticulously calculated each step along the side of the metal beast until he was crouched low beside the rear end. The faint scent of lavender rushed his senses. Her essence lingered from somewhere near his hiding place.

When he touched the end of the metal beast, a mouthlike cavern opened. Sword drawn, he jumped back, prepared to do battle. When nothing moved, he crouched forward and peered over the edge into a small crevice in the ass of the metal beast.

'Tis strange, this compartment of sorts, he thought, scouring its contents. Her scent was even stronger now. He must have imprisoned her in here. His eyes flew opened wide. *'Tis how she must have traveled*!

Ericka! Her fears washed over him with each intake of her fading essence. His nostrils flared and his heartbeat shifted into rapid speed. Did the monster know her fears? Did he feed upon them by thrusting her in the metal beast's hidden chamber and bringing her here? His shoulders flinched back and his biceps flexed as he procured his huge claymore in a fierce battle stance.

My enemy hath made a grave mistake. He inhaled deep, thriving on the scent he treasured. *I have had two hundred years of rest and every muscle hungers for revenge.*

"If 'tis my soul thee seek," Gavin whispered under his breath, weaving his way like a predator in search of prey to the door without being seen in the shadows of the night, "then ye mus' fight me for it."

Prepared to break the door down, Gavin was surprised when it opened at a twist of the knob. *A trick*! *An ambush, maybe*. He flattened against the outer wall and peeked around the door's edge into the darkness. Light filtered from a room down the hall. Grateful that the hinges spoke no squeak, he pushed the door open just enough to slip inside. After a moment to allow his eyes to adjust, he held his sword at the ready and stepped on hushed footfalls toward the room with the glow of light.

His senses told him she was there. Her scent filled the air with each step. A low male voice stung his ears, MacGillivray it must be. His jaw tightened and his shoulders squared as he craned his neck to peek around the opened door's edge. A glimpse of his enemy's back fueled the ravaged hunger for retaliation. The vision of her motionless on the floor sent an anger-tipped arrow straight through his heart.

The sight of Ericka half-naked, lying in the center of a ring of lit candles, tore at his soul. He pulled back, becoming one with the wall to gather his tactical thoughts. Though he swallowed hard, the taste of pure hatred would not recede. She lay there because of him, because of his sins of the past.

Closing his eyes tight, he tried to focus. Both hands gripped the hilt of his trusted claymore. He raised the steel-forged blade and pressed it flat against his forehead. She needed him to be the warrior he knew lived inside his skin. Though he won many battles in his past, this was different. He must not fail her as he failed Tavia and his unborn child.

With a deep breath, he sprang into the room, sword raised and battle-ready. Neither person within the circle moved. The man he knew to be his adversary sat with his back to him and did not flinch at his arrival. This showed a sign of true courage or was the sign of a madman. A quick glance showed him Ericka's likeness covered the walls and an altar sat with two pictures. One he did not know. The other…Hume MacGillivray.

'Tis madness, he decided.

"MacGillivray," he growled at the man kneeling beside his Ericka. She still did not move. The sight of her breasts bare and MacGillivray's hand upon them heightened the hatred in his gut to a point that he wanted nothing more than to remove the offensive hand from the demon at the wrist so he could no longer feel her beauty. Flexing his hands around the sword hilt, he tried to rein in the disgust boiling in his bowels. The monster would pay for the indiscretions he inflicted on Ericka.

"'Tis me ye want, not the lass."

"*Aye*." A wicked smile shot at Gavin from across the man's shoulder when he turned to look at him.

Slowly, the man rose and turned to face Gavin. Fire danced in the glint from the steel of the knife he twisted in his hand. A look of pure insanity met Gavin's across the ring of fire.

"But ye are wrong. I want ye both. Ye for the treasure your death shall provide once I've given proof to the brotherhood and Ericka..." His voice trailed off as he stared at Gavin.

Pure evil shone in the irises of the eyes he met. The golden-colored eyes glowed with hints of fire, which swirled and twisted in his glare like mini-tornadoes. Gavin stiffened when he jumped from the ring, positioning himself in a mock stance. Was the man daft? Did he think this would intimidate him?

Brother Leod tilted his chin, flipping the knife from hand to hand as he taunted. "Ericka shall be the vessel of my seed. That is, after I've taught her the ways and she learns to control the heat of my soul within hers."

"'Tis my heat that shall be the only heat within her soul," Gavin growled from between clenched teeth as his nostrils flared and his jaw tightened.

They circled one another, each sizing the other. Nothing about him scared Gavin. He watched steadily for the man to make his move. Then he would take him down. Once his back was to the circle of fire, Gavin saw the open closet for the first time. The sight of his sister's spirit imprisoned in a red globe of substance startled him. His eyes opened wide, soaking in the eerie sight.

"What sorcery is this?" he snapped.

"My sorcery, as ye hath called it. Akira is my prisoner and with you gone, so shall she be gone. The world shall be rid of two of the MacKinnon filth with the power of my blows."

Watching closely, he caught Gavin's mistake. For a moment, the MacKinnon's gaze faltered, giving him the edge. Since he could never get within arm's length of Gavin, he chose the accuracy of flight.

The hot steel of the long-bladed knife seared into Gavin's shoulder. Pain inflamed the muscle and scorched into the tendons, but he bit his tongue and refused to show any signs of pain. Blood oozed down his arm. He shifted the hilt of the heavy sword into his right hand. Little did the MacGillivray know, but he had been trained by his father so that the weapon of choice was a natural extension of either hand.

"'Tis an unfair fight. Ye hath no longer a weapon," Gavin taunted without so much as a flinch of pain in his face.

The blade seemed to have a life of its own. Upon penetration, the knife was hot, but now, with each breath he took, it intensified.

"Are ye sure about that," Brother Leod questioned, tauntingly.

Fire burned down Gavin's arm and still he held his muscles in check. He raised the ancient sword and leveled it at Brother Leod's chest. Glaring down its unwavering length into the spiraling fields of golden grain, he stated, "Ye hath no weapon."

Brother Leod snorted, making his mocking comment once again. "Ye sure about that? The beads of sweat upon your brow lead me to believe otherwise."

His eyes! Gavin saw evil dance in the swirls. The monster controlled the heat through his eyes. Swiftly, he lunged, thrusting his sword. Though his mark was true, he chose to inflict enough pain to break the devilish hold, yet not induce the gift of death to this heathen creation. He needed answers and a dead man would grace his ears with none.

"Agggh!" Brother Leod screamed, crumbling to the floor. His hands covered the gaping hole in his chest. Though the wound was not fatal, crimson blood flowed through his fingers and soaked the front of his clothes. As he lay gasping for air, he prayed to the portraits. "This should not have been."

Gavin ignored his mumbled words and lowered his sword. With one blow, the battle was over. Pulling the knife from his shoulder and dropping it to the floor, he huffed, "A warrior ye are not."

"Akira," he stated. Her spirit was trapped. Somehow, he would free her.

Tis not me who needs thee, echoed in his head. He spun around and found Ericka awake. How long she'd been that way, he did not know. Wiping the blood from his sword in one swipe, he sheathed it, leapt into the ring of lit candles and knelt at her side.

"Gavin." Her whispered word was a gift to his ears as he gathered her into his arms.

"Ericka." Pressing tender kisses along her brow, "*M'Gaol,*" followed on heated breath against her ear.

"*M'Gaol,*" she repeated in a whisper. He called her his love. Did he mean it as she had? Tears simmered in the corners of her eyes.

Moments earlier, through a fog, she heard his voice. It guided her back from the edge of oblivion. The rich timbre of his deep, Scottish brogue pulled her mind from the dark recesses of which it had crawled to be away from Brother Leod.

His scent captivated her senses. Just knowing he was in the room gave her the strength to return. Weak, she sat up and saw his blurry massive form. Instinct told her it was Gavin facing off with Brother Leod. The glint of the knife's steel flashed, catching her attention.

Parched, she could not muster enough salvia to scream. She knew his intent the moment Gavin's focus was on his sister. The monster! She had to stop him, but she couldn't move. Her wrists and ankles were still bound. It felt as if her heart shattered when the knife penetrated his flesh.

She watched through blurred vision, helpless to aid Gavin. Masterfully, he dealt with Brother Leod. He fought the devil and won. Relief washed over her. But was it for her or for revenge that he fought?

"Ericka, lass."

He cradled her in his arms, though it pained him to move the one. She felt so right, so natural against his chest. He thought he had lost her, that the evil had somehow consumed her and drained her of her spirit.

Seeing her awake and moving was the greatest sight he could think of. Never would he let anyone or anything hurt her again. Somehow he'd find a way to protect her both at night and in the day. Somehow…But not now. Now he wanted to hold her, to caress her skin and know that she was alive. Stroking her hair, he asked, "Are ye all right? Did he hurt ye?"

She shook her head. She saw his blood for the first time, soaking through his tunic and plaid.

"Gavin, you're hurt!" she gasped.

"'Tis merely a scratch, *M'Gaol*." He laughed, lifting her chin. "I'm fine, but you…"

He pulled the edges of her shirt closed, then twisted her around to undo the bindings before he continued. "You need protection, even by the light of day."

After removing the tape from her wrists and ankles, he helped her to her feet. Ericka caught the subtle blurred movement in the corner of her eye. Brother Leod slithered his way across the floor. His goal was obvious, but she wasn't quick enough to stop him from reaching the knife.

Though her muscles trembled, she leapt past Gavin, lunging at the blurry shadow of Brother Leod before he could come to his feet completely. Her swift action set him tumbling backward into the closet. The moment he made contact with Akira's prison, it sounded as if a steak had been dropped on a grill.

A sharp sizzle ripped through the air, accompanied by his screams. Smoke emanated from him as he shook violently, becoming engulfed by red fumes. The touch of his body against the magic prison was ominous. Heat intensified the room. When she tried to stand, a sudden burst of bright, red light fueled by explosive energy sent Ericka flying across the room, landing against Gavin's chest. The blow knocked him down and they tumbled backward intertwined together. His hulking frame wrapped around her for protection until they came to a skidding halt against the far wall.

Candles skittered across the floor, leaving trails of hot wax and flames in their path. Fire licked its lips and set its place at the table, devouring first the rug, then flashing its way up the curtains. The room would soon be engulfed by the demon spawn of heat and flame-riddled devastation.

The simple task of breathing caused them great pain, but Gavin would not be a victim to this avalanche of disaster. He pulled himself up, bringing Ericka to her feet with him. His arm never left her waist when she swayed and her knees almost buckled.

Gavin! *Hurry*! *This way*! Akira's spirit hovered free beside them.

Without giving her a chance, he scooped Ericka into his arms. Clutching her battered body close to his chest, he powered his way through the all-consuming havoc of the flames and intense heat with the spirit of his sister as his guide. Smoke-filled air laced each breath he took and singed his lungs but he had to get Ericka to safety. He could not lose her too.

When Gavin stumbled from the burning room, he collided with Ned in the hallway. Smoke-filled lungs made Gavin cough and his knees weak.

"This way, MacKinnon. Ye hold her. I've got ye." The older man's arm that wrapped around his waist held a strength that surprised him.

Forcing his legs to move, he followed Ned's lead, each step a painful motion, each breath a heavy effort as smoke laid its claim to the air around them and flames traced their path. The door stood opened wide where Akira's spirit shone bright, giving them the edge they needed to leave the hovel of heated death behind.

'Tis home I shall see thee again. With that said, she vanished.

It took every last ounce of muscle the two men had left to dash through the doorway. They were rushed by several of the men from the tavern, including Angus MacDonell. They helped Ned get Gavin and Ericka to the lawn across the street from the cottage.

Many of the local residents were gathered, dragging hoses and carrying buckets of water to douse the flames. Sirens screamed in the air. The village's only fire truck and volunteer crew joined in the tireless efforts to save the burning cottage from total destruction.

"This what ye had in mind, lad?" Angus nodded at the cottage as he helped Gavin lay Ericka on a blanket one of the neighbor ladies provided. The tone of his voice was not one of anger, but held a twist of humor in his words.

"*Nay*, Angus." Gavin cocked his brow and smiled. Cool air soothed his lungs, forcing him to cough as he choked out the words. "I canna say that it was."

Angus stood to return to the firefight. His hearty laugh lifted Gavin's tired spirits, but the slap of Angus' large hand on his hurt shoulder made him wince and bite back the pain. *'Tis no time for that now.* Ericka needed him.

He brushed back a strand of loose hair. She was safe. "Ericka," he whispered, kneeling closer and pressing his lips to her brow.

"Ericka," he spoke against her skin.

Her body bucked, as she hacked out deep, raspy coughs, gasping for clean air. His voice jump-started her brain into action. Her chest heavy, as was the weight of her skull. What happened? Were they dead? She forced her eyes to open, though they stung and burned when she did. Straining to lift to her elbows, every muscle ached as if she'd been stomped by a herd of cattle.

"Gavin," she rasped from a desert-dry throat, followed by a serenade of hacking coughs as she gasped for more air.

Warm arms lifted her onto his lap. One arm held her close, while the other wrapped the blanket around her chilled body. Safe, she was at last safe and in the folds of the only place she wished to be.

"MacKinnon, I've brought the car around. We needs ta be getting' ye home whilst we still 'ave the cover of the excitement an' no one be noticin' yer absence." Ned spoke quick and soft as his head bobbed in the direction of the burning cottage. He helped Gavin to his feet with Ericka still huddled against his chest and her arms wrapped tight around his neck.

Gavin followed Ned's every move. He was right. No one noticed the couple as they toppled into the backseat. All eyes and hands were trained on the battle of the fire. No one heard as Ned turned the car around and left the tragic scene behind.

No one except, for one. Severely burned, Leod disappeared into the night, unseen by anyone.

Chapter Twenty-One

ꟈ

Though at first Gavin resisted, Ericka did not listen and held pressure to his wounded shoulder while they barreled through the night with Ned behind the wheel. She ripped strips of cloth from the waist of her shirt and tied them as tight as possible across the slender, but deep, hole in his muscles. Without her glasses, the wound looked blurred, but fierce. Hopefully, it wouldn't look as bad when they reached the castle, medical supplies and her spare pair of glasses.

"We need to take you to a hospital," Ericka stated. "You need a doctor."

"What I need is you." A weak smile tugged at his mouth as he touched her cheek.

Ericka cuddled into his lap and kissed his lips. His good arm wrapped around her waist, holding her secure against his chest. Her head fit perfectly nestled in the crook of his neck with his head leaned against the top of hers. The faint scent of lavender tickled his nose, even though it was masked with remnants of smoke and soot. It felt good just to hold her, knowing she was safe.

In the driveway of the castle, Aunt May and Margaret ran out to greet them the moment the car came to a halt. Ballock MacNab had driven them home after attending to the bruised and battered, but not broken, Belvedere.

"Ericka, oh Ericka, I was so frightened. Thank God you're safe," Aunt May cried, tugging her out of the car and into an overpowering hug.

When Gavin's feet touched the gravel and he stood, Aunt May fell against him, wrapping him and Ericka in an emotional embrace. "Thank you, thank you," she gasped through the onslaught of tears.

Gavin winced. Pain shot down his arm when Aunt May grabbed it, but he did not pull back. He smiled down at the older woman. "'Tis all right, *milady*."

"Aunt May," Ericka uttered. "Gavin's hurt. We need to get him inside."

"Oh my, I'm sorry. I didn't mean to hurt you," Aunt May exclaimed at the sight of his makeshift bandage.

"Ye dinna know. 'Tis nothing," Gavin stated.

"'Tis nothing, indeed. We need to get you cleaned up," Ericka snapped, grabbing his good arm and tugging him toward the front door.

"Ned, fetch me my kit and meet us in the kitchen," Margaret shouted over her shoulder, hurrying in behind them.

* * * * *

"Where'd you learn to stitch like that?" Ericka asked as Margaret cleaned up her medical supplies.

"When ye've got two pigheaded men in the house, ye learn ta do many things ye never thought ye would. Take me Ned there…" She nodded over her shoulder as she spoke. "Stitched 'im up more times than I care ta remember."

As she handed Ericka a tube of antibiotic cream, a roll of gauze and a roll of tape, she continued. "Take this upstairs, cover the stitches good with the ointment, then wrap 'im up tight when he's done in the bath. Make sure he doesn't get those new stitches wet."

When Ericka walked into the bathroom, Gavin was out of the tub and had the towel wrapped around his waist. Water glistened on his thick muscled chest and dripped from his loose long dark hair. The scent of musky lavender soap teased her senses. He looked truly edible standing there, helplessly fighting his wet tangled mop with a comb in his one good hand.

"Here, let me help." She set the supplies Margaret gave her on the toilet lid and took the comb from his hand. As gently as she possibly could, she removed each tangled web from the thick dark mass.

He watched her every move in the reflection of the mirror. With each brush of her hand against the skin of his back, he wanted her. The sensuous flow of her fingers through his hair ignited his need. The quiet member beneath the towel awakened, he turned and caught her hand in mid-motion.

"*M'Gaol*, thy touch has me on fire," he gasped on ragged breath.

Lifting her hand to his lips, he inhaled her scent deep. His shaft twitched and he knew he wanted her. The pain in his shoulder was nothing compared to the painful need growing for her in his loins. She was his and he intended to make her see that.

Before sunrise, he planned to show her how much he truly wanted her. It was she he wanted, not Tavia. He sighed against her palm. Tavia was a sweet memory. But Ericka, she was the here and now. She was his love, his *M'Gaol*.

The touch of his lips to her palm sent heated arrows of need directly to her pussy. The warmth of his sigh thrilled her to the core. Goose bumps covered her entire body and her nipples hardened. Man, how he controlled her body. The dark green passionate glow of his eyes made her swallow hard. He wanted her. He called her his love.

Needing to think, she tilted her head back before their lips could meet.

"Gavin, I need to bandage your wound," she rasped in a throaty purr. The words had come out sounding more wanton than she intended. As she watched his gaze deepen and his lips turn up into a sensual smile, she couldn't control the shivers running up and down her spine.

Reading pure lust in his eyes, she felt her pussy clench. Her breasts felt heavy, aching for his touch and her soul brimmed with desire for this man. This ancient Scotsman, brought to life by her words, commanded her attention and ruled her body with the slightest of touch. Swallowing hard, she knew she was lost. Whatever he wanted, she would give.

"What ye need is ta kiss me," he taunted, wrapping his good arm around her waist.

He gave her no opportunity to revolt. Capturing her lips, he plundered her mouth. Her taste fueled his hunger. Delving deep with his tongue, he sampled her sweetness over and over. He cupped the back of her head, not allowing her to break their kiss.

Using the hand of his injured arm, he kneaded her bottom, pressing her tight against the hard appendage his towel barely concealed. Gently, he rubbed his shaft against her belly, barely stifling a groan from his lips. She felt so right.

Pointed nipples strained through her shirt, brushing his chest and begging him to take notice. He placed hot kisses down her neck as he answered their unspoken plea. He wanted nothing more than to tug one nipple into his mouth and suckle until she moaned.

Though every ounce of her wanted him, Ericka forced them apart. Her legs trembled and her breasts ached, but she needed to do one thing first before this went any further. Holding his head in her hands, she gazed up at him. The intensity she saw made her choke on her words. "Mind if I shower first?"

"Mind if I watch?" His smoldering gaze twinkled as he turned, moved the items from the toilet lid to the sink, then sat poised as if to watch a show.

Ericka gulped. He planned to watch her undress and shower. Could she do this? Butterflies swarmed her stomach as she started the water, then pulled the curtain closed. When she turned to face him, his eyes seemed to have deepened in their shade of green to something even more sensual than she'd ever seen.

Taking a deep breath, she decided to play his game. If his kiss and touch could turn her on, then maybe a striptease from her could do the same for him. After all, turnabout was fair play. But she'd never done anything like this before. She bit her lip as trembling fingers fumbled with the knot she had placed earlier in the tattered remnants of her shirt to keep it closed. Unable to undo it, she lifted it and the destroyed bra over her head and tossed them to the floor.

Slowly, she circled each swollen nipple with her fingertips, watching his face as she played. When his eyes widened and his lips parted slightly, she knew she had his undivided attention. Cupping the mounds in her palms, she tweaked the tender points to stiff perfection. When she tilted each one up and in turn flicked her tongue across her nipples, she wasn't sure if it was the feel of her tongue to her nipple or the deep groan from Gavin that caused the sudden moisture in her folds.

She liked the idea that it was a mixture of both. A newfound power zipped through her veins. Watching his expressions, she understood why women stripped. It was a powerful aphrodisiac for both her and her man.

Without much effort, she kicked her sneakers from her feet while continually caressing her breasts. In a sultry wave, she lifted her hands to her hair and removed the pins. One by one, she flicked them at his feet. With the last one out, she ran her fingers through the strands, letting them slither through her fingers.

Lowering her hands, she caressed the taut skin of her abdomen before dropping to the front of her jeans. Unzipping her jeans, a wicked smile teased her lips when he shifted in his seat. The bulge of his cock was obvious underneath his towel. Licking her lips, she liked the effect she was having on him.

As seductively as she could shimmy, she slid the jeans down, taking her socks off along with them, and stepped free of their restraints. The sight of his tongue slipping across his lips the moment her thumbs slipped under the lacy straps of her panties made her shiver.

The power rush from her command performance beckoned her to tease him with her panties. Ericka slinked the silken garment down her legs. Once free, she twirled it on her finger, then grasped it by its slender straps. She watched his face as she boldly slid it back and forth between her pussy lips, brushing it against her clit, again and again. Pleasure built, her legs trembled and she couldn't stop the audible moan escaping her lips. His mouth dropped open.

Before he could grab her, she tossed him the damp panties and darted into the shower.

He held the prize to his nose. Her womanly scent filled his senses and heightened his hunger. He needed to be in her, he wanted to taste her. In one fluid movement, he stood and jerked open the curtain.

His chest heaved and his heart pounded as his gaze raked up and down her body. Water cascaded from her nipples and down her belly. Licking his lips, he wanted to trace the water's path to the valley of nether curls and part them with his tongue to suckle from the hidden fountain between her thighs.

His shaft had never felt so heavy. It throbbed painfully, jutting straight out from beneath the towel. The extent of his need for her was obvious. A hungry tongue darted across his lips, savoring a hint of her taste.

"I said I wanted to watch," he growled more huskily than he meant.

The sight of his cock standing at attention, begging for her, made it hard for her to stay in the shower. Though all she wanted to do was wrap her legs around his waist and slip his cock into her pussy, she forced herself to finish washing. Anticipation rippled through her soul and heightened her need.

Ericka smiled, leaning back into the flowing stream. Suds ran across her chest as she lathered her hair. Feeling his eyes glued to her every motion, she held a captive audience. Slowly, she creamed every curvature with soap and saw his cock twitch and pre-cum glisten on its head. Her heart beat rapidly inside her chest. The need to tease him excited her beyond anything she could have imagined. She wanted him.

Meticulously, she rinsed each molecule of soap from her body and still he watched. He jerked into motion the minute she shut off the water. Wrapping her in a towel, he whisked her off her feet.

"*M'Gaol*, 'tis a hungry beast ye hath created," he whispered against her ear as he carried her into the bedroom.

He kicked the door closed. In his arms, they tumbled onto the bed. His mouth ravished her like she was the final meal of a dying man. Hot kisses and tender nibbles covered her body as his need to taste her intensified.

She had teased him with a hint of her flavor on the lacy garment she gifted him with during her strip show, but now he wanted it all. Sliding down her body, he settled his hulking form between her legs. Without any effort, her thighs opened and the treasure he sought sat spread before him. Dripping wet and pink, it begged him to taste. No other invitation was needed.

Plunging his face between her folds, he lapped at her sweet nectar. The more he suckled, the more he wanted. In and out his tongue delved. When he felt she was on the brink, he ran his tongue up her slit, clasped her hidden bud between his teeth and shoved two fingers knuckle-deep within her sheath. Her back arched off the bed and her juices flooded his fingers, tongue and face.

His name gasped from her lips, urging him on further. He couldn't control the beast she created. He nipped and licked, sucked and lapped until he feasted his momentary fill upon her resplendent rush of juices. Face dripping, he burned a trail of wanton kisses up the sensitive skin of her tummy, stopping only to suckle each breast until the nipples were swollen and red.

On heated breath, he tasted the tender spot at the curve of her neck with lingering licks, then hovered within inches of her mouth.

Teasing her ravaged bud with the tip of his swollen shaft, he rasped on ragged breath. "Tell me the truth of thy heart."

Fiery swirls of deeply passionate green fixated on her gaze and held all motion still. *The truth of her heart*. The breath hitched in her throat. *Could she tell him*?

He plunged deep within her folds, then pulled out just as quickly, holding the head of his shaft brushing against the hungry entrance of her need. Again he asked, "Tell me the truth of thy heart."

Out of the corner of her eye, she caught the first ray of morning light fight to filter in through the tightly closed window curtains. Their time was short. She chose to relinquish her heart. She clasped his face in her hands and held her gaze fixed on his.

"Gavin, I love you."

The brightest smile she'd ever seen crossed his lips. He spoke the most tender words to grace her heart in all of her lifetime.

"As I you. *M'Gaol*, I love you."

He took her mouth captive in a passionate kiss, plunging his shaft into the warmth of the treasured place he desired. Her body was his, as his was hers. Her legs wrapped around his waist, bringing him in deeper than he could have imagined.

He loved her and couldn't get enough. Repeatedly, he burrowed in and out within her heat. Her mouth's sweet taste lavished his tongue and increased his heartbeat tenfold. The moment he felt her inner muscles contract around his shaft, he knew he was a forsaken man, hovering on the verge of orgasm.

He sank to the hilt, feeling her legs and inner walls gloved around him. The sensation of her orgasm rippling the length of his shaft brought him near release, but he wanted to give her more pleasure and struggled for control. Though his balls ached and every muscle tensed, he managed to withhold his own pleasure. With the hardest shaft of his life, he rocked slowly in her slick wet sheath, taking them on another round of glory. This woman underneath him wielded some sort of magic over him that he did not understand. If her magic kept him sheathed within her, then so be it.

With each arch of her back, he plunged deeper. Over and over, in and out, faster and faster they set a ravaging pace. Sweat glistened across their bodies, breathing became haggard and still they rode the waves of their passion. Neither was able to stop. Neither wanted to. Higher and higher their souls soared on the most powerful heightened climax either could ever have imagined.

Gavin grasped Ericka's waist and plowed to the deepest level his shaft could possibly reach. Hot seed spurted as her sheath contracted around him, coating him in her molten-hot juices. His mouth covered hers, drinking in the essence of her ecstatic scream. Their souls collided in a heightened level of release neither had ever achieved.

Every muscle quivered. He released her lips and stared at the beautiful wonder of the woman he loved.

"*M'Gaol,*" he whispered against her lips.

The feel of steel jaws clamping down upon his heart shot through his chest. Pain radiated through his arms and cramped every muscle in its path. Sweat beaded his brow. Teeth gritted, Gavin collapsed.

It had to be the curse.

"Gavin," Ericka screamed beneath his dead weight. If he changed now, he'd crush her for sure. Needing to move, she attempted to wiggle out from underneath him, but failed.

Clutching his shoulders, she knew something was wrong. His skin felt fevered and clammy. His breath was ragged and shallow. Frantically, she searched his throat for a pulse, but it was so low she wasn't sure she even felt it at all.

Was he dying? What was wrong? Was it the curse doing this to him? She pressed fervent kisses to his brow.

"Oh, God! Please don't take him from me. I love him," she prayed on whispered breath across his hair. Tears slipped from the corners of her eyes and dripped into her ears. This couldn't be happening. Not after they shared so much.

The sound of her voice drifted from far away, guiding him home. She was his life. He wouldn't leave her. Not now, not ever. As the fog in his brain lifted, his senses returned. She was beneath him, holding him, caressing him and crying.

Why was she crying? The lilt of her voice carried her prayer to his ears. She loved him and that was all that mattered. He wasn't sure what had happened, but the pain in his chest had simmered to a dull throb. But at least his heart was still beating, even though it ached. Lifting his weight from her chest, he held himself up on his elbows.

"*M'Gaol,*" he managed to rasp, though his throat felt dry.

"Oh, Gavin." Ericka plastered his lips with multiple kisses.

Out of the corner of his eye, a light he had not seen in decades danced across the pillow and he froze. Their bodies were still connected. If they stayed this way, would she become stone? Before he could move, Ericka wrapped her legs around him and held him buried deep within her tight warm sheath.

"Ericka, I must..." He tried to move, but her grip tightened.

"*Nay,* Gavin, you mustn't." Smiling up at him, she pointed toward the window and continued. "I'm not sure how, but the sun's up and you haven't turned to stone."

Without giving him a chance to think, she wiggled beneath him. "But at least one part of you has."

He stared down at her in disbelief. He hadn't turned to stone. Unable to believe his eyes, he mumbled, lifting from her warm embrace and standing beside the bed. "'Tis must be some form of trickery."

Two quick strides and he held the curtain in his grasp. Seeing the confusion in her eyes, he knew she knew not what had happened, this he believed to be a truth. He pulled open the curtain.

For the first time in two hundred years, the warmth of the sun's rays coated his human form. He did not change.

"The curse is broken," he whispered. *But how*?

Ericka sat naked on the bed. No covers hid her from his sight. Her hair a tumbled mess, lips he ached to kiss thoroughly, reddened nipples stood pouting for more of his attention. A wicked smile tilted his lips as he tugged the curtain closed.

'Tis her love which saved me. He felt as if his heart would explode with the truth.

He jumped onto the bed, tumbling Ericka onto her back. Her eyes shone with pure love and her scent filled his senses with reawakened need and desire.

"'Tis a fine morning ta stay in bed."

Passionately capturing her mouth, he intended to show her the expanse of his love. In his heart, he knew it was her love that saved him from his curse and never intended to let her forget it. Not as long as his shaft could get hard and plow her voluptuous sheath.

* * * * *

Ericka and Gavin did not make it downstairs until midafternoon and would not have done so if it were up to Gavin. But Ericka wanted to share their news with the others.

Aunt May's mouth dropped and her eyes bugged at the sight of Gavin when he walked out onto the patio and into the light of day.

"Oh my God," she exclaimed. She circled him as if it were the first time she'd truly seen him.

Belvedere stopped pulling at the bandage wrapped firmly around his middle to bark, then whimpered as if it hurt. But that didn't stop him from returning to the task of bandage removal.

Gavin laughed heartily, then kissed Ericka's hand. His gaze stayed glued to Ericka's eyes, which were now covered with her spare set of glasses. "'Tis the love of a lady which broke the curse."

"'Tis a fine sight, my *brathair*." Akira's voice touched his ears. Her transparent figure sat upon the patio wall smiling at him.

"'Tis a fine sight to see thee, my sister." He stepped toward her and bowed. She held his gaze when he lifted his eyes to hers.

"Now the secret 'tis revealed. 'Tis thy burden to seek the others and set their spirits free."

"*Aye*, Akira. 'Tis not a burden, but my oath to seek and find their prisons of stone." He accepted the challenge of finding his *brathairs* with a nod of his head. Ericka moved to stand beside Gavin, his hand she took in hers.

"*Aye*, Akira. 'Tis not his oath alone. I vow to stand beside him in this search until every lost MacKinnon is returned home and freed." She smiled up at him.

"'Twill not be an easy path." He brushed her cheek with his fingertips.

"The good ones never are," she quipped as her smile grew brighter.

Before this trip, she didn't believe in anything that wasn't a proven fact. Boy, had her view of reality changed. She sighed. The love of her life was an ancient Scotsman she helped free from a curse. Because of him, she knew anything was possible.

Forgetting all others around them, he lowered his lips to hers. This woman, this beautifully different woman was his. Her love saved him from his tomb of stone. Her courage would help lead him through this new world in search of his *brathairs*. Together, he knew they would find them. Together, they would set them free.

Why an electronic book?

We live in the Information Age—an exciting time in the history of human civilization, in which technology rules supreme and continues to progress in leaps and bounds every minute of every day. For a multitude of reasons, more and more avid literary fans are opting to purchase e-books instead of paper books. The question from those not yet initiated into the world of electronic reading is simply: *Why?*

1. ***Price.*** An electronic title at Ellora's Cave Publishing and Cerridwen Press runs anywhere from 40% to 75% less than the cover price of the exact same title in paperback format. Why? Basic mathematics and cost. It is less expensive to publish an e-book (no paper and printing, no warehousing and shipping) than it is to publish a paperback, so the savings are passed along to the consumer.
2. ***Space.*** Running out of room in your house for your books? That is one worry you will never have with electronic books. For a low one-time cost, you can purchase a handheld device specifically designed for e-reading. Many e-readers have large, convenient screens for viewing. Better yet, hundreds of titles can be stored within your new library—on a single microchip. There are a variety of e-readers from different manufacturers. You can also read e-books on your PC or laptop computer. (Please note that Ellora's Cave does not endorse any specific brands.

You can check our websites at www.ellorascave.com or www.cerridwenpress.com for information we make available to new consumers.)

3. ***Mobility.*** Because your new e-library consists of only a microchip within a small, easily transportable e-reader, your entire cache of books can be taken with you wherever you go.
4. ***Personal Viewing Preferences.*** Are the words you are currently reading too small? Too large? Too... ANNOYING? Paperback books cannot be modified according to personal preferences, but e-books can.
5. ***Instant Gratification.*** Is it the middle of the night and all the bookstores near you are closed? Are you tired of waiting days, sometimes weeks, for bookstores to ship the novels you bought? Ellora's Cave Publishing sells instantaneous downloads twenty-four hours a day, seven days a week, every day of the year. Our webstore is never closed. Our e-book delivery system is 100% automated, meaning your order is filled as soon as you pay for it.

Those are a few of the top reasons why electronic books are replacing paperbacks for many avid readers.

As always, Ellora's Cave and Cerridwen Press welcome your questions and comments. We invite you to email us at Comments@ellorascave.com or write to us directly at Ellora's Cave Publishing Inc., 1056 Home Avenue, Akron, OH 44310-3502.

Cerridwen, the Celtic Goddess of wisdom, was the muse who brought inspiration to storytellers and those in the creative arts. Cerridwen Press encompasses the best and most innovative stories in all genres of today's fiction. Visit our site and discover the newest titles by talented authors who still get inspired - much like the ancient storytellers did, once upon a time.

ELLORA'S CAVE
ROMANTICA PUBLISHING